THE IMMORTAL'S ASSISTANT

J.P. FLYNN

THE
IMMORTAL'S
ASSISTANT

J.P. FLYNN

LARKFLOWER PRESS

Published by Larkflower Press LLC

First Edition: June 2026

ISBN: 979-8-9956222-0-8 (ebook)

ISBN: 979-8-9956222-1-5 (print)

Library of Congress Control Number: 2026910008 (print)

Developmental Editor: Fiona Otsu

Cover Designer: @david_gardias_designs

Formatted with Vellum

Visit J.P. Flynn's website https://jpflynnauthor.wixsite.com/home

THE IMMORTAL'S ASSISTANT

J.P. FLYNN

CHAPTER 1

Ten minutes. It took ten minutes to get to her dad's office—seven if she ran. Alice shoved through the crowd of students, barreled through the double doors, and took off across campus. The biting wind of the incoming snow storm whipped through her hair. Her clunky loafers crackled over the salted sidewalks as she dodged puddles of mud and slush. She hadn't heard from her father all day. No texts. No calls.

She pressed her cellphone to her ear. Straight to voice-mail, over and over again. Clouds of breath trailed behind her as she sped into the courtyard of East Pyne Hall, the gothic architecture a blur in her periphery. Statues of prominent Princeton University alumni scrutinized her every step from high up in their niches. She should've checked in with her dad sooner.

Alice stumbled inside. The door clanged shut behind her as the familiar melancholy crept in like the chill that seeped through the cracks in the stone. Her footsteps slapped against the tile as she ran down the deserted corridor, blanketed in murky crimson shadows from the glowing exit signs. The windows rattled in their vintage casements, either from the wind or something else. Her heart jumped to her throat. This place was haunted by more than memories.

Don't look, Alice thought. She kept her eyes fixed straight ahead as she rushed by the classrooms. When she was a child, she saw a ghost in one of the empty lecture halls. It had turned to look at her with empty dark holes instead of eyes and pointed in her direction with fingers that were too long and too spindly. Every now and then she'd still see that ghost lingering around the building, and it would disappear before she was able to make sense of it.

A door slammed. Alice froze.

Even if ghosts were real, which right now she decided that they absolutely were not, there was an actual reason she should be concerned about her safety. A student went missing last spring, and most people forgot about him when the search efforts continued to fail. But a few weeks ago, a bloody shoe was found on campus, and now the case had been reopened as a potential homicide.

Alice bolted to her dad's office, afraid she was either about to be murdered or that ghost was finally coming to drag her into the abyss. She rapped on the door.

"Dad?" Her throat tightened as she checked behind her, shaken by the mental image of ghoulish hands clawing at her feet.

She knocked again, firmer this time, and jiggled the locked handle as she feared the worst. Scrambling for her keys, she dropped them with an obnoxious metallic crash. It took a few deep breaths before she was able to steady her hands enough to unlock the door.

Empty.

Her father's desk was littered with notebooks and scrap

papers covered in scribbles of Latin and Greek and unfamiliar hieroglyphs. Tall, unsteady stacks of books spiraled towards the ceiling. File boxes overflowed with too many folders. Desk drawers were half-open with papers hastily shoved inside. Other random collectible historical items were scattered about, and a well-worn canvas map of the Mediterranean hung askew on the wall. He certainly lived up to his reputation as the quirky, eccentric professor. At least, before he got sick.

Alice chewed her lip as she tried to call him again.

Last spring, her father's cancer went into remission without treatment—a miracle, the doctors had said—and for six months he lived as if he was never dying. But recently his skin began to look just as pale as the winter sky. She knew it was too good to be true.

No answer.

Panic surged through her veins. It was only a matter of time before her dad's cancer came back. If it wasn't back already. He was the only immediate family she had left. She had no siblings. No living grandparents. And her mother—Alice's breath caught in her throat as her gaze flickered to a photo on the desk. The picture was almost a spitting image of Alice, right down to the freckles splashed across her nose and the golden flecks in her hazel eyes.

She tore through her father's mess, flinging papers to the floor, hoping to find a note about where he was or perhaps a flyer about a late evening seminar he could be attending. Her mind begged for any answer that didn't involve his declining health. She found nothing.

In a quick effort to clean up, her shaking hands knocked over a framed photo next to the one of her mother, one of Alice as a child covered in dirt and looking for bugs with a kid-sized magnifying glass in their backyard. Her heart clenched as she set it upright, remembering the first time her dad called her his Little Bug, back when life felt easy, back before everything happened.

Alice needed to get home. The mess could wait. But half way out the door, she faltered. On the floor under her dad's desk was his tattered Moleskine notebook, the one he was rarely seen without. She hastily tucked it into her bag, convincing herself it meant nothing, and slipped out of his office, locking his door with the key she definitely wasn't supposed to have.

As she stowed her keys away, she collided head first into someone.

"Oof, sorry," Alice mumbled. At least it was a solid person, no ghost.

"Is Professor Foster available?" he asked, head cocked to the side.

Alice shouldered past him with a frown. "No."

"Then why were you in there?"

She ignored him and kept walking.

"You're not supposed to have a key to a professor's office," he called after her.

Cursing under her breath, Alice stopped and faced him. "Do you work here?"

"No," he paused. "I'm a student."

Alice narrowed her eyes. He dressed like a student, with dark wash jeans, an expensive knit sweater with a collared shirt underneath, and a crossbody messenger bag. He was athletic, tall, and lean with his brown hair styled in a short quiff. He stood with an air of self-important formality, like his shit didn't stink, and probably smelled like fresh-printed money. He must be one of those trust fund preps.

"Then it's none of your business what I'm doing." She said before she stalked off.

He fell into step with her. "I thought Professor Foster had office hours this evening,"

"Yeah well, clearly he's not here today." Alice threw her body against the heavy exit door to push it open against the wind.

"I figured that," he said from behind her, stretching out his hand to help hold the door open for them. A little too close for comfort. "Which is why it doesn't make sense for you to be in his locked office. I mean, unless you're a TA, but I didn't think he had—"

Alice whipped around in the center of the snowy courtyard, her long brown hair sticking to her face. "He's my dad, okay?"

"Professor Benjamin Foster is your dad?" He blinked.

"Oh, don't act dumb." Alice sneered. She understood now. He already knew who she was and probably followed her through the building earlier with every intention to use her for information. "So what do you want? Test answers? Next semester's syllabus? Extra credit?" Other students often did this when they found out her dad was a professor, including her ex-boyfriend Noah who dumped her after he passed her father's class last winter.

"No, I—" He flinched and pulled a hand down his olive-skinned face. "I didn't know he was your dad. I was just trying to talk to you."

"Sneaking up on someone and badgering them with questions isn't the best way to make small talk." Alice rolled her eyes. This pointless conversation was wasting her precious time. She huffed out of the courtyard through the curtain of bulky snowflakes.

"I'm Leander," he said as he trailed behind her.

"Good for you." Alice waved him off.

"You're not going to tell me yours?"

She whirled on him again. "Does it matter?"

He almost ran into her from following so close behind. "I think so."

"Alice." She grit her teeth, pulled out her cellphone, and dialed.

Leander's ebony eyes tracked a few snowflakes as they fell into her dampening hair, repeating her name out loud as if trying to remember it. Before she could turn away, he spoke again. "What year are you?"

"Sophomore," she said, tapping her foot on the ground. The call went straight to voicemail again.

"I'm a Junior. What major?"

"Ecology." Alice redialed. Still nothing.

"I'm in Classics."

"Figures." She could've guessed with all of his prying about her dad.

Leander shifted on his feet. "Is everything alright?"

"I'm fine." Alice shoved her phone away. "If you're done, I have somewhere to be." She turned on her heel and darted towards Holder Hall. The snowstorm was getting worse, and she needed to grab a few things before she went home. Of course, Leander followed.

Alice rushed through the stone cloisters and into the snow-coated courtyard, leaving Leander a few paces behind her. As she entered into the stairwell, she stumbled to a halt. The stairwell ghost was in its usual spot, skulking in the corner of the landing with clawed fingers gripping the wall in distress. As much as she convinced herself these ghost sightings were sleep-deprived, stress-filled hallucinations, other students' late night stories often confirmed her suspicions. They too would sometimes claim to see the stairwell ghost or hear it mumbling and crying to itself in the dead of night. It didn't help when she discovered the building was constructed on an old graveyard. All the bodies had been moved. Supposedly.

She shook the image from her head and bounded up the stairs to her third floor single dorm. Thankfully, Leander hadn't followed her inside. As Alice darted around her room, she called her dad again with no luck. She yanked open her desk drawers in search of her phone charger, jarring the items on the surface—photos, some cool looking rocks, and a lopsided ceramic mug she made in a pottery class with her best friend Jenny.

Her pulse pounded in her ears. She shoved her charger and a few other personal care items in her bag and then barreled down the hall to Jenny's dorm room. She banged on the door.

"Alice!" Jenny said as she whipped open the door. She wore her baggy Princeton Fencing Club hoodie, and her black hair was piled on top of her head in a messy bun. "What's going on?"

"My dad—" Alice gulped. "—he's not answering his phone."

"It's okay. Breathe." Jenny cupped Alice's shoulders. "Maybe he's busy?"

Caleb, Alice's other best friend, jumped up from the small futon couch and stood behind Jenny, at least a foot taller. "Or he could've forgotten his phone," he added. "I'm sure he's okay."

"I don't know. I haven't spoken to him since last night." She cursed herself for not stopping by his office in the morning. She didn't even know if he showed up to work at all that day. "I need to drive home and check on him."

"Drive home?" Caleb asked and glanced out the latticed window. The three of them had planned to stay in and have a movie marathon due to the snow storm.

"I have to," Alice said. She'd take her chances.

Jenny pulled her in for a hug. "Do you want us to come?"

"No, I'll be fine. Thanks though."

Jenny bit her lip while spinning a gold ring on her finger. "Alright, just please be careful. Call us when you get there."

Alice clenched her teeth to prevent herself from tearing up. Those happy memories with them from freshman year felt like they belonged to someone else. The late nights where they'd get busted by the residential advisors for being too loud in the dorms. When Caleb made Alice get up and dance to Two Door Cinema Club at a party, even though she was really embarrassed. After her father was first diagnosed with cancer, her friends had helped her believe maybe life was worth living again.

"When you get home and find out everything is fine," Caleb said as he swooped in for his turn for a hug. "Tell your dad we miss him, and we're coming over for macaroni soon."

"I will." Alice attempted to smile through her sorrow. Her dad used to host Macaroni Nights for them every month when he was feeling well.

"And tell him to get his ass back to the doctor." Caleb ran a hand through his dark hair and then shook his finger. "Or we'll make him go."

Alice's heart sank. She knew there would be no convincing her father. They all knew it. Even if he did go to the doctor and found out the cancer was back, he'd probably refuse treatment again. "I'll try," she sighed. "See you Monday."

Alice almost fell down the stairs when she saw Leander

waiting for her at the bottom. He blocked the exit so she couldn't get by without speaking to him.

"What now?" She attempted to squeeze past him and failed. Her eyes darted to the bulletin board where the sun-faded missing person poster from last spring was still hanging. The hairs on the back of her neck prickled.

Leander tracked her gaze and arched a curious eyebrow at her. "You dropped these earlier." He held out some crumpled papers.

"Thanks." Alice snatched them out of his hand.

Leander didn't move.

"Well, if you're done stalking me..." Alice shoved her way past him back out into the cold and was bombarded by the heavy snowfall.

"Where are you going?" Leander asked, catching up to her.

"Home." She gripped her car keys in her hand, ready to use them as a weapon if need be, as she made her way down the sidewalk. Her car was parked less than a block away because of her dad's faculty permit. Maybe she shouldn't have mentioned where she was going.

"It's kind of dangerous to drive right now." His voice muffled in the wind.

"Will you just leave me alone? Why are you—"

She slipped on a patch of ice and stumbled off the curb. A car whizzed by and blared its horn. Leander grabbed her forearm to pull her back. Her whole body shook as the memory of the accident rushed into her mind.

It had happened right after her eighth birthday, before the longest winter of her life. Everyone always said car crashes happen in a split second, but what happened to her family had felt excruciatingly slow. Alice could perfectly recall a million pieces of shattered glass flying through her mom's hair, glittering like blood covered stars, and her father on his knees in the middle of the road in front of something, someone, covered in a white sheet as he screamed at the sky.

She remembered her little broken body in the hospital bed, the room dark with a blue-green glow from the beeping machines. Alice had asked her dad, "What happens when you don't have a mom?" He didn't answer, only cried. It wasn't until she was a teenager that she found out just how close to death she had been, that because of internal bleeding, she required emergency surgery and blood transfusions to keep her alive.

Unable to move, Alice stared out into the street. She shivered, the entire front of her coat drenched from the car speeding through the puddle of slush.

"You okay?" Leander asked.

Snapping back to the present, Alice wrenched her arm free. "I'm fine."

"You need to be careful."

"I'll survive."

Leander, dumbstruck, didn't follow her this time.

After a nerve-wracking driving home, Alice hurled herself through the front door.

"Dad?" All off the lights were off. The television hissed with static. A glass of water had been knocked off the coffee table and left a damp stain on the carpet. Her dad would never leave the television on, nor would he leave a mess on the carpet.

She called out for him again as she rushed through the house. When she reached the kitchen, she gasped. Puddles of blood and broken glass were scattered across the tile. Her heart drummed in her ears as she stumbled forward, dropping her school bag to the floor. Feeling faint, she leaned against the basement door frame. Blood splatters continued down the wooden steps.

"Oh no." Her voice quivered. He used to cough up blood during the active phase of his cancer. Once before, she found him passed out in the bathroom covered in it. That was after he had started the chemo for the first time and wasn't getting better. If the cancer was back, if her dad had been dead in the basement while she wasted time back on campus, she'd never forgive herself.

Before her tunnel vision could take over, Alice bounded down the dusty wooden stairs, wavering at the bottom. She gripped the railing to steady herself. The trail of blood led to a body lying face down on the cement floor. But it wasn't her father. It was her teenage neighbor Dillon.

"Oh my god," she said, near hyperventilating, as she crouched down and placed a hand on his upper arm. "Dillon?" She shook him gently. "Please wake up. Please." Her eyes darted around the scene, trying to figure out why he was even down here. He had a deep gash on his forearm and numerous other wounds. She leaned her face down to listen for breathing.

Cloudy, piercing white eyes snapped open. Alice staggered backwards. Dillon groaned and pushed himself up from his stomach. He moved like gravity was a hundred times stronger, swaying like he was on the deck of a ship.

"Dillon?" Alice rasped. Her taut muscles were primed, ready to launch herself out of there.

His ghastly eyes darted back in her direction. He shambled towards her like he was intoxicated and tripped into a workbench covered in tools with a loud crash.

Alice held up her hands. "Dillon, what's going on?"

He lunged at her, teeth bared. Alice cursed as she jumped out of the way, but she wasn't quick enough. His pale, bloodstained hands gripped her sweater as she struggled to break free.

The basement door slammed shut, startling Dillon enough to make him let her go. Alice took off and was half way up the stairs when a knife cut through her leggings and into her calf. She cried out, knees buckling. Dillon grabbed her ankle and pulled. White flashed before her eyes as her chin hit the steps. Ears ringing, she squirmed and rolled onto her back, screaming and kicking to keep him away. Dillon hurled himself forward and sliced the knife through the air.

She choked on her breath as burning pain radiated from a deep slash across her stomach. With her last few ounces of adrenaline, she kicked her leg upwards and hit Dillon in the face. He tumbled backwards down the stairs and split his head on the cement floor, laying motionless in a fresh pool of blood.

Alice stared. Numb. Each shallow breath she took caused the pain in her abdomen to worsen. Her quivering hand hovered above the laceration as blood soaked her ivory sweater.

She cried out for her dad again, unsure if he was in the house, or if he was okay.

The smell of smoke wafted from under the basement door.

Heart pounding, she dragged her body up the rest of the stairs. What little oxygen she inhaled was being overtaken by the thickening smoke. Her bloody hand slipped right off the door handle. Someone had locked her in.

The roaring of the fire grew closer. She hammered her fist on the door. Her cries for help turned into a coughing fit. Alice's weakened arm collapsed at her side as all hope drained, welcoming the hazy dizziness, hoping she'd lose consciousness from blood loss before being burned alive. She wanted to call out for help one last time, but no voice escaped her smoke-filled lungs.

Her body flopped onto the kitchen floor as the basement door flung open. Someone hoisted her up under her armpits, and she shrieked in pain. Her consciousness faded in and out, her vision blurry and unfocused. She remembered what it felt like to be dying.

"Alice," A male voice echoed in her ear. "Come on, stay awake as long as you can."

The person hoisted her up and carried her out the back door, walking almost straight through the flames, but they luckily didn't get burned. Once outside, the cold air shocked her skin, and the fresh oxygen was welcome to her lungs. He laid her down in the back hatch of an old SUV.

"Here." He gave her a balled up t-shirt to press on her stomach. "Keep pressure on it. Lay back and keep your knees up," he said in a panic. He shut the hatch and rushed around to the driver's side.

Alice drew in a shaking breath, her chest heavy and her throat raw. "What about... my dad?" The last thing she heard was the sound of sirens in the distance as the car sped away.

CHAPTER 2

Alice's head throbbed. Her throat burned with each breath. Something beeped beside her. She opened her groggy eyes and found herself tucked comfortably under a blue and white quilted blanket in a wooden four-poster bed. Not a hospital. A vital signs monitor was mounted on a pole next to her, and a bag of fluids dangled from a hook, dripping down into the IV in her arm. Her weak fingers traced the outline of a bandage taped across her abdomen.

The room was lined with dingy wood paneling. Across from the bed, an antique dresser supported a large wood-framed, albeit lopsided, decorative mirror. Out the window to her left, the cool winter sun reflected off the rippling water of a river, the banks still covered with fresh, undisturbed snow. In the corner next to the window was a lumpy maroon armchair, and seated in the armchair napping lazily was Leander.

The beeping on the monitor quickened. Disjointed memories flew through Alice's mind as she pieced together what happened the night before. Taking stock of her surroundings and steadying her breathing, she planned her escape. If she was quiet enough, she could sneak out before Leander woke up.

With a wince, she peeled off the medical tape and pulled out the IV. Then she picked at the electrodes stuck to her chest, but as soon as she removed the first one, an alarm on the machine sounded. Her head snapped up.

"Going somewhere?" Leander asked with steady eyes and a quirked eyebrow.

Alice threw the blanket to the floor and ripped off the rest of the electrodes. She heaved herself out of the bed with a surge of panicked energy, ignoring the screaming pain from her wounds. Her legs wobbled towards the door.

"You should get back in bed before you hurt yourself." Leander watched her with a bemused expression.

Her feet shuffled across the threadbare rug, picking up speed as her heart slammed in her chest, moving as fast as she could through the pain. She expected him to jump up and grab her any second. Alice needed to get outside, get to a neighbor or flag down a car, find anyone to help her get away before he murdered her.

Leander let out an annoyed sigh as he got out of the chair and headed her way. Alice pushed herself to run but lost her balance. Her hands clawed for the bedroom door frame. She missed and crumpled to the floor. Footsteps hurried down the hall, and a strawberry blonde head poked in the doorway.

"Oh! You're awake," the girl said, looking down at her with concern etched in her eyebrows. Then she whipped her face up at Leander. "Why is she out of bed?"

"She wasn't going to make it very far." Leander rolled his eyes and bent down to scoop Alice up in his arms.

"You lying asshole," she croaked as she pushed against his chest, the side of his face, pulled at his hair, whatever it took to get him to drop her. She'd climb out the window and jump if she had to. Anything to grab the attention of a passerby, even if she broke her legs in the process.

"Easy there, slugger," Leander said as he placed her back in the bed and attempted to cover her with the blanket.

Alice pushed it off and slapped at Leander's hands. "Get away from me!"

"You're going to hate me even more if I have to restrain you," he said through gritted teeth, grabbing for her wrists.

"No need to scare her like that." The girl stepped forward and nudged him aside. Freckles dotted her rosy cheeks, and she looked to be in her mid-twenties, dressed in a casual black t-shirt and jeans. She pulled a wallet from her back pocket and flipped it open to show off a gold badge. "I'm Natalie. And you've met Leander, my partner." Natalie elbowed Leander, and he showed off his own badge.

Alice blinked, her frantic emotions halting as she processed the information. "Wait, you're cops?"

"Criminal investigators," Natalie said as she put her badge away.

They looked a little young to be investigators. She thought someone had to be a patrol officer for a few years before being promoted to something like that. Alice rubbed her throbbing forehead and scrunched her face. "Shouldn't I be in a hospital?"

"Being that you're in witness protection, a public hospital would be too risky," Natalie said. "So we brought you here to our safe house for now."

Alice wasn't too familiar with how witness protection worked, but she supposed that was the point. They had to keep the process a secret to protect the confidentiality of the victim. *She* was the victim. Someone had targeted her and her neighbor—and possibly her dad—and she didn't know why.

Her eyes narrowed at Leander. "Were you following me around campus because you knew something was going to happen?"

"I was following a lead." Leander crossed his arms.

Alice's heart stuttered. "A lead that involved me? Why didn't you say anything?"

He ran a hand through his hair. "I was gathering information. I had no idea what was going to happen."

"You let me go home to almost get killed!"

He scowled. "First of all, I'm not permitted to discuss details of a potential case with a civilian. Second of all, do you really think you would've listened to me if I told you not to go home?"

"I—" she paused. He had a point. Alice would've told him to shut up and would've gone home anyway. "Well maybe if you showed me your badge, I would've listened."

"There are rules when working undercover, you know." He spoke to her like she was a child.

Her voice ticked up. "So your plan was just to follow me and stalk me all night then?"

"You're lucky I followed you, or you wouldn't have made it out of that fire."

A lump formed in her throat, her anger losing steam. She remembered almost passing out on the basement stairs, accepting that she was about to die. Leander had saved her. "Was my dad in there?" Her bottom lip quivered. She wasn't sure if she was ready for the answer.

"No," Leander said. "We don't know where he is."

Alice squeezed her eyes shut. "And Dillon, is he..." His bloodied, lifeless face flashed in her mind. She gulped as she remembered the cause of his death, that she was the one that pushed him down the stairs. The sound of his skull cracking on the cement replayed in her head, a sound she'll never be able to forget. No one could survive a fall like that.

"He didn't make it," Natalie said. "We're so sorry."

Tears slid down Alice's cheeks as she heaved a shuddering breath. Dillon was dead, and her father was missing. She held her face in her hands, as if she could stop the tears from flowing, as if she could keep it all in. But she couldn't. She slammed her hands down on the bed as her tears turned to anger. "You should've done something! You should've warned us that we'd been targeted—"

"It's a complicated case—"

"Bullshit." Alice tried to force her way out of the bed again. Leander held her down by her shoulders. She yanked at his wrists, her fingernails digging into his skin. He hissed in pain. "Get off me, you—"

"Hey Violet?" Natalie called out the bedroom door. "Can you come in here? Leander, let her go and chill out."

Leander stepped away with an aggravated huff, holding up his hands in acquiescence.

Before Alice could launch herself out of the bed again, a white-haired woman wearing a crocheted shawl on top of a shabby Niagara Falls t-shirt entered the room. "Hi, dear, I made this for you. It's a chamomile blend." She offered her the steaming mug.

Alice cringed away. "I don't want tea, I want..." she paused, her emotions cresting over the edge as she let out a sob. She wanted her dad.

With a warm, sympathetic smile, Violet put a hand on Alice's shoulder and gave her the mug. "Drink. It'll calm your nerves."

This time, Alice didn't flinch away. Something about the old woman felt comforting, safe. She could feel it in her bones. Alice sniffed the tea, and after a nod of encouragement from Violet, she took a chance and sipped. Its heat bloomed in her belly, warming her entire being.

"Do you remember anything else from last night?" Natalie asked, treading carefully so she didn't set Alice off again.

Alice was unsure what to say. Part of her wondered if she should say anything at all. As she drank more of the tea, it seemed to ease something deep in her chest. With an exhale, she told them everything that she remembered, starting from when she left campus up until she arrived home to the scene.

"Dillon was face down on the floor, all cut up and bloody. I thought he fell down the steps. When he woke up, his eyes were cloudy. He wasn't himself. Maybe he was on drugs. He would never attack me like that," Alice rambled, thinking out loud, wondering what the hell could've caused Dillon's bizarre behavior.

Natalie sat on the bed with her. "Was anyone else there?"

"I think so. I got locked in the basement when the fire started." She shook her head. Someone wanted her to be trapped down there, the same person who probably attacked Dillon first. "I don't know who would want to hurt us like that."

"Don't worry. We'll figure it out," Natalie said. "You're safe here."

Alice wasn't quite sure about that yet.

Violet fussed with the IV. "I'm going to hook you up again, if that's alright. You need more fluids." She opened the top drawer of the dresser, which was filled with a variety of medical supplies instead of clothes, and grabbed what she needed.

"You're a nurse?" Alice asked as Violet prepped her arm.

"Yes dear," Violet said. "Just a small pinch…"

Alice winced from the slight prick of pain as Violet inserted the IV catheter. Then she drew some medication from a vial into a syringe and administered it directly through the IV line. She did it a second time with another medication before hooking up the bag of fluids again.

"What are you giving me?" Alice asked, eyes suddenly feeling heavy. She almost spilled her half-empty mug of tea, but luckily Natalie grabbed it from her and placed it on the night stand.

"Just some antibiotics and pain medication," Violet said with another warm smile.

"Oh." Alice rubbed her head, feeling woozy, a strange cloud overtaking her senses. The medication was kicking in awfully fast. Her half-lidded eyes fluttered as a wave of dizziness slammed into her. Natalie was saying something else, but Alice couldn't understand the words. Everything went dark.

* * *

It was the middle of the night when Alice awoke again. The IV had been removed from her arm. The vital signs machine was gone. Her injuries no longer throbbed with pain, and only a dull ache lingered. When Alice attempted to haul herself out of bed, the creaking mattress springs woke Natalie who had been sleeping in the armchair.

"Hey," Natalie whispered with a cracked voice. She uncoiled her long legs and wiped the sleepiness from her eyes. "You okay?"

"Where's the bathroom?" Alice asked, her voice clipped, annoyed she was being monitored so closely overnight.

They probably thought she was still thinking about running. She was. Alice wasn't fully convinced they were who they said they were.

As Alice tested her weight on her feet, Natalie swooped an arm under Alice's armpit for extra support. She was tempted to pull away, but controlled her impulse to recoil. Alice found it strange that a supposed criminal investigator would provide care like this. The entire thing seemed weird and informal and kind of disorganized. Her identity could've been protected in a hospital. They could've had police guarding her. Instead she was stuck in this random old house with these strange people.

The two girls shuffled down the dimly lit hall to the bathroom. The walls were lined with dark walnut wainscoting, and the upper half was covered in faded crimson wallpaper that peeled in a few places. Most of the brass wall sconces had intricately etched glass lampshades, all except the one at the far end where a lone bulb flickered.

After using the toilet, Alice stared at herself in the tarnished mirror as she washed her hands. The dark circles under her eyes clashed with her pasty skin. Numbness overshadowed any lingering emotions from the past couple days. Her neighbor, Dillon, a boy she knew since the day he was born, the boy she used to babysit and tutor in science, had tried to kill her. And then she killed him. His dead white eyes were unforgettable. Maybe someone force fed him a weird, psychosis-inducing drug to make him look and act like that.

Alice shivered. Whoever trapped them in the basement and burned down her house was still out there. Her dad was missing, or worse, dead. She splashed some cool water on her face to settle herself.

"All good in there?" Natalie asked through the door.

Alice shrugged as she exited the bathroom.

"Do you want something to eat?"

"It's the middle of the night." Alice wanted to be left alone. She wasn't hungry, and her head felt too heavy on her shoulders.

"Yes, but you haven't eaten in a while. I'll make you something."

Alice couldn't say no as Natalie directed her to the stairs and helped her descend step by step. At the bottom, a soft glow emanated from the kitchen from the light above the stove. A twelve-inch box TV sat on the counter rolling commercials. Leander swigged from a bottle of beer at the kitchen table. He closed the book he was reading and pushed it aside, leaning back in his chair with questioning eyes as they hobbled closer. He looked tired, strung out, and maybe a little drunk.

"Alice is hungry." Natalie pulled out a chair with a cracked plastic cushion for Alice to sit. A few minutes later, she placed a steaming cup of tea on the table. "Here ya go, might want to let it cool first."

"Thanks," Alice mumbled. She wasn't used to being cared for, because normally she was the one being the caretaker at home. She dragged the mug across the table, the sleeves of her sweatshirt hiding her hands, when she realized it wasn't actually her sweatshirt. Looking down at her chest, she saw Princeton written across in faded orange letters. Someone must've changed her clothes while she was unconscious. She grimaced with disgust and embarrassment.

"It's mine," said Leander after another gulp of his beer. He didn't look her in the eye.

Alice's grip tensed around the mug. "So did you actually go to Princeton, or is that another lie?" She couldn't remember the details of their conversation from the other night. Her memory was too fuzzy.

He frowned. "I did."

Her fingers drummed on the table, and she pursed her lips. The night they met, he must've ben profiling her with the absurd amount of questions. Now when she wanted more information, he barely said a full sentence.

"When did you graduate?"

"Does it matter?"

"I wanna know."

His eyes flashed with annoyance. "It's none of your business—"

"How about some soup?" Natalie interrupted, holding up a red and white can. "Leander?"

"I'll pass." He finished off his beer and chucked it in the trash.

"Uh, sure." Alice wasn't actually interested in the soup. She gave a dirty look to Leander, knowing he was giving her an attitude as a taste of her own medicine.

Natalie started up the rusty Chambers stove and grabbed some mismatched bowls from the dated, dark wood cabinets which matched the dark wood walls and the dark wood floors. The kitchen decor looked stuck in a past decade, while the room itself appeared much older beneath it. The curtains, towels, and other decor were a mix of orange, yellow, and more brown. The table cloth was a matching floral covered with cracked plastic like the chairs. And it was kind of a mess, with clutter and knickknacks scattered about.

"What are you reading?" Alice asked as she snatched the book Leander had set aside.

He glared at her. "See for yourself."

She opened to a random page. The entire thing was

written in Latin. "You know how to read this?" A cop that went to Princeton and could read Latin, not the usual demographic for the profession.

"*Latine facunda sum. Potesne legere?*" Leander asked.

Alice's cheeks reddened, unable to accurately discern what he had asked her, something about if she could read it. "*Etiam...*" she stuttered as she tried to remember the phrase. "*Etiam... scio pirum.*" She only knew a few basic phrases from her parents and binomial nomenclature from her ecology studies.

Leander placed a hand on his chest and laughed at her. What an ass.

"What's so funny? I said I know a little."

"No, you said 'I also know pears.' The correct phrase would be *etiam scio parum.*" He laughed again.

She shoved the book back towards him. "Whatever."

"Leander likes to show off his Latin skills," Natalie said as she stirred the soup on the stove.

"It's a dead language," he said as he got up to grab another beer from the fridge. "Someone should remember it." He plopped back down in his seat.

There was an awkward moment of silence as Alice watched him drink, wondering if it was appropriate for him to drink on the job, if he was even on the job since it was well past midnight.

"Have you heard anything about my dad?" Alice couldn't hide the desperation in her voice. The last time she saw him, the day before the fire, he looked so sick, so frail.

"Nothing yet," said Natalie. "Unfortunately we have almost nothing to go on right now, and even if we did, a lot of it would have to remain confidential. Until we get more solid answers, you'll have to stay here a while, to be safe."

"Where is *here*, exactly?" Alice asked, her patience thinning. "Am I allowed to know that much?"

"A small town called Riverton," said Leander. "About a forty five minute drive from Princeton if you're going south down the interstate."

"Do you all live here together?" If they won't tell her about her dad, maybe they'd tell her more about themselves. And if she got them talking, they might eventually slip some information about the investigation.

"Yep." Natalie leaned an elbow on the counter as the soup bubbled in its pot. "Live together and work together. Violet is actually my grandma, and she works with us too."

Alice furrowed her brow, finding the relation a little bit strange, but it wasn't too out of the ordinary for family to work together. Her parents did. "And are you two like—" She made a motion with her hand, pointing between them. "You know."

"No, no." Natalie smiled at Leander and walked over to pat him on the back. He leaned away from her, annoyed. She scoffed and returned to the stove. "We've been close friends for a long time, eventually became colleagues. Then the police department needed a new location for a temporary safe house, and my grandma volunteered our place. After that, she came out of retirement to provide nursing assistance when needed," Natalie rambled as she set a bowl of chicken noodle soup in front of Alice. "It all kind of worked out this way."

Alice nodded mindlessly as she stirred her soup. Her attention faded, the words Natalie spoke floating away past her ears. Nothing seemed real. She was stuck in time, suspended somewhere between the seconds and minutes.

Bringing a spoonful of soup to her mouth, her trembling hand caused it all to splash back into the bowl before she could eat it. Alice dropped the spoon and rubbed her face. She couldn't stop thinking about her dad, where he was, or if he got out of the fire. She wondered what her friends knew, if they were worried. She wondered if anyone had called her Aunt Jane out in California.

The news report returned to the television. "A deadly house fire ravaged the normally peaceful town of Princeton, New Jersey last night. Officials report the cause of the fire could be arson, however no suspects have been identified. The body of a local teenage boy was found in the debris." A photo of a smiling Dillon was plastered on the screen. "The residents of the home have yet to be located. Please forward any information to the Princeton Police Department." Dillon's photo changed to one of Alice and her father.

"They don't know I'm here?" asked Alice, blinking in confusion.

"Remember what we said about witness protection?" asked Natalie. "We can't let the public know where you are right now."

"So no one knows I'm here?" Her dad, wherever he was, and her friends—they were probably worried sick about her. Her thoughts raced. "Was anyone able to grab my bag from my house? My cellphone? Can I call someone?" She needed some sort of connection, some sort of comfort, some sort of reassurance that she'd be okay when it felt like she was free-falling with no one there to catch her.

"No, unfortunately I didn't have time to grab anything." Leander said, peeling the label from his beer bottle. "The fire was getting out of control." He glanced up at Natalie. "And we haven't had a chance to return to search the scene."

"Can I at least use your phone to call my aunt? My friends?"

"Sorry," Natalie said. "But no. That's one of the rules of

witness protection, no contact until we figure out your case."

Alice held her breath as she looked back to the TV at the photo of her and her dad from their trip to the Grand Canyon a few years ago. It was before he got sick, when he was still full of vitality and the two of them were able to hike all day in the heat. No matter the challenge, he always had a bright smile on his face.

Her shaking hands pushed the soup bowl away. Somewhere out there, her dad was missing, sick and scared, and she was isolated here, unable to contact anyone. Alice clenched her teeth and cursed the tears that gathered at the corners of her eyes, embarrassed to be seen by the two strangers as she fell apart. Again. She normally only did that in private.

Natalie cupped Alice's shaking shoulders, and Leander pulled her up by her elbow as they coaxed her to the living room and onto the couch. She didn't have the strength to resist.

Sniffling, Alice picked at the pilling couch fabric to calm herself, taking in the vintage clutter sprinkled around the room. Two overflowing bookshelves flanked the fireplace. Natalie flicked on a stained glass lamp and kneeled at her side. Leander hovered in the doorway.

"Can you tell us a little more about your dad?" Natalie asked with a soft voice.

"Um…" Alice sniffed again. She supposed she should open up if it meant she could somehow help them find him. "He's a professor at Princeton, fluent in Latin and Greek." Her shoulders slumped as she told them about her dad's cancer. "But last spring, somehow he was miraculously cured." She shook her head, refusing to accept the possibility.

"Miraculously cured," Leander repeated as he made eye contact with Natalie.

"I guess." Alice shrugged. "He's just been through so much." She held her head in her hands. "And now he's missing, and no one knows if he is okay, or if he was in the fire, or if he knows about Dillon." Her breathing quaked. "He's probably so worried about me. Unless... unless he—"

"Leander. Tea." Natalie snapped her fingers and pointed at the kitchen. Leander hurried in and out. When he returned, he tried to push a fresh cup of tea into Alice's hands.

"Why do you keep making me drink this?" She forced it away and wiped her nose on her sleeve.

"It's to help with your nerves." Leander sat on the couch and urged the cup towards her again. "Please drink it."

"Fine." Alice took the cup, only to appease him, and held it in her lap. She wasn't thirsty.

Leander's eyes bored into her, waiting for her to drink.

"Are you trying to drug me or something?"

"Of course not," he said, scowling. "You really think we're the bad guys here? We'd lose our jobs if we drugged you."

"It's a mix of chamomile and valerian root. It helps people relax," Natalie added. "We know this has been really hard for you. Unfortunately, we have to ask you some more questions. So the tea will help."

Alice narrowed her eyes at them. The explanation made sense considering what she knew of valerian from her biology classes. It was an herb used as a sleep aid for centuries. But that wasn't enough to convince her to drink it.

"Here," Leander said as he swiped the mug from her

and took a gulp. "See? No drugs or poison." He handed it back to her.

Alice considered it. A calming tea did sound like a good idea since she was having trouble handling her emotions from this crazy situation. With a sigh, she finally sipped the tea to get them off her back.

"Notice anything else out of the ordinary with your dad recently?" Leander asked, his body less tense.

She paused to think, sipping more of the tea, wondering what type of information they were even looking for. "He had insomnia. Last year he was obsessed with translating an old book he found, and he would stay up all night trying to figure it out." Alice relaxed into the soft couch cushions and closed her eyes, feeling tired again even though she just slept for over twelve hours straight. "All those Greek and Latin scrap papers you found were his." She yawned. "I cleaned them up from his office."

"Anything else strange happen over the past year? Anything out of the ordinary?" Leander asked, his voice pressured.

Alice rubbed her eyes as she tried to remember. "A student went missing last spring. People thought he was murdered after his bloody shoe was found on campus."

"A missing student?" Natalie asked, eyebrows darting up her forehead. "Last spring, you said?" She looked at Leander who appeared grim.

"Do you think it's connected to what happened?" Alice asked, her anxiety bubbling up again. She might've been tracked and targeted by the same perpetrator for almost an entire year. She sipped her tea again to calm down.

Leander rubbed his chin. "Maybe. Right around the same time as—"

Natalie nudged him.

Alice knitted her brows. "Around the same time as what?" She yawned again, struggling to make the mental connections through her sleepiness.

"Nothing," Natalie said.

"Then why did—" Alice pointed at them, prepared to argue, but a flood of exhaustion washed over her. Head lolling to the side, she dropped her hand to her stomach and cringed in pain from hitting her injury.

"Why don't you lay back." Natalie took her mug and helped Alice get situated on the couch. "Relax. I'll change your bandages and then you can get some more sleep."

"Thanks," Alice mumbled through her grogginess.

Natalie's delicate hands removed the taped gauze from her abdomen, revealing red and inflamed skin around the stitches. "Leander, can you get me a damp cloth and the first aid supplies?"

"Are you a n-nurse, too?" Alice asked, her words slurring. She sucked in air as Natalie used the damp cloth to clean up her wound.

"I only finished nursing school because Violet wanted me to, but I never got my license." Natalie opened an unlabeled glass jar and slathered an earthy-smelling paste over the infected skin. Leander prepared the clean gauze and assisted Natalie with taping it correctly. "Ended up switching careers," she said with a shrug.

Alice pulled her sweatshirt back down, feeling exposed with the two of them hovering over her. "And you?"

"I just help out when Natalie needs an extra set of hands," Leander said as he bent down to help with Alice's leg bandages. "My family chose this career for me."

"It's what you make of it, right?" Natalie zipped up the bag of supplies and smiled at Leander. He ignored her attempt at connection and sat in the recliner without responding.

"Why don't you quit?" Alice asked.

Leander raised his eyebrows, chin in hand, and shook his head. He stared out the window without a word.

Natalie pulled a multicolored knitted blanket over Alice, like a mother tucking in a child, and then threw another balled-up blanket at Leander, jarring him from his daze. "He'll stay down here with you for tonight in case you need anything. Here—" She handed Alice her mug of tea. "Finish this and hopefully it will help you sleep deep enough that Leander's snores won't wake you."

CHAPTER 3

Alice opened her eyes to an eerily quiet blue gray haze, and she couldn't tell if it was dawn or if she had slept until dusk the next day. Leander was gone from his place in the recliner. At least she didn't have to deal with his grumpiness.

Led by her curiosity, she dragged her tired body off of the couch and explored the room with mostly steady feet. Her hand absent-mindedly rubbed her abdomen, surprised that her wound felt much better. She examined the cluster of picture frames lining the fireplace mantle. There was a black and white photo of two women wearing polka dot dresses smiling and embracing on a porch swing. One of them looked a little bit like Natalie. Perhaps it was her mother, or maybe it was Violet when she was younger.

Something pulled Alice's attention out the tall window. The front yard was covered in half melted snow. A woman stood in the center of the yard and faced the river across the narrow street. Her light-colored, unbound hair wafted gently in the breeze. She wore a long grey dress and no shoes. Even her skin looked ashen in the poor light. Alice blinked and rubbed her eyes, then tapped on the window to get the woman's attention. Whoever it was, she didn't seem alright.

The woman turned, mouth wide open in a silent scream. She had black holes where eyes should've been, and she pointed a gnarled hand in Alice's direction. Alice jolted back, tripping over her own feet, as goosebumps erupted across her skin. Before she could make sense of what she was seeing, the ghost faded into nothingness.

Alice covered her face with her hands, forcing the image from her mind. It must've been all the trauma she'd endured and her weird sleep schedule causing her to hallucinate. Not a real ghost. It couldn't be. She hurried out of the room, as fast as her lingering limp would allow her, looking for any of the others. Being alone was freaking her out too much.

She searched the entire downstairs, which was much larger than she expected. The last room she checked was what looked like an office towards the back of the house. Since no one else was around, she could at least distract herself with some snooping.

The room had a desk, some bookshelves, and filing cabinets like a usual office, but there was also an entire wall lined with shelves covered in sealed jars, some made of translucent glass with herbs inside and others made of thick black and brown glass with unknown contents. There were strange glass and metal chemistry instruments scattered around, and bunches of dried flowers hung upside down from strings tacked to the ceiling.

Alice poked around the disorganized room, shuffling through a stack of mail, most of it addressed to Violet O'Connell. On the desk sat a few leather books, no titles on the front or sides. She flipped through one of them and saw it was the same Latin book Leander had been reading the other night. Some of the words were recognizable. One chapter seemed to be about nature and plants, while another chapter was about something called *eligere et exsugo,* but she had no idea what that meant.

She tucked the Latin book under her arm, hoping to sneak it up to her room and translate as much as she could from memory. There was a notepad under the book, and it had a few words hastily scribbled in copperplate calligraphy across the page:

Princeton University,
Classics Department, Foster,
snow, brown hair,
house fire, blood, stairs

Her hand flattened her hair subconsciously. The night she and Leander spoke in the courtyard on campus, his eyes tracked the snow falling in her hair, saying her name out loud as if it was familiar. Alice ripped the page from the notebook, spooked by the oddly specific notes. What made it even more strange was the fact that it was dated a week ago, before the incident even occurred. It must've been a mistake.

Alice opened the desk drawer and found a collection of silver knives of different sizes. She slammed the drawer closed, suddenly feeling like she wasn't meant to know all the details of this investigation yet. Or maybe they've been lying to her about everything because they're actually the ones who tried to kill her. The details didn't line up.

She braced her shaking hands on the desk. Leander had been following her across campus that entire evening and conveniently arrived at her house just in time to save her from the fire. He said he was a criminal investigator following a lead, but it could've been a lie. Those badges could be fake. Leander could very well be the one who started the fire, but then again, it wouldn't make sense if he was the one who saved her. Unless it was a ruse, some cover story to make the public believe Alice died in the fire, while they kept her here to torment her with whatever malicious plans they had.

"Ridiculous," she mumbled to herself as she paced the room. "Just relax. They haven't hurt you." *Yet*. Alice talked herself down from a panic attack, convincing herself to trust these people for now, ignoring her gut feeling to run away. She decided if things continued to seem strange over the next day, if she found out any other damning information, she'd sneak out when they weren't looking.

Her pacing halted. On the far wall was a door with an alarming amount of padlocks, all of which happened to be unlocked. She moved closer to inspect it. The door wasn't made of wood, but bolted iron. She placed a tentative hand on the cold metal handle, and as she pulled it open, a strange breeze ruffled her hair before a firm hand slapped onto the door and pushed it closed. Alice jumped.

"Nothing to see in there." Leander angled his body between her and the door. "Besides a dusty old basement." He wore a well-tailored navy suit and held a black tie in his free hand. "I thought I heard someone rustling around in here."

"I'm sorry, I was—"

"Curious about the house full of strangers and our odd collections?" Leander's eyebrows were raised. "Use that Ivy League brain of yours." He tapped his temple. "Violet is a nurse. She likes to research and collect medicinal herbs."

Leander said as he gestured to the shelves. "She has a huge garden in the backyard. And this..." he pounded his fist on the iron door. "Leads directly to the basement, which leads outside. We don't want any intruders, due to our line of work. Must've forgotten to lock it this morning." Leander went down the long line of padlocks, his deft fingers locking each and every one of them with a satisfying click.

"Oh." She scratched her head, lips pursed in thought. Again, it was an explanation that seemed to make sense. Or it could be a good cover story that he had rehearsed all morning. "What time is it?" Alice asked.

"Almost seven." Leander guided her out of the office by her shoulders and into the kitchen. The light from the growing dawn streamed in through the windows. "I was up much earlier than you. Busy day ahead. Breakfast?" He encouraged Alice to sit at the table.

"What was with all the knives?" She knitted her brows as she sat. Leander's tone was much more cordial this morning compared to his irritability from the previous evening. Perhaps it had been the alcohol bringing down his mood last night. Either that, or he was placating her to make sure she remained agreeable.

"Hm?" He glanced over his shoulder absentmindedly before returning to his task of brewing a pot of coffee. "Knives?" He paused. "Oh you mean Violet's gardening collection?"

Alice knew a bit about gardening. "They didn't look like—"

"They're collectibles," Leander said as he placed a fresh cup of tea and a plate of buttered toast with jam in front of Alice.

"Why can't I have coffee?" She asked as the smell filled

up the kitchen. It made her miss spending time in the cafe on campus with her friends.

Leander poured himself a cup. "Caffeine wouldn't be great for your anxiety right now."

"What about decaf?"

"Well—" He halted when he noticed the Latin book on her lap. "Some light reading for later?"

"Apparently I have to brush up on my Latin," she said with a scowl, placing it on the table. "What does *eligere et exsugo* mean?"

"Oh, hmm," he tapped his chin as he sat down across from her. "That one I don't actually remember. I'll have to look it up later." He placed a hand on the book and pulled it towards him. Clearly, he didn't want her to look through it.

"Yeah well what about this?" Alice shoved the notebook paper in his face. "Why do you have these weird notes about me and my dad?"

Leander started on his own breakfast. "Well, this is an investigation." He leaned in and pointed at her with the crust of his toast. "A private investigation."

"Why is it dated *before* the night of the fire?"

"Huh?" Leander snatched it out of her hands. "Shit, I've been writing the wrong date on all of my paperwork." He folded up the paper and pocketed it. "You really shouldn't have been snooping."

"But—"

"I'm sorry, Alice. We can't tell you anything else right now."

She forced her plate away. "I deserve to know. It's about my father, and someone tried to kill us... and Dillon." She didn't continue her next thought. *She* killed Dillon. Accidentally.

Leander stopped chewing his food. "I'm legally not allowed to mention anything."

With a mumbled curse, Alice excused herself from the table. Everything was becoming so convoluted, and the knife collection and the ridiculously padlocked door were more than concerning. Tonight she'd sneak out when they were asleep.

Right as she turned to leave, she bumped into Natalie who was also dressed in a tailored pants suit and tie, her long hair twisted into a low polished bun.

Natalie grasped Alice's upper arms. "Hey what's going on? Are you okay?" She peered over Alice's shoulder at Leander who shook his head.

"No one wants to tell me anything, that's what." Alice attempted to push past Natalie, to go where, she didn't know. If she tried to leave right now, they'd probably chase her down, and she knew she wouldn't make it far because of her still-healing injuries.

"Alice found some interesting things in Violet's office this morning," Leander said, his mouth full of food.

"Did she?" Natalie asked. "Alice, you know we can't tell you anything about the investigation."

Alice wouldn't look her in the eye. She was tired of being in the dark, tired of being treated like a kid, like a prisoner. "Yeah, you keep saying that." She wriggled against Natalie's grip. And she was tired of them manhandling her all the damn time.

"Did you eat or drink anything?"

"I'm not hungry," she snapped. "Will you let me go?"

"You should have something," Natalie said, sounding more concerned. "You haven't touched your food or your tea."

"I said no," Alice said with a raised voice, finally breaking free from Natalie's hold.

"Okay, okay. Sorry," Natalie said in a flurry, then grabbed Alice again, this time by the wrist. "At least let me take a look at your injuries before we leave for the day. Your stitches might be ready to come out."

"It's only been two days." Alice jerked her wrist back. "I think." She kept falling asleep for absurd amounts of time, so she wasn't completely sure about how much time had passed.

"Can I please just take a quick look?" Natalie held up her palms.

Alice balled her fists at her sides. "Fine."

She needed to keep her temper in check until she had enough nerve to get herself out of there. Even if it meant playing nice until she could sneak out, and then begging strangers for money so she could take the three day train ride to California to stay with her Aunt Jane until her dad was found.

As Alice headed back into the living room, she stopped in her tracks, heart jumping to her throat. The black-eyed, open-mouthed ghost was back, outside and flush up against the window pane, her crooked finger pointing at a linen drawstring sachet on the sill.

"What?" Natalie asked. "What's wrong?"

Squeezing her eyes shut, Alice shook her head. "Nothing." When she opened her eyes the woman, the ghost, was gone again. Her eyes drifted to the sachet. "What's that on the window sill?"

"Oh that," Natalie said with a chuckle. "Violet likes to make little potpourri pouches and stick them in all the rooms." She walked over to the window and warily looked out in all directions. "You know how old houses can get that musty smell." She chuckled again and pulled the curtains closed.

"Right." Alice shook her head again as she laid back on the couch. Her subconscious had to have been influenced from staying in a creepy old house.

Natalie carried over the bag of medical supplies and removed the gauze bandage taped over Alice's abdominal wound. She wiped away the remaining earthy paste with a damp cloth. Alice winced in anticipation, but it didn't even hurt.

"This looks great!" Natalie pulled a pair of surgical scissors from her bag and snipped away at the stitching on her stomach.

"That was really fast," Alice said looking down at her mostly healed scar. "I thought it would take a week or more."

"You were lucky," Natalie said as she worked on removing the stitches from her leg wound. "It looked a lot worse than it actually was." She slathered on some more of the paste and covered the scars with more gauze.

"Are you ready?" Leander asked as he entered the room tying his tie.

"Yeah, let's get going." Natalie straightened her suit jacket and flattened the wrinkles from her pants. "Alice, make sure you eat something today, and make sure you're drinking enough."

"Hold on," Leander said as he disappeared into the kitchen and returned with Alice's mug. "I reheated this for you."

Alice covered her face with a couch pillow and grumbled. They were a little bit too attentive to her needs, well, her need for sustenance but not her need for information.

"Set it on the table," Alice mumbled through the pillow.

"At least try it." Leander pulled the pillow from Alice's hands and tossed it aside. He held out the mug to her. "It's a different blend with a better flavor."

Natalie eyed Leander. He dipped his chin at her, and then after a short moment of hesitation, she nodded towards Alice with encouragement. "Try it," she said with a smile.

Alice looked between the both of them with narrowed eyes. They were awfully persistent about the tea. "I'm not thirsty."

"Come on, just a sip. Violet tweaked this blend for you," Natalie said.

"Why would she go through the trouble?" Alice questioned. They all knew she didn't care for the tea, and yet they kept trying to make her drink it.

"Remember how I told you herbalism was one of her hobbies?" Leander said as he handed Alice the mug. "It's how she likes to spend her time. You don't want to hurt an old woman's feelings now do you?"

Alice frowned at the not so subtle manipulation and gave the tea a tentative sniff. It actually smelled lighter than the other tea, more refreshing and less earthy. She didn't understand why it mattered so much, but she realized Leander and Natalie weren't going to leave until she tried it. If they were going to poison her or kill her, they would've done it by now when she was in her most vulnerable state.

With a resounding sigh, Alice sipped the tea, and surprisingly it was a lot more pleasant than the other blend. It tasted so good, she actually sipped again and again and again.

"Like it?" Natalie asked with bated breath.

Alice nodded as the crease between her eyebrows softened, and her scowl turned neutral. It was like peace washed over her, and any worry or anger she had slipped out of her head. She couldn't even remember what she was upset about before. She stared up at the two of them expectantly, blinking slow, trying to remember who they were. They sure were dressed nice. She wondered where they were going.

"Well it's about time we headed to work," the girl said with a smile as she placed a hand on the boy's arm.

Natalie and Leander. That's right, they were criminal investigators, investigating something she couldn't remember right now.

"We'll be out for most of the day," Natalie continued. "I remember how much you said you like Violet's tea blends."

"I did?" Alice asked. Who was Violet again? Oh yeah, Natalie's grandma. The three of them were taking care of her here.

"Yeah, yesterday." Natalie said. "So Violet whipped this up for you as a surprise."

Alice sipped and nodded again. How sweet of her. The tea *was* really good.

"Make sure you get some rest," Leander added. "When we have more information, we'll tell you what we can. In the meantime, you can trust us. You're safe here."

Alice blinked slowly again as the statement settled in her mind. *You can trust us. You're safe here.* She believed him.

"Violet will be awake soon," Natalie said as she and Leander headed for the door. "She'll keep you company today."

But Alice couldn't remember if and when Violet might've joined her, because after she finished the tea, she napped on the couch until the late afternoon and didn't wake until Leander and Natalie came home. They convinced her to come to dinner, but she could barely eat, still groggy from her long nap. Afterwards, she had just enough energy to shower for the first time since she got there.

Back in her room, someone had left a folded pile of spare clothes for her to borrow on the bed. Once she changed into pajamas, she glanced out the window. The ghostly woman was in the yard again, standing alone in the darkness, barefoot in the snow, looking all the way up at her on the third floor with those hollow eyes. Alice yanked the curtains closed, jumped into bed, and pulled the quilt over her head. She squeezed her eyes shut, willing sleep to take her, but a tap, tap, tapping on the window kept her awake for hours.

CHAPTER 4

Violet kept a beautiful backyard, even in the dead of winter. A wrought iron fence, mature oak trees, and a line of evergreen shrubs surrounded the property, making it fairly private. The garden beds were overgrown with dry brush, but Alice assumed in the spring and summer it bloomed with a variety of flowers and greenery considering the old woman's affinity for herbalism.

Alice sat on the porch steps while Violet filled the tilted stone bird bath with the hose. She liked spending time with her. It was easy. Violet was generally in a good mood most days, happy to prattle on about normal stuff like the weather, her plants, or all the wild animals from the neighborhood she cared for, things Alice liked to talk about too. Although those conversations made her miss her studies back at college and often left her wondering what her friends and classmates were up to, if they were thinking of her, or if life just kept moving forward after the local police came up empty handed in the search for the missing professor and his daughter. People seemed to move on quickly after that other student went missing last year.

"There you go little friends," said Violet. "Splash away." She rolled up the hose and clapped the dirt from her hands. The birds chirped impatiently in the nearby bushes, and as soon as the coast was clear, they flocked over to the fresh water.

Alice cracked a small smile. For the past couple days, Violet kept her distracted, keeping her focused on little things, letting her help with the cooking and cleaning and other odd jobs around the house. Leander and Natalie on the other hand, were in a continuous bad mood and avoided Alice at all costs. She'd catch them speaking in hushed voices, and they'd abruptly stop when she entered the room. They refused to answer her questions. Early every morning, they would disappear dressed in their business attire and return for dinner, spending a little bit of time exchanging fake small talk before disappearing into the office or the basement.

A few times Alice attempted to sneak around late at night to do more snooping, but Natalie was a light sleeper and Leander was always up way too late drinking in the kitchen, so she'd be diverted before reaching her goal. She had a feeling they knew what she was up to, which pissed her off even more.

At least they stopped watching over her while she slept, but they still wouldn't let her leave the house. This morning, after a news report stated yet another Princeton student went missing on campus, they doubled down on their rules, triggering a heated argument. By the end of it, Natalie actually sided with Alice, and they graciously allowed her to spend time on the back porch for some fresh air as long as Violet was out there with her.

"Those birds really trust you," Alice said as she pulled her hoodie closer around her. She knew one thing for sure, if animals trusted a human, then the human was definitely trustworthy.

She shifted on her feet as she gazed towards the wrought iron gate situated between two tall hedges, the desire to run still simmering in the back of her mind, but deep in her bones she felt like she couldn't. *You can trust us. You're safe here.* She remembered those words, but just barely, like when she tried to remember a dream in the early hours of the morning and it drifted just out of reach.

"I've been caring for the neighborhood birds for a long time. We've got a special bond." Violet hobbled up the steps of the back porch and sat on a wooden rocking chair.

"How long have you lived here?" Alice asked. If she got Violet talking, maybe she'd divulge some information about the investigation.

"My whole life, well most of it." Violet looked up into the trees and hummed a tune.

"Where else have you lived?"

"Hm?" Violet stopped humming. "I spent a few years in Vietnam after I joined the Army Nurse Corps. I wanted to help out in any way I could."

"Oh, wow." Alice sat in the rocking chair next to the old woman, hoping to hear more. "What was it like?"

"Frightening. Saw some things I shouldn't have seen as a young girl. My sister wasn't happy I went, but eventually she got over it. A few months after I was there, her letters were mostly about her new boyfriend."

Alice sensed some bitterness in Violet's voice. "Do you still talk to your sister?"

Violet stopped rocking in her chair. "No." She stared at Alice, a somber expression on her face. "She died. A long time ago."

"I'm sorry," said Alice. It hadn't been bitterness in

Violet's voice, but grief. Maybe both. "I don't have any siblings, but I've lost family. It's hard."

"Yes, they told me." Violet put a hand over Alice's. "And now your poor father is who knows where." Violet started rocking again. "Leander and Natalie will find him eventually."

"So they *are* looking for him?"

"Oh yes, can't have someone like him running around out there can we?"

"Someone like him?" Alice blinked. "What do you mean?"

Violet turned away, tight lipped. She never answered and instead hummed another tune. After a minute she said, "Look at that one, a female cardinal." She pointed. "You can tell because she's more of a tan color except for the red tuft on her head."

Alice stood up with a frustrated sigh. That was as far as the conversation would go. If she pressed too hard, Violet might tell Natalie and Leander about her continued attempts at prying.

She paced the back porch a few times then headed towards the gate. "I'm going for a walk." Maybe she'd come back, maybe she wouldn't. Although something inside told her she *should* come back.

"Oh no, sorry dear, you can't," Violet called after her. "They said you can't leave." She got up slowly, a hand pressed on her hip as she crinkled her nose in discomfort.

Alice groaned. "I just want to go across the street to look at the river. It's not that far."

"I don't know," Violet said with a frown.

"What if you come with me?"

"Well," Violet paused as she thought it over, looking concerned but amenable. "I suppose." She eased her way down the steps and followed Alice over to the gate, and together they rounded the side of the house. Violet halted in the front yard and rubbed her hip again. "I'll watch you from here, go on ahead." She pointed across the street towards the water. "Ten minutes, okay? I don't want you out there when Natalie and Leander get back. I'll never hear the end of it."

Before Violet even finished speaking, Alice was crossing the street. Ten minutes was barely enough time to clear her head, but at least it was something. It was the first time Alice had been out, really out and away from the damned house, and it felt good despite the chilly wind. She pulled her hood up to shield her ears and to hide her face from the few people out walking their dogs before the sun set. Another snowstorm was expected that evening.

She found a place to sit on the retaining wall separating the land from the river, the cold stone biting into the back of her thighs through her jeans. Her feet dangled over the edge about a foot away from the water where she could see a few minnows darting around under the surface. A couple chunks of glassy ice from the previous storm floated in the water and scraped against the stone.

Glancing over her shoulder, Alice saw Violet watching her like a hawk from the front porch, as if she didn't trust her. It's not like Violet would be able to chase her down if she decided to take off. Alice didn't plan on running. Not now, at least.

It wasn't long before the sun dipped behind the Philadelphia skyline, sending shafts of golden light through the bridge cables across the water. A little more than ten minutes had passed by, so Alice figured she should head back before Violet started hollering for her. Violet, however, was messing with something in her garden boxes on the front porch, distracted and unaware of the time that had passed.

As Alice went to cross the street, she bumped into a woman who was walking her little Yorkshire terrier. The woman did a double take and stopped.

"Are you Alice?" She asked, reeling in her dog.

Eyes wide, Alice didn't know what to say. She was supposed to be in witness protection. People weren't supposed to know who she was. Her gaze snapped to Violet who was focused on pulling dried vines from the garden boxes.

"Some man just told me to give this to you." The woman shoved a folded up piece of paper into Alice's hand.

Brows furrowed, Alice unfolded the paper. In scratchy handwriting, it read:

> Little Bug -
> Meet me at the church on the corner of
> 4th and Main after sundown.
> Love, Dad

Her stomach lurched as her head whipped around looking for him. He had to be nearby if he was able to get someone to deliver a personalized note directly to her. Unless this was some kind of trick by the murderer to lure her somewhere. "Why didn't he give me the note himself?"

The woman shrugged.

"Did he say anything else?"

"No, sorry," the woman said. "But he looked really sick."

It had to be him.

"Do you know where 4th and Main is?" Alice didn't care if it was a lure, if there was a risk of being kidnapped, she had to at least scope it out. If her dad was sick, she needed to get to him so they could help him.

The woman turned and pointed down the road towards a dock jutting out into the river. "See the main dock over there? Right across from that is Main Street. Just follow it a few blocks and you'll see the church."

Clutching the paper to her chest, Alice thanked the woman and crossed the street towards Violet's three-story Victorian home. Once back in the front yard, she noticed how much it was falling into disrepair. The outside walls were lined with huge cut stones, but a few were missing. The wooden front steps bowed in and splintered. The porch roof sagged in one corner, and an animal made some sort of nest with a pile of leaves in the gutter.

With a grunt, Violet yanked out the last dried vine. "Oh, you're back," said the old woman as she wiped her dirty hands on her pants. "Enjoy the view?"

"Yeah." Alice stealthily stuffed the note into her pocket. "Thanks for letting me take a look."

"Of course dear," Violet said. "I know Natalie and Leander can be a little overbearing sometimes."

"You don't say," Alice said.

Back inside, Alice declined dinner and said she was going to bed early that night. Luckily, Leander and Natalie hadn't returned from work yet. Perfect. She pretended to walk upstairs, waited for Violet to be busy in the kitchen, and then she snuck out the front door without a sound. She'd figure out how to sneak back in later. And if she was caught, well it was easier to ask for forgiveness than ask for permission.

Fluffy snowflakes were already sticking to the dried grass as Alice made her way down Bank Avenue. The fresh powder also covered up the grey piles of slush from the snow plows on the sides of the road, hiding the dismal ugliness and actually made it look magical outside again. She pulled up her hood for warmth and anonymity as her hurried footsteps took her towards the docks. A few more grand Victorian homes lined the street facing the water, and she could only imagine the wealthy families who had built them a century ago.

The most monstrous mansion loomed in the shadow of dusk on the corner of the block, towering over the neighboring houses at twice their size, its silhouette steeped in a macabre aura reminiscent of a Victorian haunted house from an old ghost film. It looked uninhabited, lonely and forgotten, with no electricity and half of the windows boarded up. Patches of masonry had crumbled off the exterior wall, damaged by the crawling vines. It was a shame this historic home had been allowed to deteriorate. Surely someone could've purchased it and restored it to its previous glory. A shadow moved in one of the upper windows. Alice stopped, frozen with fear and curiosity. Perhaps the mansion was actually haunted, and that's why no one wanted to claim it. Alice sure as hell wouldn't.

Gas lamps flickered on along the emptying street, lamps that must have been there for as long as those old mansions. Feeling unsettled, Alice checked over her shoulder. Nothing was there, but still she picked up her pace. After a couple more minutes, she reached the dock and made a right onto Main Street. Just a few more blocks and she'd be meeting with her father. Hopefully. She pushed the fear of it being a ruse out of her mind.

Alice stood in front of the massive brownstone church, staring up at the stained glass rose window located at the pinnacle of the facade which glowed from the soft interior light. Her hood fell back as she craned her neck, allowing snowflakes to dust her hair as she attempted to discern the images depicted in the glass. Not being religious herself, a building with breathtaking architecture such as this still could make Alice feel connected to something greater.

Below the circular window was the narthex alcove which jutted out slightly, and it was lined with more stained glass lancet windows. The red-painted, main entrance doors were at the base of the bell tower to the right. A historic informational plaque was stationed on a podium to the side of the walkway, signifying that the church was constructed in 1855, just four years after the town of Riverton was founded.

Looking from side to side, Alice wondered where exactly her father had intended to meet. She listened for any signs of approach, the falling snow making everything quiet enough that she could hear each flake as they hit the ground. She drew in a shaky breath.

A strong hand clapped on her shoulder. Startled, Alice whirled around.

"What are you doing?" Leander asked with a deep scowl. He wore his suit and tie from work, no coat, unfazed by the cold and snow.

"Going for a walk." Alice stiffened. She didn't plan on mentioning the note from her dad.

"You know you're not supposed to leave." Leander narrowed his eyes.

Alice ignored the comment. "How did you find me?"

"We saw you sneaking out the front door just as we were pulling up to park." He smirked. "Thought you were being slick, huh?"

Alice pursed her lips as he chided her. "No one else saw me."

"You don't know that." Leander gestured down the sidewalk. "Let's go."

Alice mumbled a curse. She'd find a way to ditch him on the walk back, just to give her enough time to look for her dad. He can be pissed at her later.

A loud crash sounded from inside the church. Alice and Leander stopped mid-step, eyes locked on the front door. Someone screamed. Leander, as a police officer with duties to protect and serve, should've been rushing in to help, but he didn't even budge. There was another scream which sounded more painful than the first. They had to do something. What if it was her dad?

Throwing caution to the wind, Alice darted for the entrance.

"Don't!" Leander lunged for her but she was too quick.

The bulky red doors groaned as Alice swung them open. She paused at the far end of the nave. A man lay on the floor in the chancel before the altar, and another person was crouched over them. One of the tall golden candelabras had fallen over, candles snuffed out, and glass from a broken vase littered the floor.

Panicked, she ran towards the front before Leander could grab her. Approaching the altar, her run slowed to a walk as she took in the scene before her.

A puddle of crimson coated the floor beneath the two men. It wasn't her father injured on the floor. No, her father was the one crouched over the bloodied body. The victim's legs were bent in awkward positions, their throat slit open. Professor Benjamin Foster looked up at Alice with sunken eyes. Blood dripped from his mouth and down his chin.

"Alice," he croaked. His grayish skin was taut and dehydrated, like he was on the edge of death. Scraggly patches of facial hair covered his gaunt jawline, and ragged clothes hung loosely on his bones. He held up his blood-covered hands.

"Dad?" Her voice shook. "What's going on?"

Leander threw his arm in front of her. "Get back, Alice."

"Did you..." She couldn't say the words. Her eyes lingered on the dead body.

"It's not what you think," Ben said as he stumbled to his feet, wiping his bloody mouth on his sleeve.

"Y-you killed him, didn't you?" Alice stuttered, backing away. She didn't want to ask the next question, if he drank the man's blood. Her dad wasn't a monster, even though right now he looked like one.

"Little Bug, please... listen." He seized her hand.

Leander caught his wrist and pulled him off. "Don't touch her."

Her father tried to yank himself free. When he realized he couldn't overpower Leander's strength, he reached for something in his pocket with his other hand. Silver flashed through the candlelight. Alice screamed.

"Fuck," Leander hissed, instantly releasing Ben. He stumbled away from her father, his hand clutching the left side of his chest, blood gushing between his fingers and staining the front of his white shirt and suit jacket. He swayed on the spot, eyes squeezed shut, his breathing labored.

Alice's hands flew to her mouth.

Leander opened his eyes, and with a heavy sigh he straightened his back, as if the fatal stab wound to his chest was just a scratch.

"You should be dead!" Ben cried, still holding the bloodied knife in mid air.

With a grunt, Leander stalked towards her father. "Well, I'm not."

Ben's eyes widened as he backed away. He gave one last apologetic look at Alice and bolted for the back door.

Alice's breathing shallowed, disoriented from shock. Her gaze shifted between the back door, Leander's bloody stab wound, and the dead body at her feet, the body that looked like it actually might still be alive.

"Alice, get away from—"

The man's eyes snapped open, cloudy and white, just like Dillon. Alice tripped backwards with a scream. Leander bounded for her, putting his body between her and the man, who crouched on all fours in front of the gilded altar, snarling like an animal with rabies, blood dripping out of the gaping slash in his neck.

The flashback of Dillon slammed into her. She couldn't move.

"Shit," Leander said under his breath, urging Alice backwards step by step, his hand outstretched in front of him.

The man hurtled himself up the aisle towards them, leaving a trail of bloody handprints on the decorative tile floor.

The heat hit her before the blinding light. Alice winced as she raised her arm to shield herself from a wall of flames. Leander flourished his hand in a sweeping motion, a trail of fire in its wake, separating them from the man.

Alice staggered back and clutched her chest. Days ago, Leander had carried her out of the house fire, and the flames hadn't touched him then, like they answered to him, like he could *control* them. And now he was summoning fire from nothing. It shouldn't be possible. It couldn't. It didn't make sense. She had to be in some kind of nightmare.

Leander swiped his hand again. The fire billowed out towards the man. He yelped, cowering in pain as the flames licked his skin. Leander pressed forward as the fire engulfed him, his skin blackening with each passing second, his screams echoing off the vaulted ceiling as he collapsed beneath the pulpit.

Sirens blared from outside. Red and blue flashing lights shone through the stained glass windows.

"Son of a bitch," Leander growled. He brandished his hand again, guiding the flames around the perimeter of the church, igniting the wooden pews on both sides of the nave, and then up into the vaulted ceiling setting the rafters ablaze.

Alice couldn't breathe. Her brain couldn't make sense of what she was actually seeing, what she had already seen. A helpless whimper escaped her lips. She couldn't figure out if she was in danger, if she should try to run, if her father was the villain or Leander. Sweat dripped down her face from the heat of the fire. She wavered, feeling faint.

Leander gripped her upper arm. "We need to go."

"Get off me!" Alice struggled against him.

"I need you to trust me," he said through gritted teeth.

"You set my house on fire!"

"No, I was the one who saved you, remember?" He held her upper arms and looked her in the eye, his voice steady. "Now listen to me. We need to get out of here before the police see us."

Alice gaped at him. "I thought you were the police?"

"Yeah, about that—"

The front doors banged open, letting in the cacophony of sirens and fire engine horns. Firefighters made their way into the church, their shouting dampened by the roar of the fire. Leander sent a flourish of flame to block the way, effectively hiding the two of them from their view. He shrugged out of his suit jacket and pulled his bloodied shirt over his head, then tossed them into the flames.

"What are you—"

"Destroying evidence. Now let's go." He pulled her towards a door at the back of the church, the same one her father had used to escape. Leander waved his hand to clear a path through the flames which separated enough to let them pass through, and they headed down into the basement.

The fire thundered above them, the building shaking from ceiling beams crashing to the floor. Cinders rained down through the cracks in the floor above their heads. Heat and smoke rippled around them. They pushed their way through a storage area, tripping and falling into random objects, desperate to get out of the church before it collapsed. As they passed a coat rack, Leander snatched one and threw it on. They rushed towards the metal bulkhead doors, and he cracked them open an inch to see outside without being detected.

Alice peered through the crack next to him, the cold air blasting away the heat. Most of the emergency responders were centered at the entrance to the church, leaving the back end clear for escape.

"When I say go, I need you to run for those bushes over there. Got it?" Leander said.

Alice gulped and nodded. It was either trust him or run to the front of the church, straight to the police, the *real* police, and tell them what she just witnessed. They'd never believe her.

Before she had a chance to question it further, Leander gave her the signal, and they both bolted across the property through the memorial garden behind the church, crouched low until they were hidden amongst the bushes.

Leander led her through thick trees behind another old building, the Parish house according to the signage, and out onto the sidewalk a block away from the chaos.

"Walk fast, but act normal," Leander said out of the side of his mouth as a police car whizzed by.

Alice's entire body quaked from the insanity they just escaped. Leander hurried ahead of her on the snowy sidewalk. She couldn't keep up with him. Hot tears flowed down her stinging cold cheeks. She could barely lift her feet.

When he realized she was falling behind, he paused. "Alice you need to—"

Her bottom lip quivered and her buckling legs shuffled to a stop. She couldn't believe what could've led her father to do such a heinous thing. She heard about retired millionaires in secret cults that drank the blood of young people to slow their aging, but that was just rumors and pseudoscience. Her dad would never believe something like that. He'd never kill someone. *But he did.*

And then the man, who looked completely dead, came back to life acting like a crazed animal just like Dillon had, and Leander burned him to death with some sort of fire manipulation. She hugged herself, nails digging into her arms hard enough to cause pain through her long sleeves.

Worry flashed across Leander's face as he rushed to her side, hand bracing her lower back to keep her upright. "Come on. Only a few more blocks."

Alice didn't know how she could keep going. Everything felt like it was moving in slow motion. Her eyes scanned around her, wondering where her father could've gone, if she even wanted to know. She gazed up at the cloudy sky, snow flurries melting on her face. Leander hadn't chased after her father, even though he just murdered someone. But then again, Leander said he wasn't with the police, and he was fatally stabbed but didn't die. And some how he summoned fire from nothing. Alice had no idea what that made him. Another police car flew by followed by an ambulance. She cringed from the brightness of the lights.

"We need to keep moving," Leander urged, pushing her forward. "Or these cops are going to stop us because we look suspicious."

Another vehicle, an old beat up SUV with the headlights turned off, sped down the block and pulled up to the curb next to them. They rolled down the window.

"Get in," Natalie said in a loud whisper.

Leander ushered Alice into the back seat and slid in next to her. Natalie took off driving before Leander could close the door.

"What the fuck happened? The church is on fire!" Natalie said. "I tried calling you—"

"I was a little preoccupied with Alice's dad."

Natalie gasped. "What?" She whipped the car around the corner, going a little too fast for a residential neighborhood. "As soon as I heard the sirens, I knew something was wrong. Followed the cops to the church—"

"So if you're not cops," Alice said, her voice frantic. "Then who the hell are you? What's going on?"

"Uh," Natalie started. "You wanna answer that one, Leander?"

"Not now." Leander's gaze was fixed out the back window.

They were back at the house in less than a minute. Leander and Natalie hurried towards the front door, trailing through an inch of snow. Alice stalled on the curb. The ghost woman with black eyes stood there waiting in the center of the yard.

"Alice, what's wrong?" Natalie asked, eyes darting around to make sure no one was watching them.

To get inside, she'd have to pass the ghost. Alice wasn't sure if she wanted to go inside, if she wanted to stay with these people. But at the moment, she really had nowhere else to go, no one else to trust. *You can trust us. You're safe here.* Alice frowned, conflicted by the thought that didn't seem like her own.

The ghost floated towards Natalie, reaching out a hand as if to caress her hair, but it went straight through her. Natalie didn't even notice it, couldn't even see it. Alice tried to tell herself it was another hallucination, that it couldn't possibly be real. With Natalie standing right next to the ghost woman, Alice finally realized why she looked so familiar. She must be some deceased family member, maybe the sister that Violet had said passed away a long time ago. And for some reason, that made the ghost a little less scary.

A car turned a corner a few blocks away and headed up their road, moving slowly and shining a bright flashlight out of their window like they were searching for someone.

"We need to get inside," Leander said. "Now."

Again, Alice felt compelled to run into the street to flag down the police, beg them to help, beg them to get her away from these people. She looked back to the ghost who cocked her head to the side and then pointed to the house. Alice felt absurd that not only was she acknowledging that the ghost could be real, but she was going to trust it. She headed inside with the others, the ghost's black-eyed gaze following her the entire way.

CHAPTER 5

Alice stood rigid in the foyer. Leander locked the door behind them and tossed his stolen coat aside. Natalie pulled the curtains closed in the living room. Violet hovered in the kitchen doorway nervously surveying the scene and looking guilty.

Natalie hissed through her teeth when she noticed the coagulated stab wound on Leander's bare chest. "That looks like it hurt," she said as she prodded the skin next to it with her finger, causing him to cringe.

"How are you not dead?" Alice asked. "That knife would've punctured your lung, maybe even your heart."

Leander and Natalie exchanged a glance. Violet disappeared into the kitchen.

"You said you'd tell me what's going on when we got back." Alice raised her voice.

"How much did she see?" Natalie asked Leander.

He sighed. "Enough."

Natalie nodded. "Alright then," she said as she gestured for them to have a seat in the living room. "Time to have the talk."

So this was something they've done before. Whoever they are, whatever they do. They weren't cops. They've been holding her hostage. Leander has some sort of way to summon fire, and Alice was positive she didn't see him holding a chemical flamethrower. Her heart thundered in her chest. If she tried to run away now, she didn't know what he could do to her, if he'd turn her skin to ash.

"Leander and I," Natalie began. "We're not really criminal investigators working for witness protection. We're not with the police. We were chosen to help restore the natural order."

"Chosen?" Alice asked with a confused frown. "By whom?"

"*Eligere*," Leander said.

Alice closed her eyes, remembering the chapter title in Leander's Latin book. *Eligere et Exsugo*. "I don't understand."

"It's complicated," Natalie said as she sat on the couch, patting the cushion for Alice to sit next to her.

Leander perched on the arm of the recliner across from them, scratching his head as he searched for the words. "They're beings, like spirit beings," he began carefully. "They're commonly called daemons."

Alice flinched at the word. "Daemons? Are you kidding me?" She didn't want to believe it. However, after having all of these supernatural encounters, she had no idea what could be possible any more.

"It's not what you're thinking, not exactly," Leander said. "Daemon is a more neutral term of reference as compared to the typical Judeo-Christian demon. The *eligere* is one type of daemon, and they choose individuals to inhabit in order to provide them with certain abilities, such as manipulating elements."

Every science class Alice had ever taken never explained

something like this. Sure there were bizarre things in the animal kingdom—like electric eels that can produce low volt electricity, chameleons and octopi that can change their appearance, and bioluminescent creatures that can emit light—but the manipulation of elements wasn't supposed to be possible by anything, animal or human.

"So you're telling me," Alice rubbed her forehead. "That you're possessed by daemons that give you magic powers?"

"We're meant to protect people from evil, unnatural things," Leander said. "Like your father."

Her stomach dropped. "My dad? Is he possessed by a daemon too?" The words felt foreign on Alice's tongue. Never before would she consider such esoteric nonsense.

"No." Leander bowed his head with an exhausted sigh. "Unfortunately what's going on with your father is much worse."

"What could possibly be worse than being possessed by a daemon?" Alice asked.

"You told us that your dad translated an old book last year, and then a few months later his cancer disappeared," Leander said. "There's only one thing we know of that can cure diseases. It goes by many names, such as *essentia mortis, ius vitae*, the Fountain of Youth, the Elixir of Life..."

Alice twisted her face in confusion. She remembered reading a brief passage about Ponce de Leon in one of her history classes. "That's absurd. It's just a legend."

"Some legends are based in fact. There aren't many copies of the recipe, but there was one in that book," Leander said.

"But my dad would never believe in something like that."

"How desperate do you think he was to cure his cancer?" Natalie asked.

"I don't know," Alice whispered. Her father hadn't seemed desperate at all. Even though he was sad about the poor prognosis, he seemed to have accepted his death, especially when he refused treatment the second time around. But there had been a few nights when she couldn't contain her grief, nights when she let the tears escape in front of her father. If he had noticed how distraught she had been, maybe that's what pushed him down this path. She cursed herself for it. "Does the elixir have any side effects? Why would he—" she faltered, her throat dry. "—why would he kill someone?"

"We don't know the exact details," Leander said. "Except the main ingredient is human blood."

"Human *what*?" Alice grimaced. "Why?"

"*Sanguis est vis vitae*. Blood is the life force," Leander said. "The elixir causes the victim's soul to bind with the blood, so that when your father drinks their blood, he gains the victim's health, vitality, and remaining years. It becomes addicting after a while."

"Their soul?" Her voice trembled. "Meaning what exactly?"

"If he keeps killing, if he keeps stealing souls, he could live forever," Natalie said. "The Elixir of Life is the key to immortality, and the main ingredient is death."

"Oh my god, the student that went missing last spring. It was the same week my dad's cancer was cured. And then Dillon." Alice held her head in her hands. "And that man in the church? Is that what made them attack? My dad took their soul?"

"Yes," said Leander. "Without a soul, the bodies become shells, or as we refer to them, *Immortui*. They also feed on blood in order to function, so they're another unnatural thing that needs to be controlled."

"This is so fucked up." Alice dragged her nails through her hair. "What's going to happen to my dad?"

Leander sighed. "The more he kills, the more souls he consumes, it'll warp and distort his own soul until he forgets his humanity. Even hurt people he loves."

"Like me?" Alice's throat tightened. "Was he the one who set our house on fire?"

Natalie pulled a face. "We think so. After killing Dillon, he might've had enough sense to try and cover up the scene. Maybe he didn't know you were in there."

Alice sniffled. "He had to have known. I was banging on the door and calling out for him." Her heart broke in her chest with each excruciating beat. "But if he wanted to kill me, why didn't he come after me tonight then? He ran away."

"He was probably shocked that the knife didn't kill me," Leander said. "And ran off because he was afraid."

Alice blinked. "Why didn't the knife kill you? Does it have something to do with the daemon?"

"Essentially, yes." Leander looked down at the wound which was crusted over with dried blood. "Because it did pierce my heart, I felt it, and I definitely would've died without the *eligere*."

Violet came bustling back into the living room, two steaming mugs of tea in her hands. Leander took his gratefully and set it to the side. Alice didn't accept hers.

"Why the obsession with tea?"

"It'll help," Violet said, adamantly offering it to Alice again.

"Why isn't he drinking his?" Alice pursed her lips and eyed the mug Leander had set aside. "Have you been drugging me?" She jumped to her feet and paced the room, recalling how many times they forced her to drink it. Every time she drank it, she had passed out. "You're drugging me and it's making me hallucinate. This has all been a lie. None of this is real. You're trapping me here. You won't let me contact anyone." Alice backed out of the room towards the foyer.

"Alice, we're trying to help," Natalie said, hands raised in trepidation.

"I don't believe you!" Alice shouted.

"Please, listen," Natalie begged. "We gave you the tea to help you calm down. It's blended with another herb, a sedative. We didn't tell you because we thought it would be too much to handle at once."

"Too much?" Alice's voice cracked.

They were right, it was too much.

She dove towards the front door, hands fumbling with the handle. Alice barely cracked the door before a gust of wind slammed it shut. The potted ivy plants on the console table fluttered with movement as the tendrils lengthened and twisted over the door knob. Alice whipped around to see Natalie's arm extended, hand open wide as she manipulated the plant until the entire door was latticed with ivy.

Alice sprinted to the kitchen, but she skidded to a halt. White claw-like hands gripped the window sill, and two beady black eyes peered in through the pane. The face looked less than human, with paper thin skin stretched across angular skull bones. Fear rippled through Alice's body, hair standing on end. The creature disappeared from sight.

"Holy shit," Natalie said from behind her.

"What was that thing?" Alice was pretty sure she didn't want to leave anymore.

"Your dad." Leander ran over to the window to check if he was still there. "He's gone," he said as he closed the curtains. "I doubt he'll try to get in here, at least for tonight. But we don't know what he might decide in the next few days."

"W-why did he look like that?" Tears welled in Alice's eyes again. "He didn't look like that earlier."

"*Lux foris ostendet quid sit anima intus*," Leander said. "Light will make seen on the outside what the soul is on the inside. As his soul descends further into darkness, light will distort his appearance and become painful to him, especially artificial light."

"How will you stop him?" Alice asked, afraid of the answer. The idea of her father's soul becoming distorted into something sinister was heartbreaking. If the soul was real, she hoped there wasn't a dark afterlife waiting for him.

"We're not sure yet," answered Leander.

"Can he be saved?"

"We don't know." Natalie said. "All we know is he's dangerous."

"Can he get in here?"

"We have sachets of banishing herbs in the four corners of the house and at all the windows, so it should deter him," Natalie answered. "If he continues to consume blood, he could get strong enough to break in, but hopefully it won't come to that."

Violet peeked her head into the kitchen with the second mug of tea in her hands. "I think it's time for the tea," she said.

"You're still trying to give me that sedative?" Alice snapped.

"I'm giving it to both of you." Violet nodded her head towards Leander. "It's not just a sedative. It accelerates healing."

Alice looked down at her body and realized her jeans

were torn open at the knees revealing nasty scrapes. Her palms were all cut up. The left sleeve of her hoodie was sliced open showing off an ugly gash. Through all the trauma she didn't even notice she had been hurt.

"It's why we had to give it to you every day when you first got here," said Natalie.

Violet handed her the mug. "It helps you heal faster, that's why it makes you so tired. You lost so much blood the other night, and you had a terrible infection. Without the tea, you wouldn't have made it. You can trust us. You're safe here."

You can trust us. You're safe here.

There were those words again. It strummed something deep in her mind, and she believed it to be true. Alice met Violet's shining blue eyes and felt a strange surge of love for the old woman, because she had such a motherly comfort about her, something she hadn't felt in a long time. These people really did save her life. Leander saved her from the fire and protected her from harm. Violet and Natalie saved her from her injuries. Maybe she could trust them. Maybe she could be safe there.

Alice finally nodded in agreement. After hearing everything and seeing her father and his twisted face, the idea of passing out and having a dreamless sleep seemed like a good idea.

"We'll tell you more as time goes on, but for now you need to rest," Natalie said.

"Okay," Alice said with a strained voice. She still felt a little hesitant, but she had no energy left in her to argue or question. After a few sips of the tea, she quickly felt herself become unsteady from the fatigue. Natalie and Leander helped her upstairs to her bedroom, and she passed out as soon as her head hit the pillow.

CHAPTER 6

"Why can't I call my friends?" Alice asked, poking at her chicken pot pie with a fork. Violet had to convince her to come downstairs and have dinner. "I'll make sure they don't tell anyone."

"It's not a good idea," Natalie said. "If they let anything slip, it could mess up the whole situation, especially if the real police got involved." She sighed and loosened her tie. Natalie and Leander had spent the day scouring the town while impersonating law enforcement, questioning locals to see if there were sightings of her father after the church fire. Nothing noteworthy had been reported.

"Would your friends even believe you?" Leander asked, too snarky for Alice's liking.

"It doesn't matter if they believe me," she snapped back. Alice wasn't even sure if she believed all of it, and she had seen it with her own eyes.

"Surely it couldn't hurt to let her have a short conversation with her friends," Violet chimed in, patting her mouth with a napkin. "Just so that they know she's okay."

"It's too big of a risk," Natalie said.

"Please, I promise they wouldn't tell a soul." Alice was desperate to talk to someone who didn't live in this house.

"It's not happening," Leander said as he leaned back in his chair. "End of discussion."

Alice had enough of him. "Seriously, why—"

A sharp knock on the front door interrupted Alice's retort. Violet jolted in her seat. Natalie choked mid-sip on her drink. They exchanged confused glances around the table. Another knock cut through the silence. After an uneasy look with Leander, Natalie left to investigate.

"Were you expecting company?" Alice asked.

Leander shook his head. "We never expect company." He craned his neck to listen for any bits of conversation.

Natalie reappeared in the kitchen doorway with her arms folded. "Your brother's here."

Leander dropped his hand to the table, rattling the glasses and utensils. "Of course he is."

"Am I letting him in?" Her eyebrows arched in tentative anticipation. It seemed like she'd already made up her mind.

"I don't want him here." Leander clenched his jaw.

"I know how you feel about him, but we could use his help," Natalie said. "The two of you are the only ones who've actually handled this type of situation. He said he saw the church fire on the news and came to see if we needed assistance. So I told him what's going on." She sighed. "Why don't we bring him in and at least see what he has to say?"

"We could use the help," Alice pressed. She wasn't going to let Leander's attitude get in the way of helping her father.

Leander drummed his fingers with resignation. "Fine."

Natalie returned moments later with a man following close behind. He was classically handsome, with dark hair and olive skin just like his brother, and only looked a few years older. His clothes looked casual but expensive. Curiosity flashed in his eyes as he scanned the room.

"William, you can have a seat next to Alice," Natalie said, beckoning him to the table.

On his way to his seat, William nodded at Alice, and she forced a weak smile. Then he greeted Violet by kissing her on the cheek. The old woman flushed and giggled.

Leander rolled his eyes.

William's friendly expression hardened. "Little brother," he said, his voice flat. He pulled out his chair, the metal screeching on the linoleum floor, and sat down.

Violet passed an extra dish with a serving of pot pie to their new guest. Natalie fetched a couple beers from the fridge and handed them to the brothers. Leander drank his immediately, pitched the bottle cap towards the trash can, and slammed his bottle on the table.

"Leander. Stop," Natalie said.

"Am I supposed to act like everything is fine?" Leander asked. "Last time he was here, he punched me in the face."

William scowled. "If I remember correctly, you punched me first."

"And I told you to never come back. Yet here you are."

"Hey!" Natalie slapped her palms on the table. A gust of air blew past them, sending a pile of napkins swirling to the floor. The flame of the candle at the center of the table swelled in size. "Knock it off. Both of you. The sooner we figure out how to handle this, the sooner you can get back to never talking to each other again."

Alice was stunned by Natalie's ferocity and the magic that spilled out because of it. The brothers glowered at each other but said no more. Violet abandoned her half-eaten meal and went upstairs to avoid whatever situation was about to unfold. Alice watched William out of the corner of her eye. He gave her a questioning gaze in return, studying her.

"So Natalie said you both have experience with this kind of thing?" Alice asked, her voice quiet, not wanting to provoke any more arguments. But she needed to know more.

Leander looked like he forgot she was even there because he was too busy being pissed off. "Uh, yes. A while ago."

"Our father, Thomas Montgomery, also made the elixir," William said. Leander shook his head, warning his brother.

"What happened to him?" Alice played with the plastic tablecloth. Their demeanor didn't bode well.

"He," Leander paused. "Died."

Alice's breath hitched. "How did he die?"

Leander's eyes pierced into William as if he was mentally threatening him to keep his mouth shut. William ignored him and said, "We killed him."

Her fork clanged onto the table. "Killed?" Alice squeaked. She bit the inside of her cheek, forcing herself to maintain composure as heaviness sank in her chest. If the two of them couldn't even save their own father, how could she possibly hope they could save hers?

"What the fuck, William?" Leander rubbed his temple. "We didn't want to tell her yet."

"It's better than being lied to," William said. "She deserves to know the truth."

Leander scoffed. "Because you're so honest?"

"You're calling me a liar?" William raised his voice. "You've probably been lying through your teeth since the day she got here."

He was right, they had been lying to her since the very

beginning, when Alice would've preferred the truth up front, no matter how ridiculous or frightening it was. Although, she really wasn't quite sure how she would've handled it if Leander had told her that her dad was a blood-drinking murderer as soon as she woke up after the fire.

Leander shoved himself up from his chair, knocking into the table and almost spilling everyone's drinks. "We did what we thought was right." His fists clenched at his sides. "To protect her. We would've explained it eventually."

"You should've told me," Alice said.

William crossed his arms. "I rest my case."

"You should've never come back." Leander stomped out of the kitchen. The front door slammed.

"The two of you are insufferable." Natalie grumbled a slew of curse words under her breath as she stood. "Now I have to go make sure he doesn't do anything stupid." She hurried outside after Leander.

After an exasperated sigh, William went back to eating his food in silence. Alice, feeling awkward and over-whelmed, left the table without a word and curled up on the couch in the dark living room, the flickering of the dying fire the only source of light. Any hope to save her father was ripped out from under her. He was a murderer descending into madness with each passing day, and the only way to stop him was to kill him. She hugged her knees to her chest, as if she could protect her heart from shattering.

William appeared in the doorway, interrupting her private lamentation, and leaned against the frame. "That went just as bad as I thought it would. Not a very good first impression of me." His voice was much softer than it had been back in the kitchen. He ran a hand through his hair, looking a little sheepish.

"No, it wasn't," she said.

"Mind if we start over?" he asked.

Alice narrowed her eyes. "Do I even have a choice?"

"Of course you do," William answered, sliding his hands into his pockets. "Say the word, and I'll leave you alone."

She stared at him, brows furrowed, shocked that he of all people was the first one to give a shit about her choice. It piqued her interest enough to not immediately shoo him away. "Is it always like that between you two?" Alice asked, swallowing her emotions.

"Unfortunately," William said. "He's probably halfway to the bar and three shots of whiskey away from getting into a fist fight with a stranger." He sat next to her. "Are you okay?"

She scooted away from him, surprised how quickly he was making himself comfortable next to her. "Obviously not."

"I didn't mean to be so harsh about your father. I'm sorry." He rested his elbows on his knees, hands clasped together. "I know I'd want the truth."

After a week of endless questions, William seemed like the most straightforward out of everyone, even if it was harsh. Perhaps that's why Leander hated him so much, because William said things he didn't want to hear. Then again, Leander wasn't very tactful either.

"You really had to kill your dad?" she asked, tears forming in her eyes. She blinked them away before he could see. Alice couldn't imagine doing such an abominable thing. There had to be something, anything, that could prevent her father from meeting the same fate while also ensuring that no others died by his hand.

"Yes," William said, fidgeting with the band of his watch.

"He was a terrible man who did terrible things, and the elixir made him even worse. He had to be stopped."

"My dad's not terrible though." Alice wiped her nose on her sleeve, the weight of hidden grief forcing her guard down. "It has to be the elixir making him this way. He's not a killer. This isn't who he really is."

The lump returned to her throat. Alice held her breath, afraid more of her feelings would escape if she breathed too deeply. She should've paid more attention to her dad's behavior months ago. She should've noticed something was wrong. "I never imagined him to be desperate enough to believe in some supernatural cure for cancer, especially if it required him to kill people."

"Sometimes bad things happen to people who don't deserve it, and they make regrettable choices driven by their grief," William said, eyes closed as if holding onto some grief of his own.

Alice tried to imagine what she would do if the situation was reversed. If she was dying of cancer and leaving her father behind, maybe she would've made similar choices out of desperate grief. Or not. Killing someone else in order to stay alive wasn't right. But still, she didn't want to blame her father. He was under the influence of the elixir. When he looked at her last night, right before he ran away, she could see it in his eyes that the real him was in there somewhere.

"Is killing him really the only option?" Alice knew in her heart that her dad must be stopped somehow.

"I'm honestly not quite sure," William said. "This type of thing doesn't happen often because of the rarity of the elixir." He closed his eyes as he recalled the memory. "With my father, everything happened so fast. He was insanely strong, and my brother and I were still struggling with learning our abilities."

"So you have elemental abilities like the others?" Alice asked.

William nodded and hummed under his breath. "My brother and I were chosen by *eligere* shortly after our father created the elixir."

"But how do the *eligere* know who to choose?" For a brief moment, Alice wondered why *she* hadn't been chosen in response to her father's actions. Not that she wanted to be chosen. It carried too much responsibility.

"We think it has something to do with proximity to the unnatural event," he said with a shrug. "But that's all we know. Everything else is speculation."

"Are there a lot of people like you out there?" Alice felt silly asking it, but it blew her mind to think there could be others like him hiding in regular society.

William chuckled. "Oh yes, there are more of us. Not a lot, but enough to do what needs to be done when necessary. A long time ago, we were referred to as *dominus elementorum*, otherwise known as master of elements, a term which has cropped up in a few ancient texts. There are other names of course, different languages have different titles that have accumulated over the years, some not so nice. We generally go by *Eligere* or Chosen."

Alice wondered how long people with magical abilities have roamed the Earth, what types of events they have influenced, which fairy tales that might actually be true. Fairy tales that seemed more like nightmares. Blood magic, daemons, the undead—Alice shivered.

"Why did your dad make the elixir? Was he sick?"

William scoffed and hung his head. "No, his only goal was to live forever. It didn't matter what price he had to pay, or who he had to hurt in the process." He clenched his hands together, his face somber.

Alice searched his face. "He hurt you."

He finally met her gaze, his eyes glassy in the firelight. "My fiancée was his first victim. I was the one who found her."

"Oh my god," she whispered.

William handed her the left side of a black and white photograph that had been ripped in half. A man and woman stood side by side, both dressed for a fancy occasion, if the occasion happened a century ago. The man looked like William, a top hat covering most of his dark hair, and the woman had an ethereal beauty about her.

Alice scrunched her face, puzzled. "Is this from a costume party?"

"No," William tilted his head, studying her expression. "They didn't tell you anything about our past?"

"No, just the magic part." Alice felt sick to her stomach. "Where was this photo taken?"

"At my old family home, down the street from here," William said plainly, not acknowledging Alice's growing tension.

"And when?" The words almost didn't leave her mouth. It was a preposterous idea, but after all of the unbelievable things Alice heard this week, anything seemed believable now.

"It was a few weeks before Victoria was killed," William answered. "In 1876."

Alice leapt off the couch, rubbing her forehead as she looked between the photo and William. "How?"

His face was youthful, not a wrinkle or age spot in sight, no gray hair. He looked like an otherwise normal human. Part of her felt like he was lying, but looking down at the photo again it was hard to ignore the identical features. She wondered if the photo could be a fake, but it was weathered and worn, and on the back it had the date and names written in fine calligraphy: *William A. Montgomery* and *Victoria York*. The possibility began to seem more real, especially remembering her father's recent entanglement with immortality and how Leander was able to survive a knife to the heart.

"The *eligere* siphons small amounts of life force from our body in order to provide us with our abilities. This causes our cells to regenerate much faster than normal so we can provide continuous energy. Because of the increased cell regeneration, it accelerates our healing and affects the aging process." William spoke like he was simply describing the weather. Of course, it probably felt more normal to him, since apparently he had been living this truth for over a hundred years.

"Like a symbiotic relationship? This is crazy—" Alice halted when she noticed Violet in the doorway, unsure how long she had been listening. "Do you know about this?"

Violet walked over to the fireplace, plucked a picture frame from the mantle, and handed it to Alice. It was the black and white photo of two young women on a porch swing.

"That's me," Violet said. "And my sister."

Alice pulled a face. "Your sister that died?"

"Well, that's what it felt like after she was Chosen."

"Who is your sister Violet?" Alice gulped. She already knew.

"Natalie," Violet said, wringing her hands. "She's technically my big sister since she's older than me. I was born in 1934, and she was born two years before that."

Alice's mouth hung open, gaping at the two old photos

she was holding, and then looked back at William. "And you?"

"Born in 1848." William stood up and pointed to his photo. "I was twenty six when this was taken."

And if Leander was truly his brother, then that meant—

The front door slammed. Leander stopped mid-stride in the foyer when he noticed Alice, William, and Violet huddled in the center of the living room. Natalie stumbled into his back. Leander's eyes landed on the old photographs in Alice's hands. "What did you tell her?" he asked.

William snatched his photo from Alice and replaced it in his wallet. "About our past."

"There's nothing from our past she needs to know." Leander stepped forward, bristling with annoyance.

"Violet," Natalie said with an accusatory tone that made the old woman flinch. "How much did you say?"

"She told me enough," Alice answered in attempt to defend Violet from Natalie's scorn.

"It wasn't your place, either of you," Leander said, pointing a finger at them.

"Alice asked me," William said as he smacked his brother's hand away. "I wanted to be honest."

Leander's mouth quivered, like he was struggling to contain his words. "This entire situation is a very delicate matter—"

"Who cares?" William interrupted. "She already knows most of it anyway. No sense in lying about the details."

Natalie stepped forward. "Yeah, but we can't let any of this information get out—"

"Who would I tell? It's not like you let me talk to anyone else," Alice argued.

Leander stiffened and glared at his brother. "Fine. Tell her what you wish," he said. "But only if it's your story to tell." He stormed out of the room, his heavy footsteps pounding up the stairs.

Natalie folded her arms in defense. "Violet, listen, I—"

Violet turned away to replace the picture frame on the mantle. "I don't want to hear it, Natalie. Not until you stop speaking to me like a child."

The silence was taught between them.

"I never meant for it to be this way." Natalie heaved a breath, her face full of regret, then she went up stairs.

A tear slid down Violet's cheek, but she swiftly wiped it away. Her aged hands lingered on the picture of her and her sister smiling together, a snapshot of what their relationship used to be. There were about a dozen other pictures on the mantle. One of the photos featured the sisters along with two other people who Alice assumed were their parents, a smiling man in an army uniform who could've been their father, and a familiar looking woman with light-colored hair wearing a long dark dress.

Alice's heart skipped a beat. The woman was identical to the ghost who had been wandering around the yard the past couple days. By this point Alice assumed it was a real ghost, not a hallucination, along with every other ghost she had seen throughout her life. A chill ran down her spine. The ghost woman had to be Violet and Natalie's mother, lingering around in the afterlife because she missed her daughters. Two weeks ago, Alice would've dismissed any comment about the supernatural, but now her head felt like it was about to implode with all of the extraordinary evidence proving that the supernatural was quite real.

Violet cleared her throat. "William, if you're planning to stay the night, your old room is available."

"*My* old room?" he asked, scratching the back of his head.

"You always have a room here." Violet gave him a kind smile, patting him on the shoulder and leading him towards the stairs. "Come, I'll get you some fresh linens."

"Thank you," William said with a smile. "You're too kind."

The three of them headed upstairs, stopping on the second floor so Violet could fetch the linens from the closet before retreating into her own bedroom. Alice headed for the next flight of stairs, and William followed with the folded linens in his arms.

Up on the third floor was Alice's current bedroom, a bathroom, and two other rooms, one of them she now knew belonged to William. The last room, Leander's room, was at the end of the hall. His bedroom light shone underneath the door, but was blocked by a hovering shadow at the sound of their arrival. Alice knew he was listening.

"Let me know if you need anything," William said, pausing at his door. His kind eyes searched her, and it made her stomach tumble from the vulnerability.

She paused at her own door, attempting to smile. She heard the phrase many times throughout her life and realized most people say it to be nice but don't actually mean it. People could never give her what she needed anyway. And even if they could, she'd never find the strength to ask.

"Thanks," she said before disappearing into the room.

CHAPTER 7

"I'm picking up Arthur from Philly this afternoon," Natalie said as she sat on the formica countertop and ate her bagel with cream cheese.

"Who's that?" Alice kept her voice neutral. She worried about sounding too desperate, because then they might continue to withhold information, especially if they were still angry from last night. She had to work this the right way if she was ever going to get them to talk more.

"An old friend with valuable connections." Leander stared out the kitchen window as he drank his coffee. "He's been around for a while."

"Like you?" Alice spread jam on her toast, feigning causal interest.

Leander narrowed his eyes and kept half his face hidden behind his mug. "Longer than that."

"Arthur is old as hell," Natalie said with a laugh. "Like, Revolutionary War old. He taught us everything we know, and we still don't know everything."

"It was the French and Indian War, actually." Leander arched an eyebrow at Natalie.

Natalie waved him off. "Yeah, yeah—"

"Is he coming to help you kill my dad?"

Leander choked on his coffee.

"Uh," Natalie's wide eyes darted between them. "We're not sure what we're going to do yet, so we need his advice."

William strolled into the kitchen, helped himself to a cup of coffee, and leaned against the counter. "Arthur?" He blew away steam from the top of his mug. "You called him?"

"We're going need the extra help. We think Alice's father made a mistake with the elixir." Leander moved to the other side of the kitchen, away from his brother. "Because he's stronger and more volatile than expected."

Alice flinched. It sounded like he could be talking about anyone else but her father. Benjamin Foster wasn't supposed to be a murderer, he was a quiet, unassuming professor. Well, he used to be.

"Stronger?" asked William. "Like the doctor from London?" His eyes unfocused, haunted by some memory.

"It seemed that way." Leander gulped down the rest of his coffee and set the mug in the sink with a forceful clunk.

"The doctor?" Alice asked. "Were there others who made the elixir?"

"Yes, a few have tried over the years," William said as he refilled his mug. "Back in the 1880s, there was a string of murders in London. Turns out it was an old acquaintance of our father, a well-known and highly respected doctor. We found a copy of the recipe scribbled in his journal, but it had some mistakes in the translation."

"What happens if there are mistakes?" She assumed it was bad.

"The doctor became feral, animal-like," Leander said. "He left a trail of mangled bodies across the city."

Alice gagged at the horrific image. "Will that happen to

my dad?" she asked. She feared he was already halfway there.

Leander scrunched up his face. "We don't know, but we won't let it happen again."

"There has to be something we could do," she said. "Help him somehow."

The others didn't seem convinced.

"Anything?" Alice continued. "You're telling me there isn't some other magical thing that could help my dad? Couldn't we just catch him and keep him hidden away somewhere?"

"He'll still have the urge to kill," Leander said. "And if he doesn't, the cravings would be so strong it would drive him insane."

Alice racked her brain. There had to be a way it could work, even if it meant capturing him and finding blood for him to drink in the meantime, not killing people, but something. "We can figure it out."

"But what kind of life would that give him, Alice?" Leander folded his arms across his chest. "Would it be worth it?"

"I don't care." Alice clenched her jaw. "He's still my dad."

William rubbed his chin. "Maybe we don't have to kill him."

She sucked in a hopeful breath. Anything was better than the alternative. Months ago, she prepared herself for her dad's imminent death. But now that she knew magic was real, there had to be something to save him.

"And let him continue murdering innocent people?" Leander asked with a scoff.

William held up his hands to quell his brother's rising temper. "Like Alice said, what if we captured him until we figured out a way to help him."

"Capture him? Maybe. Reverse the elixir? That's never happened. Ever." Leander said.

"But what if it was possible?" Alice asked. "What if there was something to slow him down and keep him subdued until we found something to prevent him from going mad. Would your friend Arthur know?" She'd get on her knees and beg if she had to.

Leander's face soured. "I doubt it."

"She has a point though." Natalie tapped her mouth as she thought. "We can research and ask around. There might be something that could weaken your dad temporarily, long enough for us to capture him. We can figure out the rest from there."

William nodded in agreement. "Our father had hoards of books and artifacts from his travels. He could have information tucked away somewhere." He sounded like he actually cared about trying to save her father, and Natalie seemed to be coming around. Whereas Leander sounded like he had given up from the start.

"It's settled then." Natalie hopped off the counter and dusted crumbs from her pants. "Why don't you check your old house today? Bring Alice with you. The more eyes the better."

"Absolutely not," Leander said.

"I want to help," Alice said. "It's for my dad." Going to the old Montgomery manor might also bring up more conversations about their past, more about what happened with their father and whoever the doctor was which could lead to potential clues for her own dad. Most importantly, Alice needed to get out of this house before she went mad herself.

"Whatever," Leander grumbled.

Natalie rolled her eyes. "I'm off to get Arthur." Natalie

clapped Leander on the shoulder as she headed out. "Can you be nice for a day?"

"Because you asked," Leander said. "No, I won't."

* * *

The Montgomery brothers, with Alice between them, walked along the recently snow-plowed road towards the monstrous ramshackle mansion on the corner of Bank and Lippincott, the same one Alice had passed by the other night. Montgomery Manor, the brothers' childhood home, had been left empty and falling apart, and she didn't know if they even cared.

As they rounded the curb down the side street, she pulled her thick cardigan tighter around her body to shield herself from the icy air, wishing she had the sense to grab a coat. The mansion's wrap-around front porch was lined with decorative columns except for the rounded corner portico, which was supported by an ugly wooden post due to damage. Snow-dusted English ivy, hardy even in the winter months, crawled upwards through the cracks in the sage-tinted serpentine stone masonry, and in some areas the ivy was so dense it covered entire windows. The frozen snow crunched under their feet as they approached the side door. Leander jangled through a ring of iron skeleton keys to find the correct one.

Alice's gaze traveled upwards, and she almost stumbled backwards from how tall the mansion was. It rose three stories above them, and the corner tower might've been four stories at one point. The mansion was preternaturally beautiful even in its ruined state. She couldn't imagine how magnificent it would've looked a century ago, and what it could've been like to live in such opulence.

"So this was your house?" Alice asked as they entered through a small foyer and stepped down into the galley kitchen. Crisp winter sunlight beamed through the open side door, illuminating a flurry of dust floating through the damp interior air. The scent of musty aged wood and moldy parchment swirled around her. The house was finally able to breathe for the first time in decades.

"It was," Leander said, avoiding eye contact. He locked the door behind him, dousing them in gloomy shadow and uneasy silence.

"Do you still own it?" She stood in the center of the neglected kitchen, inspecting all of the unkempt details. The century old oven was missing most of its doors. A long wooden table with only three legs was flipped upside-down. The crumbling fireplace at the far end of the room over-flowed with dented pots and debris.

"No, a distant relative owns it." Leander shoved past them, his stern eyes focused forward, and went through a doorway where the door barely hung on by a hinge.

William kicked some broken pottery shards and exchanged a furtive glance with Alice before following his brother into the formal dining room.

"You have relatives still around?" Alice asked, coming up the rear. Considering how old the brothers were, she wondered if they had anyone left who remembered their actual identity.

"The man who owns it is our first cousin thrice removed," Leander said in a bored voice. "But he thinks I'm his grand nephew. He's eighty-something years old now, so I offered to oversee the property for him while he tried to sell it. The neighbors think it's cursed."

"It probably is," William said under his breath. "So

many bad things happened here." He managed to give Alice a small smile, though his eyes seemed sad.

She couldn't smile back.

A humongous brass chandelier hung from the vaulted, twelve-foot ceiling, distracting Alice enough to cause her to trip into a squeaky-wheeled serving cart. William helped her regain her footing, his warm hands on her upper arms a welcoming comfort in the chill of the house. Leander, unfazed by Alice's near tumble, kept moving.

A film of dust covered the long dining table and chairs, still situated neatly in their proper positions, each seat set for dinner with expensive china. Faded floral wallpaper peeled off the walls, and another fireplace stood at the end of the dining room. The air thickened the deeper they traveled in the house. Alice sneezed, cutting through the quiet.

Leander disappeared through the next door, as if he was trying to get as far away from them as possible. Alice pattered after him to keep up, with William close behind.

Because of the boarded up and ivy-covered windows, the next space enveloped them in almost complete darkness. Leander clicked a lighter to life. He directed the flame upwards to light the half-melted candles of a three tier chandelier, partially illuminating the two-story entrance hall and grand staircase. The room was so large, the light couldn't reach far enough to uncover everything hiding in the corners.

"This place is creepy." Alice felt like a dozen eyes watched her in a place she didn't belong. She thought she saw a shadow sneaking behind a broken chair, or maybe it was just the flickering candle flames playing tricks on her. With the knowledge she had now, it really could be a ghost or daemon, though she wasn't sure daemons could be seen with the naked eye, and she was too afraid to ask. Alice inched closer to William, and he touched a tentative hand on her back. Such a simple gesture made her feel safe. Protected.

"That's why no one wants to buy it, so it's been left to fall apart for a hundred years," Leander said, his voice sharp, as they headed up the grand staircase.

The rickety wooden stairs creaked under their footsteps. Alice couldn't imagine living in this mansion a century ago. She stared dumbfounded at the men walking in front of her, realizing they were tracing their footsteps back through time. She wondered how often they came back here, if ever.

At the top of the main staircase was a painted portrait of a tall, austere man standing with pride and a tight-lipped woman seated rigidly next to him. Two smaller portraits of young boys with dark hair hung on either side of the large painting. One had a playful smirk and a gleam in his eyes, while the other looked lost in melancholy with a half smile.

A knot formed in her throat. The little boys' faces, William and Leander's faces, looked so innocent. It pained her to imagine them growing up to endure the trauma of killing their father, although it could've been a relief considering the man was evil enough to kill William's fiancée. Neither of the brothers spared the portraits a passing glance, years of suffering long forgotten or ignored.

"Did you like it here?" Alice asked.

Leander ignored her, fist clenched at his side.

"I liked it," William said. He glanced over his shoulder and gave a smile. "Before everything happened. Not so much anymore, too many bad memories. But, we did have some pleasant moments here."

This time, Alice smiled back. She admired his ability to

find some positive in anything, amazed that he could hold on to hope despite the horrors he lived through. Alice didn't think she'd be able to do it.

They leveled out onto the mezzanine which wrapped around the second level of the entrance hall. Leander made a quick turn and led them down a dark hallway, disappearing into one of the rooms. Alice hovered outside the door, afraid the gloom would swallow her. William gave her an encouraging nod and followed his brother. She followed shortly after.

Leander clicked his lighter again and used his magic to light an array of candles situated on a heavy oak desk. Built-in bookshelves, half empty, lined the walls from floor to ceiling. More piles of books and papers were strewn about the room. Two ripped and tattered armchairs were positioned in front of yet another fireplace. One of the chairs had a huge slash in the seat cushion, stuffing spilling out onto the floor.

"What are we looking for?" Alice asked as she carefully stepped through the mess.

"Anything Greek or Latin, like books or handwritten notes, or anything that seems related to the occult. This was our father's study, so there might be some additional research hidden in here," Leander said as he busied himself with perusing the bookshelves. William did the same.

Alice couldn't figure out where to search first. She felt like she was trespassing, and if she touched anything it could disturb some ghost from the past. She decided to begin with the desk drawers and rummaged through some wrinkled papers. When she lifted up a mildew covered portfolio, she found the right half of a torn black and white photo underneath. In the photo was a light-haired woman in a white dress holding a bouquet of flowers, and standing next to the woman was a man in a tailored suit and top hat. Alice held it up to one of the candles to look more closely. Her breath hitched in her throat.

"You were married?" she blurted out.

Leander hesitated, arm extended mid-grab for a book, and kept his back towards her. The air seemed to be sucked out of the stuffy room. With no answer for an entire minute, he walked over and swiped the photo from her hand. He clenched his jaw, closed his eyes, and left, leaving Alice alone with William in the haunting candlelight of the study.

"I'm guessing I shouldn't have brought it up?" she asked, wincing from her guilt. Leander was going to be even more annoyed with her because she didn't know how to keep her damn mouth shut.

"It's not my story to tell." William shuffled through a stack of papers with averted eyes.

"Should I apologize?"

"You can try." He pulled a face and nodded his head towards the door. "You'll probably find him down the hall on the left."

With a heavy sigh, Alice stepped out of the study. Something slammed at the far end of the hall. Swallowing her fear, she hurried towards the sound. Last time Leander was this upset, Natalie had chased after him to make sure he didn't do anything stupid, whatever that meant. Alice needed to apologize before it got worse.

A hazy shaft of daylight came from the cracked door all the way at the end of the corridor on the left. The hinges creaked as she pushed it open. Leander braced himself against a chest of drawers, arms stiff and his head drooped between his shoulders. In the center of the far wall was a large four poster bed, and the wall to the right of the bed was lined with tall skinny windows covered with moth-eaten drapery. A lonely bassinet sat in the corner.

"Yes." Leander's voice was soft. "I was married."

Dirt and dust scuffed under Alice's feet as she stepped inside. Leander turned his face to look at her, his eyes damp. Her heart sank. The only emotion she ever saw from him was either anger or stoicism, but now he was cracked open in front of her. He appeared to sense her appraisal of him and promptly turned away to hide his anguish.

"I'm sorry," Alice said in a rush, picking at the hem of her sleeve. If Leander had been married over a hundred years ago, his wife wouldn't be alive anymore if she hadn't been Chosen with him. She would've died from old age decades ago. However, his reaction made Alice believe something terrible happened to her before she had a chance to grow old. "I didn't mean to bring it up. I didn't realize—"

"It's fine." Leander pulled a hand down his face and stalked out of the room. "Let's go. We have more places to search."

She wasn't going to push him.

They headed back into the hallway to find that William had left to go search on his own somewhere, perhaps his own old bedroom to get lost in sorrowful memories. Leander directed Alice through the endless maze of hallways and doors, carrying a lit candle to light the way.

Alice tiptoed behind him, afraid to make too much noise, afraid to wake up any lingering spirits in this long dead mansion. They were alone, but she didn't feel alone. She squeezed her arms to her chest. They went through another door which opened up to a narrow spiral staircase that led to nowhere. It was boarded up.

Leander set the candle on the steps and fussed with the planks of wood. He ripped them off with his bare hands, causing rusted nails to clatter down the stairs below. A gust of freezing air greeted them as he pushed up the makeshift trap door. They were on the roof, but it didn't look like it was supposed to be a roof.

"This used to be the workshop where my father worked in secret, up here in the tallest tower. It burned down after..." Leander trailed off, his jaw tight. "After everything happened."

Leander traipsed across the loose, charred floorboards, his hair whipping in the winter wind, while Alice stayed in the stairwell shivering from the cold and barely poking her head above the threshold. He pulled up a singed floorboard revealing a small hidden compartment, untouched by the fire. "Nothing of importance," Leander grumbled as he rummaged through the hiding place in the floor. He shoved a few loose scraps of paper in his pocket. "There's one more place I'd like to check."

Back through the grand foyer on the first floor, they traveled down the main hall which opened up into a lavish ballroom. A replica of the entrance hall chandelier hung in the center of the room. It too was illuminated magically with fire by Leander. The walls of the ballroom were made of carved wood panels interspersed with arched windows. Between each window was a matching candle sconce, and at the end of the room was probably the largest fireplace in the whole mansion.

"Your family had to be filthy rich," Alice said, taking in the decadence of the room.

"Thanks to generations of Philadelphia businessmen." Leander walked across the center of the ballroom. "The wood is from the Black Forest in Germany." He waved his hand apathetically. "My father obtained it during one of his frivolous expeditions. He liked to show off our wealth, and so he hosted many parties here." He stopped at the fireplace and placed a hand on the cracked marble mantle. "Including my wedding. My father and her father arranged the match." Leander held up the photo of himself and his wife, the same fireplace in the background.

"Like an arranged marriage?" She asked, shocked by how much he shared.

"Not officially, but it was fairly common for prominent families to pair their children together." He dusted off the corner of the mantle, but it hardly made a difference.

"Did you love her?" Alice might've pushed him too far with that question.

"I—" He blinked a few times. "Yes, of course I did. Despite the arrangement, I courted her the proper way to ensure she felt the same. I didn't want her to feel forced into it. Because knowing my father, he would've forced it for business reasons, regardless of our feelings." He made a bitter face. "The original plan was to match Elizabeth with William since he's the eldest, but he refused. He was already seeing Victoria at the time, but our father didn't know about it. Not that any of it mattered in the end." Leander shook his head like he was ashamed of how much he let slip. "Come on."

He led her through more hallways and doors. So many different directions, she'd get lost if she didn't have Leander to guide her out. Hopefully she didn't end up pissing him off enough for him to leave her there.

Eventually they reached a flight of stairs that descended below. The last place they needed to check was the basement.

Alice grabbed the railing as her knees buckled. Her

other hand shielded her abdominal scar in reflex. Leander was already halfway down the stairs, taking the candlelight with him, so Alice had no choice but to keep up with him or get left in the dark.

Dampness clung to the stone walls and dirt floor of the basement, and as they walked further Alice swore she saw claw marks gouged in the rock. It smelled like rotten wood and low tide. The flame of the candle diminished due to the limited oxygen, barely leaving enough light for them to see to the end of the cold hall.

Leander used the full weight of his body to heave open a colossal iron door with a six-pronged wheel lock. The vault was almost bare besides the shelves around the perimeter which were littered with scraps of paper, empty cigar boxes, and some water damaged books. Leander set down the candle and shuffled through a few loose papers before pushing one of the shelves away from the wall to expose another iron door with a wheel lock.

The arched door was shorter and wider than average size, and when Leander opened it, the other side revealed a tunnel that had been cut through raw earth and filled with ankle deep water. The soft ripple of waves could be heard in the distance.

"It leads out to the river," he said, ducking his head under the low door frame and stepping over the ledge into the freezing water. "During high tide, the water travels up here, but not enough to flood the whole thing. The door is water tight. Although there have been leaks in the past from heavy storms." He tapped it twice with his knuckle. "There's an off-shoot ahead with a small chamber, protected by another watertight door, where my father hid more secret things. You can wait here. I'll go check."

Alice crossed her arms as she waited, protecting herself

from the wet chill leaching in from the tunnel. Leander had only been gone for about a minute when she became antsy. She plucked the candle from the shelf and peered back into the hall, curious about some of the other rooms they had passed on the way in.

There were a few doors back in the main hall of the basement, possibly servants quarters judging by the size of this house and the time period. One of the doors had a sliding bolt latch strangely located on the outside of the door. It was relatively high up though, so perhaps it was only installed to prevent wandering children from getting inside, the type of place their father might've hidden important things.

She slid open the latch, waving off an annoying black fly that kept buzzing by her ear. When she opened the door she was hit with an awful, rotten stench. She held up the candle to illuminate the little storage room. It was cluttered with old furniture, heaping piles of water-logged clothes, and rodent skeletons. A ring of demarcation encircled the room, about a foot high, from a previous flood. She stepped inside, grimacing when her shoe squished into the soaked carpet.

"Yeah, I don't think so," she said as she backed out, closing the door behind her. One of the brothers could go in there later and search for themselves.

Leander still hadn't returned when she got back to the vault. She had enough of this dank basement. Alice leaned against one of the shelves, shuffling her feet impatiently, but the sound of shuffling didn't quite match up with her movement. The back of her neck prickled. Her feet stopped. The shuffling continued.

"William?" she called, heart pounding in her throat. Alice gazed into the darkness. She hadn't seen him since they were up in the study. Gravel crunched somewhere in the basement. "Hello?" She stepped out into the hall, silently hoping it was the other brother.

The shuffling grew louder, and in the flickering candle light, Alice watched in horror as dirty, pale feet with blackened toenails shambled forward. A malnourished woman approached, crooked and thin, wearing a ripped and stained dress. When the woman's ashen face was finally visible through the murky darkness, her cloudy dead eyes stared straight into her. *Immortui.*

Alice stumbled backwards, tripping over the iron door frame. She fell flat on her back, the wind knocked out of her. The horrifying woman hissed and positioned herself on all fours, her gangly fingers clawed into the dirt, and she propelled herself towards Alice.

"Leander!" Alice breathlessly cried. "Help!" She scrambled across the floor to get away.

The woman screeched and bounded forward faster. Finally on her feet, Alice threw her weight against the iron door to shut it, but the freakishly strong woman pushed her way in. Alice screamed and fell against one of the wall shelves. The candle knocked to the floor, snuffing out the flame, leaving her in the dark. She screamed again.

Leander cursed as he splashed back through the partially flooded tunnel. He struggled to light his lighter, precious seconds slipping away, until flames finally swelled through the room. The woman cried out and cowered in a corner. Leander pushed Alice to stand behind him, but when he got a clearer look, he froze.

"Marie?" he asked with wide eyes. His flames dwindled. "What happened to you?"

She growled and catapulted herself at Leander, slamming him into the floor. His flames disappeared, blanketing them in darkness once again with only a shaft of dusky light coming in through the tunnel. Marie's blackened fingernails slashed open Leander's shirt and sank deep into the flesh of his chest. He howled in agony. "Alice," he groaned, blood sputtering from his mouth. "My lighter."

Alice scrambled across the floor searching for it, dirt lodging under her nails and rocks cutting her palms. Leander cried out again. Marie licked blood from one of her hands while the other clasped around Leander's throat, fingernails puncturing his neck. He flailed beneath the woman's grasp. His blood soaked the floor. Alice was about to find out if someone like Leander could actually die.

"I can't find it!" Alice yelled.

Marie's head whipped towards her with a snarl. The woman sat on her haunches, then growled as she stalked closer. There was a sharp crack. Alice went rigid. Marie crushed the lighter beneath one of her clawed hands.

Alice gasped. "Leander, she—"

"Get out," Leander said, choking on blood. "She's... stronger now. She drank my blood... Go find... my brother." He clutched his open wounds.

Alice turned to run, but Marie's claws sank into her leg. She shrieked and fell to her knees. A weak gust of air swirled through the room. Leander held out his bloody hand, using his waning energy to knock Marie off of Alice with the last bit of his magic. Alice crawled away and tried to get to her feet, but the creature pulled her down. She let out a pathetic whine as she hit the ground.

A roaring flame erupted into the room, so hot it caused the dampness of the stone walls to sizzle into steam. Alice, face first in the dirt, shielded her head from the fire. When she looked up, William had his arms open wide as he manipulated the flames to surround Marie. Her gray skin blackened as she screeched in pain. Once the fire receded, she collapsed to the floor. Blackened patches of burnt skin flaked off as new skin regenerated underneath. That didn't happen with other *Immortui*. Fire was supposed to kill them.

"Shit!" William yelled, throwing his body onto Marie's legs. "Hold her!"

Leander, still profusely bleeding on the ground, reached out in an attempt to pin down Marie's arms. He struggled to keep her still as his strength wavered.

"Alice, I need you to hold her arms," William ordered.

She took over for Leander and pinned Marie's arms to the floor. The woman weighed less than a hundred pounds, but had the strength of a fully grown man. "I can't do this for long," Alice said, her voice shaking. The woman's upper arms were so thin, just bone and no muscle, yet she squirmed beneath them with vigor.

William kicked a silver knife towards Leander, his face distraught. "It has to be you."

Leander dragged himself to Marie's flank, a look of grim understanding passing between the brothers. He grasped the knife in his hands. "Please forgive me," he whispered before slamming his fist into her sternum, breaking her ribs, and impaling the knife deep into the woman's chest. A blood curdling scream filled the basement as Leander sawed and hacked through her ribcage, blood splattering across their faces.

He tossed the knife aside, plunged his hand into her chest cavity, and retrieved her still beating heart, holding it in his hand until it stopped. Leander's shoulders slackened, and he rolled the heart to the floor with a nauseating squelch. The body lay lifeless. William let go of his hold, and Alice did the same. The sound of their ragged breaths and the smell of singed flesh filled the room.

"Everyone okay?" William asked, using the back of his arm to wipe the blood from his forehead.

"Getting there," Leander said as he rubbed his hand over the deep lacerations on his chest and neck. The wounds would've been lethal to any other person, but the bleeding had already stopped and begun to clot thanks to the *eligere* inside him. His torn, blood soaked shirt dangled like ribbons from his collar.

"Alice?" William reached out to put his hand on her shoulder, trying to shake her out of her shell shock.

She looked down at her blood splattered hands, then the corpse with the gaping hole in her chest, and then the lump of muscle that once was a beating heart. Alice's entire body was cut and bruised from the ordeal, yet she couldn't feel a thing. She started shivering, her empty eyes looking between the brothers.

"We need to get her out of here," Leander said, groaning in pain as he forced himself to stand. He ripped the remains of his shirt from his neck and used the scraps to wipe as much blood from his face as possible.

Alice's body remained as limp as a rag doll when William tried to pull her to her feet. She couldn't control her limbs. All of her strength had been used up in the fight. It took both of the brothers to keep her standing, and she swayed on the spot even with their support.

"Come on," Leander said as they headed for the stairs with Alice hoisted between them.

"Did you know Marie was down here?" William asked. He slid his arm around Alice's back, keeping her steady as they ascended to the first floor.

Alice dragged her heavy feet up each step. If William

hadn't been holding her, she would've tumbled back down the stairs. At this point, she didn't care.

"I had no idea," Leander said. "I thought she died back then."

"Me too." William's voice was quiet and laced with grief. "It's a shame she didn't."

CHAPTER 8

Night had fallen by the time they made it outside, and the blustery streets were mostly clear of people. They hurried along the road to get back to Violet's as quickly as possible before they were seen. When they stumbled in through the front door, haggard and bloody, they found the house empty. Alice mindlessly followed the brothers into the kitchen, and William handed her a glass of water. A note sat on the counter, and William read it aloud.

> *Drove Arthur and Violet down to the cabin to ask*
> *M + J to help us out. Meet us there tomorrow.*
> *- Nat*

"Why does everyone need to be involved in this?" William rolled his eyes.

"I asked myself the same question when you showed up," Leander said, washing the blood from his hands and arms in the kitchen sink.

William crumpled the note and tossed it in the trash. "Good thing I did show up."

"We would've been fine." Leander dried his hands on a small towel.

"Marie sunk her claws inch deep into your chest. Your ribs would've been cracked open if I showed up a minute too late." William crossed his arms. "Not the first time I've saved your ass. A thank you would be nice."

Leander cursed and threw the towel at his brother.

Alice limped up the stairs, ignoring the escalating argument in the kitchen. Her ears rang with white noise. She needed to wash the blood from her body. She needed to wash the memories of the past week from her mind. Everything.

After finding some pajamas from the pile of clothes Natalie had given her to borrow, she headed across the hall to wash up. In the bathroom, Alice kept her gaze averted because she couldn't stand to see her blood-stained face in the mirror. When she accidentally caught a glimpse of herself, fear seized her.

There was more than one set of eyes looking back at her, cloudy lifeless eyes sunken in a shadowy skull. They disappeared when she blinked. She looked over her shoulder, searching for the source of the grim face. She yanked back the shower curtain and found nothing. She was alone.

Alice spent less than ten minutes in the shower, scrubbing painfully to remove the blood stains as fast as possible. She kept peeking outside the shower curtain to make sure no one else was in there. The steam of the hot water thankfully fogged up the mirror, preventing her from seeing those eyes staring at her again.

As she turned off the water, she heard more muffled

arguing followed by a door slam from the hallway. Even though the loudness startled her, it was a comforting reminder she wasn't alone in the house with some scary creature, just the brothers storming around after their argument. In the cabinet, she found some of the earthy medicinal paste she used before and slathered it on her fresh wounds, waiting for it to dry before she dressed.

William, still dirty and bloodied, leaned against the wall in the hallway while waiting his turn for the bathroom. He perked up when she came out and asked if she was doing alright.

Alice kept her head ducked low as she slipped into her room. Of course she wasn't okay. She had just watched some undead human get her heart carved out of her chest. So she stayed quiet and ignored him. It was easier that way. Because her whole life she had learned to lie about being okay, especially after her mother died, and she just didn't have the strength anymore.

As she tossed her blood-stained clothes to the hamper in the corner of the room, she froze. The same graying skull with horrific eyes stared back at her in the dresser mirror. She stumbled and fell against the footboard of the bed, the wooden post jabbing into her back. The eyes appeared again in the black glass of the window pane. She cried out, hunched over, pressing the heels of her hands into her own eyes to rid herself of the vision.

"What is it?" William asked as he rushed into the bedroom.

She shook her head, whimpering. "The eyes. They're looking at me. Make them stop looking at me." Her body trembled, and she kept her face covered.

The curtains rustled as William closed them, followed

by the flutter of a sheet. He guided her to the bed and sat next to her. Alice refused to uncover her eyes until he pulled on her wrists.

"It's alright," William said. "You can look now."

The window was completely covered by the curtains, and there was a white sheet flung over the mirror. Leander braced himself in the doorway of her room, drawn by the commotion, and he held a cup of steaming tea. He still wore his stained pants, his ruined shirt long discarded. His chest and neck lacerations were at least no longer bleeding.

"What happened?" Leander asked, eyeing the sheet covering the mirror. "What did she see?"

"I'm assuming it was the *exsugo* that had been possessing Marie," William said.

"What? She wasn't an *immortui*?" Alice asked.

"No, although they are easily confused," said Leander. "*Exsugo* are another type of daemon, a type that drains life by possessing others."

Alice clutched her heaving chest. "Is it in the house? Can it get us?"

"No, it can't get in," Leander said. "But it knows we're here now. It probably followed us since it was after sunset when we walked back."

"And Marie injured you while she was possessed by it. So it'll remember you," William added. "But it can't get you. It's stuck on the other side without a host."

"The other side?" Alice instinctively looked over her shoulder.

"The Grey. The in-between where souls and daemons and other things reside while in limbo," Leander said as he sipped his tea and rubbed his eyes from the sedative effect kicking in. "But it could find a way through eventually, if it grows strong enough, which is why it's a good idea for us to wait to go to the cabin tomorrow morning. It won't be able to trail you in the daylight." He turned to leave and glanced over his shoulder at William who remained seated next to Alice. When William didn't move, Leander rolled his eyes and left with a huff.

Alice took a shuddering breath, waiting for William to leave too. She knew what she wanted, but she was too afraid to ask, too embarrassed, because she was used to dealing with her feelings alone. Alice wasn't sure if she even knew how to ask for help.

"I don't want to impose, but..." William paused and cleared his throat. "Do you want me to stay?"

She picked at a loose thread on the quilt and nodded, grateful he offered.

"Then I'll stay," he said as he stood. "But let me clean up first." He gestured down to his stained and ripped clothes.

Alice chewed her lip, afraid of the daemon that lurked in the mirrors and windows, that it would find a way to escape from the Grey and possess her while she was alone.

"Only a few minutes, okay?" He nodded towards the open door. "I'll be right across the hall, and I'll leave the door cracked so I can hear if you need me."

She didn't move the entire time. Her body remained stiff as she repeatedly surveyed the corners of the room, double checking every shadow, waiting for the demonic eyes to reappear. Her fingers cramped from clasping her hands so hard, and she didn't relax until William came back, clean and dressed in sweatpants and a T-shirt. After closing the door, he pulled back the window curtains a little to check outside.

"Nothing out there," William said as he ruffled a towel

through his wet hair before tossing it into the hamper. He made himself comfortable in the armchair in the corner.

"What about the woman? Is she out in the yard?" Alice asked as she laid down in bed, pulling the quilt up to her chin. William was the first person she trusted to tell about seeing those things, because she knew he would tell her the truth.

"What woman?"

"I see her standing out there sometimes. Her eyes are black holes. Is she an *exsugo* too?"

"Black holes for eyes?" William asked. "No, that's another type of daemon, a *vagari*, a wanderer, a typical ghost."

Alice's stomach dropped. A ghost. That confirmed every single ghostly encounter she had was real, the classroom ghost in East Pyne, the stairwell ghost in her dormitory, and all the others. "Can everyone see them?"

William cocked a curious eyebrow at her. "No, not everyone. And some people can see them much more clearly than others. I'm assuming you've seen other *vagari* throughout your life?"

Alice nodded. "Ever since I was little. They notice me too. They watch me and try to get my attention."

"Interesting," William said, leaning his chin against his hand. "They can't hurt you, so don't worry about them. They're just lost souls in the Grey, and their image is being reflected into the physical world. Although if they linger too long, sometimes they descend into madness and become *exsugo*."

"How does someone get possessed by an *exsugo*?" If it was stalking her, Alice needed to figure out how to keep it away.

"They use fear to grow stronger, breaking down their

target mentally and emotionally, until they're strong enough to cross over and possess them."

She shivered knowing the daemon could be sentient enough to manipulate its prey. "I don't know how to not be afraid of those things."

"It'll get easier once you realize they can't actually control how you feel." William sounded unbothered by the thing. "They want weak and unstable hosts because they're easiest to possess. Those *immortui* you encountered, they're the perfect host for an *exsugo* because they have no soul at all to protect them from it."

"Was that what happened to Marie?"

Something flickered across William's face, and he looked away. It took him a minute to finally answer. "I believe so. She was likely one of my father's victims, and maybe he hid the body down there." He hung his head. "Poor girl. She was one of our servants. Although she was more like a friend."

"I'm sorry," Alice said. The more trauma she heard about their past, the more she was concerned about her own father's future.

William heaved a sigh and shrugged. "Not much we can do about it now."

"How could she even stay alive for that long?" Alice grimaced. Probably drinking blood.

"*Sanguis est vis vitae*," William said, the same Latin phrase Leander quoted before. "All blood has some magical properties, but immortal blood is the strongest," William said as he motioned down to his own body. "An *immortui* can survive for a short amount of time when ingesting blood, but eventually their body will die if they aren't possessed before then. An *exsugo* can survive longer when drinking human blood, and if it drinks immortal blood, it can regenerate its body, making it harder to kill. They need blood, because the main function of the *exsugo* is to drain the life force to keep itself alive. Without blood, the daemon will destroy the host's physical body over time."

Alice's mind ran through reels of television shows and movies, all with dark creatures that drank blood and undead monsters that stalked the living. None of them compared to the horrors she experienced or learned about so far. She never imagined she'd be living in a world where monsters and ghosts were real.

"I can't believe more people don't know about this," Alice whispered.

"Where do you think all of the vampire and zombie lore comes from?" William asked, flashing her a grin. "We do our best to keep most of it hidden. That's the job of the Chosen."

"Sounds exhausting."

"Trust me, there are plenty of other things I'd rather spend my immortality doing." William leaned back in the chair, hands behind his head. "None of them involve dealing with blood-thirsty creatures."

"Obviously," Alice said, the corner of her mouth quirking up. "What would you rather be doing?" She didn't know what she'd do if given the opportunity, if she would even want it. Being immortal sounded awful.

"Travel more. Eat, drink, and be merry," William said with a smirk. "You know, the basics." His smile faded. "If you really want to know what I'd rather be doing, by this time I'd already be six feet under and forgotten. I would've preferred to have a normal life, get married and have a family. But of course, my father stole that from me. I suppose that's why I stick around and help others when I can, so they don't have to go through what I did. "

"Thank you," Alice said. "For helping me. It's very noble of you." After everything he lost, he still had a heart to help others.

William chuckled. "Noble?"

Alice shrugged. "If you didn't show up the other day, I don't think I would've been able to convince them to save my father on my own."

"Honestly, anything is possible. We discover new things all the time. Not only are there blood-thirsty *immortui* and *exsugo* we need to manage, but there are also some people out there who dabble in all sorts of magic, discovering things regularly. Of course, then you have the really fucked up people who mess around with blood magic. It's perverse, often involving rituals with the living and the dead, and it has nefarious consequences."

Alice grimaced. Just like her dad decided to mess with blood magic. "Why would anyone choose to do that?"

"They think the benefits outweigh the risks." William gave her a pained look as he reached for the desk lamp to turn it off. "But they always seem to forget the cost."

* * *

Alice opened her eyes to the soft light of dawn glowing around the perimeter of the window curtain. William was asleep stretched out in the armchair, his head lolled to one side and arms folded across his chest. Her blanket fell away as she sat up and stretched, a chilly draft breezing through her bones, and she kicked herself for not offering him an extra blanket.

As if he could sense she was staring, his eyes fluttered open. "Sleep okay?" He asked with a yawn, his hand flattening his slightly unkempt hair.

"Better than I have recently," Alice answered. It was helpful to have him there watching over her all night, different from when Leander or Natalie would stay in her room, because their main goal was to make sure she didn't run away, not for her comfort. "Besides when they knocked me out with the tea. But even then, it wasn't good sleep. I'd wake up like I was hungover."

William frowned. "Did you have a choice?"

"Nope," Alice said. "And they lied to me about it."

"Hmph, sounds about right." William stood and stretched again. "Why don't you get yourself ready and pack up your things. I'll drive us down to the cabin in a little bit."

"I don't have anything to pack." Her throat tightened. She'd lost everything in the house fire. She had nothing. Not even the clothes on her back were hers.

"Oh, right," William said. "I'm sure they wouldn't mind if you borrowed some more clothes." He pointed to the dresser.

Alice fidgeted under his pitying stare.

"I'll meet you downstairs," he said stiffly before he left.

The few sets of clothes Natalie had lent her over the past week were already used, so Alice needed to find some clean items. The dresser was full of a variety of clothes, some delicate with patterns of flowers while others were bigger and boxier. Some of the clothes were aged and retro-styled, probably Natalie's from the fifties. Alice found a backpack in the closet and shoved some plain shirts and jeans into it, along with a bulky sweater, a cardigan, and some pajamas. She dressed herself in something equally plain and pulled Leander's Princeton hoodie over top.

Before leaving, she took one last look at the bedroom where she spent the past week. The window curtains were still closed, so she mustered up the courage to pull them open. She cringed from the sudden brightness of the sun reflecting off the calm river below. If it wasn't for the frightening things that went on in this neighborhood, she thought it would be a nice place to live. Her hand hovered over the white sheet covering the mirror, but her courage faltered, and she left it there.

CHAPTER 9

Alice slipped into the back seat of William's black luxury car, and Leander took the front. Maybe the brothers could talk during the ride, sort out their problems. Leander slammed the door. William glared at him as he shifted into gear, then turned on some metalcore music to drown out any possible conversation. Maybe not.

They drove through small towns and tree-lined streets until they reached rarely traveled back roads. The cabin was somewhere deep in Wharton State Forest, outside of Batsto Historic Village. Alice had been there once on a field trip in elementary school where they learned about early settlers and the Jersey Devil. She wondered if the Jersey Devil was based on reality too, a blood-sucking *exsugo* prowling the Pine Barrens, or perhaps it was something more sinister. Alice remembered learning that the Jersey Devil was supposedly the thirteenth child of the Leeds family, born with a goat's head and bat wings. She hoped a grotesque creature like that didn't exist, but at this point she wouldn't be surprised.

Alice picked at her nails and turned to check out the

back window a few times to make sure there wasn't a daemon or creature chasing after them. William's dark eyes caught hers in the rearview mirror. Her stomach flipped, and she looked away.

William turned down the music. "You okay back there?"

"I'm fine," she said. When she looked back, the flicker in his gaze showed he knew she wasn't.

After about an hour, the car rolled down a twisting road through a thicket of pitch pine trees which still held their green color in the midst of winter. At the bottom of the hill they turned onto a hidden driveway. Alice wasn't sure what she had expected at the end of it, perhaps a modest-sized cozy log cabin. Her lips parted in shock when a grand two-story building made of log and stone appeared around the bend. It was clearly old, not modern by any means, and was likely used as some sort of hunting lodge or summer retreat for the wealthy during the gilded age. She could almost picture the well-dressed men and their dogs parading through the trees preparing for their hunt.

Leander knocked on the side door of the cabin, and they waited. Alice, shivering in the cold, focused on inspecting the grounds, making sure nothing had followed them, no ghosts, no desiccated bodies. Her eyes traveled across the yard, noticing a few outbuildings, including a neglected horse stable, and a rippling cedar creek with some lingering snow drifts along the banks. The property was well hidden and tucked between the valley of two forested hills. It seemed private enough that it would be hard to find if someone didn't already know its location.

After a minute or so, the oversized door opened a few inches and a set of brown eyes peeked out. Upon noticing who it was, the person opened the door wide and smiled. "Leander, hi! So great to see you." She paused. "Both of you." She nodded at William, and he gave a warm smile in return.

The woman's gaze passed from the brothers and landed on Alice. "Is this our new friend?" she asked, tucking a lock of black hair behind her ear. "Alice, right?"

Alice nodded, shifting on her feet, anxious to get inside

"I'm glad you're here. I'm Michelle." She stepped aside, practically glowing with kindness, and allowed the three of them to enter. "Come in, come in."

As Michelle led them into the heart of the house, Alice was hit with the scent of aged wood, smoke, and leather. The interior was warm but dark, with thick tapestries, heavily framed paintings, and even a few unnerving taxidermies hanging on the paneled walls. Every piece of sturdy furniture looked like it was from a different century, a mix of time periods and culture. And almost every surface was lined with antiquated curios from around the globe, like a painted ship in a bottle, a cracked lion bust, and a clockwork orrery with models of the sun and planets.

"Are they here, *lǎo pó*?" asked a man's voice from the other room. A tall man with tousled auburn hair appeared from around the corner. He dried his hands with a dish towel and hustled towards them. "How is everyone?" he asked with a hint of concern, his hand resting on Michelle's lower back. "Natalie told us to expect you this morning."

"We've been better," William said. "Thanks for having us, James."

"Like we said last time, you're always welcome with us," said Michelle, more so to William. Leander failed to hide the frown forming on his lips.

She motioned for them to follow her into the lofty living room. Tall picture windows stretched upwards towards the vaulted ceiling and lined the long side of the room that faced the tree-covered hill. A stone fireplace, surrounded by plush couches and leather chairs, glowed on one end of the room, and above it was a wood-carved coat of arms with inlaid swords. A rustic chandelier made of iron and wood hung in the center of the ceiling. Opposite the wall of windows was an interior balcony running along the second floor hallway. In one corner of the room was an upright piano with a calico cat snoozing atop the keys, and in the other corner was Natalie who was conversing with an older man who had graying hair and a scruffy beard.

"What happened last night?" Natalie asked as she hurried over to them. "Your text was really vague and oh my god—" She reached out and pulled on the collar of Leander's shirt, revealing his scars.

"It's not a big deal." Leander swatted her away.

"That looks like a big deal! What happened?"

"We found our old servant, Marie, in the basement." William folded his arms. "Possessed by an *exsugo*. We took care of it."

Shock flashed across Natalie's face, and she turned to Alice. "Are you okay?"

Alice stared at the floor, cringing from the bloody memories. "I'm fine."

"I thought Thomas killed Marie," the gruff looking man said as he joined the group in the center of the living room. He had a smooth London accent and a scar through his right eyebrow. He wore clothes from another century— fancy slacks, a button down shirt, and a tweed waistcoat with a silver chain leading to his pocket.

"So did I," Leander said. "Somehow she was getting enough blood to stay alive."

"Hmm, unfortunate for the people that wandered into her path," the man said, rubbing his bearded chin deep in thought. His attention was eventually directed at Alice. "And this young lady must be the one whose father is currently... afflicted." He held out his hand, and Alice shook it. "Arthur Haverleigh. So sorry."

His offer of condolences wasn't a good sign. Alice was starting to believe no one thought her father could be saved. She dug her nails into her palm and clenched her teeth.

"Come on, let me show you your room," Natalie said as she led Alice up the stairs.

Alice looked over the railing down into the living room below. The men were huddled together, faces stern, deep in hushed conversation. William's eyes trailed Alice as she walked. She hoped he would convince the others of the plan to capture her father and not kill him. And if that didn't work, she'd cry, scream, and beg them to give him a chance.

There were a couple doors along the right wall, and a door straight ahead. The hall turned the corner and came to a dead end with two more doors across from each other. Natalie led her through the door on the right. It was a tiny and poorly lit room, minimally decorated, with just enough space for a bed, nightstand, and dresser. An upholstered bench was built in the recess of the dormer window.

Out the window, Alice saw nothing but the creek and endless trees. She couldn't quite remember the route they took to get them deep into the state forest. Hopefully the *exsugo* didn't follow them. She shivered, wondering if it would be stalking through the trees searching for her after nightfall.

Natalie started unpacking Alice's bag into the dresser for her, like she was distracting herself from something, avoiding something. Her eyebrows were furrowed, her movements stiff.

"I'm sorry we lied to you," Natalie said after a long silence, inspecting one of the old shirts Alice had picked out. "We haven't figured out the right way to talk to people about this stuff, if there is a right way."

"Yeah I guess that makes sense," Alice said. If they were so old, they should've had plenty of time to figure it out. Hearing everything up front would've been better than the frustrating dance of lies.

Silence hung between them as Natalie continued unpacking.

"I hope you don't mind I borrowed some more clothes," Alice said in an attempt to disrupt the awkwardness.

"Of course, I don't mind." Natalie smiled as she held up the bulky cable knit sweater.

"Was that yours?" Alice asked.

Natalie's smile faded. "It was my mother's."

"Oh, I didn't mean to—"

"Don't worry about it," Natalie said as she placed it in the drawer. "This was her favorite sweater. It took her ages to save up for it. I'm glad it'll get some use again. She only got to wear it once before she died." After a heavy sigh, she sat on the window bench. "She was possessed."

"I'm so sorry," said Alice as she sat on the bed.

Natalie took another breath to prepare for what she was about to say. "My dad was traumatized after the second world war, but wouldn't talk to anyone about it. He acted like he was fine until one day, he wasn't. My mom found him after he..." Natalie trailed off. "My father was so depressed he took his own life."

Alice's eyes widened in shock, not just from the story but the fact that Natalie was opening up to her like this. But before she could say anything, offer any condolences, Natalie pressed on. "For the next few years, my mother worked so hard every day to make a life for us, and she drank a bottle of wine every night to numb the pain and loneliness. That's when the *exsugo* caught her. I was twenty three at the time." Natalie stared off into the distance.

"We had no idea," she continued. "One day, something snapped and she went mad. She was muttering gibberish. Her eyes were glazed over and bulging out of her head. She attacked my sister and I with a butcher knife, and we had to barricade ourselves in the basement for three days."

Alice held her hand over her mouth, horrified as she pictured them being attacked by their own mother. She knew humans could be capable of heinous crimes, even without being possessed. But the *exsugo*, they were powerful enough to change kind people into monsters willing to kill people, even their own children. And other dark magic, like the elixir her father drank, could do just the same.

"We didn't come out until the pounding on the door stopped," Natalie said. "We found her body curled up in a fetal position at the base of the door, blood oozing from her eyes, nose, and ears. She had splinters under her finger-nails, and her knuckles were all bloodied and bruised from trying to break in."

"That's horrible," Alice said. The *vagari* back at Natalie's house in Riverton, it had to be her mother, unable to let go, unable to pass on, forever waiting outside in the yard for her daughters to notice her. She shuddered, hoping the spirit of Natalie's mother somehow found peace before descending into madness and becoming an *exsugo* herself.

"It gets worse. If the *exsugo* kills the host body, they have the ability to come back stronger and possess someone else. And who better than my traumatized little sister as its next target. I walked into Violet's bedroom to check on her the next day, and she was hanging upside-down from the ceiling foaming at the mouth. Before I could do anything, I passed out from an agonizing headache. That's when I was Chosen. I woke up to Leander shaking me, of course I had no idea who he was or what was happening at the time. I heard screaming and growling in the background. I watched Arthur strap my sister to the metal bed frame, writhing in torment, yelling curses. He was force feeding her some liquid concoction. Once she drank it, Arthur sliced her arm open and black sludge oozed out instead of blood. He told me it was a daemon. He caught it in a flask to dispose of later."

Alice had no words left to say. She wondered how someone could remain sane through such trauma. She wondered about it for Natalie, for Violet, for Leander and William, but also for herself. "Was Violet okay?" Alice asked. She didn't realize it was possible for a person to survive being possessed.

Natalie shrugged. "It was really hard for her. She pushed through it, maybe too hard. She signed up to be a nurse in the Vietnam War. I think she wanted to help the world somehow. Especially since she wasn't Chosen like me. But the war traumatized her even more. When she came home, she struggled to adjust. And as she got older and I stayed the same, she became more withdrawn. Other *exsugo* still targeted her, but they couldn't get her. We made her some leather jewelry inscribed with repelling sigils," Natalie stopped and studied Alice's face. "We'll make you some things for protection if you need them, don't worry."

"But what about you? How do you deal with it? With everything?" Alice asked.

"Me?" Natalie looked shocked, but as it ebbed away it turned to weariness. "I just do. I'm the big sister. I have to." The conversation died after that, with Natalie falling into pensive silence. She shook her head as if to rid herself of whatever terrible thoughts were haunting her, and encouraged Alice to come back downstairs to get more acquainted with the others.

Alice would've preferred to crawl into bed, feeling worn out from the weight of her emotions, but she went downstairs with Natalie anyway. They overheard the tail end of a discussion as they came into the living room.

"We have to at least try," William demanded in a loud whisper.

Arthur seemed doubtful. "I've been around much longer than you, William." His voice didn't waver. "Not once have I heard of reversing dark magic like this. It does not seem likely to find something to help him, especially when time is of the essence."

"He has a point," Leander said. "We really don't have a lot of time." He made eye contact with Alice as she drew nearer. "Which is why we need to act fast to apprehend him. We found no sign of him around town the other day. Who knows where he could've run off to."

"Very well," Arthur said, giving a curt nod. "However, if things become worse, I'm sorry, but I will do what I must."

Fresh anger bloomed in Alice's chest. She barely knew Arthur, but she was ready to snap at him for being so dismissive about her father. Did he even care? Did anyone care? Or was this just another job to them? Arthur seemed ready to simply eliminate the threat and move on.

"Understood," William said. His jaw tightened, and he glanced at Alice as if to say he would never let that happen. It was enough to persuade Alice to keep her mouth shut, for now.

Michelle entered the room carrying a tray with a decorative pot of tea and matching cups. "Please, sit," she said.

James and Violet trailed in behind her, immersed in quiet conversation. A low fire crackled in the fireplace.

Alice did a double take at the tea, remembering the numerous times she had been sedated in the past week. As the others found seats on the couches surrounding the coffee table, Violet patted the spot next to her for Alice to sit.

"It's not that type of tea," Violet whispered as she leaned into Alice's ear.

Michelle took care to prepare and steep the tea before pouring a serving for each of the guests. She seemed to have tenderness radiating from her. Alice held her cup to her lips, watching as the others took their first sip. Michelle noticed her hesitation. "It is only green tea, *péngyǒu*."

Alice recognized the term of endearment her best friend Jenny often used for her, and a pang of sadness wrenched through her chest. She missed her friends. She missed her dad, at least, the old version of him that she so desperately wanted to get back. Alice eventually sipped her tea with the others.

"Thank you so much, Michelle," Arthur cleared his throat. "So neither of you have heard of any ritual to reverse the Elixir of Life?"

Michelle replaced her cup on the tray with her delicate hands. "I have not." She sighed and looked to James. "Not specifically at least."

"We've heard whispers of different types of magic over the years, perhaps something that could alter it," said James as he threaded a hand through his hair. "It could be possible, but it will be hard to find."

"This could take a very long time," Michelle said. "But I'm willing to try." She reached over and touched Alice's knee. Alice swallowed the lump in her throat and gave

Michelle a half smile, glad she actually seemed to care about helping her father.

Arthur leaned back on the couch with a heavy exhale. "We'll need to collect as much information as possible, as soon as possible."

"As you know we have stacks of books in our office and more in storage," said James. "Michelle has some hand scrolls from her village."

"Yes, those would be helpful. But the things we need the most I'm sure Thomas Montgomery had already collected," Arthur said grimly as he looked over at the brothers. They both looked uneasy.

"You didn't find any of his belongings?" asked Natalie.

"A lot of his things were cleared out," Leander said. "Including his private collection which I thought would still be in the basement."

"Sounds about right," Arthur said. "Those were coveted artifacts. I wouldn't be surprised if they were stolen and lost through secret exchanges over the years."

"You could check the farm," Natalie said. "Maybe he had some things there. Leander, would you want to head out there to look later today?"

"I'll go now," Leander said as he started to get up from the couch, so eager to leave he looked like he was about to jump out of his own skin.

William held up a hand to stop his brother. "Actually, it's best if I go. Alone. Too many bad memories for you."

Leander blinked away his confusion as he processed William's words and fell back in his seat. He stared out the window lost in his thoughts. Alice was surprised he didn't argue back.

"Good idea, Will," said Natalie with a sympathetic smile. "Besides, Leander, you're still healing from last night.

Arthur and I were talking earlier, and we decided we'll go up to Princeton to search for signs of Alice's father, the book, or his research, either at their old home or around campus."

"We'll head out to Riverton to search for him, since that's the last place he was seen," James said. "It's best if we go, since he wouldn't recognize us and run off."

"Indeed, you make a good point," Arthur said as he stood and flattened the wrinkles from his pants. He pulled out a silver pocket watch to check the time. "Best we get moving."

"And me?" asked Leander, returning from his daze.

"We need someone to stay with Alice and Violet," Natalie said. "You can start going through the books here."

"Of course," Leander said with a flat voice.

"Couldn't I help look for my dad?" Alice asked. She shrunk in her seat from everyone's disapproving stares.

"No. It's not the safest idea," said William.

"Don't forget, that *exsugo* is out there looking for you still," Leander mumbled.

Alice shivered at the memory. If the *exsugo* found her, it could haunt her, feed off of her fear and vulnerability, and eventually possess her.

"The *exsugo* is still out there?" asked Arthur, annoyed. "You killed the host without doing an exorcism? I taught you both better than that."

"My brother was a little busy getting his chest ripped open," William said. "The situation needed to be controlled. Besides, we didn't have the proper supplies." As William recounted the tale, Alice chewed the inside of her cheek, wincing a few times during the more gruesome parts of the story, and Violet did her best to comfort her.

Arthur's demeanor suddenly became much softer. "I

apologize, I spoke too harshly. Are you okay, my boy?" He touched Leander's shoulder.

Leander's body language softened too. "Better now, mostly healed."

"I'm glad to hear it," Arthur said, his hand briefly resting on the back of Leander's head. Alice could sense a deep familial closeness between the two of them. William shifted uncomfortably in his seat. Alice wondered if he was jealous, because *she* was definitely jealous of the comfort, the connection, and the history between all of them. Something she might never experience again.

CHAPTER 10

After they were done drinking their tea, the others dispersed to prepare for their tasks. Alice followed William outside to his car.

"When will you be back?" she asked. Alice didn't want to admit how much she needed him after one night of sound sleep.

"Not tonight. Possibly not for a few days." He rummaged through his trunk, rearranging his things to make more space. "Our family's farm is out in the middle of Pennsylvania."

"You told Leander not to go. Is it because of whatever happened with his wife?"

"You know it's not my story to tell." William straightened his posture.

"He didn't tell me much. I just assumed it was something bad."

William frowned. "It was. He rarely speaks about anything from the past."

"Maybe he has no one to talk to," Alice said.

William shut the trunk and rested his hand on the car.

"He has Natalie and Violet. And Arthur." He sounded bitter. "And everyone else."

"Maybe he needs his brother."

"Doubtful."

"And what about you?"

"What about me?"

"Do you need your brother?"

William didn't answer at first, his face pained, probably due to over a hundred years worth of unspoken grief. "No."

"I think you're wrong," Alice said.

He looked away.

The others filtered out of the cabin, loading a few duffel bags into Natalie's truck and Michelle's nondescript sedan. "You'll be alright," William said when he saw Alice's distressed face.

"How do you know?" Alice's heart pounded, remembering Leander's near fatal wounds. "How do you know it didn't follow us?"

"It can't in the daylight. See this creek?" William pointed to the winding water surrounding the right half of the property. "It's cedar water, full of iron ore. Also, Michelle planted some herbs along the bank upstream, imbuing the water with more magical properties to deter such things." He turned and pointed to the other side of the property. "Out there is an iron fence, which does the same. That's why we came here. This cabin and its grounds are protected."

Alice felt some of the growing tension leave her body from his explanation and returned her attention to Michelle who was helping Natalie load a few more things into the vehicles. "What are they bringing with them?" Alice asked.

"Most likely herbal tinctures, inscribed leather bindings, other things that could either inhibit your father's strength or enhance theirs."

"Isn't elemental magic enough?"

"We're not invincible," William said. "But your father is *almost* invincible, which puts us at a disadvantage."

"Almost?"

"The more he kills, the stronger he'll become, the faster he'll be able to regenerate. We'd barely leave a scratch, let alone be able to bind and contain him. That's why Arthur is so concerned with the amount of time your father is left out there."

"Arthur wants to kill him. I think everyone does."

"I won't let them." William grasped Alice's shoulders. "We'll save your father. I promise."

* * *

Alice meandered back inside, unsure where to go and how to spend her time. As she drifted down the main hallway, she passed an unsettling taxidermy deer head whose beady eyes seemed to follow her until she turned the corner. The hall opened up into a spacious kitchen with heavy antiquated cabinetry mixed with sleek appliances. At one end was a massive stone inglenook fireplace with a wide hearth. On the other side of the room sat a circular dining table, and in the center was a hefty wooden prep table that doubled as a kitchen island surrounded by stools for extra seating.

Leander stood next to the stovetop as he waited for a kettle to boil and spooned a heaping pile of loose leaf tea from an unlabeled tin into the tea strainer in his mug. "Did my brother have anything important to say?" He kept his back to her.

"Why do you hate him so much?" she snapped in return.

His shoulders tensed. "Who said I hated him?"

"You don't have to say it. It's obvious."

"I'm sure he hates me even more."

"He doesn't." She paused. "It was thoughtful of him to go to the farm instead. He cares about you."

Leander scoffed. "Sure." The kettle whistled, and he poured the hot water into his mug. He drummed his fingers on the counter as he waited for the tea to steep.

"You should talk to him," Alice said.

"I talk to him when I need to. No more, no less." He tossed the used tea leaves in the trash.

"But you're family."

"Can you drop it?" Leander huffed out of the kitchen.

She chased after him into the living room where she found him sitting back on the couch. "What's your problem?" Alice asked, hovering in front of him.

"You are." Leander pressed his fingers into his temple.

Alice cringed but didn't stand down. "What did I ever do to you?" she asked. "You have all this resentment bottled up. Why can't you let it go already? Hasn't it been long enough?"

Leander slammed his mug on the side table. "You know nothing about what I have had to endure all these years."

"That doesn't give you the right to take it out on me!" Alice yelled back.

He grit his teeth. "Just leave me alone, Alice."

"But—"

"Go away."

Alice balled her fists, stomped out of the room, and headed out back to find Violet. She needed to let off some steam before she exploded.

Right outside was a worn brick patio covered with a wooden pergola. Dry winter vines climbed up the posts into the overhead beams, and raised wooden flower beds encircled the perimeter of the patio. A flagstone pathway led Alice between some winding bushes and through an arch tunnel which was also overgrown with more dried vines.

On the other side of the tunnel, the path brought her to a large conservatory. Its walls and roof were made entirely of corrugated glass supported by a wood frame. Through the windows, Alice could see the abundant greenery stretching through almost every inch of the space. She walked in, the dewy air significantly warmer from a wood burning stove in the corner, and headed towards the pleasant humming she heard through the dense garden.

Violet stood at a workbench repotting a plant in the back corner. She smiled as Alice drew nearer and said, "They're lucky I'm here, it's about time these little ones got new homes. Couldn't let their roots get too crowded. Isn't that right?" She lovingly held up her freshly repotted plant and patted its top leaves.

"Gardening is definitely your calling," Alice said, the anger from earlier dissipating.

"Oh yes, and I'm quite jealous of their setup here." Violet waved her hand around, gesturing to the windows above their heads. "Although if I had something like this, it would take ages to manage. Michelle and James can easily care for the plants with their, you know..." she wiggled her fingers. Their magic.

Alice raised her eyebrows with realization. "Does it matter?" Alice asked. Violet stared at her, not quite understanding her meaning. "Does it make a difference how the plant is grown?"

"Ah," Violet nodded as she caught on and selected the

next plant to be repotted. She pulled it out and shook the dirt from its roots. "See here, the roots are short, the stems are long, and the leaves are way too big. That's how I can tell they used their magic to rush it. The poor thing didn't have a chance to collect nutrients properly. And that causes its effectiveness to be decreased. If we give it more time to grow naturally," she said as she placed it in a bigger pot with fresh soil. "Then it should be okay."

"Makes sense," Alice said as she watched Violet continue her work.

"That's why I always say—" She wagged her finger. "Don't rush it. But do they listen? Hmph." Violet pushed the repotted plant aside and picked another small one.

Alice noticed a dirt-splattered notebook with dainty cursive writing on the table open to a page with what looked like a recipe. "Leander said you make the teas?"

"I do. At first I simply followed the old recipes and helped them prepare the different blends. Eventually I started tinkering and came up with a few of my own." She inspected the small roots of the next plant and gave another huff.

"They're really good," Alice said automatically. As the words left her tongue, there was a wisp of confusion floating in her mind. She couldn't really remember having any specific opinion of the teas. Regardless of the strange feeling that left as soon as it came, she was happy Violet found something she enjoyed, something meaningful. Alice thought maybe she could find a way to be more helpful too. If Violet could create new magical herbal recipes, then maybe Alice could figure out something for her dad.

"It's one of the only things I can do to help," Violet said, eyes unfocused.

"Why did you tell me your sister died?" Alice asked.

Violet snapped out of it and sighed. "It felt like she did. After everything happened, she spent so much time with Leander. It's why I joined the service. I had to find a purpose in life, or at least find something to occupy my time." She continued her repotting, her frail hands shaking. "Of course, that didn't work out how I expected it either. Just more death. I was medically discharged because of my... troubles. When I came home, I was sent off to an institution." One of the terracotta pots crashed onto the floor.

Violet bent down to pick up the pieces with trembling fingers, shooing Alice away. There were fresh tears on her cheeks. "You can only talk about daemons so much before people start to think you're crazy." She gave a small laugh. "So they put me on all these drugs. Natalie said it was for my own good."

Alice knelt down, grabbed the old woman's hand and squeezed.

Violet quickly composed herself as she picked up the last of the broken pieces. She tossed the pieces on the workbench and dusted off her pants. "I don't take them anymore, the pills. I never really needed them. I spoke my truth and everyone thought I was crazy, but I'm just a person that crazy things happened to." Violet wiped her hands on a rag. "I can't reverse the damage they did to my brain though." She tapped on her temple. "My memory isn't what it used to be after the shock treatments at that wretched hospital."

"Why didn't Natalie stop them?" Alice asked, pushing the horrific images of electric shock therapy from her mind.

"I told you, Leander took all of her time." Violet gave a suggestive look over the top of her reading glasses. "She forgot about me for a little while."

"I thought there was nothing between them." Alice wasn't surprised to discover yet another lie.

"Well, there isn't." Violet shrugged as she brushed the remaining dirt from the table with the rag. "Not anymore." She shimmied sideways to a cluster of more plants and began trimming the leaves. "They seemed very much in love. I think they still are, only different now. I don't know, it's been almost fifty years." She clipped away at the leaves mindlessly. "I can't believe Michelle let these plants get this overgrown." Her hands moved to her hips. "They're very lucky I'm here."

The conversation circled back to plants, and Alice knew it was unlikely for her to hear any more about deeper topics. Violet's disturbing history in a mental hospital explained her tendency to be easily distracted. Sorrow washed over Alice. Natalie shouldn't have treated her sister that way.

Alice meandered her way back into the cabin. Leander, lightly snoring on the couch, had passed out from drinking the tea. At least he wouldn't be bothering her for the next couple hours. It was getting later in the afternoon, so Alice decided to finally venture into the basement to search for some books before it got dark.

She stood at the top of the stairs, heart in her throat. Even though these stairs were well lit and relatively clean, she couldn't shake the memory of mildew and blood. With a deep breath, she descended, gripping the railing until her knuckles turned white. At the bottom of the basement stairs, there was a laundry room directly to her left and a storage room with towers of dusty cardboard boxes to her right. Alice walked straight ahead, and at the end of the long hall was a cramped office. There were wall to wall shelves and cubbies overflowing with books, stacks of papers, glass jars and instruments, boxes, and weird metal trinkets, similar to the office back at Violet's house in Riverton.

A long desk was built into the left wall, and in the corner of the room was a tall vase made of beautiful blue and white porcelain. Inside the vase, Alice found a variety of walking sticks, a cane with an intricately carved brass pommel in the shape of an eagle head, and a sword encased in a dragon embossed sheath. She grasped the hilt of the sword and pulled, just enough to reveal about an inch of the blade, and was shocked to see that the blade was not the typical color of silver metal but an iridescent white. She'd never seen metal that color before, if it was even metal. Alice swiftly replaced it, not wanting to touch or damage something that could be incredibly rare or expensive.

Open on the desk was an oversized ledger with a list of names, dates, and locations. Alice gulped. Her name and her father's name were at the very bottom. She flipped through the filled pages at the front of the book, seeing decades worth of entries. Of course they would keep records of all the people they saved, or at least tried to save. All the way to the right of each page was a column labeled "Deceased," and at least half of the rows had a check mark. Although judging by the dates, most of them would be dead by now anyway unless they had been Chosen.

Alice opened another ledger, but this one seemed more like an almanac with coordinates, weather patterns, and astronomical events. The book beneath it was a hand-written encyclopedia of plants which she tucked under her arm thinking there might be some useful recipe or ingredient inside.

In the built-in storage unit next to the desk, there were rows upon rows of older looking leather-bound books, except for one shelf which had stacks of scrolls with red and gold tassels on the ends. Not knowing where to begin, she pulled out a random book, but it was written in a language she couldn't recognize. She continued to search the books until she found a few written in English. The first book was about herbal medicine, another was a journal of a sea traveler's stories, and the third was a collection of European fairy tales. She figured if these books were in their huge basement collection, they had to be of some importance, so she stacked them up in her arms and headed out of the room.

Pausing in the doorway, Alice looked to her left. The hall continued a bit farther with an alcove to the right side with a enormous wooden chest squeezed into it, and above the chest there were even more shelves lined with opaque bottles and jars. At the end of the hallway was a heavy iron door with a sliding bolt and a narrow slot for items to be passed through. Alice tiptoed closer, not sure what to expect on the other side. When she was close enough to peek through the barred window, she was relieved to find it empty besides a rusted metal cot with a lumpy stained mattress. There was a tiny barred egress window in the top corner of the room. Her eyes darted to the stone wall where iron loop hooks jutted out, and there was a pile of chains on the floor.

Alice lurched backwards. They had agreed to find her father and capture him while they looked for a remedy, but did they plan to keep him in this dungeon? Would those iron chains be strong enough to hold him? She remembered the supplies they loaded into Natalie's truck, and how William mentioned her father's impending invincibility, how he would become much stronger than them. It broke her heart to imagine her father wasting away in this basement dungeon, going mad with his craving for blood. They needed to help him before he was lost forever.

She stomped her way back upstairs in a rush and rested against the basement door to catch her breath, clutching the stack of books to her chest. Dusk was falling, and out the window she could see the glowing light of the conservatory in the distance where she assumed Violet was immersed in her gardening. Back in the living room, Leander remained unconscious on the couch. The calico cat, Ming, was perched on the armrest next to his head.

As carefully as she could, she set the bulky books on the coffee table with a muffled clunk. Leander didn't stir, however Ming opened her eyes and lifted her head for a moment before returning to her slumber. Alice craned her neck to take a closer look at his scars, and noticed they were mostly faded. It was unbelievable to her, the idea that he had advanced healing abilities which were improved even more by a magical herbal tea. It reminded her of the little green lizard she had as a pet when she was younger. One time it lost its tail after an injury, and it took two months for it to grow back. She wondered what would happen if Leander lost a finger or an arm. Would it grow back? She shook her head to rid herself of the peculiar image.

Alice made herself comfortable on the opposite couch, and she spent the next couple hours perusing the faded pages of the journal in the dimming light. It detailed the experiences of a seafarer traveling through the Indian Ocean. There was a bit of parchment with the seal of the East India Trading Company pressed between the pages. Out of curiosity, she checked the inside of the cover and noticed the name and date scrawled in the bottom left corner: *J. Clarke 1637.*

Reading through his journey was exhilarating, and

judging by the content of his entries, he wasn't a law abiding citizen. By the time his crew had reached the coast of East Asia, their cargo hold was full of valuables obtained by dishonorable means, and they planned to obtain a little more before returning to England. As he snuck aboard a local ship in the middle of the night, he had been cornered by a village woman who threatened to kill him for stealing and—

"Anything interesting?"

Alice jumped, so immersed with the seafarer's tale, she didn't notice Leander had woken up. She eyed him, unsure what type of mood he was in after his nap. "The adventures of J. Clarke, whoever that is," she said.

Leander yawned and stretched his arms overhead. "So you found one of James' journals?"

At least his grogginess prevented him from starting up an argument again. "Wow," Alice whispered, holding the book a little bit more delicately. She hoped Leander's half-awake state meant he'd be more likely to answer some questions, although she'd steer clear of asking anything specific about him. "And this woman he mentions, is that Michelle?"

"Yeah, they're really old." Leander said, rubbing his chin. "Probably two of the oldest remaining Chosen."

"And they decided to settle down in New Jersey after three hundred years?" Alice asked with a quiet laugh. He seemed much more relaxed.

"They said they craved a quiet life," he paused. "New Jersey is pretty inconspicuous."

"Why not move out west?" Alice asked. That's where she'd go to get away from it all. Someplace like Wyoming or Montana, out in the mountains, and she'd have a horse. Her mother had loved horses.

"They wanted to stay close enough to lend a hand if needed. This is a central location to three of the biggest cities on the east coast, which are hot spots for our type of work." As Leander spoke, his grogginess faded. He sat up, fluffed the throw pillow, and Ming took that as an invitation to jump into his lap and beg for attention. "What made you decide to look through his journal?"

"I only grabbed what I could read." Alice shrugged. "A lot of their books are in different languages, and I don't really know that much."

He furrowed his brows, mulling something over in his mind, as he scratched the cat's head. "I thought it was you, you know," he finally said.

Alice tilted her head. "What do you mean?"

"Being Chosen by an *eligere* gives us other abilities. When something requires our attention, we get strange visions or dreams. You were in mine for weeks. So when I saw you on campus and when you dropped those scrap papers, I was convinced you were the one who translated the book and completed the elixir." Leander tried to hide his embarrassment.

Her eyebrows jumped up her forehead. "Me?" She chuckled, but it quickly subsided. "If you thought I was dangerous, why didn't you leave me there in the fire?"

"The fire wouldn't've done much if you had been the one to create the elixir. And I couldn't bring myself to cut your heart out right then and there without asking you for the truth first. You were nearly unconscious and didn't seem like a threat, so I brought you to Natalie's and decided we'd figure it out later."

"Cut out my heart?" Alice grimaced. "Is that the only way to..."

"Kill an immortal? Yes, unfortunately. *Sanguis est vis*

vitae. Remove the heart, remove the life force." Leander averted his eyes.

She glanced at the faded scars on his neck. Marie had gone straight for his chest, his heart, like she instinctively knew that was the only way to kill him. And that was how they killed Marie. It was how the brothers killed their own father. How they would have to kill hers.

No, she wouldn't allow that to happen. No one was cutting out her father's heart. She couldn't imagine how many hearts Leander had cut out in the past century. It made her sick to her stomach.

"I'm sorry," Alice said with a quiet voice. "You were right. I really have no idea what you've had to endure."

Leander tilted his head, surprised by her words, like no one's ever apologized to him before. "I—" he stuttered. "Thank you, uh, it's a lot."

"Do you wish things were different?" Alice asked.

His eyes moved back and forth, searching the corners of his mind for an answer. His shoulders softened as he sighed. "I wish lots of things were different. I never wanted this life, and I blame the choices of my father for forcing me into it. People like me, we're just here in the background, holding up the world, while everyone else gets to keep living."

Alice tried to imagine the timeline of Leander's life, the losses he experienced and the incomprehensible terrors he faced. He lived countless lives, searching for daemons to eradicate over the past century, with never a breath to pause, to live. Never a chance to destroy the mental demons that resided within him. Leander and the others only existed to serve a purpose, lingering endlessly as time wore on.

CHAPTER 11

The winter air wasn't going to keep Alice from being outside. Now that she was stationed at the cabin, she was allowed to have a little more freedom. She could roam the property without fear of being seen since there were no neighbors for miles. Being cooped up made her nerves worse, so she preferred to be outside in nature, no matter what the weather was like.

The others had found nothing on their searches the day before, so they were out again looking for signs of her father's whereabouts. And if they weren't searching for her father, they'd be digging for any piece of magical lore that might weaken him enough for captivity. Either way, Alice was always stuck impatiently waiting for answers at the cabin.

This morning, her eyes had blurred from the hours of reading scrawling words on old parchment. She had scoured each page of the old handwritten encyclopedia of plants and ended up writing down a few notes about plants with detrimental cardiac, coagulation, or paralytic effects such as monkshood, oleander, and lily of the valley. If an immortal's life force came from blood, perhaps temporarily slowing or stopping the heart could be the key to her father's capture.

Alice crouched down next to the rust-colored creek, flicking chunks of days-old frozen snow into the water with a stick revealing the detritus and hardened dirt beneath. Her thoughts wandered to the etymology of Leander's name, pondering if he was purposefully named after a poisonous plant. He'd been avoiding her since their talk last night, and she could only guess it was because he opened up more than he would've liked when he generally seemed to be a man of few words.

She continued to poke around in the soggy leaves, using her stick to dig up a couple interesting rocks like quartzite and some others she couldn't identify because she forgot the names. An oblong ivory rock was lodged more firmly in the ground, and it took some maneuvering to get it out. The edges were slightly flared at each end, and when she brought it to her face to get a closer look, she almost puked up her breakfast. She threw the bone to the ground and wiped her hands off on her pants, hoping that it had been an animal bone, but knowing the nature of the Chosen's work, it could've been something much more disturbing.

The gravel driveway crackled as two cars approached, Natalie's truck followed by Michelle's sedan, returning just in time for dinner. Once parked in front of the garage, Natalie hopped out of her truck and hurried over to Alice. There was a messenger bag slung over her shoulder— Alice's messenger bag.

"We didn't find any leads about your dad, but I found this while searching through the debris of your house," Natalie said as she held out the soot covered bag. "Threw in a couple extra things I could find."

"Thanks," Alice said, her heart stuttering as she took the bag, a small piece of her life before this nightmare started. She opened the flap and withdrew a small stuffed dinosaur, a turquoise brachiosaurus which smelled like smoke. She shoved it back in her bag and pulled out a picture frame with a photo of her childhood self with her parents, the three of them all wearing Princeton hoodies. Tears crested in her eyes as her bag dropped to the ground. She almost dropped the picture frame, but Natalie caught it for her.

"Let's walk," Natalie said as she picked up Alice's bag and led her further along the creek.

Alice appreciated Natalie's suggestion. She didn't want to go back inside with her eyes all puffy. She was tired of the way everyone looked at her when she was upset. "You really didn't find any signs about where my dad could be?" Alice wanted this to be over.

"No, nothing." Natalie frowned. "He might not have been back up in Princeton at all. He could be anywhere, even across the country for all we know. But we think he's still nearby judging by the increase of missing person cases in the local area. We'll keep looking. How was it here while we were gone?"

"Fine." Alice said tightly, unsure if she wanted to bring up the conversation she had with Violet yesterday. "Did some reading, even though I don't know what I'm looking for." She kicked a rock into the water in an attempt to quell her attitude. It didn't work. The way Natalie had treated her sister was too upsetting not to mention. "I talked to Violet," she paused. "She told me some things."

Natalie stopped walking. "Like what?"

"About how you sent her to the hospital." Alice stopped too as she waited for a response. "Why would you do that?"

"She needed help," Natalie whispered, looking down. "I

didn't know what else to do. She said she was seeing daemons, but we didn't find any evidence of *real* daemons. I figured it was the trauma from the war that was getting to her. She would be up all night pacing the halls. If she slept, she'd wake up screaming. She wouldn't eat. I worried that if she got more depressed, she'd get possessed again. I thought the hospital would help." Natalie looked ashamed as she rambled. "It was a mistake. She needed me, and I sent her away. I had no idea how bad it was until it was too late."

Alice clenched her teeth as she mulled over Natalie's side of the story. She could understand her point of view, but Violet was the one who suffered. What would become of Alice once this was all over? If she was so traumatized by daemons and death, would she get sent away too? No one would understand what she had been through, and she'd never be able to talk about it with anyone.

The girls started walking again. "It sounded like a difficult situation," Alice said with a weary exhale. It was the most neutral thing she could think of, because she had nothing kind to say about what Natalie had done. Violet needed her sister during her lowest point in life. No wonder she said her sister died long ago.

"Yeah," Natalie said, shoving her hands in her pockets. "The only thing I can do now is try to make up for it."

They were silent for a while as they continued to walk along the creek. Alice looked up at the overcast winter sky through the barren tree branches. When her gaze returned to eye level, she almost jumped out of her skin. A gray-faced woman with sunken eyes swayed back and forth on the opposite side of the creek, her baggy clothes hanging loosely on her frame. "Natalie..." Alice croaked.

Natalie threw a protective arm out in front of Alice as

the woman shambled forward. "Get out of here. Go get someone," she said. "Now. Hurry."

Alice ran as if the creature was on her tail, each step kicking up clouds of dirt behind her. When she looked over her shoulder, she saw the woman had waded into the water, hovering in the center of the creek in a silent stand off with Natalie.

"Natalie needs help," Alice huffed as she stumbled in through the open garage door where Michelle and James were unpacking supplies from their cars. She bent over, clutching her knees to catch her breath. "There's someone out there... something..."

Arthur appeared in the doorway that led into the cabin kitchen, and Leander peered over his shoulder. "What's all this about?" Arthur asked.

Michelle and James had already taken off running across the yard.

"A woman... gray skin." Alice couldn't catch her breath as panic crept in. "She looked dead, but wasn't. I think... *Exsugo*."

Arthur muttered something to himself as he moved into action. He dug through one of the duffel bags and pulled out a coil of leather rope before running after the others.

When Alice went to follow, Leander grabbed her wrist. "I wouldn't," he said in warning.

Alice yanked herself from his grasp. A blast of fire flashed in the distance. The others were already using their flames to corral the possessed woman. Leander took off running. Alice chased after him.

The possessed woman had made it to their side of the creek, but she seemed considerably weaker being within the perimeter of the property. Michelle, James, Leander, and Natalie positioned themselves in four corners surrounding her. She growled and clawed at the dirt. Every time she tried to escape, they'd ignite a ring of fire around her, keeping the flames a safe distance so they didn't harm the woman's body any more than it already was.

Arthur stood poised as he unfurled the rope, a lasso, waiting for the perfect opportunity. When the creature finally stood up straight, Arthur swung the lasso around over his head before releasing it in the woman's direction.

The lasso, perfectly targeted, circled around her and pinned her arms to her sides. Arthur gave the rope a yank, and she fell to the ground with a wail. He used the tail end of the rope to bind her flailing legs. From his pocket, he pulled out another leather strap inscribed with sigils and gagged her mouth. The woman stopped thrashing, her energy suddenly depleted, but a low rumbling growl continued from deep in her chest.

Alice snuck a little closer to take a look, arms hugging her chest, wondering if she was about to witness another heart get ripped out. She swallowed, nausea roiling in her stomach, suddenly regretting following them out there.

The woman's cloudy eyes darted around at everyone. Her dehydrated, graying skin was stretched thin across her face and limbs from the *exsugo* draining the life from her. A shudder coursed through Alice's body. *Exsugo* weren't supposed to be able to travel in the daytime, but somehow this one managed it. Even through the overcast clouds, the daylight had burnt her skin causing it to start flaking off in certain places. And her ankles, they seemed singed like a chemical burn from standing in the creek that had been imbued with herbal magic.

Michelle and James moved to either end of the woman and scooped her up. They carried her sagging body into the garage, gently laid the woman on the concrete, and removed the gag. The others circled around.

The woman started wailing and screeching again, head rolling side to side. Michelle knelt down, grasped her by the jaw, and pried her mouth open. James uncorked an unlabeled bottle and forced a liquid down her throat. The woman gurgled and gnashed her teeth, but eventually her erratic movements slowed and her chest heaved with exhaustion.

Leander spun open a silver butterfly knife with a flourish as he knelt by her other side. "Ready?"

"Be quick about it," Arthur grunted and loosened the rope enough to free one of the woman's arms. Leander took her wrist, pushed up her sleeve to expose the graying flesh of her forearm, and slashed.

Alice gasped. No blood came from the wound, and she could see almost all the way down to the bone. She couldn't look away. Slowly the wound filled with a black sludge. Leander squeezed the woman's arm below her elbow to hasten the flow. Arthur held an empty jar under the wound, and the black sludge slid in with a sickening plop.

A second later, fresh red blood started gushing out of the wound. The woman's skin regained a tinge of color. Natalie and Leander fumbled to wrap the woman's arm in a bandage. Arthur rummaged through another supply box and unscrewed a silver flask, ready to pour. Michelle placed her hand gingerly on the woman's face. "You're going to be okay," she said. "You need to drink. It'll help you."

The woman struggled to speak, gulping a few times as she tried to find her voice. She rocked her head back and forth. Blood was already seeping through the bandage on her arm.

"Please, you need to drink this now. The tea can heal

you." Michelle continued to persuade the woman, one hand cupping her face and the other flattening her matted hair. Arthur held the flask closer to her mouth, encouraging her to drink.

The woman's lips, which were now turning blue, parted as she groaned. She spit up blood followed by something like coffee grounds. Michelle gasped and wiped the woman's face with a ragged towel. Arthur pulled the flask away with a sigh.

"What are you doing?" Alice asked with a shaking voice. "Make her drink the tea."

"She's bleeding internally," Natalie said with a solemn face. "The *exsugo* drained her so much it already started consuming her vital organs."

"Can't the tea save her?"

"There's a point of no return where it can't help anymore." Natalie shook her head. "The healing effects can't work fast enough."

Arthur leaned in closer to the woman. "Can you tell us anything? What do you remember?"

The woman gulped again and gasped for air. Blood dribbled out of the corner of her mouth, and then from her nose and ears. She lolled her head to the side and made eye contact with Alice. She couldn't lift her arm, but raised a shaking finger.

"Alice?" Arthur grunted. "What about her? We need to know."

The woman trembled, gagging and choking. Her mouth gaped open but no words came out. Arthur was about to start pressuring the woman again, but Michelle silenced him with her hand.

"It's okay," Michelle said. "Shh... don't speak. Rest." She

continued caressing the woman's hair. "Someone get a blanket."

Alice rushed over to a box full of old laundry and handed Natalie a few quilts from the pile, but then she returned to the boxes, frantically digging through them. "There has to be something that can save her. Something stronger than the tea." She moved on to the next box, looking for medical supplies. Anything. "What about Violet? She could slow the bleeding, couldn't she? Then we can still give the woman the tea to see if it works."

Natalie had covered the woman's body up to her shoulders, and James rolled up another blanket to place under the woman's head. Michelle used her fingers to comb through the woman's hair. Leander wiped his knife on his shirt and put it away. Arthur stood and stepped back with folded arms.

"You're just going to give up?" Alice cried, jutting out her arms.

They stared at her, silent and unmoving.

"In the back of the truck is one more bag," Michelle said to Alice, her voice quiet. "Can you grab a bundle of dried flowers from there?"

With bubbling hope, Alice sprinted over and popped the hatch of Natalie's truck. The bag was in the back corner on top of a deep red stain covering most of the carpet. She couldn't move. It was her blood from when Leander put her back there after saving her from her house fire.

A gentle hand fell on her shoulder to move her aside. "I never got around to cleaning it," said Leander. He reached past her and withdrew the bundle of dried white flowers from the duffel bag.

"I didn't realize it was that bad," Alice said, her body tense.

"It was." Leander closed the hatch, and they hurried back to the garage. He handed the flowers to Michelle, and she held them under the woman's nose for a moment before placing them on her chest. Leander urged Alice to back away with him so that her view would be obstructed.

"Are they going to save her?" Alice asked Leander in a whisper.

"No," Leander said. He looked down at the floor. "Like they said, there's nothing we can do anymore. The flowers are to help soothe her and assist her soul with passing through the Grey so she doesn't become a *vagari*."

Alice saw such deep sorrow in his expression, sorrow he carried every day for his extraordinarily long life. He had seen situations like this regularly, but it seemed like it hurt just as much each time. She couldn't imagine what it must be like for him, for any of them, to carry such a heart-breaking burden.

Arthur, on the other hand, looked detached. He was older, so maybe he became desensitized over the centuries. But Michelle and James were even older than him, and they seemed to be overflowing with compassion for the woman. The same with Natalie who had tears streaming down her face as she rubbed the woman's hand.

It didn't take much longer for the woman to pass away. Natalie pulled the quilt up to cover the woman's face, and they all held a moment of silence for her. Alice's bottom lip quivered, feeling helpless as she imagined her father underneath the sheet.

Alice couldn't understand how they gave up so easily. Someone could've called emergency services to airlift the woman to the closest hospital. It didn't matter what ridiculous story they'd have to make up to explain her condition to the doctors, it was their job to try and save the life of every human that came through their doors. Even if the woman wouldn't have made it, the Chosen still could've tried harder.

After a somber dinner, everyone sat together in the living room, either reading or chatting quietly to decompress. Violet asked Alice if she wanted the sedative tea, but she declined. The idea of being knocked out was tempting, but Alice didn't want to feel checked out anymore. She felt compelled to face her new reality, especially after watching how the others managed it, knowing this was their normal life. She hoped she could eventually become strong enough to get through everything she already endured and every dreadful thing still yet to come.

Looking for a distraction, she dug through the messenger bag Natalie had returned to her earlier. She avoided bringing out the family photo again, ignored the few notebooks, and instead clawed for the smaller things tumbling around at the bottom which was where she found her silver flip phone. She kept it hidden in her hand as she got up and walked into the kitchen. Luckily, the others paid her no mind.

When she turned it on, she discovered there were over a hundred missed calls and texts. Feeling breathless, she called the first person she could think of.

"*Alice? Oh my god! Are you okay? Where are you?*" Jenny's frantic voice sounded through the phone.

"Jenny! I'm okay. I'm safe. I—"

Before she could even say anything else, Leander snatched it out of her hand and hung up. "Shit, Alice. What were you thinking?"

"Hey! What the hell?" Alice snapped as she tried to get the phone back from Leander. He held it above his head.

"Give it to me!" She lunged for him, but he easily avoided her.

"You need to chill out," Leander growled under his breath and tucked the cellphone into his back pocket. The phone started ringing, probably Jenny trying to call back. Alice tried to reach around him to get it, desperate to hear her friend's voice again, but he smacked her hand away.

"Let me talk to her!"

"You're being stupid, Alice," Leander said, his volume matching hers. "Knock it off."

"Oh, now I'm stupid? I've been trapped with you people for weeks! We've gotten nowhere!" Alice lunged at him again, but he was faster, sidestepping out of the way like he could predict her every move. Leander gripped her upper arms and forced her to stand still.

"Don't you get it?" Leander's voice was low and steady. "You have to stay hidden, not only from the daemons but from the public. The police can track your location on your phone. And now that your friend heard from you, she'll alert the authorities, and they'll come searching for you here."

By this time, the two of them had an audience. The others gathered in the hall leading to the kitchen, Michelle in the front, arm out to hold a furious-looking Arthur back. None of them dared to speak.

"So what! Let them come," Alice hollered. "They'd probably be more help than you!" She tried to free herself from Leander's grip, but forgot how strong he was.

"Alice, *listen*," Leander said through gritted teeth, his patience waning. "If the police come here, they're going to find out real quick that all of us aren't who we say we are. That we've been grifting our way through society. Do you know how many dead bodies we have buried in the yard?"

Alice gulped. She didn't think of that. She hadn't been thinking at all. She had been so numb, she didn't even stop to think what they did with the woman's body earlier. She grimaced, recalling the bone she found earlier and how it was very likely a human bone. Her eyes snapped to the others and felt a pang of guilt when she noted their concerned faces. She really screwed up. She cursed herself for being so impulsive.

Leander finally let her go, and she hugged her arms to her chest, eyes downcast.

Natalie took a deep breath and pushed herself forward through the crowd. "I'll go handle it. Who did you call, Alice?"

"My friend Jenny," Alice replied, her voice small. "What are you going to do?"

"Talk to her, convince her not to say anything," Natalie said as she eyed Leander who gave her a sharp nod. "Where would I find her?"

Alice looked between them, wishing she could shrink away. Wishing she could take back everything that just happened. "Probably at school, in our dorm." She told her the details, and Natalie took off out the side door, snatching her backpack on the way.

Arthur stepped forward with his hand out, brows heavy over his condemning eyes. "Give it to me."

Leander handed over the cellphone, and Arthur snapped it in half. Alice yelped at the blatant destruction of her only lifeline to the outside world, the texts and voice-mails gone forever.

"I'll head to the police station to intercept anyone that might've gotten word," Arthur said as he headed toward the door. "May I take your car, Michelle?"

"Whatever you need," Michelle said. "Call us if you need backup."

"It should be fine," Arthur said with a tired sigh before leaving into the night.

Violet came and put an arm around Alice to lead her back into the living room. "Come sit, dear," she said. "It's okay. Everyone makes mistakes."

As she was led away, Alice glanced over her shoulder at Leander, who stood rigid in the center of the kitchen, the two broken pieces of her cellphone clutched in his hand. He looked pissed. Or worried. She wasn't sure which and definitely didn't plan on asking him to find out.

"It was a really bad mistake apparently," Alice mumbled as she slumped into the couch.

"They'll handle it. They always do." Violet offered her another mug of tea, but Alice declined. She couldn't stomach anything else after ruining everyone's night after an already horrendous day.

"Don't worry," Michelle said as she and James joined them in the living room. "We've dealt with worse."

There was a rustling in the kitchen and the clang of bottles as the fridge was forcefully opened and closed. Leander didn't make eye contact with anyone as he headed up to his room while chugging a beer, a second unopened one in his other hand. Alice waited to hear a slammed door, but surprisingly she didn't.

"Would it really be that bad if the police found out about you guys?" Alice asked.

"We're technically criminals," James said, attempting to joke. "Documentation forgery, identity theft, fraud, money laundering."

"It's hard work shifting identities every few decades," Michelle said. "And we've been doing it for centuries." Her eyes were fixated on the crackling fire in the fireplace. "We're lucky to have connections that help us."

"Connections?" Alice asked, heart fluttering with nervous hope. She remembered what William had said before, how there were hundreds of Chosen people across the country. "Have you called all of them? There has to be someone who knows something that could help my dad."

Michelle and James shared a tentative glance. "We've called some people," Michelle said. "Unfortunately so far no one's able to help."

"Well, keep calling!" Alice snapped. Michelle winced, and Alice immediately felt bad. Michelle had been nothing but kind to her this whole time.

James gave an awkward laugh to ease the tension. "Some connections are complicated. But, there is someone Arthur knows. I think he's been avoiding contacting him."

"Is there any way to convince him?" Alice asked.

Michelle sighed. "When he gets back, I'll try."

CHAPTER 12

Once sunrise came, Alice dragged herself downstairs to the living room, suspended between extreme exhaustion and hyperawareness. She had slept with the lamp on and woke up almost every hour with a racing heart, feeling like something was in the room with her, trying to convince herself that the shadows on the walls weren't moving. Whenever she did fall asleep, in her dreams she would see two cloudy eyes staring right into her soul.

From the window, Alice could see there were no cars in the driveway. She had no idea if Natalie found Jenny last night, or what they might've talked about, and Arthur hadn't returned from scouting the police station. She hoped she didn't mess things up too bad if it took them the entire night to fix the problem. She also wondered what fixing the problem actually entailed. Could Natalie and Arthur be charismatic enough to spin believable lies for Jenny and the police?

Violet pattered quietly in the kitchen, but Alice didn't disturb her as she tip-toed into the living room. Instead she crawled onto one of the couches next to the fireplace and curled up under a crocheted throw blanket. The comfort of daylight and knowing Violet was near helped her to finally get some restful sleep on the couch.

She woke again sometime in the afternoon to the soft sound of the back door closing as Violet headed for the conservatory to care for the plants as usual. On the couch across from her, Leander reclined against the armrest reading a huge, ancient-looking tome which he had propped up on his knees.

"You doing alright?" Leander asked without looking at her.

Alice sat up and pulled the blanket tighter around her. She narrowed her eyes. "Depends on if you're still going to be an asshole."

Leander blinked and huffed out a breath. "I'm sorry about last night. You're not stupid. You didn't know."

Alice opened her mouth but said nothing for a moment, speechless that he didn't bite back. "I'm sorry too. I should've known better not to make a phone call." Her emotions had been making her more impulsive. She needed to use her brain more.

"It's fine. They'll fix the problem, and we can move on. I know this is a lot to handle," he said as he closed the book, a small plume of dust wafting into the air, and set it aside. "Some nights are still hard for me, depending on what happens. This... *job* has a lot of responsibility."

Their previous conversation entered her mind, about how he wished he never had to live this life. "How did you get Chosen?" she asked.

His head bobbed back from the direct question, even though he should expect these questions from Alice by now. "It was triggered by my father's first kill."

"Victoria," Alice said as she remembered William's story.

"Yes, my brother's fiancée," Leander continued, looking sour. "William was hysterical. After he found her, he spiraled as the evening wore on, drinking an endless amount of liquor locked away in his room. Nothing could console him."

Alice couldn't imagine William so distraught, so outwardly rife with misery. He seemed private with his feelings, showing what he wanted others to see. He must've truly loved this woman if he was so devastated by her loss.

"I stayed awake, trying to monitor him in any way I could since I've known him to be reckless. In the dead of night, he slipped out the front door without my notice. But through the window, I saw him running towards the docks by the river. I pursued him, and he was there with our father's pistol, preparing to take his own life."

Alice's hand flew to cover her mouth. The bright winter sun shone through the window, and birds sang in the trees, but the atmosphere was dimmed by the mental image of William contemplating suicide after the murder of his partner. It was a shocking and deeply personal story that perhaps William should have been the one to tell himself.

"My pleading caused an argument, but then we were interrupted by excruciating headaches. The next thing I remembered, it was dawn and we were flat on our backs. An older gentleman was nudging me in the face with his walking stick," Leander said. "That's when we met Arthur. He helped us get adjusted to our new lifestyle, and we worked to decode the mystery. It took us some time to figure out it was my father committing all the murders in town."

"But why was it so hard figuring out it was your dad?" Alice asked. "Didn't he look different or act different?" Her own father's demeanor had drastically changed in a short amount of time at the beginning of winter. Although, she wasn't even mindful enough to notice the severity of the change.

"No. He completed the elixir perfectly, so there were no obvious side effects. And he was very good at covering up his tracks, for a while at least." Leander ran a hand through his hair. "He had us all fooled."

"How did you finally discover it was him?"

"Confusing circumstances and alibis that didn't add up," he said, shaking his head. "He had unusual vitality and strength for his age, compared to how he had been just a few months prior. He became more secretive and suspicious. William eventually snuck into his tower workshop and found compelling evidence against him, such as items he collected like trophies from his victims, including a few of Victoria's belongings and a lock of her hair. We cornered our father up there one evening. He admitted it and," Leander paused. "It was a harrowing fight. William set the entire room ablaze in his fury."

Alice pictured the two brothers, face to face with their own murderous father, and making the choice to kill him, to cut out his heart. If Alice was in that situation, she wouldn't be able to drive a knife into her own father's chest. Even if her own life depended on it, she would refuse, because it wasn't his fault he was turned into a murderer. She knew they had to stop him somehow, but she could never imaging killing him.

The rest of the day was spent reading in silence, anything to keep her mind busy instead of spiraling while being stuck at the cabin. Alice kept skimming through the books, jotting down magical properties of plants, the significance of certain celestial events, and more. Somehow she would find a way to connect these things in a way to help her father.

Natalie returned later in the afternoon. She didn't say a word to Alice about what happened with Jenny and hurried off with Leander to speak somewhere privately. Alice stalked after them with a few choice curse words on her tongue, but Violet intercepted her before she had a chance to let them have it. Instead she ended up helping Violet make dinner.

As Alice chopped up some vegetables, Violet sang a classic tune from her youth as she boiled some potatoes on the stove. It almost felt normal, a glimpse of what life could've looked like if her father wasn't out there killing people for another fix of blood.

The singing stopped. "Oh my..." Violet raised a hand to her mouth.

A little television on the counter played the news. Violet turned up the volume and stepped aside to reveal Benjamin Foster's face and name plastered across the screen. He was the number one suspect in the murder case for Dillon, a few other murders and missing person cases speckled across New Jersey and Pennsylvania, and the disappearance of his daughter. Of Alice.

To make matters worse, the body of a fatally stabbed police officer was found next to a stolen car on the side of the highway, and Ben's fingerprints were all over the scene. They had hard evidence that he was the murderer, and now they were on the hunt.

The room spun. Alice desperately grabbed at the counter top, but instead knocked over the five-pound bag of potatoes as she fell to her knees. Natalie and Leander came running in, eyes wide, transfixed on the news report.

"Shit." Leander stomped over to the TV and turned it off.

Natalie and Violet knelt by Alice's side as she crumbled. Her shoulders shook from her sobs, inconsolable, unable to hold back the flood of emotions anymore. Seeing her dad on the news as a wanted murderer made everything so much more real. He was out there, all alone, sick and distorted by the evilness of that elixir. More murders meant her dad was stronger. They were out of time.

Alice couldn't eat dinner, as much as they tried to convince her. In a daze, she retreated to her bedroom. She wondered if her father could still be saved. He had to be. She didn't care how impossible the others made it seem. She'd find a way. He wasn't going to be another body buried in an unmarked grave somewhere in the middle of the forest.

Curled up in bed and unable to rest, Alice retraced her steps from the night of the house fire. She thought back to being in his office, if anything there seemed out of place or different that night. Alice sucked in a breath and jumped out of bed. She clawed through her school bag, flinging things out of the way—a couple notebooks, her ecology textbook, a few scrap papers from her dad's office. Tucked away in a separate pocket, she found his Moleskine journal. She snatched it out of her bag and thumbed the pages. She kicked herself for forgetting about it.

With shaking hands, she opened it to the first page which was dated about a year ago.

February 9 -

Generally, I'm not one to keep record

of my personal thoughts in a journal, but I decided it might be time to do so considering my circumstances. After failing at hiding my symptoms, Alice finally convinced me to see my oncologist for further follow up testing. I should have heeded her advice sooner. Regrettably, the cancer has returned and metastasized to my brain. Due to the severity of the malignancy, it has been deemed inoperable. I was offered the options of chemotherapy and radiation once again, however I have decided to decline. Alice will not be happy with me once I tell her of my decision, and it will break my heart to do so. The treatment was terribly burdensome last time. I feel if I choose to endure it again, the treatment might be the thing that kills me and not the cancer itself.

It was a shame that the horrible news came the day after I made an extraordinary discovery in the basement of East Pyne. A student had been sneaking around the storage rooms, however they ran off before I could reprimand them. While ensuring that no objects had been disturbed or stolen, I noticed a file box out of place. Behind the file box, I found an ancient textbook, likely dating back centuries judging by the condition of the vellum pages. It appeared to be written in a cryptic form of Greek which lies beyond my area of expertise. My wife would have loved the challenge, and I'm sure her brilliant mind would have been able to easily decipher it.

So of course, my excitement regarding this historical find was instantly diminished with the news about my declining health this afternoon. Now instead of getting lost in my love of research, I must focus on getting my affairs in order before my time inevitably runs out.

Alice had to put the journal down because the tears pouring down her face made it nearly impossible for her focus. Reading her dad's words broke her. What terrible timing it was that he discovered that damn book with that nefarious recipe less than a day before he got the news about his cancer returning. It was like he was cursed, and his fear of death pushed him towards this nightmarish fate. She wiped her nose on her sleeve and continued reading.

In the cafe before I left for my appointment earlier, I unexpectedly met up

with one of my former students, Alexander—
his last name escapes me at the moment.
He informed me that he was applying to a
PhD program in the upcoming year, and he
requested that I be his doctoral advisor. I
told him I was honored and I would
consider it. Regretfully though, I will have
to decline since I only have six months to
live. It's quite a shame because, like
myself, he seems captivated by Classical
history and linguistics. I am utterly disappointed that I won't be able to pursue this
fascinating work with him. Perhaps I could
entrust Alexander with the task of deci-
phering the old textbook once I'm gone.

At the bottom of the page were a few Greek to English translations, some crossed out and corrected. If her dad was willing to leave the book with his former student to decipher, perhaps this student helped him decode the elixir recipe. She rubbed her eyes and turned the page.

February 11 –

I'm not doing well. It's as if the
confirmation of my cancer's return has
exacerbated my symptoms—fatigue,
headache, nausea. I had to cancel all of

my classes today. Besides the physical symptoms, I also find myself in a profound state of dread. I haven't yet told Alice of my decision to refuse the treatment. I cannot find the strength to do so for the fear of seeing the despair etched on her face once again. Even if I agreed to the treatment, it might only extend my life for a few months at best, and it would not be an enjoyable existence. Although I might be tempted to try, if only to have a few more precious months with my Little Bug.

I can't begin to fathom how she must feel, and I can't help but blame myself for stubbornly not following up with my doctor. If I had gone sooner, perhaps we would've caught the cancer at an earlier stage. I might've had more time. Now Alice must suffer the consequences of my actions, and she'll be left parentless at such a young age.

Alice slammed the journal closed and fell back on the bed, crying into her pillow. How had she been so clueless about the intense pain and self loathing her father had been hiding? She wished she never found his journal. She wished it had burned up in the fire. Part of her felt ridiculous though, because she knew the journal could have clues about what happened to him, what he went through to create the elixir. She just didn't think her heart could handle reading any more right now.

Suspended in the limbo of being half asleep, her father's journal clutched to her chest, a sudden knock jarred Alice awake. It was almost midnight. She rolled out of bed, tossing the journal on the nightstand, and opened the door a crack.

"Still awake?" William asked, leaning his forearm on the doorframe above his head.

Her heart skipped a beat from the shock of seeing him there. She stepped aside allowing him to enter. "Off and on," Alice said.

"I can't imagine getting much sleep with that light," he said, nodding towards her lamp.

She closed the door behind him with a shrug and sat on the edge of her bed. "I'm not sleeping much to begin with." Alice wasn't about to admit that she had a new fear of the dark.

"You could always drink the sedative tea." He arched an eyebrow at her.

"I don't want it."

"I'm not forcing you, only a suggestion." William held up a hand before sitting next to her on the bed. "I heard about what happened yesterday with that *exsugo*—"

"You told me they can't come out in daytime," she said as she wrung her hands. "It tracked me."

"I know," he sighed. "I didn't think it could follow us during the day. I'm sorry I wasn't here to help."

Alice swallowed her emotions, unable to forget the sound of the woman's final rattling breath, the desperation in her eyes. "After the exorcism, they just let her die," she whispered.

"Unfortunately, they can't be saved once they reach a certain point." William shook his head. "One of the more difficult parts of this type of life."

"There has to be some sort of magic out there that can—"

"You can't bring people back from the dead, Alice." William locked eyes with her. "I'm sorry." He tipped his head towards her nightstand. "What's that?"

"My dad's journal," Alice said. "I found it in his office the night of the fire and stuffed it in my bag. Natalie brought it back with her yesterday after searching the debris of my house."

"Did she? That could be really useful." William's eyebrows raised as he rubbed his mouth. "How much have you read so far?"

Alice picked at a loose thread on her blanket. "Just the first few pages. I couldn't get past the part where he found out his cancer came back." She closed her tear-rimmed eyes.

"Don't force yourself to read it if you're not ready." He placed a hand on her upper arm.

Her tense shoulders slumped from the touch. "I don't know if I'll ever be ready."

"It's okay. You can take as long as you need." William rubbed her back.

"But we're running out of time." Her voice shook. "William, he's killed even more people. I saw it on the news." She couldn't believe what she was saying, what she was willing to forgive, just to have her dad back. She wouldn't give up on him.

"Then we'll figure it out," he said as he pulled her close for a hug.

She settled into the warm comfort of him that she so

desperately craved, trying to convince herself that they'd find a way. "Do you really think so?"

William pulled away from the hug and brushed a tear from her cheek with his thumb. "Yes, there has to be something out there. People have been experimenting with magic for centuries. If the right ingredients are mixed together and the right ritual performed, someone could've come up with something by now that we could utilize. If not, we'll come up with it ourselves."

Alice nodded. It seemed believable enough, even though she didn't completely understand magic and how it actually worked. Violet, an average human forced into this magical world, had been able to create new types of herbal tea blends with different magical effects. Perhaps magic was more like science than she realized. Maybe that's why her father had believed in it too.

"I think my dad could've been working with someone," she said. "In his journal he mentioned an old student of his who was also proficient in linguistics."

William blinked, the words sinking in. "That's an important lead. If your father had an assistant, then that's another person we can track. Was there a name?"

"Alexander. No last name. But I haven't read far enough yet to know for sure."

"It's enough to start somewhere," he said. "I can go up to Princeton and check through the enrollment records."

"You can do that?" Alice asked. Princeton's academic records were extremely secure.

"I have my ways," William said with a half smile. "Do the others know about the journal?"

She shook her head. "I just found it tonight."

"Best to not mention it yet. They might take it from you."

Alice frowned. "You're right." Especially remembering how Arthur treated her other personal property, she wasn't eager to hand something so important over to him or anyone else. Let them keep searching for her father while William explored the lead on the student.

"You'll read more when you're ready, and then you can decide when to tell them." William gave her thigh a soft pat and stood up.

"Where are you going?" Alice asked in a rush, her nerves ticking up again.

"Well," he started as he directed his gaze around the room. "I'd offer to keep you company again, but that window bench doesn't look very comfortable to sleep on. There's always the floor—"

"No, I—" Alice felt too awkward to say it. "I wouldn't mind if you..." She glanced down at her bed, ears growing hot.

"Oh," William said, clearing his throat. "If you're okay with that, then I'll stay."

"Please."

He dipped his head in agreement, very gentlemanly of him, as he emptied his pockets onto her dresser— the usual items like his wallet, car keys, and cellphone, but the last thing he pulled out was a slim switchblade. It didn't surprise Alice at all considering cutting out hearts was a main part of his job.

"If you don't mind," William said, his hands pausing on the top button of his shirt. "I have an undershirt on under this."

"Oh," Alice said, blushing. "Of course." She made herself busy by laying down and making herself comfortable, keeping her eyes averted. She heard the clink of his belt buckle and the shuffle of his shoes getting kicked off.

When she looked back, she saw him unfasten his gold watch and set it on the dresser next to his folded up shirt and other belongings

William rounded the other side of the bed and slid under the blanket with her. "You okay with turning out the light?" He asked, rolling onto his side to face her.

Alice blew out an unsteady breath. If William was there, then maybe she could be okay in the dark. So she reached over and turned off the lamp, blanketing them in almost complete darkness. As her eyes adjusted, her mind played tricks on her, making her see flashes of those ghastly white eyes. She gripped the blanket, pulling it up to her chin, her body rigid.

"You okay?" William asked in a whisper.

Despite the space between them, Alice felt the warmth of his breath along her skin. She swallowed. "I don't know," she said. It felt too vulnerable to say anything more.

"Do you want to come here?" he asked.

In the shadow, she was able to make out the silhouette of his arm lifting up. An invitation.

Alice tensed at the gesture, feeling self conscious. She barely knew him, yet she already felt so safe around him. It had been so long since she had been held, something she knew she needed. She scooted closer and curled into him, face against his chest as she breathed a sigh of relief. Every muscle in her body melted as his arm wrapped around her. His presence felt like an anchor holding her steady in a stormy sea.

"You'll get through this. I'll make sure you're safe," he whispered.

She believed him.

CHAPTER 13

Alice and William slept in late the next morning, and it was almost eleven by the time they descended the stairs together. They received a few curious looks from the others mingling in the kitchen and living room. William seemed unbothered by the attention. Alice wanted to go back up to her bedroom and hide. Instead of running off, she grabbed one of the fresh muffins Arthur had brought back with him and hovered at the edge of the kitchen.

"When did you get here?" Leander asked from his seat at the table.

William started a fresh pot of coffee, not bothering to look at his brother. "Late last night."

Leander pulled a face, probably about to make a rude comment, but Natalie interjected. "Did you find anything at the farm?" she asked.

William made a lazy gesture toward a small pile of textbooks stacked on one of the stools next to the kitchen island.

"Seems like a waste of a trip," Leander said as he hopped out of his seat and inspected the pile. "Herbalism, precious metals and minerals..." The books slapped against the countertop as tossed them aside one by one. "A book on weather patterns, bronze age weaponry. Things we have already."

"I brought everything I could find," William said, his fist clenched at his side. "Did you forget I went in your stead? As a favor?"

"I would've been fine."

"Do you want my help or not? Because I will leave."

"Then leave."

William bristled, doing his best to withhold his simmering rage. With a sigh, he slammed down his coffee mug and excused himself from the kitchen. The screen door banged shut behind him. Alice watched him through the window. He passed his car, and she relaxed knowing he wasn't actually leaving. She saw him disappear along a path through the side garden.

"Leander, please," Natalie said. "Can you keep it civil when he's here?"

"That was civil," Leander responded as he re-stacked the books on the counter and shoved them away.

"He's doing his best to help," Alice said.

Leander raised his eyebrows in contempt. "We don't need his help. No one even wants him here."

"I want him here."

"He made you think you want him here. That's what he does."

"And what are you even doing to help?" Alice snapped. "All you do is sit around reading and being miserable."

"Kind of like you," Leander spat back.

"You're the one keeping me trapped inside!"

"By all means, Alice, go ahead." He motioned toward the door. "Good luck out there."

"Maybe if you weren't such an asshole all the time." She huffed and walked off. Maybe she *would* leave. Her stomach twisted as she remembered the danger that lurked in the woods. Unfortunately the cabin was the safest place for her. So even if she didn't actually leave, it was a good idea to at least go outside for some air. Stopping at the back door, she slipped on her shoes and grabbed a random coat hanging from the rack. Then she headed out into the garden.

William was seated on a bench along one of the paths. Tall evergreen hedges stretched upwards behind him. He scribbled something in a small notebook and tucked it in his pocket when he saw Alice arrive. "Nice of you to bring me my coat," he said with a cocked eyebrow and a smile.

"Your coat?" Alice asked, looking down at the heavy black wool coat that was about two sizes too big. She started on the buttons, about to remove it to hand it over, but he declined it.

"It's fine, you can wear it for now. I don't really need it." He was wearing a sweater and didn't appear too fazed by the cold air. Alice wondered if improved cellular function and regeneration also included resistance to frost bite.

"He's so mean to you," Alice said as she sat next to him on the bench.

"I might deserve it," William said as he made a bitter face. "I wasn't the nicest big brother. I bullied him a lot when we were kids."

"Is that why he holds a grudge against you?"

"Amongst other things."

"He said some terrible stuff about you while you were gone." Alice swung her leg back and forth, kicking up some gravel. She felt bad bringing it up, but she wanted to know.

"As expected," William said as he shrugged.

"He told me about the night you were Chosen, after

Victoria died," she paused. "About what happened on the docks."

William hunched forward, hands clasped, his nonchalance turning into tension. "What part?"

"Well..." She paused, unsure how to broach such a personal subject. "All of it."

"I see." William hung his head and let out a long sigh. "One of my darker moments. It was not a very good time for me. I had just discovered the body of my dead fiancée. I think anyone would've been equally distraught." After a minute, he sat up straight again, his face moved from sadness back to anger. "How hypocritical of him. Leander asked me to not tell you his story, yet he goes and tells mine." There was ice in his voice. "And he calls me the uncaring one. All I do is care, sometimes too much. I've spent so many years trying to make things right," he paused. "I'm still trying to make things right."

Emotion dripped through his normally reserved voice. Alice wanted to reach out to him, comfort him. A low buzzing came from her coat pocket. She pulled out a flip phone and held it up to William. "Yours?"

"It is my coat, so that makes it my phone," he said playfully as he took it from her hand. "One of them anyway." He narrowed his eyes at the number on the screen and silenced the call. "This is a burner phone I use for certain contacts. I'll call them back later."

"What kind of contacts?"

"People helping me locate things that could be useful."

"You seem like you're the most invested in this out of everyone," she said. "Thank you for caring about me and my dad instead of wanting to kill him."

"Of course," he said with a smile. "If I had a father like yours, I'd want to save him too."

"You say that like you know him," Alice said.

William shrugged. "He must be an amazing person, judging by how much you love him, how much you want to save him. I wish my father was half as decent as yours." He took her hand. "I'm sorry this happened to him. To you."

Tears filled her eyes, and she held her breath until the wave of sorrow passed over her. William had a way of breaking through her emotional walls, no matter how vulnerable it made her feel.

"Do you want to walk?" he asked as he stood, taking her hand and guiding her to stand with him.

She didn't let go.

They strolled along the path further into the garden, their hands comfortably clasped together. The trees and dried brambles grew thicker, the hedges high, and Alice could barely see the roof of the cabin. At least she could hear the splashing of the near-by creek which calmed her anxiety knowing they remained mostly protected from daemons if they stayed within the border of the property. And William was with her too. He'd protect her.

The walking helped dispel some of the heaviness she felt in her heart. She distracted herself by taking interest in the winter foliage. It probably tripled in size in the spring and kept the area well hidden. She pointed out a few of the species of trees and plants, including their Latin names which impressed William, as well as the call of a song sparrow. She also told him about the pitch pine trees, and how their pine cones actually required natural forest fires in order to spread their seeds.

Eventually she trailed off, staring blankly ahead. Talking about the plants and wildlife made Alice realize how much she missed her studies at the university. She missed visiting her father in between classes and listening to him ramble about ancient Greece. She missed spending the evening studying with Jenny and Caleb in the common room.

William sensed her melancholy. "Hey," he said with a soft voice. "You seem far away."

"Huh?" Alice blinked. "Oh, I..." There was so much she could say, and yet she couldn't form the words. "I just miss my normal life."

"I get it," he said.

Their eyes met. She knew he understood.

"Will you tell me a story?" she asked, in need of a distraction.

"A story?" he asked. "About what?"

"I don't know," she said with a shrug. "From back then."

William smiled. "I suppose I can think of something," he said as he mulled it over. "My brother and I used to go sailing together. The only time we actually got along was when we were out on the river. Well, most of the time."

"You were a sailor?"

"You could say that," William said with a chuckle. "It was more of a hobby than a lifestyle. Leander was much better at it. In fact, so good, we won the town's first sailboat race because of him. I, however, often struggled with it. Once I accidentally heeled the boat too hard and sent Leander flying overboard."

Alice laughed. "I'm sure he was pissed."

"He was," William said, grinning.

The conversation lulled as they continued to walk along the path.

"What was Victoria like?"

"Uh—" he stuttered from the unexpected question. "She, uh, she was one of a kind, the type of person that made the world feel brighter. We met when a traveling circus came to town. She was one of the performers—an acrobat, equestrian, gunslinger, and more. She had no family, and was forced to find a way to make a living at a young age. Victoria had learned all of the skills needed to become self-sufficient, which was rare for women of that era. And after all of the struggles she had been through to make a life for herself, she still had a smile that shined."

"She sounds remarkable."

"Very," William said. "I went to see her perform every night until she agreed to go on a date with me. The master of the troupe was not thrilled when she chose to stay behind when it was time for the caravan to leave town. He challenged me to an illegal duel." He smirked, staring straight ahead as they walked. "And I would've won if he didn't back down last minute."

Alice could see the wistfulness in his eyes as he reminisced about his past. There was sorrow there too. William stopped walking. His expression looked heavier, the memories of a thousand lonely nights lost on his face.

"I never met anyone else like her," he continued. "She chose me, not because she needed a man to take care of her, not because of my money or status, but because she loved me for me. When I lost her, I didn't know how I could go on."

Alice lightly touched his arm to show how sorry she felt, knowing no words would ever be able to alleviate his mourning, and pulled him for a hug. His eyes fluttered, surprised by her action, and then tucked his face into her hair.

"I can't help but wonder what my life would've been like if we had decided to run away together, before my father returned, before he had the chance to..." William stumbled on his words. "We could've had a life together, a family. I wouldn't have been damned to this wretched existence. It's been such a long time." He took a deep breath, parting slightly from the hug enough to look down at Alice. "Thank you for listening to me. I don't talk about her much."

"Of course," she said. "You can always talk to me." Alice meant it. She wanted to be there for him like he had been there for her, because it really seemed like he had no one else.

"I guess I got used to the loneliness," William said, eyes downcast.

"You don't have to be alone though," Alice said. If only he would make up with his brother or connect more with the others. Or even *her*.

"I know," he said with a sigh. William reached out and tucked a piece of her hair behind her ear. His hand lingered there. "But it's easier this way."

Alice felt something flicker between their eyes. Her breath caught in her throat, and she stilled from the gesture. She tried to discern the words he didn't say out loud, unsure if his actions implied something more.

"I'm sorry," he said, drawing back and releasing her from the hug.

"It's okay, I—" Alice searched her mind for the right thing to say. She had felt so much over the past week, fear and horror and uncertainty and desperation. There hadn't been space for anything else, although somehow this connection with William had squeezed in. She began to crave the nights he'd spend with her, comforting her as she slept, but the intensity of her feelings intimidated her. "Everything is really confusing right now."

"I understand," William said, clearing his throat.

They continued their walk in silence until Alice's teeth

chattered from the cold. He kept his hands stuffed in his pockets and didn't look at her for the rest of the walk.

Once they returned inside, William spent most of the day avoiding her, which was more hurtful than she'd care to admit. Maybe he was avoiding everyone else too, specifically his brother. He isolated himself in one of the guest rooms at the top of the stairs, presumably reading through the books he had brought from the farm.

They crossed paths once more before the end of the night. As she was coming out of the bathroom, she saw him down the hall returning to his room. They made eye contact, and she thought she saw something like longing there, but he disappeared quickly behind his door.

Alice laid in her bed, lamp still on, waiting for William to come to her as he did the previous night. Because without him, she couldn't sleep. He knew that. She watched the minutes tick by on the clock. Every movement she heard outside her door caused her to perk up, but it was her other housemates going in and out of the bathroom as they turned down for the evening. The disappointment in her chest deepened, and that was a clear enough answer for her. She had gone through so much in her life alone, pushing everyone away or never letting them get close in the first place—her father, her friends, and even her ex-boyfriend Noah. William made her realize how much she didn't want to be alone anymore.

She peeked her head out the bedroom door. The hallway was dark like the living room below. Dying embers glowed in the fireplace downstairs, and it looked as if everyone was off to bed. Her socks muffled her footsteps as she tiptoed down to the other end of the hall. When she reached William's door, she waited. She listened for any sound or sign of movement. There was a dim light glowing underneath the crack of the door. She heard the flutter of papers and the sound of him sighing under his breath. She knocked. His voice beckoned her to come in.

William sat at an elegant writing desk by the window, back to the door, illuminated by the small antique lamp which cast him in a shadowy silhouette. He barely glanced over his shoulder to look, like he already knew it was her. "Is everything alright?"

Alice stepped inside and shut the door. The bedroom was larger than hers, but somehow the gravity between them made it feel much smaller. She swallowed and picked at her nails as she tried to understand his diffidence. "I was waiting for you."

He placed his pen on the desk and turned to the side in order to face her more, but his expression remained hidden in shadow. "I wasn't sure if you wanted me there."

"Of course I do," Alice answered, a little too quickly for her liking. She inched closer and saw the corners of his mouth turn upwards in a slight smile.

He didn't respond right away, like he was suspending the silence on purpose. "Since you're already here," he finally said as he gestured outwards. "Make yourself comfortable. I have a few translations to finish up." William picked up his pen and began writing again.

Alice crawled into his bed and pulled the comforter up to her neck as she rolled on her side. It smelled of him, and instantly she felt more relaxed. She studied William as he finished whatever research he was doing. He looked through one of the old textbooks and scribbled down some notes, the pen scratching on the paper from his brisk handwriting. He dipped the end of his pen in his mouth as he paged through the book, his hair falling in front of his face as he pondered some distant thought. Then he was writing again.

Eventually William was satisfied with whatever he was working on and stretched back in his seat with a yawn. He turned off the lamp and stood, his figure doused in moonlight as he pulled his shirt over his head and tossed it back on the chair.

He slid under the comforter with Alice. As they scooted in closer to each other, her heart rammed in her chest. They'd already spent a couple nights together, but this time it felt different because of their conversation earlier, and because of the things he might've admitted between the lines. Unless she was assuming too much.

"Earlier in the garden..." she began, her voice quiet, wanting some sort of confirmation of his true intentions, about what he did or did not feel about her.

"Don't worry about it," he said as he brushed her hair out of her face. His hand didn't linger this time. It was as if he wanted to dismiss everything that happened between them since the afternoon, since they first met, as if he wanted to ignore the electricity building between them right now in this moment.

Disappointment twinged in her stomach as she second guessed herself. The only thing Alice was sure of was that she felt safe around him, that she trusted him to take care of her, to be there for her through one of the hardest times in her life. She realized when she said she wanted him there earlier, that wasn't completely true. She *needed* him there.

"It's not always easier being alone," she whispered. Even though the message was meant for him, it felt true for her too. They were both so similar, pushing people away thinking it would protect them from their emotions, when what they both needed most was comfort.

"Alice, you said it yourself, everything is too confusing right now. Things could get complicated."

"I don't care," Alice said, her voice sounding a little more desperate than she intended.

Something flashed in William's eyes, taken aback by her confession. He searched her face, looking for some sort of silent permission. His hand lifted back up, letting his fingers rest along the side of her neck, thumb smoothing across her cheek. That breathless feeling found her again as she looked up into his deep, brown eyes.

She tensed when he drew his whole body closer to her, their knees brushing. His gaze didn't leave hers as he traced his hand down the length of her arm until it met her waist, wrapping around her back to pull her into him even more, entwining their legs. She could feel the heat rising between them, their breathing slow, heavy, matched.

Her hand pressed against his bare chest, feeling his own pounding heart under his skin, and her other arm wrapped around his torso. The inviting movement from Alice was the signal he needed to incline his head down, his face inches from hers. They hovered there, breathing in each other's breath. She inched her mouth closer, feeling the pull of him, impatience and urgency gnawing at the pit of her stomach. He smiled, as if he could see it in her eyes, as if it was all the confirmation he needed of how she truly felt.

He moved in devastatingly slow, his mouth soft upon hers, but only for a moment. This time it was Alice who pulled him in closer, because it wasn't enough. He obliged by pressing his mouth down on hers, his kiss fully enveloping her, his tongue dipping in for a taste. She gasped into his mouth.

His hand that had wrapped around her waist was now splayed across her stomach, pushing her back into the bed.

They kissed for what felt like an eternity. Their hands roamed each other's bodies, the heat escalating with each passing second.

When William broke away from the kiss, he hovered over her breathlessly, his eyes hungry but his composure controlled. His hand brushed her messy hair from her forehead. "Maybe we should slow down," he said, moving to lay on his side next to her.

Alice's chest heaved and she nodded, even though she didn't want to stop. She needed to be close to him, to feel him and connect with him in a way that reminded her she was still alive. But he was right, and she could wait. So instead she shimmied closer to him, and he held her while they fell asleep.

CHAPTER 14

Morning sunlight streamed in through the huge picture windows of the living room, brightening up the array of eccentric, old-world relics scattered around the space, making it feel less like a museum and more like a home. Alice and William sat thigh to thigh on the couch by the fireplace as they read through some herbalism books. She shared her idea with him about creating an herbal blend that could slow or stop the heart temporarily to use on her dad. William was intrigued and eager to learn more.

Alice leaned into him as he pointed something out on the page. His other arm rested on the back of the couch behind her as he rubbed her shoulder. She felt eyes on her, and noticed Natalie staring at them from the kitchen. A flush bloomed across Alice's chest and neck, as if Natalie could see the truth of her newfound closeness with William.

A door opened and closed from upstairs. William removed his arm and inched away from her. Leander's hand trailed along the second floor banister as he headed for the stairs. Clearly William didn't want his brother to know. Even though Alice understood why, considering Leander's testy demeanor, it hurt just the same.

Natalie noticed the body language shift as well, judging by her raised eyebrows. Leander, completely ignoring Alice and William, made his way downstairs and into the kitchen. They engaged in some sort of conversation, and Natalie's eyes kept flicking between Leander, who had his back towards them, and Alice's sheepish expression.

William cleared his throat, startling Alice out of her daze. "Something more interesting in the kitchen?" he asked in a low voice, his breath dancing around her ear.

Alice shook her head, unable to squeak out any response. There was something about the daylight that made secrets feel less secretive, as if any word she'd say might give her away. Even if no one would be able to hear her from across the living room or all the way in the kitchen, her face would betray her.

William's buzzing cell phone saved her from her awkwardness. He took one look at the number on the screen and sighed. "I have to answer this." He put a hand on her knee before taking the call privately on the back porch. Alice had the urge to follow him, but decided against it because she didn't want to draw any more attention to herself.

She attempted to refocus on the task of reading but was interrupted by Natalie plopping down on the couch next to her with a smirk. "What?" Alice asked, the blush returning to her chest and now rising up to her cheeks.

"What's going on between you two?" Natalie leaned in closer to Alice, her voice quiet.

"Nothing."

"It doesn't seem like nothing."

"Okay, something."

"Hmm." Natalie eyed her up and down.

"Please don't tell anyone," Alice said in a rush.

"Oh trust me, I won't." Natalie looked back to the kitchen. Leander was drinking his coffee and reading through a book with a tense fist crumpled in his hair.

Alice wondered what he was so mad about this time, and hoped he didn't notice how close she had been sitting next to his brother or how often they spent the night together. Not that it was any of his business to say the least. She didn't want to be on the other end of his wrath. She dealt with his anger enough already. He hated his brother and constantly gave him grief, and Alice could very well end up being a recipient through association.

Through the glass panes of the back door, Alice watched William pacing and gesturing as he spoke on the phone. He pulled a hand down his exasperated face, hung up, and stared off into the forest.

"Who was he talking to?" Natalie asked with a frown.

Alice shrugged. "I don't know, he said he has contacts helping him with information."

"He looks stressed out."

William indeed looked stressed, like he received some bad news. Alice wondered if it was another dead end, another piece of hope lost in the fight to save her father. He strode back inside at a brisk pace.

"I have to go," he said to Alice.

"Go where?" Natalie pressed.

William barely acknowledged she was sitting there. "I have to meet up with someone." He blinked a few times. "They have information, and it's time sensitive."

"What kind of information?"

"That's the magic question isn't it?" William said with a little too much disdain.

Natalie scowled.

"I'm sorry," he said, checking his watch. "I'm stressed, and I need to get to this person before they leave."

"Keep us updated this time," Natalie said with a firm voice.

"I'll try my best," he grumbled.

Alice stood to face William, closing the space between them. "When are you coming back?" she asked, hoping she didn't sound too needy.

"I don't know." He touched her arm briefly, letting his hand trail down to grip her fingertips.

"Will you take me with you?" It was a foolish request.

"I don't think it's a good idea," William said with an understanding frown.

"But—"

Natalie coughed. Alice and William stepped back from each other as Leander entered the living room, inspecting them with narrowed eyes as he approached. "Something amiss?"

"I was just leaving," William said as he stepped away from the crowd. He disappeared upstairs to gather his things.

"Good," Leander said under his breath. He gave Alice a look. They hadn't spoken since their last argument the other day. But he stayed silent, jaw clenched, and turned on his heel to return to the kitchen. Natalie followed after him talking about something or other.

By the time William returned downstairs with his packed bag, everyone else was picking at breakfast in the kitchen. James cooked some fried eggs and pancakes which he laid out on the kitchen island with some assorted fruits, breads, jams, and cheese. He stood to the side, arms folded and beaming as he watched everyone enjoy the meal.

Alice helped herself to a few pieces of fruit at first, but James strongly encouraged she at least try his pancakes. She was glad she did, because they were the most delicious pancakes she'd ever eaten in her life.

"My mother's recipe," James said with a smile as he untied his apron and hung it on a hook inside a tall pantry cabinet. "Try them with the honey."

Alice followed his suggestion. "Wow," she said as she chewed. She tried to do the math in her head to figure out how old the recipe could have been and made a mental note to ask him for a copy. They were way better than the boxed stuff from supermarkets.

William didn't touch the food, only coffee which he poured into his travel mug, and paused by the side door with his bag slung over his shoulder. "I'm heading out to meet up with a contact about some potential information." After a glare from Natalie, he added, "I'll reach out if I'm successful."

Arthur drummed his fingers. "I'll also be reaching out to one of my contacts today."

Michelle's eyes lit up and she gave a quick wink to Alice, indicating her convincing worked. Alice felt a smidgen of hope return.

"Don't get too excited," Arthur added. "He might not be too keen to assist us. My last interaction with him didn't end well. But I shall try." He clapped a hand on Leander's shoulder, jarring him enough that crumbs fell from his toast. "In the meantime, we'll be heading back up to Princeton to continue the search for our person of interest."

"Can I come?" Alice asked, eyes darting between the two men. She had a gut feeling that she didn't trust Arthur and Leander to go off alone searching for her father, because they were the ones most likely to kill him on the spot.

"No," Leander said shortly, not even bothering to look up at her as he dipped his toast into egg yolk.

Alice squeezed her fork in her fist, fighting the urge to throttle Leander, when Arthur spoke up. "You'd be too much of a familiar face if you went back to your home town," he said delicately.

She didn't care to admit he had a valid point. "Well if I can't go with you," she said tightly as she gestured at Arthur. "And I can't go with you." She gestured to William. "How long do you expect me to stay sane while cooped up here?" Her voice ticked up a notch. "I can't sit around waiting forever. There's only so many books I can read before I lose my mind—"

"You can come with us," Michelle said. The others all snapped their heads to look at her.

"What?" Alice stuttered, shocked at the offer. "Yes. Please. Anything."

Everyone looked wary, especially William. "I thought the priority was keeping Alice safe and hidden," he said.

"She'll be fine," Michelle continued. "James and I are heading up to New Hope today. We have a friend who acquired an incomplete manuscript that was found in storage at an old library. We'll be in a different state, almost two hours away. No one will recognize her, and we won't even be there long."

"Michelle..." Arthur said, his voice tense. A warning. The two held stern gazes, and Alice wondered if Michelle was about to use her seniority to make him agree.

James stepped forward, arms out in suggestion. "Let the girl get some fresh air. She'll stay in the car with me while Michelle runs in to get the manuscript." At this point, it really did seem like they were covertly using their seniority, because James was next oldest. Then Arthur, the third. She wondered if their disagreements were always settled in a tense fashion like this, going by seniority, or if it ever got worse. Volatile. With Leander's temper, she was sure the others have faced his wrath before too. Especially considering Leander and William had engaged in more than one fist fight in the past.

"You don't want to stay here and hang out with me and Violet today?" Natalie asked with a forced laugh.

"No," Alice said.

Violet's hopeful smile disappeared.

"I need to get out of here, even if it's only a few hours. It'll help me feel like I'm actually doing something to help. Please." Her voice cracked.

Leander and William remained tight lipped. Arthur waved his hand dismissively, scoffing under his breath, and took his plate of food out to the living room to finish eating by himself.

After breakfast, Alice hovered in the driveway as everyone loaded up their vehicles with any supplies they might need for their planned errands. Arthur carried the eagle pommel walking stick with him, the one she had seen in the basement, and he stowed it away in the back of Natalie's truck.

William was rooting around in the trunk of his car looking for something. He walked over to Alice, hand out to display a braided leather cord in his palm. "Here," he said. "Give me your wrist."

"A bracelet?" she asked, one eyebrow popped in curiosity.

"It'll keep you safe once you leave this property," William said as he tied it around her left wrist, holding her hand for a little bit longer than he needed to. "To deter any daemons that might try to latch on to you."

She inspected the bracelet. It had tiny symbols burned into the three leather strips of the braid, and there was a pressed metal bead in the center. Iron. "Thank you," she whispered. "No one else thought to give me anything like this." Her eyes drifted over William's shoulder to see Leander giving them a spiteful look as he flung a backpack into the truck.

"They should've given you something for protection on the first day they found you." William's voice was quiet with disdain. "We all have something." He pulled a necklace out from under his sweater, a thin leather cord with an iron pendant stamped with some type of sigil. "They should've known better."

Alice glanced over to where Natalie and Violet stood on the porch, saying their goodbyes to Leander and Arthur. Her stomach turned. Natalie had said she'd get her something for protection, and yet she never got around to it. She frowned and looked back at William. "Chosen can get possessed too?" she asked.

"Yes," he said. "Not very often. I haven't personally seen it, but it's better to be safe." William took her hand in his again, worry written across his face.

"Are you mad that I'm going?" Alice asked.

"No, not mad," he said, his thumb rolling across the back of her hand. "Concerned. But I trust Michelle and James to keep you safe. Besides, I think you should be allowed to make some of your own choices after everything you've been through."

She smiled. "You have no idea how much I appreciate that."

William smiled back. "While I'm gone, I'll try to stop by campus to dig up records of your dad's classes and see how many students he had with the name Alexander." He paused. "If you're up to it, and by no means am I pressuring you, consider looking through more of your dad's journal."

"I'll try," Alice said. William's support helped her feel a little more confident in her ability to handle this. If he was strong enough to go through the loss of his fiancée, almost committing suicide, killing his own father, and even more awful things over the past hundred or so years, then Alice could be strong too and read a couple more pages of her dad's journal.

"Hey, you ready?" James called as he opened the driver's side door of Michelle's car. "We have a long drive ahead of us." He slapped the roof of the car and got in.

"I guess I'll see you when I see you," William said. He hooked a finger under her chin and lifted it. He didn't kiss her though, he wouldn't. Not in front of everyone. So he instead gave her a charming smile before he climbed into his own vehicle.

With a blush spreading across her cheeks, she slipped into the backseat of Michelle's car. As Michelle got into the passenger seat, she gave a sly glance over her shoulder at Alice. Her closeness with William wasn't much of a secret after all.

"Thanks for bringing me," Alice said as they drove onto the main road.

"We figured a day out would be helpful for you." Michelle said.

"You're not worried?" Alice fiddled with the leather bracelet on her wrist, searching the passing trees for anyone, or any*thing*, that could be following them.

"Nothing to be worried about," James said.

"But the *exsugo*, it came for me in the daytime—"

"A rare occurrence," he said simply. "But now it's gone."

"Even if something did come after us, we'd be able to handle it," Michelle added.

Alice had a hard time believing them. "Then why was everyone else so against it?" she asked. "It seemed really tense back there. Arthur—"

"—has control issues sometimes." Michelle interrupted. "Same with the boys."

Alice noted the informal way she referred to William and Leander. She spoke of them like they were her own sons. "How long have you all known each other?" Alice asked.

"Oh, goodness," Michelle mused as she shared a glance with James. "What year was it? When we were back in London?"

James rubbed his chin, eyes concentrated on the road ahead as he drove through the winding roads of the forest. "A few years before the thing with the doctor, whenever that was."

"The London doctor?" Alice gulped, recalling the brief story the brothers mentioned about the doctor that turned feral after drinking the elixir.

James flashed a guarded glance at Alice in the rearview mirror. "They told you about it?" he asked, sounding much more serious than usual.

"Not much. Only that he was like an animal." She squeezed her eyes closed, forcing out the image of her father with blood dripping down his chin.

"Hmm, you probably know more about it than you think," he continued. "The doctor was more famously known as Jack the Ripper."

"What? Really?" Alice was stunned. Her brain flicked through a series of random historical events, wondering if magic or daemons could've played a part. Michelle and

James probably had answers to hundreds of unsolved mysteries in their basement library. Maybe when this was all over, they'd let her read through some of it if she promised to keep it a secret.

"Unfortunately," said Michelle with a sigh. "It was a dangerous case."

"How did it end?" Alice asked, even though she already knew what they'd say.

"We had all split up, tracking him through the city one night. The boys found him first." She paused. "They stopped him."

"By cutting out his heart," Alice whispered.

"Yes, exactly that," Michelle said.

Alice didn't respond. She only stared out the car window with a ball of dread in her stomach. If they didn't find a cure, her dad would meet the same fate.

"We'll try our best to make sure it turns out different this time," James said.

After they finally drove through Trenton, the terrain became rougher with higher elevation and more dense trees. The northern part of New Jersey was more mountainous, full of trails Alice used to hike with her dad. But surprisingly, Alice had never made it across the river to the town of New Hope, Pennsylvania. She knew her mother used to love it up here, with all of its little cozy shops, and it saddened Alice that she never got to come here with her.

As they crossed the old truss bridge, they entered into the quaint town with its main street lined with stores selling handcrafted items, gifts, apparel, and more. There were also quite a few restaurants, ice cream parlors, and coffee shops with wooden, hand-painted signs hanging at their doors. It seemed like an average tourist type of town older adults would spend a lazy Sunday browsing through, something her mother would've really enjoyed, especially any place that sold kitschy crafted items.

They drove over the train tracks of the historic railroad and pulled into a public parking lot. Once the car was off, James twisted around to look at Alice, hand resting on the back of Michelle's seat. "You ready?"

She blinked. "Ready for what?"

"To take a walk with us." James gave a smirk. "No one will recognize you up here."

"You're sure?" Alice asked.

"Here," James said as he rummaged through the center console, pulled out a pair of sunglasses, and handed them to Alice. "Keep them on until we get there."

She held the sunglasses in her hands, looking between them as if she couldn't believe they'd actually let her come out with them. With a deep breath, she put on the sunglasses and smiled. "Alright, let's go."

The three of them headed down the sidewalk, which wasn't very crowded due to the cold February air. Alice imagined it was much busier during warmer months. Besides all of the cute shops and restaurants, there was a surprising amount of occult stores selling crystals and tarot cards, and there were multiple psychics and palm readers for hire, an interesting and unexpected combination. After a couple short blocks, they paused in front of a store with skeletons, taxidermy, and creepy dolls in the bay window display. The sign above the door read: The Gallery of Oddities.

"He knows we're coming today, right?" James asked Michelle. She nodded.

They headed inside, the jingling of the bell above the door announcing their arrival. James made a point to spin the open sign to closed so they wouldn't be disturbed by new customers trying to browse the shop.

It was a cramped space that smelled of incense, lined floor to ceiling with a variety of bizarre looking knickknacks and collectibles. In a glass case were a few skulls, real human skulls, for sale. Alice gasped. The entire display case was full of human bones, animal bones, and teeth. There was a shelving unit next to it lined with wet specimens in jars—dozens of snakes, rats, bugs, eyeballs, dissected body parts, and more preserved in formaldehyde. All available for purchase. Anyone from the general public could walk in and buy these human or animal remains.

In another display case, she saw an old briefcase opened to show off a variety of bottles, knives, an old pistol, a bible, and a wooden stake. It was labeled as a real vampire hunting kit. There was a bookshelf full of dusty vintage books and weather-worn leather journals, and sitting atop the shelf was an unnerving porcelain doll, a crack running down her face, with a tag that said "Haunted: Do Not Touch."

Alice fidgeted with the leather bracelet on her wrist before she tucked her hands into the pockets of her coat. She wouldn't dare to touch a single thing in the store. Now that she had experienced the supernatural, any of this stuff could actually be real and not a gimmick. James arched his eyebrows at her. "Cool, huh?" he asked.

"You could say that," Alice said.

Luckily the store was mostly clear except for one lingering customer, an older woman with short blonde hair carrying around a taxidermy owl with mismatched glass eyes. She awkwardly placed the thing up onto the counter so she could pay for it. The man at the register had a bright smile as he made the sale. He wore all black, including his painted finger-nails and the makeup lining his eyes. Dangling from one of his ears was a silver earring in the shape of a dagger. He bid the woman farewell and waited for her to leave before speaking.

"You're a bit late," the man said in playful jest. "I was starting to wonder if you'd bail."

"Sorry, Trevor. We had a last minute change of plans this morning," Michelle said.

Trevor's eyes lingered on Alice, who was doing her best to stay hidden behind the others, still wearing the sunglasses. Her heart rate picked up. Maybe she should've stayed in the car.

"You don't have to worry about me spilling any secrets," Trevor said, leaning his hands on the counter top. Most of his fingers had heavy silver rings on them, his knuckles tattooed with a variety of symbols like snakes and skulls and crosses and astrology glyphs. He wore black wristbands with spikes on them, and both of his forearms were covered in more tattoos. "My ass is mixed up with enough crazy shit that I don't want to be bothered with anything else."

James nudged Alice and gave her an encouraging nod. Alice took off the sunglasses and tucked them away in her coat pocket. Trevor's eyes widened as he seemed to recognize her, which made sense considering her face had been all over the news. Alice gave him a cautious smile, hoping he truly meant they could trust him.

"So, about the manuscript," Michelle started.

"Right, let me grab it for you." Trevor disappeared through a black-curtained doorway behind the counter. A few moments later he returned with a cardboard file box and heaved it onto the counter with a thump. He pulled off the lid to show a disarray of papers and notebooks and journals.

"This is it?" James said as he took in the mess.

Alice inched closer to look inside. It reminded her of the mess of forgotten scrap papers at the bottom of her father's filing cabinet back in his office. Trevor eyed her curiously as she started to fish through it.

"I told you it was an *incomplete* manuscript." Trevor shrugged.

"We might be able to find something in here," Alice said as she pulled out a notebook with a few drawings of plants and mushrooms within its pages. She was trying to stay optimistic, even though it was more scribbled notes for her to decipher that might lead to nowhere.

"How much?" James asked.

Trever squared his shoulders and tapped his fingers on the counter. "Twelve hundred."

"For this?" Michelle said, gesturing at the box as if it was a pile of junk.

"I paid eight hundred for it at a private auction," Trevor said, folding his arms. "Not to mention how difficult it was to secure an invite to one of those things."

James clicked his tongue. "Makes sense," he said as he exchanged a look with Michelle. Dejected, Alice returned the notebook to the box and took a step back. She couldn't imagine them spending that kind of money on something that might end up being a waste of time, something that could end up being another dusty box in their basement.

"We'll take it," Michelle said as she pulled a thick bundle of cash from her purse. She counted out twelve hundred-dollar bills and handed them to Trevor, who recounted it for good measure.

Alice gawked at Michelle. "Really?" she asked. "That's a lot of money."

"It's worth it." Michelle smiled as she put the lid back on

the box and hoisted it off the countertop. Alice couldn't believe they'd spend that type of money on something like this, something that wasn't guaranteed to be useful, for Alice and her father, a man they never met. If Alice hadn't gone with them, they probably would've declined the purchase.

"Let me, *lǎo pó*," James said sweetly as he took the box from Michelle and headed for the door. Alice followed behind him.

"Thanks so much, Trevor," Michelle said with a polite wave. "Please tell Kenneth we said hello."

Trevor chuckled and tilted his head in agreement. "He'll be pissed he missed you guys. You need to come for dinner soon."

"We will," James called over his shoulder. "It's been too long."

"It really has," Trevor paused. "Good luck with your uh... situation."

The bell jingled above the door as the three of them left the oddities shop, and they headed back to the car. James plopped the box in the back seat with Alice. She tore off the lid to forage through the contents on the ride back to the cabin.

"Is Trevor Chosen?" Alice asked as she opened one of the random notebooks.

"Nope. He's a regular human," James said. "And he really is ass deep in a bunch of magical problems, but that's what happens when you start collecting artifacts like he does. People eventually come looking for them."

"Oh," Alice answered, deep in thought. She herself was a human mixed up in this magical nonsense, and it had her wondering what might become of her and her father in the future. If they even made it out of this mess.

She spent most of the car ride trying to organize some of the papers and notebooks, but it became increasingly difficult to concentrate while sitting in the back of a moving car. Michelle and James stayed quiet for most of the ride. They held hands across the center console, and Alice noticed the wedding band on Michelle's ring finger. She had assumed they were together, but didn't stop to think they would be married. If someone was alive for centuries, she didn't think they would concern themselves with such things. Wouldn't they get bored or annoyed with each other after the first fifty years? Maybe stuff like that didn't matter to them, because living for hundreds of years probably got lonely.

CHAPTER 15

For the next few days, Alice spent every waking moment going through the musty old box of scrap papers and notebooks and journals. Thankfully it was all written in English, besides the Latin names of plants, so she was able to organize most of it. Combined with her previous research, she compiled a list of promising plants and few interesting tincture, tonic, and extract recipes, including one that was generally used to reduce the subject's heart rate in order to treat tachycardia. Then she brought her ideas to Violet. Privately.

They'd spend the afternoons together in the conservatory experimenting with different combinations and methods. Violet shined as she focused on her herbal work, and Alice scribbled down as many notes as she could while the old woman described the delicate processes of infusion, decoction, and distilling. Some of these recipes would usually take weeks or months to complete, but Violet had access to some esoteric information which helped magically expedite their experiments. Thankfully, Violet agreed to keep their work a secret from the others, because she knew how brash and impulsive Leander and Arthur could be.

Everyone else spent the week going in and out of the cabin, continuing their search for any signs of her father. They'd go back up to Princeton, or they would go to local crime scenes where a person was either found dead or reported missing. William, he still hadn't returned. So Alice's sleep suffered without him.

Every night, Alice would lay awake in bed with the lamp on, staring at her father's journal until she finally mustered up the courage to crack it open again.

February 19 -

    With his ability to expertly decipher the cryptic text in the ancient tome, Alexander discovered a supposed natural cure for medical ailments. He suggested we try it out to see if it could work for my cancer or perhaps prolong my life a bit more. I scoffed, but decided to at least humor him since he seemed so enthusiastic. I figured it could be a helpful distraction since I'm living on borrowed time anyway.

Alice choked on her breath, scolding herself for waiting so long to read more. She had been right. Her father's old student somehow managed to encourage him to make the elixir.

March 21 -

    I've been tasked with cultivating a plant for the recipe for weeks, only to find out I must feed it my blood, an absurd and downright nauseating request. I was ready to refuse, however Alexander surprised me with an astonishing feat. He had deciphered another alchemical ritual from the grimoire, and he transmuted a silver coin into gold right before my eyes, proving to me that perhaps this arcane book might hold the secret to regaining my health.

    My extensive knowledge of ancient history would have never prepared me to believe in such things. All historical accounts of alchemy had seemed to be mere fiction, and yet I have observed it. Now that I reconsidered my stance on the subject, I have found myself cutting into my skin weekly to feed this plant my blood in hopes that it will cure me.

Alice wanted to throw up. She couldn't recall seeing him caring for any plants or doing any gardening, and she never noticed any self-inflicted wounds on his skin. All she could remember was how often he'd stay late at his office, claiming his students really needed his help that semester, when all that time he had been working with Alexander. Not once had he mentioned the name to her.

May 1 -

It is done, but at what cost. If Alice ever found out, she would never forgive me. I don't think I can forgive myself.

Ex nihilo nihil fit.

The same week the student went missing. His first victim. Her hands shook as she continued reading.

May 12 -

In an incomprehensible turn of events, my cancer has disappeared. My oncologist was just as baffled and asked if I'd be interested in participating in a study about spontaneous remission. I declined. I cannot risk researchers asking too many questions. What Alexander and I had to do in order for this elixir to work, it is not something I am proud of, nor would I have initially agreed to it if I knew beforehand. But it is in the past now, we've achieved our goal, and all that is left is to move on.
In a gesture of gratitude, since

Alexander would not take my money, I offered him the ancient textbook to keep for himself since he had become so fond of it. I've invited him to lunch because I'd love to introduce him to Alice, as I am confident they'd discover they have much in common. Unfortunately Alexander said he has been quite busy and often does not have time to return my calls. I wouldn't care to admit out loud that I miss him. He had been such a good friend, and I might go as far to say that he was almost like a son to me, staying by my side during my darkest moments.

October 19 -

The absence of recent journal entries has been due to the wonderful summer I had spent with my daughter, living life with my full health returned. It has been amazing to feel so youthful again, to be able to keep up with Alice on our favorite hiking trails. And yet, with the incoming autumn season, I have started to feel a bit odd. Not weak or sick or physically unwell. It's my mind that concerns me, especially due to the fact that I am no longer able to sleep, one side effect of the elixir. I can't quite place my finger on what exactly feels off, perhaps just an edge, or an uncertain foreboding feeling in the back of my mind. Some evenings, I've seen shadows dancing in the dark with hollow eyes watching over me. I blink and they disappear, so I assume they are simple hallucinations. I've tried to contact Alexander to ask him about it, but he hasn't returned my calls.

December 4 -

I'm endlessly haunted by my thoughts, day and night. I'm starting to believe that creating this elixir was a grave mistake. I am not well. I am not myself. I cannot escape the guilt of what I have done. Alexander and I, we killed a student and I drank his blood. His soul. That is what it cost me.

I desperately need Alexander's assistance, and I don't know why he is avoiding me. He has the grimoire, which could have a solution.

These shadows, I see them more often now. They crawl in the corners, stalking me, watching me with their hollow eyes, as if they can see into my very soul and they know what I've done. I can never rest, because I'm never alone.

I have this craving deep inside. My mouth is dry, and I have a hunger that is never satisfied. Food tastes like dust. Water provides no relief. I'm afraid there might only be one thing to satisfy me.

There was one more journal entry, no date, but she assumed it was sometime this past January. It was a jumbled mess, incoherent words and phrases in scribbled handwriting next to drawings of eyes and shadow figures. At the bottom was what she assumed was a bible verse:

Submit yourselves, then, to God. Resist the devil, and he will flee from you.

Alice slammed the journal closed and flung it onto the nightstand. Her father had always been an atheist, but his madness seemed to make him desperate enough to pray to a god that he suddenly believed might save him. She remembered when he started acting strange, just a couple months before the incident with Dillon, yet she had no idea it had come to this at the time. How could she have been so blind? He hid it from her so well.

Curling up under her blanket, she cried, stifling her sobs in her pillow. She didn't want to draw anyone's attention. There was only one person who could make her feel better, one person that made her truly believe they might be able to save her father. Alice played with the leather bracelet meant to keep her safe from daemon possession, given to her by William because everyone else seemed to either forget or not care. Alice was just another job to them, a case to solve, and then they'd move onto the next one.

* * *

Arthur was in a sour mood the next day, so sour he even snapped at Violet when she simply offered him a fresh cup of coffee. He had the sense to apologize, because if he didn't, Alice would've been the one snapping at him next. She hated how Violet was sometimes treated by the others, despite all she had done to help them with her skills. Everyone was on edge these days, and more often than not, someone was arguing or being short with someone else.

Alice sat at the kitchen table with Arthur and Michelle, while James and Violet worked on cleaning up from cooking breakfast. Leander was seated at the kitchen island, nose in a book. The television was purposefully left off to avoid any distressing news segments. They ate in silence, with the running of water and the clinking of dishes the only background noise.

"So," Michelle started. "Did you talk to that old contact of yours?"

"I did," Arthur snipped, hiding behind a newspaper.

"I'm assuming it didn't go well," she continued.

He folded down the newspaper, revealing a fresh scowl. "What ever gave you that idea?"

"Look, I'm sorry if it was difficult to reach out to your friend because of your history, but we were running out of options."

Arthur clenched his jaw at the brief mention of his personal life. "Lester no longer considers me a friend at this point." He sighed. "And now we might truly be out of options."

Natalie strolled into the kitchen, grabbed an apple from a bowl, and sat down with them. "Lester said no? Damn it."

"Unfortunately," Arthur said.

"How was this person going to help?" Alice asked, wondering what made him so special.

Arthur sipped his coffee, looking to the others for permission to continue. Michelle nodded. "Since we've had such difficulty in locating your father with normal means, I was hoping Lester would've offered his services to aid us. He's a Greywalker."

Alice furrowed her brow. She knew about the Grey and could only assume what he meant. "Does that mean he could somehow travel there?" she asked. It didn't seem like a place anyone would want to visit voluntarily.

"Indeed," said Arthur. "With a specific ritual, one can detach their soul, enter the realm of the Grey. Time works differently there, many have claimed to see the past and the future. But it's dangerous, some have gone mad due to what they've seen, some souls have become trapped there. Lester refused to help because it started to take a toll on him after all these years."

"Could someone else do it if they knew the ritual?" Alice asked.

"It's a little more complicated than that," Michelle said.

"To be a Greywalker, one must already have a foot on the other side," Arthur explained. "Which means the person must have a history of a near death experience or being dead and brought back to life. It gives them a stronger connection to the Grey, and because of that connection, some of them can even see *vagari* and other daemons reflected in this realm."

Alice stopped breathing. After the car accident when she was eight years old, she almost died, and right after that was when she started seeing ghosts for the first time. Although, she didn't realize they were actual ghosts back then. She had one foot in the Grey her entire life and never even knew. Before she could offer herself to be the Greywalker, no matter what that entailed or how frightening it might be, Natalie spoke up.

"I know someone who might do it," Natalie said, cutting through the heavy silence. "I haven't spoken to her in years though."

Arthur leaned forward again. "Contact her. Now."

"Uh," Natalie stifled her uncertainty with a laugh. When Arthur didn't return the humor, she steadied herself. "She's kind of hard to reach, but I'll try."

"You sure you want her to help?" Leander asked with a scowl.

"We don't have a choice at this point," Natalie said before she headed into the living room. She returned to the kitchen table with her laptop, opened it to a webpage for the local Social Security Administration, and began the process of scheduling an appointment.

"She never answers my calls, so we'll have to go to her," she said as she typed. "This is the only guaranteed way to see her, that is, if she doesn't kick us out of her office."

Natalie selected 'Other' under the reason for appointment, and typed in a little note in the comment box. When she was done submitting the online form, she shut the laptop and said, "Appointment is in two days. It was the soonest time available."

"Is she Chosen as well?" Alice asked. Perhaps only Chosen people with near death experiences could be a Greywalker.

"Nah, she's a regular human with an affinity for plants and sticking it to the man." Natalie laughed. "Hopefully she'll agree to help us. If we're lucky."

That meant Alice could be a Greywalker too, if it came down to it. If this person refused, then she'd offer herself. She was willing to take the risk, not just to save her father, but also to stop the killing of innocent people that were caught in his path. It had to end.

In the silence that followed, Alice wondered how many of them were out there, people who were either Chosen after experiencing some sort of horrible fate or other non-magical people who were somehow involved in this world. If they had regular jobs and lived in regular homes across the country. Alice was amazed at how it had been kept hidden from society for so long when it had been right under her nose this whole time. Not only that, but she had been unknowingly part of this world since she was child.

A few minutes later, the side door opened and closed, and William walked into the kitchen. Alice's heart fluttered in her chest at the sight of him. He looked exhausted, and stubble had grown on his chin.

"Anything new?" He asked as he snatched up a pastry and sat next to Alice, knocking his knee against hers under the table in a private greeting.

"Arthur asked his friend, I'm sorry, *ex*-friend Lester to Greywalk for us, but he wouldn't agree to it," Natalie continued. "So I've reached out to Miss Dee instead."

William paused mid-bite. "Has she agreed to Walk?"

"We have a meeting with her in two days," Natalie said. "I'm bringing Alice to hopefully sway her."

"What?" Alice asked, echoed by the others around the kitchen.

"You can't bring her there," Leander said, his hand jutting out. "That's crazy."

"Natalie, she's a missing person," Michelle chimed in. "You can't walk her into a crowded government building. She'll definitely be noticed. Going with us to New Hope was one thing, but this would be too risky. Too many eyes."

"I'm not going in there to meet with Miss Dee by myself, and I'm sure as hell not bringing either of you," Natalie said as she pointed at the brothers. "And she doesn't really know the rest of you well enough to use as leverage. We need to work some sort of emotional advantage, or she'll refuse to help. She's the only other Greywalker we know."

"Still not a good idea," James said. "If anyone recognizes Alice, we'll have a bigger problem on our hands." He folded his arms and rubbed his chin. "Unless you've forgotten what happened the last time the government was sniffing after us."

Natalie adjusted herself in her seat, straightening her back. "I know, I know. But I'm telling you, going with the sentimental route will work on Miss Dee. I was thinking," she paused. "Maybe we'd give Alice a disguise. A hat, some glasses..."

Leander scoffed. "A disguise? Really?"

"It'll work!" Natalie said, throwing her arms up in the air. "Look, if someone recognizes her, I'll take care of them. But I'm certain it won't come to that."

Alice frowned. Even though she was willing to do anything to help her father, she hated how she wasn't even asked her opinion before being volunteered for this task.

And she was especially concerned about what Natalie meant when she said "take care of them." Whatever happened, this was another chance for her to actually feel useful, another chance to get out of the house. Saving her dad was the priority, and if this brought them one step closer, it was worth it.

The others seemed to resign to the decision, because Natalie was right, this was the only way forward. Either that or Alice would offer herself to be the Greywalker, if someone taught her how to do it.

William had been quiet for most of the discussion, which was surprising considering it involved Alice doing something else potentially risky. After he was done eating, he stood from the table and headed for the stairs, tipping his head in request for Alice to follow him.

"You're not happy about this either," Alice said as they entered his bedroom.

"Not really, no." He shut the door behind them and pulled his hands through his hair. "This could get messy."

"What did Natalie mean when she said she would 'take care of' anyone that notices me?" Natalie didn't seem like the type to kill first and ask questions later.

"It's not what you think. There's another type of herbal blend that makes the target more agreeable."

"What kind of plant does that?"

"Henbane," William answered.

Alice blinked a few times as she racked her brain through the endless list of plants she read about over the past week. "That's poisonous when ingested." Her eyes widened. Perhaps Natalie *would* resort to violence.

"Yes, but—" He held up a hand to stop her from freaking out. "When prepared correctly with a blend of a few other herbs for the effect, it's able to open the mind enough to insert new beliefs. So when someone is under the influence of it, they're more likely to believe the lies we tell them in order to get them to forget what they saw."

"So you drug and manipulate them."

"When you put it that way it sounds worse. But yes." William shrugged.

"Can they feel it? Can they figure out what's happening to them?"

"No. It's calming and peaceful, and their mind goes blank. Then they believe everything that's said to them. It's another blend that can be easily disguised as a very pleasant, light flavored tea, but sometimes we make it into a small edible."

Alice's mouth gaped open as the betrayal hit her like a hot knife in the back. She remembered drinking a tea like that once, back during her first days with Violet and Natalie and Leander, and of course she couldn't remember any of the conversation that happened afterwards. They could have said *anything* to her. "I think they gave it to me. The henbane tea. They manipulated me."

"You're fucking kidding me," William growled under his breath. "That stuff can be dangerous when not brewed or administered correctly." He rubbed his forehead.

Alice gasped. "Dangerous?"

William sighed. "You heard what James said. The last time the government got involved, we had to use the henbane to take care of an entire department, change all of their minds, and also destroy the paper trail and video evidence. It took a ridiculous amount of time and effort. Miss Dee had a lot to clean up too, which is why she's not the most fond of us. But still, even with all our work, a few things slipped through the cracks, and a few people ended up not so lucky in the end."

"You mean, they died?"

"We never want innocent people to die, but sometimes it ends badly. If the first dose doesn't work, we need to steadily increase it, but there's the risk of giving them too much. Sometimes they die from overdose of the poison, and sometimes they die from a magical side effect which causes them to attack. Then we have to stop them. And sometimes, if they get too out of control and violent, we have to kill them." William grumbled as he paced around. "I can't believe they gave that to you knowing the side effects."

Alice wished she could say she couldn't believe it either, but she did believe it. Leander and Natalie worked extra hard to withhold the truth from her when she first got there. *You can trust us. You're safe here.* Those words had kept floating in and out of her mind, as if they didn't belong to her, and her gut feeling was right, because these words didn't belong to her. It was a belief implanted into her mind to control her. She balled her fists.

William closed the space between them with two long strides and wrapped her in his arms. "I won't let it happen again."

Alice nodded into his chest, a few angry tears streaming down her cheeks as her trust in the others continued to wane.

They spent the rest of the day sitting against the headboard in bed next to each other reading through a stack of textbooks and notebooks, only stopping for a quick dinner before returning to their research. But Alice was too distracted by her thoughts.

"They told me how someone becomes a Greywalker earlier," Alice said. It had been on her mind all day. "I think I'm one of them."

William looked up from his book and stared at her for a

moment. "I had a hunch after you told me you could see the *vagari*." He took her hand. "When did it happen?"

When meaning, when she almost died. "I was in a really bad car accident with my parents when I was eight. My mother didn't make it."

"Alice, I'm so sorry that happened to you," he said as set aside his book so he could pull her in close. "You don't have to be a Greywalker if you don't want to. It can be a frightening experience. Every step you take in the Grey, the more connected you become to it. You'll be like a beacon of light, attracting all sorts of things, both inside the Grey and back in the physical realm as well."

"But if it doesn't work with Miss Dee—"

"Then we'll find someone else if we have to." He furrowed his brows. "Do the others know this about you? Have you told them?"

"No, I didn't want to bring it up. Not yet."

"Good," William said as he shook his head. "They'd force you to do it."

"But if I have to do it to find my dad—"

"I know Alice, I know." He cupped her face in his hands. "We'll cross that bridge when we get there. If you have to Greywalk, then I won't stop you." William kissed her forehead. "But if someone else is willing to do it to keep you away from that awful experience, then I think we should try that first."

Alice hung her head. He was right. Greywalking wasn't something she felt eager to do now that she knew how terrifying it could be. She'd rather have no part in any of this magical world and the emotional trauma that came with it. But she'd do it for her dad if she had to. She'd do anything. Maybe this was how her dad felt when he was desperate for a cure for his cancer, desperate to do anything to stay alive, because there was only one reason she could think of that would make her father desperate to keep living. He'd do it for her.

"I read the rest of my dad's journal," Alice said as she absently riffled through the pages of the musty textbook on her lap, her eyes fixed on an indiscriminate corner of the room.

William perked up. "You did?"

Her throat tightened. "He admitted to killing the student." She paused. "With Alexander's help."

"Wow, good thing the police didn't find that journal first." William ran a hand through his hair. "Any other details?"

"Apparently, Alexander stopped returning his calls after that, and then he disappeared."

William rubbed his chin. "Strange. I wonder what his motive was."

Alice shrugged. "My dad's been a skeptic his entire life, but somehow Alexander was persuasive enough to convince a desperate dying man to kill someone in order to stay alive." She huffed out a breath. "Did you find any school records?"

"No," William said as he shook his head. "I didn't have a chance to go to the campus yet."

"Do you think you could take me with you next time you leave?" Alice asked. If the others were willing to let her start venturing out, it couldn't hurt to go on errands with William. She needed to get away from the cabin, and she wanted some privacy, just the two of them.

His eyebrows flashed to the top of his forehead. "I don't know about that."

"You were gone for a whole week. I barely slept."

William's expression softened. "I know. I'm sorry I left

you, but please understand these are delicate and potentially dangerous matters."

"You think I would get in the way."

"That's not what I meant."

"That's what it feels like."

"Alice," William sighed. He threaded his fingers with hers. "Sometimes I have to lie and steal and coerce. I have to use the henbane and sometimes it goes bad, like I said before. I don't want you to be involved in any of that. I don't want to put you at risk." He brought her hand to his mouth and kissed her knuckles. "After this is all over, we can spend every night together, if that's what you need."

She nodded. A blush crept up her neck. William reached across her lap and planted his hand next to her hip. Alice inhaled sharply as he leaned in, dipping his head to kiss along her jaw all the way to her neck, his breath hot under her ear. There were other reasons she had missed him too, but she was too embarrassed to say it out loud.

Eventually his mouth found his way back to hers, his tongue trailing along her bottom lip. She lost herself in her senses as he ran his hands along her waist and tangled his fingers in her hair. Alice didn't understand what was going on between them, or how it happened so fast. They had barely spent any time together over the past couple weeks, with him being gone for most of it. Yet she felt magnetized to him, because he was the only thing that made her feel safe through the chaos. His hands and his mouth helped her forget too.

Her fingers ruffled through his hair as she pulled him closer, causing him to almost fall into her lap. Their heaving chests pressed against one another, like they couldn't get close enough. Alice's hand found its way to his thigh and gave it a light squeeze, causing him to chuckle into her mouth.

"Eager, are we?" William asked breathlessly. His dark eyes searched hers, asking permission as his own hand drifted to the hem of her shirt, teasing the bare skin of her stomach.

Alice, feeling bold and impatient, answered by swiftly removing her shirt and tossing it to the floor.

"I'll take that as a yes." He smirked and pushed himself off of her, just so he could make sure the bedroom door was locked and to turn down the lights. William pulled his own shirt off before he climbed back into bed, crawling his way up her body and trailing kisses along her stomach, her chest, her neck, until he reached her ear and whispered, "You're gonna have to be quiet."

CHAPTER 16

"You'll be fine," Natalie said, giving Alice a reassuring smile from the driver's seat of her truck.

"If you say so," Alice sighed. She tugged on the black knitted hat which had most of her hair tucked inside and adjusted the thick-rimmed reading glasses that kept falling down her nose. She wore an extra large shirt, bulky winter coat, and baggy jeans. It didn't feel like much of a disguise. If anything she thought she looked like an awkward teenage boy since her slender frame was hidden in the heaps of fabric. Before she left, William embarrassingly called her cute in front of everyone, causing her to rush out the door before they could see her face turn red.

Natalie and Alice drove for about an hour until they finally reached their destination, a boxy corporate building, mundane and ugly. The parking lot was packed. There would be dozens of people inside, dozens of people that could recognize her. As they walked through the main entrance and passed the police officer standing guard, she pulled the hat down even more.

"Take a number," the secretary at the kiosk desk said.

She chewed her gum and nodded at the ticket dispenser, not bothering to look up from her cell phone.

"We have an appointment with Dolores Dixon at three," Natalie said.

The secretary grumbled, finally looking up from her phone with an annoyed look on her face. "Name?" she asked as she typed into her computer.

"Natalie Jones."

A few clicks of the keyboard later, the secretary asked, "You have ID?" Natalie handed over a driver's license. The secretary gave it an apathetic once over before handing it back. "Have a seat, I'll let her know you're here."

The waiting area was crowded with people, and it took them a few moments to scan the area to find two open seats next to each other. Alice sat down in the rickety plastic chair, keeping her chin tucked down in order to not draw too much attention to herself.

The room was poorly decorated, with sun-faded posters about rules and regulations hanging haphazardly on the walls, the lamination peeling at the corners. One poster had fallen to the ground, curled up against the grimy baseboard, and it seemed to have been hiding a huge hole in the drywall that had probably been there for years. There was a shoddy table off to the side with an out-of-order coffee machine on top, and next to it was a half empty vending machine full of overpriced snacks.

"Jones?" Alice asked out the side of her mouth.

"Natalie O'Connell technically died a while ago," Natalie said, showing Alice her fake ID with her fake last name.

"Right." Alice remembered what they said about fake identities and wondered how many times they all had to change their names over the years. It sounded like it would be an annoying process. They had to have connections on the inside who helped them with the paperwork, maybe even Miss Dee.

In the seat next to Alice was a haggard looking man, possibly around her own age, but the bags under his eyes made him look even older. He had a patchy beard trying to grow in over his pasty skin, and his hoodie looked like it was three sizes too big. He cleared his throat with a phlegmy cough and leaned in closer to Alice. "Either of you ladies have a smoke?"

Alice leaned away from him. She could smell the stale scent of cigarettes on his breath. "No, sorry."

"How about any spare cash? A couple dollars?"

"No," Natalie said with a purposeful look of disgust on her face. She whispered to Alice. "Don't talk to anyone."

A little girl came running from the hallway into the waiting room. "Daddy!" she squealed as she ran over to the man they were just speaking with. The little girl jumped into his lap, a crinkled coloring page in her hand. A woman walked up behind her shortly after, a manila folder clutched to her chest, and told him she and their daughter were finally approved for a government assistance program. Alice criticized herself for judging the man so harshly. She didn't know his story, but she did know he had a family that loved him.

Luckily Alice and Natalie only had to wait in the busy waiting room for about five more minutes before the secretary called them up and directed them down a hall to Miss Dee's office. The placard on her door indicated she held some sort of management position.

The secretary led them in and gestured for them to sit in the two chairs in front of the heavy desk. Miss Dee, a black woman who looked to be in her late forties, continued to hastily type on her computer without looking up. She had long braids tied back and was dressed in a chic and expensive looking suit.

"Thanks, Naomi," said Miss Dee. "Are we ordering lunch from People's Pizza?"

"Yeah. Want me to order your usual?" the secretary asked.

"Absolutely," Miss Dee smiled. When the secretary left, her smile faded. "What are you doing here?"

Natalie squared her shoulders. "We, uh—"

"When I saw you pop up on my schedule, I knew it was going to be more of your funny business. You know how busy I am." Miss Dee's eyes looked Alice up and down. "Does it have to do with whoever this is?"

"Yes, um," Natalie stuttered, very unlike her usual confident self. "This is Alice." She waved at the hat, encouraging her to take it off.

Alice removed it, smoothing out the frizz and static in her hair. She took off the glasses next.

Miss Dee steepled her hands in front of her face, brows furrowed. She looked down her nose and said, "Alice, huh? I've seen you and your dad on the news."

"Yes, that's him," Alice said softly, looking at the floor.

"I should've known it was one of *those* types of problems," Miss Dee scoffed. "He's causing quite a mess out there, you know."

Natalie coughed. "That's, uh, why we're here."

"You're playing a risky game bringing this one to my office." Miss Dee arched an eyebrow and pointed a finger at Alice. "Are you trying to get me fired? Or arrested? What if she's seen?"

"We're running out of options," Natalie continued. "We need your help locating her father."

"You're bold," Miss Dee said, leaning back in her chair. "Coming in here and asking that of me. Why is this my problem? Who started the mess? It sure as hell wasn't me."

Natalie looked to Alice, silently begging her to talk. "My dad was sick." Alice said, picking at her nails. "He had cancer and was trying to cure it. I don't think he knew what he was getting into, but he was desperate." Alice cast a glance at Natalie and continued. "My mom died a long time ago, so if I lost my dad, I'd have no one left." Alice's hands trembled in her lap.

Miss Dee's face softened, shaking her head as she clicked her tongue. "Well, damn. People always seem to make poor choices when they're suffering, don't they."

"He made the Elixir of Life, but we think we could find some sort of cure," Natalie said. "I know it's a long shot, but we want to try."

"A cure for the elixir? Never heard of that before," Miss Dee said out loud, more to herself.

"Please help us find him." Natalie said. "We've had no luck, and every day that goes by is another opportunity for him to kill."

"I know," Miss Dee sighed. "I told you I've seen him on the news, all those murders and missing people. So I know he'll do it again. I'll help you. I won't like it, but I'll do it." She pulled out her pocket calendar and flipped to the present week. "I'm not available until this weekend. Friday night after my shift. And we'll need an anchor." She looked up at the girls discontentedly.

"I got a handful of things from the remains of Alice's old house," Natalie said. "A photograph should work right?"

"No, I'm talking about Alice. She'll be my anchor."

"No way," Natalie protested. "You're not taking her Grey-walking with you."

Alice dug her nails into her palm. It looked like she would have to go Greywalking after all. But Natalie had no right to speak for her. It should be Alice's choice. And she had decided before, she'd do anything to help her dad, no matter how scary or dangerous.

"The bond of blood makes the strongest anchor. I'm not staying on the other side for longer than I have to. If we use Alice, we'll be in and out of there."

Natalie frowned and stared at Alice. "You don't want to do it, do you?"

"I'll do it. I need to. For my dad." Her stomach tumbled with queasiness as she met Miss Dee's gaze.

"That settles it then." Miss Dee stood from her desk and walked over to her filing cabinet, unlocking the drawer on the very bottom with a key she kept on her lanyard. From inside the drawer she withdrew a drawstring sachet and tossed it to Natalie. "Have her drink this blend throughout the day on Friday. No food. I'll be over after sundown."

"No food?" Alice asked. Not that it would be hard. She didn't have much of an appetite lately anyway.

"In case you get sick, don't need you puking everywhere," Miss Dee said, flattening her suit jacket as she sat back down. "Who's all gonna be there? My two favorite boys?"

Natalie snorted. "I thought you hated them."

"They're annoying as hell and caused me a lot of problems. But that William," Miss Dee hummed to herself. "Him I can tolerate, because he's so good looking."

Alice bristled in her seat, wondering what exactly their history was and how far it went back. Even though it wasn't really her business. Alice didn't even know what was going on between herself and William. They hadn't even spoken in detail about it or discussed how something could actually work between them.

As they left Miss Dee's office, Alice fussed with the drawstring pouch in her pocket, mulling over her newest obligation. Natalie tried her best to reassure Alice that she would be fine during the Greywalking, but Natalie had no room to talk since she had never done it herself.

When they made it to the end of the hall and rounded the corner, they walked right into the wiry man from the waiting room as he came out of the men's bathroom.

"My bad," he stuttered. His face contorted in confusion as he looked over Alice's appearance. "Hey, you're the missing chick that's been all over the news." He pointed at her.

Alice snatched her knit hat from her pocket and rushed to pull it back over her head. She'd forgotten to put her disguise back on. But it was too late for that. Natalie placed two hands on the man's chest and shoved him back into the men's bathroom, his head slamming into the door as they entered. A wide-eyed Alice followed them in, locking the bathroom door behind her on instinct.

"What the—" the man tried to yell, but Natalie clapped a hand over his mouth as she pushed his back against the hard, tiled wall.

"Shut up!" she hissed.

The man thrashed against her, trying to speak, so Natalie removed her hand from his mouth. "Damn girl, how're you so strong? You some sort of gym freak? HEY!" he shouted.

Natalie covered his mouth again, "Shhh! Shut the hell up, and we'll tell you what's going on." The man continued to squirm against Natalie's grasp. "Alice, in my coat pocket is a tin. Grab it for me."

Alice retrieved an old tin of mints, but on the inside instead of mints she found some brown balls about the size of a marble that looked like dirt and herbs rolled together.

"Put one in his mouth." Natalie ordered. The man thrashed even more, eyes wide.

Alice hesitated. "Is this the henbane?"

"Do it, Alice," Natalie demanded through gritted teeth, her hand moving to the man's neck to keep his head still. He gagged. "Now. Or this situation is going to get a lot worse." She sounded breathless, like she was losing her strength trying to keep him pinned to the wall.

Feeling a sense of panic, Alice pushed the herbal ball between the man's teeth.

Natalie forced her hand over his mouth. "Swallow." She held him there until the man's muscles slackened and his eyes glazed over.

"What happens if—"

"Wait," Natalie said as she held up her finger. "Say nothing. Fix your hat and put the glasses back on." She turned her attention back to the man, grasping the front scruff of his shirt. "What happened today?"

"I went to the Social Security office with my family to apply for assistance," the man said in a monotone voice.

"What else?"

"I saw the missing girl from TV."

"No you didn't."

"I didn't?"

"No."

The man's glazed over eyes stared at Natalie and then looked over to Alice who was wearing her mediocre disguise again. "What d'you mean? I thought... ain't that her?" His words began to slur together.

"It's not. You made a mistake."

"I…" he said, his head drooping, eyes fluttering closed.

"Shit," Natalie hissed under her breath. "It's not supposed to go into effect that fast." She used her finger and thumb to pry open one of his eyes. "Fuck." It was so dilated, the color of his iris was almost gone. "Alice, quick, give me another—"

The man launched himself off the wall, grabbed Natalie by the neck, and threw her. She stumbled and fell, hitting her head on the bathroom sink on the way down. Then he was on top of her throwing punches as she tried to shield herself with her forearms. A violent wind whipped through the room, Natalie's magic, but the man didn't even flinch.

Numb with shock, it took Alice a minute for her mind to catch up to what was happening before she jumped into action. She barreled towards the man, using all of her strength to try and push him off of Natalie, but he didn't budge. He swiped a fist to the side and clocked Alice right in the shoulder.

"He's too strong," Alice cried as she stumbled back, clutching her arm.

"You need… to give him… another…" Natalie choked from the man's hands strangling her neck, asphyxiating her. Her eyes blinked slowly, blood dribbling onto the tile floor from her forehead. The ferocity of the magical wind diminished as Natalie's consciousness faded.

Chosen couldn't die like this. The man would have to rip out her heart, and Alice was pretty sure he didn't know that. But if the man got Natalie unconscious, he'd be after Alice next, and she most certainly would be killed by his madness.

From her pocket, she pulled out William's switchblade that he gave her to borrow, just in case. She flipped it open. The blade was made of pure silver which she recently learned had the ability to slow down magical effects. Alice didn't know how it would affect someone like this man though, a regular human under the influence of a magic poison.

"Alice—" Natalie gagged.

She had to do it. She had to save Natalie. Or at least distract him enough so Natalie could get the upper hand in the situation. With no weapons training except from Jenny teaching her the first four fencing positions, Alice awkwardly lunged forward and swiped the knife at the man, slashing a deep cut into the side of his upper arm. He yowled, gripping the wound, as he tumbled off Natalie. She lunged again, brandishing the knife to intimidate him. He snatched her wrist in mid air, the knife clattering to the floor, and he yanked her towards him.

With a yelp, Alice fell to her knees, the pain reverberating up her legs from the impact. The man pinned her to the floor, his bloody hands on her neck. Natalie scrambled to her feet and with a raised hand, she blasted him off Alice with a gust of wind. He crumpled and slid across the floor into the wall. Natalie shoved another henbane edible in his mouth.

The man's body became limp instantly as he babbled incoherent nonsense. Natalie dragged him into the handicapped stall, grabbed him by the collar of his hoodie, and shook him. "Hey! Look at me!" She shook him again. "You came into the bathroom, got into a fight with some random stranger. You stole their drugs, got high, and passed out."

"Drugs?" his voice slurred. "I don't even do drugs anymore, been clean for four years."

"Well, you relapsed." Natalie let him go.

He dropped to the floor, then gripped the toilet with one

hand to push himself back up. His strength failed him as the herbs took effect, and he fell flat on his face.

"We need to leave," Natalie said. She shut the stall door as the man lost consciousness. She rushed to wash the blood from her face and hands, encouraging Alice to do the same. Then Natalie pulled Alice out of the bathroom by her elbow. "Quick."

They hurried down the main hall and back through the waiting room, avoiding eye contact with everyone. The police officer at the front door narrowed his eyes as they passed.

Once they were back in the truck and Natalie was speeding away, Alice ripped the hat and glasses off. "That was insane. William said the henbane was dangerous!"

"I did what I had to do," Natalie said.

"Is that what you told yourself when you gave it to me?"

Natalie's face slackened with obvious guilt. She didn't deny it.

"Don't you care about the consequences of using that stuff?"

"He'll be fine."

"Sure he won't remember what happened, but now everyone will think he's using drugs again. His whole future is going to be messed up. He has a *family*, Natalie. A *daughter*." Her breath hitched in her throat.

Natalie's hands clenched the steering wheel.

"You manipulated me like that! You could've made me believe anything."

"Alice, it's not a big deal!" Natalie raised her voice. "We made you trust us so you wouldn't run away."

"Yeah well how am I supposed to trust you at all now?" Alice turned her face away to hide her tears, stinging with anger. She stared out the window as the buildings and trees blurred together in the orange hue of the setting sun.

The whoop of a siren shocked Alice out of her daze.

Natalie looked in the rearview mirror. "Fuck."

Red and blue lights flashed behind them. Alice's heart leapt to her throat as she whipped back around. "What do we do?"

"Put your hat and glasses back on. Relax." Natalie said as she pulled over to the side of the tree-lined rural road. She didn't look relaxed. "And don't say a word."

CHAPTER 17

The police officer, wide and muscled with cropped brown hair, strolled up to the driver's side and asked Natalie for her license, registration, and insurance. As she sifted through the glovebox, the officer called in some codes on his two-way radio and then bent down to peer in through the window.

"Where you ladies headed?" He asked, shining his flashlight in Alice's face.

"A friend's house," Natalie said with a casual smile as she handed him her papers.

"Coming from where?"

"Oh just shopping, Officer..." She arched a brow at him as she eyed his badge.

"Officer Spector." He hooked a thumb on his belt. "Do you know why I pulled you over?"

"Uh, speeding?" Natalie gave a guilty smile, fingers tightening around the steering wheel.

The officer huffed a laugh. "No, actually. Failure to signal before a turn."

"Ah, damn. Sorry sir, I must've been distracted. Won't happen again."

"Mhmm." He inspected her documents. "Natalie Jones, it says here this vehicle is registered to Violet O'Connell."

"Yeah, that's my grandmother. She uh, doesn't drive much anymore."

"I see," he said. "You sure you didn't make any other stops today?"

"I'm sure," Natalie said with another laugh, more awkward this time. "Just shopping."

"Hmm," Officer Spector's footsteps clicked on the asphalt as he rounded the front of the car. He knocked on the glass of Alice's window for her to roll it down. "Do you have identification?"

Her heart pounded. "N-no, sir."

"Can you confirm your name and date of birth?" He got out his notepad and pen.

Alice looked to Natalie for help, who shook her head barely an inch.

"No." Alice dug her nails into her leg. She was never one to disobey authority, but she knew she could incriminate herself with anything she said. She thought she remembered something about not having to provide information if no crime was committed, and she didn't commit a crime. Well, the cop didn't *know* she committed a crime.

Officer Spector blinked and looked up from the notepad. He calmly tucked it away and cleared his throat. "I need you to step out of the vehicle ma'am."

"What?" both girls asked in unison.

"For what reason?" Natalie asked, nose up.

Another cop car pulled up and parked behind the first one.

"A man was found unconscious in the bathroom at the

Cherry Hill Social Security Office. When he finally came to, he said he got some drugs and relapsed. He was also pretty beat up with a deep laceration in his bicep. Know anything about that?"

"No, sir." Natalie's throat bobbed as a second, younger looking cop walked up to her window. This one was tall and skinny with buzzed blonde hair and a snide expression.

"Interesting. We have security footage of two young women forcing him into the restroom. An eyewitness described these same young women leaving the premises in this specific truck." He slapped the roof.

"You must be mistaken. That wasn't us. We didn't go there today." Natalie said in a rush.

"Mhmm. And would you like to explain that gash on your forehead?" The officer pointed his flashlight at her face.

Natalie's eyes widened as she touched the dried blood. "I fell."

"Sure you did. Please, exit the vehicle. Now."

"Natalie..." Alice squeaked, mind racing.

"Do as they say," Natalie said under her breath, then made a minuscule gesture like she was zipping her lips.

Alice stumbled out of the truck, confused about why Natalie wasn't trying to get out of this, why she wouldn't use her magic against them. Officer Spector forced Alice against the side of the truck and patted her down, pulling out the satchel of magical herbs Miss Dee had given her and William's bloody switchblade. Shit.

"Drugs and a weapon? Hands behind your back. Now."

Alice's face was pressed against the cold metal of the truck as the officer cuffed her and read her Miranda Rights. "Now sit down over here," he said, directing her to the ground. "No funny business."

Natalie was seated next to her, also cuffed, as the two officers searched the truck. Natalie blanched when they pulled out more bags of dried herbs, a couple of silver knives, and an unlabeled flask of liquid the officers couldn't identify. The worst thing they found was a box of fake security, police, and FBI badges in the glove compartment.

"Fuck," Natalie said under her breath.

"Can't you do anything like, you know..." Alice whispered, fidgeting from the uncomfortable squeeze of the handcuffs.

"Too risky right now." She tilted her head towards the police car and spoke out of the side of her mouth. "Dash cams. It would get us in an even bigger mess. And it's too public." She jerked her chin towards the road where cars continued to drive by. "We'll figure this out." Natalie heaved out a breath, as if she didn't believe her own words. "It'll be fine. We'll just go along with it until I can make a phone call. Say as little as possible. Don't tell them who you are."

Officer Spector walked back over to them. "You've got some interesting stuff in there." He grabbed Natalie's arm and tugged her to her feet, then Alice, who hissed in pain from the forcefulness. "You're both under arrest for aggravated assault, possession of a weapon for an unlawful purpose, possession of an illegal substance with intent to distribute, and judging by all those fake badges, impersonation of law enforcement." He pushed Natalie by the shoulder and led her to his patrol car. "Bet we're gonna find a lot more things to charge you with once we run your prints, Miss Jones. If that's even your real name."

Alice gave Natalie a panicked look before she was escorted by the blonde officer, Officer Griffin according to his badge, to a separate car. He shoved her in the back seat, not caring that Alice's head bumped against the roof.

Besides a few derisive comments from the cop, it was a painfully quiet ride to the police station, a small building located at the edge of a forest out in the boonies. Inside it was cold, and Alice had to squint due to the harsh overhead lights. After fingerprinting her, Officer Griffin ushered her past Natalie, who was handcuffed to a bench and refusing to answer questions for Officer Spector, and led her into an empty holding cell in the back.

Officer Griffin removed Alice's handcuffs and locked her in, the clanging cell door rattling her pounding head. She rubbed her wrists to relieve the lingering pain from the cuffs and sat on the cold metal bench in the corner. She still wore the baggy, uncomfortable disguise from that morning, minus the coat, knit hat, and fake glasses which had been confiscated.

"Can I get a blanket or something?" She asked before Officer Griffin walked away.

He laughed. "You gonna answer our questions?"

Alice stared at him, tight lipped.

"That's what I thought." The officer laughed again as he left.

She cried as soon as she was alone, angry silent tears that she had hidden away for far too long. She cried for her dad, Dillon, the wiry man from earlier that day, the man from the church, and even those possessed women who died. She cried about the horror and blood and gruesome deaths she should've never seen. She cried for all the other missing and murdered people. She cried because she missed her friends and her old life. She cried because she missed her mom. She cried until her shoulders ached from shaking so much.

Alice wiped her nose on her sleeve and took a deep breath. In the numb silence that followed, she overheard

Natalie's voice escalating down the hall, demanding a phone call. After some arguing back and forth with the officer, Alice hoped Natalie got what she wanted. If Natalie was able to call the others, maybe they'd find a way to break them out before the two of them were transferred somewhere else.

A few moments later, Natalie shuffled down the aisle of cells, hands cuffed behind her back with Officer Spector guiding her by the elbow. She gave Alice a wink as she was dropped off into the cell across from her. She must've figured something out.

Alice stood and gripped the bars. "Did you—"

Natalie shook her head and held a finger to her lips. She tapped her wrist where a watch would be and then whispered, "Tomorrow. Early."

Alice's mouth gaped open.

"Low profile, remember?" Natalie shrugged as she sat on the bench, chin in her hands.

Alice figured it made sense. If the others came rushing in, blasting their magic to break them out, it could cause a lot of problems that they'd have to clean up later. It was probably the smartest move to come in casually in the early morning before shift change, slip a low dose of henbane in the officers' coffee, get them to do their bidding, and wipe their memories when it was all over. Easy. Now all they had to do was get through the night.

Eventually Officer Spector returned, sauntering up to Alice's cell with a scowl on his face. "So, you're Alice Foster, huh?"

She clenched her jaw to hide any reaction.

"We ran your prints. You've been missing for quite some time."

Alice blinked.

"You wanna tell us where your dad is?"

She didn't flinch. Didn't move. Didn't breathe.

"Turns out, they found your prints all over that bathroom at the Social Security office, and they have reason to suspect you or your father were involved in the death of that kid found in your house. Thought you could burn it down to hide the evidence?"

Alice trembled.

"You and your dad some sort of serial killing duo?"

She was going to faint.

"The detective from Camden County will be here in a few hours. Better make yourself comfortable."

Officer Griffin joined them, a manila file folder tucked under his arm. "Still don't feel like talkin' Alice?" He smacked the bars with the folder. "Ya know, if you talk, we can make this easier for you. Maybe I'll get you that blanket." He cackled.

Alice stood in the center of the cell, arms wrapped around herself, glaring daggers at him. What a bastard. If she was the one with magic, she would've burnt up that paperwork and singed his feet until he ran off yelping.

"Leave her alone, will you?" Natalie said. "She's not talking."

"Yeah? And are you the one who told her that? As her accomplice?" Officer Griffin sneered at her, itching for a fight.

"You can go fuck yourself."

Even Alice was taken aback by Natalie's insult, but she kept going.

Natalie batted her eyelashes. "Are you two boys so bored and so insecure that you have to pick on someone to make yourselves feel tough?"

Officer Griffin laughed again. "Should we be picking on you instead?"

"Don't you have some paperwork to do?" She looked him up and down in disgust. "Some donuts to eat? Tax dollars to waste?"

"Do you ever stop running your damn mouth? How about—" The officer was cut off by a message from his two-way radio, which reported a disturbance at the nearby high school, something like breaking and entering and possibly arson. After a beat, a second message came through indicating there was indeed an uncontrolled fire started on the school premises, and back up was needed immediately.

"Shit, don't these kids have anything better to do than to vandalize the school?" Officer Griffin said with a grumble.

"We're in the Pine Barrens, Mike," said Officer Spector. "There's nothing for them to do except drink Budweiser around bonfires and then act like idiots in the woods. You going or am I?"

"I'll go," Officer Griffin said. "I'm bored. You can stay with the lovely ladies." He pulled his lip up like he smelled something disgusting before turning on his heel to leave.

Officer Spector strolled over to the desk in the corner, sat down, and kicked up his feet. "He's right, complying with questioning would make this easier for you both."

Neither of the girls spoke. They only had to deal with the heckling cops for twelve more hours, that's it, and then they'd get out of there.

"Nothing, eh? How about—"

Officer Griffin returned in less than five minutes. He strolled back into the holding area with a smirk on his face. "The detective's here."

"Already?" Officer Spector placed his feet back on the floor and adjusted his uniform.

Footsteps clapped against the tile as the detective walked in, dressed in a sleek black suit and tie.

"Evening, gentlemen," William said as he adjusted his cuff link. "Ladies." He winked at Alice. "I hope you're prepared to answer some questions."

Alice almost choked out a cry when she saw him there. She bit the inside of her cheek to stay quiet, and she kept her face neutral, because she knew she had to play a part until this was over. Natalie was wide-eyed, surprised or angry or both. This mustn't have been part of the plan.

"I thought Detective Brinkman was coming in?"

"I'm covering for him." William said with a pleasant smile.

"Right," Officer Spector said with narrowed eyes. "Want us to get the interrogation room set up?" He jerked his thumb over his shoulder.

"Sure." William walked towards Alice's cell. "And a coffee, black," he said over his shoulder. "It's going to be a long night."

Officer Griffin mumbled something under his breath as the two of them left the holding area, leaving William alone with Alice and Natalie.

"What the hell are you doing?" Natalie hissed.

"What does it look like?" William said, paying her no mind as he faced Alice.

"I thought you weren't coming until tomorrow," Alice said, clutching the bars as she looked up at him.

William sighed. "The others weren't planning on coming until tomorrow." He hooked his finger under her chin. "I wasn't keen on waiting. I couldn't leave you here." He kissed her lightly through the bars.

Someone cleared their throat. "I didn't realize how common it was for detectives to hook up with their suspects." Officer Spector stood at the entrance, gun drawn and pointed at William. "Brinkman wasn't supposed to be here for another hour, and he had no one covering him tonight. Griffin ran your plates, then called the Chief over in Cherry Hill who said he doesn't know anyone by your name."

Officer Griffin showed up behind his partner, drawing his gun as well. "Hands where we can see 'em, buddy."

William put his hands in the air and stepped away from the cell. "Listen, gentlemen, perhaps you've called the wrong person. Let me get you the right number—"

"Bullshit," Officer Griffin spat. "You obviously know each other, seeing how cozy you are with this one." He jerked his chin at Alice, who flinched. "Clearly you're in cahoots with these murder suspects."

Officer Spector pointed to the ground with his gun. "Get on your knees. Now."

William glanced at Alice, took a deep breath, and closed his eyes.

"I said get on your damn knees!" The officer took a step forward.

"You first." William's eyes snapped open as he thrust out his hand. A gust of wind blasted down the hallway, scattering papers everywhere. He formed a fist and pulled as if he was yanking an invisible rope in midair.

Both officers dropped their guns and clutched their throats, gagging and coughing as they fell to their knees. The air had been sucked out of their lungs. With another wave of his hand, William pressurized the air just enough to burst the lenses out of the security cameras, raining glass onto the floor. He strode towards the officers, picked up one of the guns and kicked the other out of reach. He pulled the hammer back and pointed it at Officer Spector. "Keys. Now."

The officers, on their knees, clawed at their necks as they attempted to catch their breath. Officer Spector fumbled with the keys on his belt and handed them over to William.

"Stay down and don't move." William kept the gun pointed at them as he backed towards the cell doors.

"W-what the hell was that?" Officer Griffin wheezed, finally released from suffocation.

William tucked the gun into the waistband of his pants. "Shut up or I'll make it worse next time," he said through gritted teeth.

Alice staggered back a few steps as William approached her cell. "Y-you... why did..." she sputtered, eyeing the gun on his hip.

His face softened as he flipped through the keyring for the correct one. "For you."

"William, I—" Alice's eyes darted over his shoulder.

A bunch of stuff clattered to the floor as Officer Griffin dove for the desk phone. William was on him in a second. He grabbed him by the back of the head and slammed his face into the desk. "I said—" William pushed the officer back to the floor who clutched his profusely bleeding nose. "Don't fucking move." He whipped the gun back out and fired off a round at the brick wall right above their heads, the sound deafeningly loud in the close quarters.

"Jesus Christ!" Officer Griffin yelled as he cowered on the floor, shielding himself with his arms. "You're insane!"

"If either of you move again, I won't miss." William kept the gun pointed at the officer for a few more seconds, making sure they both stayed still, then he returned to letting Alice out of her cell. He reached a hand out to comfort Alice. She flinched away.

"Alice, it's okay. I—"

"What the fuck, Will?" Natalie shook the bars. "You *are* acting insane. Leander and Arthur were coming tomorrow. I had it all figured out."

"Did you?" William grimaced as he unlocked Natalie's cell next.

"This is gonna take days to clean up." Natalie pushed her way out and grabbed Alice by the arm. "Are you alright?"

Alice shoved her off and hugged herself. "Let's just get out of here."

William approached Alice again, cautiously this time. "I have to do some cleaning up before we go." He tucked a strand of hair behind her ear.

Alice gulped, suppressing her fear. She thought she'd be appalled by his callous behavior. But if she was being honest, even though it had been shocking, she understood it. Since this entire mess started, no one else had shown such tenacity to help her. William, though, he fought for her. As for the violence, she'd seen so much, even participated in it. Alice wasn't sure she knew who she was anymore, or what she was willing to do in order to get her old life back. Maybe she was more like her father than she realized.

William hauled Officer Griffin up to his feet by his bloody collar and shoved him into the chair at the desk. "Now listen, we can do this the easy way or the hard way." William pointed the gun to his head and held out his hand revealing a ball of henbane. "You're going to eat this so I can wipe your memories, or I can shove it down your fucking throat."

"M-my memories?" Blood splattered out of the officer's mouth.

"Not all of them, just the ones I tell you to forget." William smirked. "It'll be like we were never here, got it?"

Officer Griffin looked between them and then down at the ball of herbs, his face disgusted. "And if I refuse?"

William pointed the gun at Officer Spector. "Then I kill your friend and frame you."

"Will!" Natalie grabbed at his arm, and he shooed her off.

"Stay out of this. Unlike you, I get shit done." He cocked the hammer. "What'll it be?"

"I'll take it! Please, don't kill him." Officer Griffin snatched the herbal ball and shoved it in his mouth, chewing and swallowing without protest. His eyes instantly glazed over.

William fed him a bunch of instructions to destroy any documentation that mentioned either of the girls and to erase the security footage from the station and dash cams. He told him he'd forget ever seeing any of them that day and that he tripped and fell which caused him to break his nose. The officer started losing consciousness after about a couple minutes, so William talked fast to wrap it up. Then he rounded on Officer Spector, who eagerly took the herbs, and did the same.

Once both officers were unconscious at their desks, Alice felt like she could finally take a breath. "Can we go now?" She clutched William's arm.

He fumbled through the key ring again. "Right after we get your belongings." It was like he'd been in this exact situation before and knew what to do. They went to a side room where evidence was kept to collect all of the items that had been confiscated before heading out.

They were almost to the exit when the real detective walked in, an older man with salt and pepper hair and mustache. He scrunched his brow and pointed. "Who are you?" Then his wide eyes landed on Natalie and Alice. "Where the hell are you taking them?"

"Doesn't matter." William took two swift steps towards the man, grabbed his outstretched arm, and flung him to the floor. With a knee pressed against the man's chest, he shoved henbane into his mouth. "Forget you were ever here. Forget you were ever called. If anyone asks, lie." He dragged the man to his feet and directed him out the front door of the station. "Where's your car?"

The detective pointed and stumbled towards it, his consciousness fading.

William yanked open the driver's side door and pushed him in. "After you wake up, drive home. Never speak of this again." Then he slammed the door shut as the detective passed out.

CHAPTER 18

The three of them piled into William's car so he could take them back to Natalie's truck which was still parked on the side of the road a few miles away. Alice opted to stay with William for the ride back. Before he drove off, William leaned across the center console, grabbed Alice's face, and kissed her.

She gripped the lapels of his suit jacket, adrenaline surging through her veins as she desperately kissed him back. His fingers threaded through her hair as he tilted her head for better access. Alice was about to climb onto his lap in the driver's seat, but he pulled away.

"Not here," he said, breathing heavily.

Alice nodded, disappointed but understanding.

William shifted the car into gear and took off. Thankfully his radar detector allowed him to speed back to the cabin without any further police interference.

Natalie was just getting out of her truck when they pulled up. Once William and Alice joined up with her in the driveway, the side door of the cabin slammed open.

"What the devil!" Arthur stomped down the steps of the

porch looking more disheveled than usual, as if he had been interrupted from his personal time relaxing in his room before bed. "William, if you—"

"Everything has been handled," William said, holding up his hand.

Leander pushed his way past Arthur to get to his brother. "Are you fucking stupid? We would've handled it tomorrow!"

"Tomorrow would've been too late." William crossed his arms. "The detective arrived right after me to take Alice to a higher security location. She's a suspect. Or did you not stop to think about that?"

"She— what?" Leander looked at him, baffled.

"That's your problem, little brother, you never think and you're always too late."

Rage flashed across Leander's face. "Asshole." He shoved William in the chest.

"Back off," William growled as he shoved back.

"Boys!" Arthur stood between them, arms outstretched. "It's done."

The two brothers backed away but remained tense, not taking their eyes off one another.

"Were you at least successful in the original plan?" Arthur asked as he rubbed his eyes. "Or did you go and get yourselves arrested for nothing?"

"There were some complications," Natalie stepped forward, running a hand through her long hair. "But Miss Dee did agree to help us. That is, if she doesn't hate me after what happened at the office today."

"You need to make this right tomorrow morning, Natalie." Arthur chided. "We desperately need her help."

"I will, I will." She waved him off and looked towards Alice. "There's one condition."

Alice stiffened. "I have to be the anchor."

"No," the brothers said simultaneously.

"I already agreed to it." Alice pushed past them to go inside, pissed at their attempt to control her. Her mind was set.

"You're not doing it," William said as he grabbed her arm, spinning her to face him. "It's not safe."

Alice wrenched herself from William's grasp. "I'm doing it," she snapped. He had promised he wouldn't stop her from Greywalking if it was their last resort. "It's the only way to find my dad. If I didn't agree, Miss Dee wouldn't have offered to help. All of this would've been for nothing."

Leander's frown deepened. "Actually, she has a point."

"Are you serious right now?" William said, rounding on his brother, panic rising in his voice. "You know what the Grey can do to people."

Leander stayed silent, and Arthur looked like he agreed with him.

"I think Alice can handle it," Natalie said as she stepped closer. "Right?"

Alice had no idea if she could handle it. She was barely handling everything that already happened. But she was still determined to do it. She had no other choice. "We need to find my dad," she said. "We have to stop him before he hurts more people."

"There has to be another way, like something else to use as the anchor," William said, his eyebrows lifted. He reached out to touch her shoulder. "Alice, think about it."

She backed away and crossed her arms. "I said I'm doing it."

"But—"

"We've wasted too much time already!" Alice stormed off into the cabin, ignoring William's pleas for her to stop.

There was no way she was changing her mind, no matter how frightening Greywalking might be. She headed upstairs to her bedroom. William was close on her heels and followed her inside. She didn't object.

"Please," he said as he shut the door behind him. "I'm just worried about you."

She kept her back to him, squeezing her fists at her sides. "I know." She sighed and turned to face him. "And you're the only one who seems to be worried about me." Tears pooled in her eyes.

William closed the space between them and swept her up in a tight hug. "I care about you, and you've already been through so much." He cupped her face. "It hurts me to see you hurt. And Greywalking, it can be traumatizing, even as an anchor."

"I'm already traumatized, how much worse could it get?"

"Alice..." William's thumbs brushed the tears from her cheeks.

"I have to do this."

William nodded, resigned. "Okay." He kissed the top of her head.

"Thank you," she paused. "For caring about me. I don't think they care about what happens to me at all. They just want to find my dad and kill him."

"I think so too." He took a breath. "I overheard when Leander got the phone call earlier, that they didn't plan on coming to get you until tomorrow. They weren't even going to tell me what happened. So I snuck out." The corner of his mouth quirked up.

"I'm glad you did," she said. If William hadn't come for her, she'd be sleeping in that cold jail cell all night with those awful cops harassing her. Or worse, that detective could've carted her off to a detention center, and it would've been even more difficult to break her out of there.

William brushed a hand through her hair. "Sorry if I scared you today."

"You didn't." Alice played with the hem of his suit jacket. It was a half truth. She was raised to believe that violence wasn't the answer, that violence breeds more violence. But these days, she wasn't so sure anymore, because violence had saved her many times since being tangled in this magical mess. "You did what you needed to do to get me out as fast as possible. No one else was willing to do that."

"I couldn't leave you there." He rested his forehead against hers.

"I know," Alice breathed, eyes looking up into his, and somehow she knew he would tear down the world to make sure she was okay.

* * *

The next morning Alice woke up later than normal in an empty bed. William had left a note on her nightstand stating that he was heading back to the police station to cover up any final tracks. She found Violet and James in the kitchen prepping lunch, and they informed her that after an enraged phone call from Miss Dee, Natalie returned to the Social Security Office to help her clean up the mess. Miss Dee had already handled most of it, spiking the coffee of a few of the workers who were aware of the incident yesterday. And luckily, Miss Dee still agreed to Walk for them.

Alice snatched a granola bar from the pantry and slipped away before she was roped into a longer conversation. She wanted to hide in her room for the rest of the day, but she ran into Michelle who was coming up from the basement. "Alice! How are you feeling today?" she asked with a caring smile.

Alice clammed up. She wasn't sure how she felt.

"You don't have to talk about it." Michelle's smile disappeared into unease, and she placed a hand on Alice's shoulder. "How about a distraction? I'm organizing some things in the basement."

Alice gave a single nod and followed her downstairs into the office, the one she had been in before with the overflowing shelving and storage. One entire shelf was emptied out, leaving the books, files, and papers spread across the long desk on the far wall.

"I was trying to research, and it got too difficult to rummage through this mess. There are so many loose papers stuffed in these shelves, some we haven't looked at for decades. So I'm trying to categorize them by date and topic. Want to help?"

Alice said nothing as she bit into her granola bar and shuffled through one of the closest piles of papers and parchment, which all seemed to be related to nautical celestial cartography. There were charts and maps, some dated from hundreds of years ago, and most of them signed with the initials J.C. "Did James draw these?"

"Hm?" Michelle looked up from her task to see what Alice was referring to and smiled. "Oh yes, those are his." She took one from the pile and admired it with a smirk. "One of his more honorable jobs over the years."

"Instead of pirating across the seas?" Alice asked.

Michelle threw her head back and laughed. "I heard you read some of his journals. But yes, he was a cartographer. He charted the sky, the sea, and the land. Selling his charts was probably his most legitimate source of income. He was also a botanist, cataloging local flora and fauna he encountered. So sometimes he would sell his collections of illustrations too. Of course, when it didn't pay off," she paused, arching an eyebrow, "he resorted to other more scandalous means of making a living."

Alice continued to finger through the stack of maps and charts, blushing slightly at the idea of James debauching his way through towns to scrounge up some money. He was handsome and charming, and Alice could picture him being quite the philanderer.

"How did you two meet?" Alice asked, recalling the passage she read in his journal.

Michelle rested against the desk, arms folded and eyes gazing upwards in thought. "His ship arrived in my village almost four hundred years ago. I caught him trying to steal provisions from the other boats along the river in the middle of the night. He tried to seduce me to get out of trouble, even as I held my knife to his throat. Mind you, he only spoke a handful of words from my language at the time. But, he was the least of my problems when we stumbled upon something else in the cargo hold."

"Something else?" Alice stopped organizing and looked up, unblinking.

Michelle rifled through a pile of ragged journals until she found the one she was looking for. She flipped to a page and handed it to Alice—a rough sketch of a hulking beast, a canine looking creature with obscenely muscled forearms, chest, and haunches. Its long teeth hung past its bottom jaw, and its claws were more like hooked talons. Its hackles were wild and sharp across its back, covered in spines and scales and coarse hair. Most frightening was its long skinny tail which looked like it could whip around and skewer someone with its barbed tip.

"This thing was on the ship?" Alice asked, color draining from her face.

"More than one, actually. Wolverns, from the Grey. Along with a half dozen possessed and bloodthirsty crew mates."

It sounded like a death sentence. "Were you and James both Chosen back then?"

"At the time I was. He was not," Michelle said with closed eyes. She maintained her soft smile, but her head hung slightly. "James helped, but he could only do so much as a human. So while I fought the beasts and *exsugo*, I also had to make sure he didn't get his dumb ass killed. Although, I had half a mind to let him, considering he had been stealing from my village."

"How do you stop creatures like that?" She couldn't imagine getting close enough to one of those things to cut out its heart.

Michelle walked across the room to the blue and white porcelain vase and withdrew the sword Alice had seen last time she was down there. She unsheathed it from the dragon scabbard, flourishing the slightly curved white-colored blade that seemed to glimmer in the light. She handed it to Alice, who took it gingerly in her hands.

"What type of metal is this?" Alice asked as she inspected it.

"It had been regular steel before it was touched by someone more powerful than those who are Chosen. The metal had been unmade and remade, infused with some sort of magic strong enough to kill *exsugo* and the creatures that escape the Grey." She took the sword back from Alice and sheathed it. "This *dao* was an heirloom in my family, and they never understood it had more abilities than a normal blade. I discovered it by a lucky accident on the

night I was Chosen, which will be a story for another time."
She sighed. "I learned its lore much later."

Alice saw the grief flicker on Michelle's face, but respected her wishes to discuss the story at a later time. "Are there many blades like it?"

Michelle smiled. "Not many." She replaced the sword in the vase and pulled out the cane with the brass eagle pommel. "But we were lucky enough to obtain two." She gripped the pommel and detached it with a swift movement, revealing a hidden dagger with a narrow blade made of the same white metal. "This is Arthur's. We store it here for safe keeping. It has a similar story, passed down in his family through generations. Unbeknownst to them it had special power."

"That's how you killed those creatures on the ship?"

"Yes. Without the sword, we would've died. The whole village would've died. A white blade through the heart is one of the only things that can kill an immortal or dark creature without going through the trouble of immobilizing it and cutting out the heart."

"And how often do these things escape?"

"Not very often, thankfully."

"Can the wolverns hurt someone when they're in the Grey?" Alice's voice shook.

Michelle knitted her brows as she considered the question. She walked over to Alice, cupping her face gently like a mother would do to a child. "I heard you've been asked to be the anchor."

Tears crept from the corners of Alice's eyes as she nodded and leaned her cheek into the comforting touch of Michelle's palm.

"I was in your shoes once, long ago." Michelle pulled Alice in for a hug. "Nothing can physically hurt you in the

Grey. It can be frightening in there, but you will be safe. We're here for you."

* * *

Alice spent the rest of the afternoon helping organize the office and listened to Michelle tell more lighthearted stories about her adventures with James, skating over the event which triggered James to become Chosen. Another story for another time. After he had been Chosen, Michelle and James traveled the world together before settling in England and then eventually the United States. They had so many stories woven throughout history, and Alice was thirsting to know more.

Violet came to retrieve them for dinner once everyone else had returned back to the cabin from their errands. She had made Alice's favorite, rosemary chicken and roasted potatoes, a thoughtful gesture to help ease Alice's anxiety from the day before and of her upcoming commitment with Miss Dee.

As everyone ate, James took over the dinner table with his boisterous storytelling, fueled by the beers he continued to gulp down. The drunker he got, the more his native Scottish accent slipped out. By the time dessert was served, Alice couldn't understand a word out of the man's mouth. He had everyone bellowing with laughter. There were even a few times Leander and William shared a funny story from their childhood, exchanging smiles, and everything seemed fine between the two of them, their previous arguments forgotten, like brothers who actually cared for one another.

Surprisingly, Alice ended up having a couple beers herself and became a little more touchy with William in front of the others. He flirted back, if not more. When

William handed Alice her final beer of the evening, he whispered something quite inappropriate in her ear, causing her to turn bright red in front of everyone. Fortunately the only one who noticed was Natalie, who smirked and wiggled her eyebrows at them.

At the end of the night, Alice headed upstairs to shower. When she returned to her room in just a towel, she was surprised to find William looking fairly comfortable sprawled across her bed reading a book and looking a bit smug. Alice had already planned to join him in his room for the evening, the first part of what he whispered to her downstairs, but they didn't even make it that far. He then proceeded to pin her down and act out the second part of what he had whispered to her earlier that night, which was to show her exactly what else he could do with his mouth.

Later, they lay in Alice's bed wearing nothing but their skin and catching their breath. Alice curled into William, tucking her head into his chest as he drew lazy circles on her lower back. "I need to tell you something," he said.

"What is it?" Alice propped herself up on her elbow, trying to read his face.

"I heard some of the others talking earlier." He brushed a piece of hair from her forehead. "I don't think they have the same goals as us," he paused. "With your father."

Alice swallowed and inhaled a shaking breath. "They said they wanted to help him." Deep in her heart she knew they probably already lost hope.

"I know," William said as he pulled her in closer. "Now I'm not so sure. That's why after you Greywalk, you should be careful with what you tell them. You're going to see some things in there, scary things. But also things that will likely lead us to your father. I'm worried if you give them all the information, they might hunt him down without telling us."

"You really think they'd do that?" Alice thought of each and every one of them. Natalie seemed to care enough to try to save her dad, also Michelle and James. Leander and Arthur, not so much. It was obvious they wanted to kill her father. They might convince the others to agree. It sounded like they already did, judging by whatever William overheard earlier. And poor Violet, Alice knew she cared and would stand up for her, but the old woman didn't seem to get much of a say in anything at all.

"I'm not sure," William said, sounding a little too hopeless. "I wish it wasn't true, but we should still play it safe with them. At least for now. So when you come back from Greywalking, and when they ask you what you saw, try not to give them everything. Only tell me, and we'll figure it out on our own."

CHAPTER 19

"Well, well, well..." Miss Dee said as she walked into the living room. She wore casual jeans and a knitted cardigan with her long braids tied neatly at the nape of her neck. Her eyes scanned the faces, taking stock of the situation. "Didn't think I'd have a crowd tonight." Her gaze stopped on William, who was leaning against the wall, arms crossed. "Nice to see ya, Will." She gave a sly smile. "You haven't aged a day."

"Dee," William said, tipping his head in greeting, his body rigid and his face neutral.

She clicked her tongue at him, then turned her attention towards the other brother. "Leander," Miss Dee continued, looking him up and down. She wasn't thrilled to see him.

He cleared his throat. "Thanks for coming."

Miss Dee walked into the center of the room, inspecting the space they had prepared for the evening. "This'll do just fine," she said. The couches surrounding the fireplace had been pushed back, and the coffee table was moved to another location. In the center of the open space were a couple blankets rolled out on the floor along with some pillows.

"You remember Arthur, Michelle, and James?" Natalie asked.

"How could I forget?" She put her hands on her hips. "You all caused quite a problem at the office back in 1987 thanks to those two boys." She nodded in the direction of Leander and William, who avoided eye contact. "Although what happened the other day could've been just as bad. I should know by now to clear my calendar whenever you folks come knocking on my door."

Violet entered the room with a fresh kettle of steaming hot water. "Good to see you, Miss Dee," she said, placing the kettle on the side table next to two mugs.

"You as well." Miss Dee leaned in to hug Violet, who was clearly the one she liked most in the room. She turned to Alice. "Did you prepare today?"

Alice fidgeted with the long sleeves of her shirt. "Yes, I drank the tea throughout the day and had no food." She felt like she was about to vomit bile from not eating, and the tea she had to drink earlier left a nasty taste in her mouth.

"Alright, let's get to it." Miss Dee sat herself in the center of the blankets and Alice joined her.

Violet busied herself with steeping some more tea in the kettle, yet another special blend Miss Dee brought for the occasion. Alice watched in dread, feeling repulsed by having to drink another strong, and probably bad tasting, tea.

When it was done, Violet poured it into two mugs and handed them to the women. Alice's stomach gurgled with nausea. The others filed in the area, taking seats on the couches around them. William found a spot directly behind Alice and placed a hand on her shoulder in comfort. The touch did little to settle her nerves, but it was welcome all the same.

Earlier that day, Alice had asked Michelle to describe what to expect when Greywalking, what it would feel like, hoping it would help ease her anxiety. Michelle compared it to the feeling of being in a dream, where the jumble of images and scenes might not make any sense at all. Michelle also went over the ingredients of the morning and evening teas with Alice, and answered all of her questions to the best of her knowledge. It still didn't calm her down.

Miss Dee and Alice sat cross legged facing each other and drank the disgustingly bitter tea. They finished quickly in a few large gulps, as it was intended. Violet took the cups from them and set them aside. Alice and Miss Dee clasped their right hands, and Michelle knelt next to them in order to tie a braided leather strap around both of their wrists, connecting them. Alice crinkled her brow.

"A tether," Michelle whispered. "You're the anchor, and this will keep Miss Dee tethered to you on the other side as you search for your father."

The two women laid back on the blankets, their heads at each other's feet, and their tied hands in the middle between them. Alice stared at the wooden rafters of the lofty ceiling, chest heaving with nervous breaths as she felt the magic of the tea vibrating through her bloodstream. William looked down at her, forearms resting on his knees as he hunched over. He tried to give her a reassuring smile as he brushed a piece of hair out of her face, but she saw the distress in his eyes. She wanted to cry. She wanted to quit. She had no idea what waited for her on the other side, the daemons, the creatures, the horrors. But she had to do this for her father. They had to stop him from hurting people. It was the only way.

Time slowed, like the breath before drawing an arrow. Her body became heavy, limbs numb. Her mind swirled as she melted into the floor. Her eyes fluttered closed as she drifted off to sleep, like she was going under anesthesia, except deeper.

When she woke up, she was still laying on the floor of the living room. Alone. The fire was out. It was dark, but the full moon illuminated the room just enough for her to see. The blankets and pillows on the floor were gone. The tea kettle and mugs were gone. The house was empty. Why had they left her there?

Her eyes scanned the room. The clock on the mantle read midnight. A figure hovered in the hallway. A wave of fear shuddered through her as it walked, no, it floated towards her. Completely silent.

It was Miss Dee, but not really. Her form wasn't solid. She was partially translucent, and the edges around her body were fuzzy. It was hard to tell where her skin and clothes ended and the air around her began. She looked like a ghost, a *vagari*, except her eyes weren't black holes.

All of the objects surrounding them had a similar quality. Hazy, only half there. She looked down at her own hands which shimmered like gossamer. There was a glowing band around her wrist, the leather strap linking her with Miss Dee. She saw a thin cord stretching and floating, like a delicate spider web, connecting them.

"Come." She heard Miss Dee's voice, but her mouth didn't move. "You will need to lead the way."

Alice tried to walk, but instead her body simply floated closer, and together they moved towards the side door. No sound of footsteps. No creaking floorboards. Not even a breeze to ruffle through her hair. That was when she realized she wasn't breathing. That she didn't need to breathe. She tried to inhale through her nose and caught the faint smell of something metallic, like a burning wire, but then it was gone.

Instead of opening the door, they floated right through the wood. But when they were outside, it didn't look like the usual front yard of the cabin. It was a thicket of tall trees with a winding dirt path looping around and twisting through the trunks. Looking up at the night sky through the spindly branches, she was able to identify the constellation Ursa Major along with some of the other bright stars. It didn't quite make sense, since those stars shouldn't be that high in the sky at this point of the year. She remembered what Arthur said previously about being in the Grey. She could be in the past, present, or future.

"Do you recognize this place?" Miss Dee's voice sounded from her eerie unmoving mouth.

When Alice tried to speak, she couldn't, because she was focusing too much on her mouth, which wasn't moving no matter how hard she tried. So she tried to speak with her mind.

"Can you hear me?" Alice asked inside of her head.

"Yes."

"I don't know this place."

"Try to remember as many details as possible."

The trees swayed in the silent wind. There were a few moss covered boulders scattered across the ground, some carved with whorls and symbols, but most of the markings were hidden by patches of green. A cluster of white forget-me-not flowers blanketed the ground in one area at the base of a thick tree. The dirt path circled and twisted between the trees, inching closer to the edge of a rocky overhang that sloped down to a pebbled beach where there was a figure on their knees, hunched over.

With the desire to get closer, Alice's mind instantly transported her spectral form to the beach. She looked behind her. Miss Dee was no longer by her side. "Miss Dee?" she called out through her mind. No answer. The tether was still there, but it was stretched thin, disappearing back into the trees to wherever Miss Dee was waiting. Her brain was telling her she should be worried, yet her body kept floating silently forward, drawn towards the unknown figure.

The rippling water crept up, lapping against the figure's legs. The tide was coming in and the whole area would be underwater soon. Across the river she saw a glimmering city skyline in the distance, and above the skyline was a stretch of rolling clouds flickering with ominous lightning.

The silence was interrupted by strangled sobs escaping the figure as they clutched their chest. Then it stopped. They sensed her. A gnarled hand whipped out as the figure twisted around, reaching with crooked knuckles stained with blood. There were black holes where his eyes should've been and a sinister hiss escaped the gaping abyss where there was supposed to be a mouth.

"Dad?" Alice recoiled from the twisted soul of her father.

"Help me." His gravelly voice rang through her mind. He was on all fours, crawling towards her. The tide was coming in fast now, licking its way up his legs. He clutched his chest again, his heart. "Help me," he begged.

Then he disappeared like smoke, the wisps dissipating into nothingness. "Dad!" she cried out in her mind, spinning around trying to find him. What could it have meant?

His horrifying appearance, his empty eyes. Was it too late for him to be saved?

The rustling of bushes caught her attention. When she looked back at the thicket of trees up on the rocky ledge, she saw at least a dozen sets of glowing eyes. Watching. Waiting. There was a low rumbling growl coming from that direction. A pack of wolverns.

"Miss Dee!" she screamed in her head. But Miss Dee was still nowhere to be found. The tether on her wrist was still there, along with the delicate cord connecting them, but it was stretched even thinner than before, and its light was faint. Alice tried to pull on it, to somehow signal to Miss Dee that she needed her. When she turned around, she was faced with another figure on their knees.

William.

His face was battered and bloody, hands bound behind his back. He was crying. "Please," he whimpered. "Don't." A dark ghostly figure appeared in front of him, pointing a narrow blade at his chest.

Alice lunged for him, feeling compelled to save him, but he too dissolved into mist. More rustling was heard from the trees, then a growl. A woman screamed. Miss Dee was in trouble.

She suddenly felt countless hands on her, invisible claws scratching at every inch of body, ripping at her iridescent skin with unforgiving force. Her blood felt as if it had turned to ice. She flailed her arms in panic as she battled against the invisible creatures. Something sharp tugged on her navel, like she had been hooked by a fishing line, causing her to fall to her hands and knees. Her fingers dug into the pebbles as the river tide crashed in around her. The claws sank deeper into her incorporeal body, yet the pain felt physically real. Michelle promised her nothing would harm her in the Grey. It had to be a lie. Alice was about to get ripped apart.

She screamed but no sound came out as she tried to scramble to her feet. She couldn't move underneath the crushing weight of some invisible force keeping her pinned down. And for a moment, Alice truly believed she was going to die in this parallel realm.

There was a slight thrumming sensation on the tether tied around her wrist. Miss Dee was trying to reach out. She couldn't give up. Not yet. She had to keep going for her father, to save those innocent victims. Somehow Alice managed to roll over onto her back under the invisible crushing weight, the water of the incoming tide splashing into her face. If she could just get back to Miss Dee. But as she tried to push herself up, she saw Leander hovering above her, his eyes empty dark holes. She gasped in horror.

The tugging on her navel increased, like she was getting pulled through the earth. And then she was free falling through nothingness, unable to scream. The tether was stretched so thin, it seemed like it might snap. She'd be lost in nothingness forever.

Her free falling slowed and the black nothingness flickered with an indiscernible image. Alice heard muffled voices, as if she was underwater, and someone called her name, echoing in the distance. They were so far away. She felt hands on her again, not claws, but soft, comforting hands. Her eyes flickered open, her blurry vision taking a moment to focus on the faces that surrounded her.

Searing pain throbbed in her gut and her head. Sweat dripped down her forehead and soaked her back. Alice clawed at her shirt and yanked it off, leaving her in a damp tank top as she gasped for air.

William knelt next to her, saying her name over and

over as he cupped her face. "Are you okay?" he asked, offering her a glass of water. She pushed it away. Alice rubbed her arms, trying to stop her shuddering. Trying to forget the pain. Trying to erase the memory of her father's distorted soul. She couldn't stop sobbing.

"What did you see?" Arthur asked.

"Give her a damn minute," William barked, brushing a few sweat-soaked strands of hair off her forehead.

"The longer we wait, the more information will slip from her memory," Arthur snapped back.

"She needs to rest."

"She can rest later."

William glowered at Arthur, but before he could argue back, Alice spoke up. "My dad," she whispered with a trembling voice. "Near a river. I could see the city. There were trees and a path and..." She finally looked up at William. His eyes narrowed slightly, reminding her of their conversation from before, reminding her to keep the details a secret.

"Anything else?" Arthur prodded. "Details. We need details."

"It's fuzzy," Alice lied, her throat tight. She couldn't tell them what her father looked like, how deformed and sinister he was. That would give them more of a reason to hunt him down and kill him without question, because they'd believe he was too far gone.

"Was anyone else there?"

"No." Another lie. "Just Miss Dee, but she disappeared."

"There were some wolverns in there stalking Alice, along with some *exsugo* and other dark creatures," Miss Dee said, sipping a glass of water. She was sitting up next to her on the rumpled blankets as Violet pressed a damp cloth to her head. "I wasn't able to see much because I was busy distracting them, trying to pull them away. They don't usually act like that unless they have a reason, unless they recognize someone." She cocked her head at Alice. "You've been to the Grey before." It wasn't a question.

Alice's heart lodged in her throat. She knew. Miss Dee knew.

"What?" Arthur snapped. "Are you a Greywalker? And you didn't tell us?"

"I didn't know." Alice's voice was small. Ashamed.

"When did you die?" Miss Dee asked.

Everyone gaped at her as she told the story of the car accident, how she needed blood transfusions in the hospital to save her life. She told them of the ghosts she had seen since then, of how she saw Natalie's mom in the front yard back in Riverton. Violet started crying. "I'm sorry," Alice said at the end of her story. "I didn't realize until recently, but I wasn't sure."

"Greywalkers are like a signal fire in the Grey," Miss Dee said as she shook her head. "And there were two of us this time, drawing a crowd. Did any of them touch you?"

Alice nodded. "They clawed at me. Pulled me down. I..." Her voice quivered as she started to cry again, the phantom pain aching throughout her body. She gripped William's shirt and buried her face in his chest.

"Damn it." Miss Dee rubbed her forehead.

"What else do you remember?" Arthur pressed, not caring about what Alice went through. "We need to know."

"Let her sleep," Natalie said quietly, as if she regretted the entire thing. "Let her rest. She can write down what she saw, and we'll go over it tomorrow."

"But—" Arthur tried to argue.

Michelle silenced him with her hand. "Let Alice rest."

In a swift moment, William scooped Alice in his arms as

he got to his feet. "I'll make sure she writes it down." He strode across the room and carried her up the stairs.

She kept her face hidden in order to avoid the disappointment on everyone's faces. She knew she would have no problem remembering what she saw because it was so frightening, she might never forget.

William took Alice to his room and carefully placed her on his bed, being sure to cradle her head until it was on the pillow. He covered her with the blanket. "What can I get for you?" he asked. "Water? Something to eat?"

Alice groaned as she curled onto her side. "No food." She felt sick to her stomach. "Water, some medicine for my head. No tea."

He disappeared into the small bathroom attached to his room and returned with a cup of water and a bottle of pills. "I'm not sure how well medication will work on something like this." He handed her the glass of water. "I can go back downstairs and ask them."

"No," Alice grumbled, sitting up in order to take the pain pills with a swig of water. "Don't leave me." There was more to her words than he likely understood.

"I won't," he said as he sat next to her on the bed, placing a tender hand on the back of her neck.

When she was finished with her water, they laid down facing one another as she tried to figure out the best way to explain the visions. "I saw you in there," Alice whispered, her lip quivering. "You were hurt."

William stiffened. "What else?"

"Someone was threatening you, but I couldn't see their face." She tried to stifle a sob. "You were begging them not to kill you." Her tears finally escaped as the thought of losing William overwhelmed her.

"It doesn't mean it's true, Alice," he said as he held her.

"Is there anything else you remember? If we figure out when and where this happens, then we can do something about it."

"I don't know," Alice said with a sniffle. "I've never been there before. I could see the Philadelphia skyline in the distance. It was like an island sticking out into the river. There was a path winding through a forest and moss covered boulders with carvings, like whorls."

William exhaled through his nose and rubbed his eyes. "I might know the place. Which means the others might also know. Keep this between us for now, until I look into it more."

Alice nodded, more inclined to keep this a secret knowing William could get hurt. "There was someone else," she added. "Your brother."

"What was he doing?" William scowled.

"Nothing except standing over me as those invisible creatures clawed at me. He had no eyes." She shivered.

"More of a reason we shouldn't trust him."

"You're right." Alice didn't need any more convincing. From the very first night she ran into him on campus outside of her dad's office, Leander had been lying to her. He sedated her, drugged her, manipulated her. And it was quite obvious he didn't care about saving her dad.

"What about anything regarding Alexander?" William asked.

Alice shook her head. "Nothing."

William loosed a breath. "Alright, well tomorrow I'll start looking into this, but I'll have to leave. You'll have to cover for me."

"Why can't you take me with you?" Alice was desperate. She couldn't be alone.

"That would be too obvious. We can't let them catch on

that we're withholding information. So when they ask for more details you need to lie or say you don't remember."

Alice would normally feel guilty about blatantly lying. She didn't even know if she'd be good at it. But they all had lied to her in one way or another. Maybe they deserved to be lied to. And if they were planning to kill her father behind her back, then they definitely deserved it.

CHAPTER 20

Alice kept her eyes on the sky every night, watching and waiting as those stars inched closer to the position they were in when she was in the Grey. It felt like a countdown, a countdown to the end. Her father was still missing, no cure for the elixir had been discovered, and Alice was still working with Violet, trying to come up with some sort of tincture to weaken her father enough to capture him.

In the evenings, Alice would have her nose in a book searching for any mention of a cure for immortality, or she'd be rereading her father's journal looking for anything she might've missed. William had managed to get some records from the university and discovered that over the past ten years, her father had a total of seven students with the name Alexander in his classes. Since then, William had been attempting to track down each of them to no avail.

The others were still on the hunt for her father, based off the little information she provided them from her Grey-walking experience, with some of the details either purposely vague or downright incorrect. The information had them scouring the entire west coast of southern New

Jersey along the river. Alice even went with them a few times on their excursions, in disguise, suggesting random locations that she knew were wrong. At one point, William suggested perhaps it wasn't the Delaware River at all, but the Schuylkill River instead, which sent them on another wild goose chase in the opposite direction through eastern Pennsylvania.

It seemed like everyone in the cabin was on edge, the situation getting worse by the hour. Leander was more miserable than usual. Natalie's attitude became more prickly. Violet was more detached. Michelle and James mostly kept to themselves. Arthur avoided the cabin half the time, electing to stay in his townhouse in Philadelphia when he wasn't following a lead.

Every now and then, they would approach Alice to ask if she remembered anything new from her Greywalking experience, or if she had any meaningful or symbolic dreams. It kept Alice walking on eggshells. She was afraid to slip up and say something that didn't line up with her lies. Judging by Leander's constant suspicious expression, he didn't trust her. But that was fine, because she didn't trust him either. Alice also began to wonder if there might be another more incriminating reason as to why Leander had been sneaking around East Pyne Hall on the night they met.

Benjamin Foster's face was still all over the news, along with some new faces of recently missing or murdered people, which brought the probable victims list up to around ten or so. It was difficult for Alice to avoid her guilt about keeping her father's journal a secret from the others. If the others knew of the journal and Alexander, perhaps with more people searching they'd be able to find her dad sooner and more people could be saved. Yet if they found her father before her, they might kill him before giving

Alice a chance to save him. Maybe she was being selfish, caring more about saving her dad instead of the innocent people that might be killed if their search went on any longer.

William somehow maintained his optimism, believing they'd find her father or Alexander before any more deaths occurred, and Alice was thankful for it. When he was around, he helped Alice and Violet in the conservatory with their tincture project, and he even volunteered himself to be the test subject.

"Are you sure?" Alice asked with an uncertain frown. "You don't have to drink it."

"I'm not going to drink it," William said with a popped eyebrow. He whipped out his switchblade and sliced open his palm before Alice could even protest. She gasped.

"I've had worse," he said with a smile. He clenched his fist and let his blood dribble into a small dish. When there was enough, he pushed the dish across the workbench towards Violet and wiped his hand clean before wrapping it in a cloth.

"Will," Alice said as she touched his arm. "You didn't have to do it like that."

"It'll be healed by nightfall," he said with a shrug.

Violet uncorked a dark glass bottle holding their most recent tincture sample and used a pipette to drop a small amount into the dish with William's blood. The three of them leaned in, eyebrows furrowed as they watched with bated breath to see if it had any effect. After about a minute, Violet swirled the blood in the dish.

"Well I'll be damned," Violet whispered. The blood had thickened to a gelatinous consistency, and there were a few clumps of blood clots in the center. Alice recalled watching a nature documentary as a kid, and the blood looked exactly how it would look if it had come into contact with snake venom.

"Shit," William said as he pulled a face. "I'm glad I didn't drink that."

"What do you mean?" Alice asked, clutching her chest, worried the tincture might be too strong. "Would that have killed you?"

"No, I don't think so," William answered as he rubbed his stubble-covered chin. "But I'm sure it would be unpleasant. Blood is what helps the magic flow through an immortal's body, so if the blood is slowed, the magic is slowed. I think this could work to reduce your father's strength enough for us to capture him and keep him subdued until we figure out the cure."

"As long as it won't seriously hurt him," Alice said. "Right?"

"It shouldn't do any lasting damage," he said, shaking his head. His hand found the small of her back. "I'm impressed, Alice." William smiled. "Nice work."

"She knows her plants," Violet added, also smiling.

"I researched everything I could find," Alice said as her cheeks reddened. "Anything to stop my dad from hurting others so we can help him." She paused. "Violet did most of the work though."

"Now don't go and discredit yourself like that," Violet said as she cleaned up. "You helped a lot more than you realized. And you caught on quickly to the process. Hopefully this will be the thing that helps us help your dad."

William left later that night without much explanation. Alice wasn't able to argue because one, they had an audience when he announced his departure at the dinner table, and two, she didn't want everyone else to know about the tincture she and Violet created. Not yet. Alice had followed him into the foyer with the intent to convince him to take her with him, but he was already halfway out the door. He gave her a swift kiss and promised to return in a few days.

* * *

"What if we tried Greywalking again?" Leander asked the group at breakfast one rainy morning.

"Miss Dee is out of town on vacation with her daughter," Natalie said, slumping down in her chair.

"Couldn't Alice just go alone?" Arthur asked. "Being that she is a Greywalker herself."

"I'm sitting right here," Alice grumbled. They spoke about her like she wouldn't even have a choice.

"I don't know if we should send Alice in there alone," Violet said.

Alice partially agreed. Going into the Grey was one of the scariest things she ever had to do in her life, and that time she had someone accompanying her. She wasn't sure if she could handle it alone, but she already knew she'd say yes anyway.

"We need more information," Arthur said. "This has gone on for too long. Her father must be stopped. Too many people have died because of our insufficiency."

"So then let's do it this weekend," said Leander.

Alice slammed her hands on the table. "Doesn't anyone care about *my* decision?"

"Of course we do," Michelle said, her voice soft and placating.

"We're just running out of time," James added, his usual kind demeanor hidden behind tension. "Please consider it."

Her nails dug into the wood. "I am considering it," she spat. "You know I'd do anything for my dad. I just hate how you all talk about me like my choice doesn't matter. Like you don't even care what happened to me in there!"

They were silent.

Alice gritted her teeth. "No one else here is eager to Greywalk."

"None of us have died." Arthur said. "No one else here can do it."

"Do what?" William asked as he came in through the side door, dropping his backpack, and immediately going to Alice's side. "What's going on?"

"Alice is going to Greywalk for us this weekend," Michelle said as she stood, her head high, taking on her leadership role. "Miss Dee is unavailable."

William's head snapped to Alice. "What?"

She met his gaze, trying to mentally urge him to stand down. "I have to do it," she said. If she didn't agree to it, the others would get suspicious. So she'd agree to do it and lie about what she saw. Then hopefully in the meantime William will be able to find either her father or Alexander on his own.

"Do we even have the ingredients for the blend?" William asked with an edge to his voice. "We can't do it without the—"

"We have all the herbs," Violet said quietly. "It will only take me a few days to prepare."

Alice didn't know why, but for some reason, she had hoped Violet would fight more for her, stand up for her, want to protect her from experiencing those horrors again. Even though Alice still planned to Greywalk again, she wanted the others to empathize with her more, to understand just how hard this has been for her, instead of looking at this like another job, another nuisance. The only person who actually cared about how Alice felt was William.

* * *

The days came and went faster than Alice had anticipated. She had hoped for some sort of breakthrough before she had to Greywalk again, but William kept hitting dead ends in his search for Alexander.

"Why don't we at least tell the others that my dad had someone helping him? Then we'd be able to cover more ground," Alice said, swinging her legs off the edge of William's bed.

"No, not a good idea." William stretched out in his desk chair with an exhausted grunt. "They're getting more impatient. Who knows what they'd do to the poor kid if they found him before we did."

What *were* they going to do with the student when they found him? Anger simmered in her stomach. She needed someone to blame, and Alexander would be a perfect target. It was his fault her father completed the elixir in the first place. She balled her fists, pushing down the violent thoughts that slipped into her mind. Perhaps they should be more worried about what Alice would do to Alexander once they found him.

"Are you ready?" William stood as he held out a hand for Alice to help her to her feet.

She shrugged, her nonchalance amplified to hide her nervousness. "There's no turning back now."

"Whatever you see in there," he started as he kissed her head. "Remember it can't actually hurt you. And when you come back, remember to keep the details vague."

Alice nodded and leaned into his chest for a hug. "I just want this to be over."

"It will be soon," William whispered into her hair.

They headed down to the living room, everything

moved out of the way like before. Alice sat on the blanket in the center, and Violet handed her the mug of tea. William sat on the couch behind her, rubbing her shoulders as she drank.

It was strange the way the others stared at her, like an animal on exhibit at the zoo, waiting for her to do some sort of trick. Except the trick was her crossing over into the realm of the unliving and hopefully returning with answers. She had no idea what to expect this time, if she'd be taken back to the river bank to find the tormented soul of her father crawling towards her in the rising tide.

Alice took a shuddering breath as she laid back on the blanket and closed her eyes, the familiar heaviness washing over her and pushing her down into the floor.

When she woke up, she was still laying on the floor of the living room. Alone. The fire was out. It was dark, but the full moon illuminated the room just enough for her to see. The house was empty. The clock on the mantle read midnight. A figure hovered in the hallway. Completely silent.

The familiar metallic smell of the Grey twinged in her nose. The skin of her hands and arms were like gossamer, except brighter and more clear than before. Alice allowed herself to float towards the hallway where the shadowy figure had disappeared. Alice drifted through the side door, but instead of being in a forest, this time she was facing the river. Gas lamps flickered along the unpaved road. A crescent moon now hung in the sky. She knew this place, except it was different.

Slowly she turned around, face tilting up as she took in the grand manor before her. No ivy crawled up the sides. Candlelight fluttered in the unbroken windows. The fourth floor mansard tower was completely intact. A horse and carriage was parked along the curb at the side of the house, and out of the carriage stepped William Montgomery wearing a swallowtail coat and top hat.

With a simple thought, Alice was instantly transported next to William's side. Somehow the image was clearer than her previous experience Greywalking. She could see his perfect skin and the youthful spark in his eye, exactly the same as he looked in the present. He held out his gloved hand and helped a gorgeous woman exit the carriage. She wore a beautiful corseted gown and had long billowing red hair, vibrant even in the dimness of the Grey. William quickly ushered her into the side door of the mansion, peering over his shoulder to ensure they weren't seen.

The setting dissolved around Alice, like rippling water, and then reformed. She hovered in a resplendent bedroom with gilded furniture lit by candlelight. Tangled in the sheets of the four-poster bed, William held the red-haired woman as they passionately kissed, both in various stages of undress. Alice wanted to look away, but couldn't. She heard him whispering the woman's name under his breath. Victoria.

Footsteps could be heard in the hallway drawing nearer, and in laughter-filled panic, William hurried to hide Victoria in his closet as she clutched a bedsheet to her chest. They shared one more quick kiss before he hid her away. He straightened his clothes and replaced his tailcoat as there was a knock on his bedroom door.

The next scene dissolved into a study. William stood before the heavy oak desk, hands clasped behind his back, and an imposing yet handsome dark-haired man was seated on the other side. A familiar book lay open on the desk, large and old with the scribblings of an ancient language.

Curious instruments of metal and glass lined the shelves behind him.

"As the eldest son, it is your responsibility to uphold the family name," the man said as he lazily spun a brass armillary sphere on the corner of his desk.

William gulped. "Yes, father."

"Do not disgrace me."

"I can assure you, I have not." William raised his chin.

"Then what of these rumors of you gallivanting around town with a whore? Some circus freak left behind by her own troupe?"

"Only rumors, nothing more."

"Regardless, please ensure to keep your dalliances private. I do not want the Montgomery name to be ridiculed."

"Of course, father."

Alice was transported to the bank of the river at dusk. A fierce wind whipped through the trees overhead. William paced along the stone retaining wall, distressed as he flung rocks into the water. Then he froze, eyes trained on a smidge of pale white peeking above the surface—a hand. He jumped off the ledge onto the gravelly bank below which had been revealed by the low tide. William splashed into the shallows and fell to his knees, cradling Victoria's dead body in his arms as he sobbed. Her cloudy eyes stared up into nothingness. Her wet, tangled red hair clung to her ashen face. Her graceful neck, slashed open.

It was dawn in the next scene, and fog hung in the morning autumn air. Three men walked along the river— William, Leander, and Arthur with his eagle-pommel cane, each of them dressed impeccably.

"The fortieth parallel is a place where great magic lingers," Arthur said. "Why do you think such prominent families chose to build the town precisely in this location? Someone must have been drawn to practice dark magic here."

"You believe the murders are related to this dark magic?" Leander asked as he adjusted his top hat.

"Indeed, and if it continues, more darkness will be drawn to this place." Arthur said.

"They must be stopped," William said with a stone face.

Arthur nodded, his mouth a thin line. "It will be difficult if my theory is correct."

"Is our magic not enough?" Leander wrung his fingers into a fist.

"I'm afraid not. To kill individuals with such magical strength, one must cut out their heart or stab them through the heart with this." Arthur withdrew the hidden blade from his cane, the white metal glimmering, even in the mist.

Alice was transported to the fourth floor tower of the manor, the walls ablaze around her as ceiling beams crashed to the floor. A hole had been blasted through the roof to reveal part of the night sky. Three men were locked in a stalemate, and Thomas Montgomery had a wicked smile on his face.

"You sick bastard!" William yelled over the roar of the flames.

His father laughed as flames licked his skin, uninjured and skin unmarred.

The brothers tackled him to the ground in a flurry of fists and blood. Leander pinned down his father's shoulders as William, with tears of rage in his eyes, hacked out Thomas Montgomery's still beating heart.

It was morning, and only a small wisp of smoke rose from the charred remains of the tower. William argued with his brother and Arthur in the front yard of the manor, their words muffled and unclear.

Leander stepped back, the ancient grimoire tucked under his arm. "I promise, the book will be destroyed."

William responded with a stiff nod "As it should be."

Alice's surroundings changed once more. Her father sat in his dark office, the lightbulb in his ugly beaded lamp flickering. His back was hunched, and his shoulders shook as he cried. The grimoire was open on his desk. Crumbled scrap papers littered the floor at his feet.

"Alexander," her father said through his cries. The student was nowhere to be seen. "I don't think I have much time left. Please tell me it'll work." He spun around in his desk chair, his eyes black holes, his mouth slack, his hand clutching his chest. "Help me." Her father tumbled out of the chair and scrambled towards Alice on all fours.

She fell backwards, floating in slow motion like she had fallen into the deep end of a pool. Gasping for air, she broke the water's surface. Alice was back at the river, at that strange place she visited during her first trip to the Grey. She sat on the pebbled shore as water lapped around her. A man stood on the rocky ledge above, watching.

"The fortieth parallel," Arthur said, standing over her but staring straight ahead into nothingness. His eyes were black holes. "A place of great magic." His voice echoed strangely.

Scrambling to her feet, she cried out. "What does it mean? Where?"

Arthur cocked his head at her and gestured downwards. Floating in the shallows around her ankles were dead bodies. Victoria. Thomas Montgomery. Her father. Each of them with black holes for eyes, mouths open in silent screams.

"What do I do?" She begged. "How do I save him?"

Growling could be heard in the distance. Wolverns. They were back. They were hunting her again. She could see their eyes between the trees.

Arthur pointed behind her.

Leander stood there, with black holes for eyes like the others, the white blade in his hand dangling at his side. "*Sanguis est vis vitae. Cum morte sua finiet.*" He pointed the blade into the distance, to the rolling storm clouds flashing with lightning above the city skyline across the river. "With his death, it will end."

"Whose death?" Alice asked, her panic rising.

Arthur pointed to the sky, to the stars.

"Who?" She cried.

A wolvern howled.

Her father's dead body sat up rigidly in the water. "Run," he said.

So Alice ran, trees whipping past her as she followed the path through the forest. Someone grabbed her arm. William. His eyes were black with tears of blood dripping down his cheeks.

"I'm still trying to make things right," he said.

Claws slashed into her back, and Alice fell to her knees with a painful wail. The wolverns had found her, and this time they weren't invisible. She saw them as they surrounded her, the big hulking beasts with sharp talons and teeth. She tried to call for help. William's figure dissipated into nothingness. The trees around her swirled and blurred.

"Alice!" someone yelled from the distance.

The claws burned every inch of her skin. Her vision faded. The tide had come in, a wave so high that it crested over that rocky ledge and reached the forest, drowning everything in its path. Alice flailed. She was underwater. She couldn't breathe.

Alice choked in attempt to cough up water, except no water came out. She sucked in a breath as her eyes fluttered open. Someone was shaking her by the shoulders, but she couldn't tell if she was awake for real or in another vision in the Grey. "Help!" she cried out. "They've come for me!" She scrambled in the pile of blankets on the cabin floor, her weak legs failing to gain purchase.

"Alice, you're out. You're safe," William said, the real William, as he held her firmly by the shoulders. "I'm here."

She collapsed in his arms, her quaking body slick with sweat.

"What did you see?" Arthur asked. "We need to know."

"Damn it, can't you see she's been through a lot?" William hissed. "Give her a break."

"Last time, she barely remembered anything," Arthur snapped back. "We need to know what she saw. Now."

Alice took a deep breath to subdue her crying, her eyes fixed on Leander. "I saw you." She nodded towards him. He stiffened. "And you." She looked up at William. "I was in the past. I watched you kill your father."

"You saw Thomas Montgomery," Arthur said as he rubbed his chin. "Anything else about him?"

"He had the book," she continued. William's intense gaze focused on her, and she faltered. "Everything else is fuzzy. It's hard to remember."

"It should have been more clear," Violet said, scratching her head. "I adjusted the recipe to hopefully allow you to see better in the Grey and remember more clearly."

What Alice saw in the Grey was exceptionally clear besides the minimal fuzzy haze that surrounded figures and objects. The visions she saw were more coherent, instead of muddled imagery like before. "No, it was actually harder for me to see things this time," Alice lied. "I could barely make out the details."

Arthur grumbled. "Did you see anything about your father at all? A location?"

"Well," Alice started, giving a brief glance to William. "Just an image of him in his office on campus with the book. That's all I remember."

"Then we'll circle back to the campus," Michelle said. "First thing tomorrow morning."

"What about the river you saw last time?" asked James.

Alice shook her head. "No, there was no river this time."

"If this doesn't pan out," Arthur said as he stood up. "We're going to need you to Walk again. Every day that goes by, your father is out there killing. Violet, keep tweaking that recipe."

Alice was too exhausted to fight. She knew they would keep forcing her to Walk if they didn't get the answers they were looking for. It was up to her and William to figure this out before it happened again.

"Anything else you could remember? Signs or images?" Michelle asked.

"No, I'm sorry," Alice said as she feigned sleepiness. "I'm just so drained, I can barely think."

William helped Alice to her feet. "Let's get you to bed," he said, wrapping an arm around her waist to support her as they walked up the stairs.

The others watched her leave, their faces laced with wariness. Clearly they were getting fed up with this chase and the blood that was on their hands for being unable to locate her father.

Up in William's bedroom, Alice collapsed into his bed, and he joined her. His expression was soft and patient, waiting for Alice to be ready to open up more about her experience. She knew he wouldn't inquire if she wasn't ready yet. He brushed his hand through her hair, and she closed her eyes. Without him, she'd be a mess.

"I was in the past," Alice started. "I saw you and Victoria." She told him everything she could remember, every crisp detail.

William scowled at the mention of his father and again when she mentioned the scene where he found Victoria's body, as if reliving the traumatic memory himself. After a moment, he said, "The fortieth parallel? I remember discussing it back then."

"Do you think we could find my dad there?" Alice asked hopefully.

"It's a possibility. The strength of the magic would draw him in. I'm pretty sure I know exactly where it is." William cupped her cheek. "We're getting close, Alice. We'll find him soon."

CHAPTER 21

William didn't allow Alice to go with him, no matter how much she argued and begged. He said it wasn't safe, so he'd go first to scope out the scene, to check for evidence of her father or Alexander before reporting back. He theorized that her father's student could be dabbling in dark magic, using her father as a guinea pig, a poor desperate soul who would say yes to a magic cure.

It had been a week since William left, no updates, no phone calls. That weekend, Alice noticed William's car had finally returned to the driveway sometime earlier in the day. She rushed out of her room to knock on his bedroom door. When he didn't answer, she let herself in. His bag was on the floor next to the desk, but he was nowhere to be found. Through the window, she saw him walking along the garden path into the conservatory. She frowned, wondering if he was avoiding her.

With a huff, she bent down and unzipped his bag, digging through books and papers, before she let herself question the integrity of her actions. At the bottom of his bag, she found a wallet-sized notebook with W. A. Montgomery written in cursive on the inside cover.

Flipping through it, she found pages upon pages of Greek to English translations, along with another similar looking language she had never seen before. William was a skilled linguist, so it seemed. There were even a few pages with a scribbled copy of her new tincture recipe. He must've been so impressed, maybe he wanted a record of it for himself.

As she continued to search the pages of the notebook, a small scrap of paper fluttered to the ground. It said *one fortnight* in scribbled handwriting, quite unlike William's elegant cursive script. When she turned over the scrap paper, she saw the black and orange emblem of Princeton University in the bottom corner.

Alice pulled a face, unsure why William would have Princeton stationary. Leander said he had been a student at Princeton years ago, so perhaps William had gone there too. But why did this handwriting look so familiar? She held it closer to her eyes, inspecting it, trying to convince herself it was nothing but a coincidence.

She darted out of his room and back to hers, snatching her father's journal off her nightstand and flipping to a random page. The handwriting matched.

Stuffing the paper in her pocket, she stormed down the stairs and out the back door. She huffed into the conservatory and found William standing at the workbench alone, bundling some herbs.

"You didn't come say hello," Alice said, her voice flat.

William looked over his shoulder, and when he saw her aggrieved face he went to offer a hug, but she stepped back. "I had a lot to do in here and didn't want to disturb you."

"Of course." She couldn't hide the bitterness in her voice.

"What's wrong?"

"Have you been lying to me?" Alice asked. There was no skating around it.

"Why would you think that?" He looked offended.

She shoved her father's scrap paper into William's face. "Why do you have this?"

He paused, studying the paper with narrowed eyes. "Why were you looking through my bag?"

"Why do you have my dad's paper, William?"

"How do you know it's his?"

"I'm not stupid!" Alice yelled, pushing him in the chest.

"Whoa," William said as he held up his hands. "Alice. That's not what I meant."

She jutted her hand out. "What do you mean that's not what you meant? I'd know his handwriting and stationery anywhere." Alice tensed her muscles to control her rage. "You've been lying to me."

"Alice," William said as he took a tentative step towards her. She backed away. "Please, trust me. I'm not lying to you," he paused and took a deep breath. "But, there are some things I haven't told you."

"That counts as lying!" She tried to push him in the chest again but he grabbed her wrists before she had the chance.

"Calm down and listen to me for a second," he said as he let her go. "There are things I didn't tell you because I didn't want to upset you."

Alice crossed her arms. "Well, it's not working, is it? Because here I am, upset." She sniffled. She hated how often her anger turned to tears. "Everyone has been lying to me, this whole time. I thought you were different."

William put his hands on her shoulders to steady her. "Alice, I promise I'm not lying to you. I'm trying to help you." He sighed, eyes darting to the ground. "I broke into your father's office looking for information about that student. I got caught by a security guard and had to use the henbane. Things ended badly. Okay? I'm sorry. I shouldn't have kept it from you."

She buried her face in his chest as she cried, unable to think of any words to say. He cradled her head, flattening her hair as he comforted her. So many people have gotten hurt or died because of this mess, and there was no indication it was going to get any better.

"Come on," William said, leading her out of the conservatory and back to the cabin. He guided her to sit on the couch. "Let me get you something to drink and we'll talk. Violet made some raspberry lemonade earlier while you were napping."

Alice nodded and sat there feeling completely numb until he returned. "Where is everyone else?" she asked as he handed her the glass.

"They're all out in Pennsylvania following the false lead we told them about before." He sat down, inviting her to lean into him as he put his arm around her.

"Even Violet?" Alice asked as she took a few sips of her lemonade, which was extraordinarily delicious, light and refreshing. She'd have to ask for the recipe when Violet got back.

"Surprisingly yes," William said, rubbing her upper arm. "I told them it might be best to have as many eyes as possible on the lookout. Violet was itching to get out anyway."

"Makes sense." Alice yawned. His fingers traced along her forehead, lightly pushing back some loose strands of hair. She closed her eyes, feeling at ease. It had been a long week without him there. Now that he was back, she could finally rest.

"Why don't you take a nap?"

"A nap?" Alice asked.

"Yeah, try to relax for a bit." William said.

Alice sipped her lemonade. Actually a nap sounded like a great idea.

When she woke up, she was still lying on the couch in the living room. Alone. The fire was out. It was dark, but the full moon illuminated the room just enough for her to see. The house sounded like it was empty. Her eyes scanned the room. The clock on the mantle read midnight. A figure hovered in the hallway. Completely silent.

Alice jolted up, bracing herself on her forearms. The scene felt familiar, but she wasn't in the Grey. Her wide eyes stared at the shadowy figure in the hall and watched them slip out the side door. She launched herself from the couch and followed them outside, feet crunching on the gravel as she ran through the darkness.

William was about to open his car door when he spun on his heel at the sound of Alice barreling towards him. She lunged at him, fisting the lapel of his shirt. "You drugged me," she hissed at him. "You—"

His hand covered her mouth, and he pinned her against the car. "If you promise not to scream and wake everyone up," he whispered. "I'll tell you what's going on."

She squirmed against him, throwing muffled insults into the palm of his hand. William's grip on her grew tighter, almost painful, forcing her to tense up with fear.

"This is serious," he grumbled through his teeth. "Alice. Stop." His eyes looked wild, as if compelling her to submit to him. She gave a meek nod, and he removed his hand. "I found your dad," William admitted. "I'm going after him. Alone."

Alice's heart skipped a beat. How dare he go after him alone without telling her. She opened her mouth, sucking in a deep breath getting ready to object, but he cut her off.

"You're not coming."

"Is that why you drugged me?" She snapped.

His face remained flat, but his wide eyes intimidated her. "I'm running out of time. Get back inside." William grabbed her by the upper arm and hauled her towards the door. He had never been this rough with her before.

She planted her feet into the gravel driveway, digging grooves in the rocks as she tried to resist. "I'll tell them we've been lying," Alice threatened.

William stopped dragging her and yanked her closer so their faces were inches apart. "What?" He hissed.

Alice gasped from William's harshness. "If you don't talk to me," she started breathlessly. "I'll tell everyone we lied about where to look for my dad. I'll tell them you made me lie to them about what I saw in the Grey. I'll tell them you drugged me."

"You wouldn't."

"Then talk to me."

"I don't have time."

"Then take me with you."

He growled under his breath, his fingertips gripping deeper into the flesh of her arm. She winced from the pain. There was a moment of hesitation where Alice thought he was going to physically force her back inside.

"Get in the car," he demanded and pushed her towards the passenger door.

She stumbled on her feet and nearly threw herself into the car before he changed his mind. He got into the driver's seat, a solemn darkness washed over his face, his eyes fixated ahead of him. He kept the headlights off as he crept his car down the driveway. Once they were on the main road, he sped off.

Alice wrung her hands in her lap as William drove through the night. Her head jerked forward and back each time William roughly switched gears. He wouldn't look at her. "You drugged me," she said.

He ignored her.

"You're just like them."

William finally looked over at her, scowling. "No, Alice, I'm not."

She could feel how angry he was. It chilled the air around them. His anger was different from his brother's. While Leander was impulsive and fiery, William's anger was sharp, lethal, and cold. Not something she expected to feel from someone who had been so warm and compassionate over these past few weeks.

"I knew this," he waved his hand, "would happen if you knew where I was going. I hoped to leave before you woke up. Then the others arrived back at the cabin much earlier than expected, and I couldn't leave until they were all in bed or I'd risk being questioned by them."

"Why, though?"

"Because it's not safe, like I told you before. And I knew you wouldn't take no for an answer."

"My dad wouldn't hurt me." She tried to convince herself, even though the memories of the house fire and the blood dripping down his chin still haunted her.

William held a grave expression. "Oh, but he would."

"You don't know that."

"He's killed enough people to make him invincible,

which brings him to the edge of darkness. I doubt he has any humanity left."

"Then why face him alone?" Alice choked. "If he's so strong, so dangerous, how can you possibly believe you can capture him? What if my tincture isn't enough?"

"I have a plan." William sighed. "What do you think I've been working on all this time?"

"Oh I don't know," Alice scoffed. "It's not like you tell me anything anymore."

"Because this wasn't supposed to involve you," he paused and looked at her with a pained expression. "It couldn't, because I didn't want you to get hurt. But now I have to improvise."

She didn't know how far they drove, but they had been in the car for about an hour going back west towards the river. William turned down a few narrow residential streets and parked on the side of the road under some trees.

"Stay in the car," William said as he got out and grabbed his book bag from the back seat.

Alice unbuckled her seatbelt to get out. She couldn't be left behind, no matter how dangerous her father was supposed to be. She had to be there. To see him. To help him.

William was faster than she was. He rounded the car and pushed her back into the seat. "I said stay."

"I can help. He'll recognize me."

"That's exactly why I need you to stay here." He braced himself against the roof of the car as he hovered over her, barricading her inside with his body. "I don't need to be babysitting you."

"Please," Alice said. "Please let me come with you." She was desperate. She wanted to see her father, and something within her told her she needed to be there.

"Don't make me force you to stay, Alice," he threatened, about to close the car door on her.

"Wait! The vision from the Grey," she said, looking up at the night sky. "In my vision, the stars were like this, and it was a full moon, just like tonight." The words tumbled out of her mouth. "And you were hurt, remember? What if you need me? I think I'm supposed to be there."

William exhaled, tapping his fingers on the roof of the car as he considered it. "If you come with me," he began, eerily calm as he stared down at her. "I need you to remember this was your choice."

"Fine."

"And you must do as I say."

"I'll do anything."

William stepped aside and finally let her out. He slung his bag over his shoulder and led her down the dark street. There were houses to the right and a few warehouse-like buildings on the left. Alice saw signage for Riverside Marina and some boats parked on trailers along the fence.

They passed more boats which were dry docked on the left and some more warehouses for boat storage on the right. At the end of the road was a dead end, and to their left was a simple wooden barrier gate blocking off a gravel road with a sign that said Amico Island Park. William was tall enough to hoist himself over the gate, while Alice had to crouch down underneath it.

The gravel road went on for a little bit until it opened up to a narrow parking area. It was almost pitch black, but there was a bit of moonlight streaming through the tree branches overhead. Alice inched closer to William.

"How do you know he'll be here tonight?" she asked, shivering. Even though it was technically the first day of spring, it was freezing in the middle of the night.

"I didn't at first," he said. "But your visions from the Grey made me believe otherwise."

"Did you bring a flashlight?" she asked. They started down a dirt hiking path which was even more obscured by trees and brush. "Or can you use your fire to light the way?"

"I don't want to draw attention."

Alice looped her arm through his, getting as close as she possibly could without impeding their ability to walk. It was more quiet in the forest than Alice expected. There were no crickets chirping or sounds of frogs or nocturnal birds. There was barely the sound of rustling leaves, just the soft shuffling of their footsteps on the dirt and the faint rippling of water nearby. Alice could even hear her own heart pounding in her ears.

"Why is it so quiet?" she whispered.

"He must be near. Creatures can sense him."

It reminded Alice of an old myth she heard long ago while hiking in the Appalachian Mountains with her father. The forest should be teeming with the sounds of life, even in the dead of night. If it was silent, it meant danger. It meant a predator was near, such as bears, bobcats, or wolves. According to local legend down south, it could be something worse, like a cryptid that stalked humans in the night.

As they descended deeper in the forest, she recognized the area from her vision. She sucked in a breath. Her eyes frantically scanned the area, trying to spot any sign of movement. She prayed to whatever god above that her father hadn't devolved into some sort of a predator, like the terrible creature she saw in the Grey. She prayed he still had some humanity left, enough humanity to recognize his daughter and trust her to save him.

The trees became a little less dense, and it looked like

they were on some kind of peninsula that stuck out into a harbor along the river. The path came to a point ahead of them before switching back to the right and looping around through some more trees. In the distance she saw the Philadelphia skyline across the river. That must be where the rocky ledge was, and her father might be waiting on the beach below.

Alice gripped William's arm with a shivering hand. "That's it," she whispered. "That's where I saw my dad." Her chest tightened with anticipation.

His response was a quiet grunt as he led her away in the opposite direction. Alice stumbled, their feet moving off the path and into the tall weeds and undergrowth. The shadowy outlines of a few large boulders became clearer, and in some areas she was able to see the carved whorls etched in the stone in the moonlight.

William guided her over to the largest boulder, the one by the largest tree and the bed of white flowers, the forget-me-nots which were blooming a little early for the season. He tossed his bag to the ground and knelt next to it, digging through and pulling out some tiny glass jars, a metal flask, and his small notebook. Alice knelt with him, peering over his shoulder as he reviewed a couple pages.

"Aren't we going down to the beach?" she whispered. "That's where my dad is supposed to be."

"I'm going down to the beach," he said without looking at her. "You're staying here. Out of sight."

Before Alice could argue, the sound of something ruffling through the brush caught their attention. William gripped her shoulder and pushed her to hide behind the rock. But when William stood up to leave, he froze. There was another figure there now, standing in shadow a few paces away.

CHAPTER 22

"You came," said a raspy voice, like they had been strangled. It sounded familiar, but hollow. Empty. Hopeless. The sound of it broke Alice"s heart.

William took a moment to give Alice a threatening look over his shoulder, forbidding her from moving or making a sound. She was so frightened she didn't dare disobey, because if that truly was her father lurking in the shadow, he could be feral and unpredictable.

"Of course I came," William said gently, hiding a flask behind his back.

The shadowy figure shambled closer. His elbows bent awkwardly at his sides, and his spindly hands dangled like limp claws. When he was positioned in a beam of moonlight, Alice could finally see his hollowed features. He looked like a living skeleton. There was barely any muscle left on his bones and no color left on his skin. No life. Just dull, ashen grey. The raggedy clothes he wore hung like oversized drapes on his small frame. His face, gaunt with sunken eyes. But there was something left in his eyes, some sort of emotion. A very human emotion. Despair.

Alice cupped a hand over her mouth to silence herself. When her father was in the throes of his cancer treatments, she thought he had looked terrible. Thin, frail, and weak. But this was even worse. His body looked like a bag of bones, barely held together by paper thin skin, and there was some sort of darkness floating around him, the air almost crackling with sinister energy.

"You sure this'll work?" her father asked, his voice trembling as he wrung his hands.

William nodded and handed him the flask. "First, you'll have to drink this."

Benjamin frowned as he unscrewed the cap with a disgusted look on his face. "You know the last time you made me drink something it ended badly."

"Do you want to get better?"

"Of course I do," Ben hissed, wrath flashing in his eyes.

"Trust me."

Ben scowled. "I've been trusting you this entire time." He wavered for a few seconds before he chugged whatever was inside the flask. He doubled over with a coughing fit and clutched his neck. "It burns..." He sputtered up blood into his hand. "W-what... what is this?"

"Dad!" Alice scrambled out from her hiding place behind the boulder. Her father hunched over again, coughing up more blood.

Alice reached out a hand to touch him on the shoulder, but she paused, unsure. This was her father, and he didn't seem that feral or dangerous. She took a deep steadying breath and gently touched his frail upper arm. Ben jolted, shocked from the comfort, and settled when he realized it was his daughter.

"Alice," her father whispered, blood-tinged spit dribbling down his chin. "What's going on?" Benjamin wiped his face on his dirty sleeve and looked at William. "Why the hell is my daughter here?"

William's face was blank as he considered his next choice of words. "We're here to help you, Ben." He held out his hands, palms up as if to say he wasn't a threat so he wouldn't trigger the darkness within. The shadowy air simmered around Benjamin as his panic and rage increased. A growl rumbled in the professor's chest, suggesting he might actually be a little more feral than Alice first thought.

She backed away from him, but her father didn't move, didn't attack. Alice rubbed her forehead, trying to put together the pieces. "How do you know each other?" She clenched her teeth, body shaking as her nervousness boiled over into anger.

Ben took a wavering step towards Alice. "How do *you* know each other?" He pointed his gnarled finger between his daughter and William. "Does she know about me? About... what we did?" He wrung his hands again.

"What did you do?" Her quiet voice trembled. "William, what did you do?"

"William?" Benjamin blinked, confused.

"Alice... listen..." William's chest rose and fell with heavy breaths. He reached for her hand and grimaced when she recoiled.

"Alexander is one of my old students," her father started, his voice even more raw than before, blood still dripping out of his mouth. "He's helping me."

"Alexander?" Alice narrowed her eyes at William as the story unraveled. "One of your old students?"

"Yeah," Ben said, scratching his almost bald head where only a few wisps of hair remained. "He helped me decode that old book I found. There was a recipe in there, an elixir. Alexander said it would help me get better and—"

"You..." Alice hissed. "You did this to my dad?" Her hands curled into fists as she stomped forward, and this time it was William's turn to recoil.

"I was trying to help," William said, holding his hands up.

"You turned him into a murderer!" Alice yelled as she jabbed her finger into William's chest. "You ruined his life." Her voice got louder. "You ruined both of our lives! You liar!" She pushed against his chest as a sob escaped her lips. Her fury was uncontrollable as her fists pounded into him. He barely stumbled, her desperate wrath no match for his strength.

Something broke within William, his blank mask of innocence morphing into blatant disgust. He rolled his eyes with an annoyed groan as his hand snatched one of Alice's thin wrists. He yanked. Hard. She fell over from the force. Before she could steady herself, dirt exploded beneath her feet as tree roots burst from the ground, whipping dangerously before they twisted around both of Alice's wrists, ensnaring her and pulling her down until her face slammed into the dirt. She couldn't even scream before another thick vine wrapped itself around her neck, almost closing off her windpipe. Her legs kicked until they too were tied down to the earth.

"Alice!" Benjamin cried, followed by a series of hacking coughs. "Alexander, what—" He was interrupted by a roaring burst of flames.

Alice craned her neck to try and see, but the tree roots gnawed against her skin. Her father stumbled backwards into a large tree as he shouted confused curses, shielding himself from a billowing plume of fire erupting from William's hand.

Alice writhed against her earthen restraints, her screams stuck in her throat. William promised he wouldn't hurt her father. He promised to help him.

With another flick of his wrist, William magicked more roots to burst from the ground. They twisted around Benjamin's body until he was tied to the tree, the final root coiling around his neck to silence him.

Now that they were both silenced and immobilized, William let his arms go slack at his sides. He rolled his neck with an exasperated sigh and ran a hand through his hair. He knelt down to pick up a small glass vial from next to his bag and carried it over to Ben. William allowed the root strangling Ben's neck to loosen.

"Let her go," Ben croaked as he struggled to free himself, his strength minimized from the first concoction he was given moments ago. Blood stained his chin. He was supposed to be invincible, and yet whatever internal injury he suffered, it wasn't healing. "Alexander, why—"

"It's William actually," he said, his face unflinching. "Alexander is my middle name."

"W-why lie?"

"To protect my identity, considering the amount of murders that happened because of this elixir. I didn't need anyone tracking me down if someone caught wind of what we did."

Benjamin coughed up blood. "I thought you were going to help me."

"I am helping you. So is Alice. You can thank her for creating the tincture you drank. It made this much easier."

Her father looked at her with confused and devastated eyes. Alice wished she could cry out, tell him that she never intended on hurting him, that the tincture was only meant to slow him down, that she had nothing to do with whatever William was planning. She wished she could strangle William for betraying her. For harming her father. For making her seem like she was part of this.

"What?" Ben asked as he spit out even more blood. "How... how is this supposed to help?"

"You have to trust me," William said. He clutched Ben's jaw with his fingers, prying his mouth open to tip another tincture inside. "Now drink." His hand covered Ben's mouth until he reluctantly swallowed.

Muddy tears streamed down Alice's face as she watched helplessly, her body limp from exhaustion. Had this been another example of what William meant when he didn't want her to see the terrible things he did? Did he lie this entire time so Alice wouldn't find out it was him who damned her father to this fate? Is this what he meant when he said he was trying to make things right? But how could this be right when he was causing so much pain?

Benjamin's body slackened against his restraints, his sunken eyes drooped with sudden fatigue. William crouched down, placing his hands on the earth in front of the patch of flowers and the boulder with carved whorls, and with a pulse of magic the weeds, brush, and flowers slithered back. The greenery retreated into the ground and disappeared until there was only dirt. His fingers slid into the earth, and slowly it started to recede, forming a crater in the ground that grew wider and deeper in a matter of seconds.

When William seemed satisfied, he knelt there as he assessed his work. It was hard to discern the size of it, but if Alice had to guess, it was about six feet deep.

Her father didn't stir. His head lolled forward, and his

chest barely moved. This felt wrong. It didn't look like William was helping him at all. She tried to break free again, but to no avail. Her struggling drew William's attention.

His face softened when he looked at her, apologetic even. He moved and crouched down next to her, taking her chin in his hand. "Remember, Alice, this was your choice." His voice was a whisper. His eyes, empty.

She groaned, trying to get enough air. She wasn't suffocating, not yet. Her neck would be bruised and scathed in the morning. If she made it until morning. The trust she had for William was gone, only to be replaced with loathing and terror.

William emptied bottles and jars and sachets into the hole in the ground, occasionally checking his watch or the position of the moon and stars in the sky. He stood in front of her father, grasping under his jaw to tilt up his face to inspect Ben's reaction to the last concoction.

"I-I feel... different. Are you... helping me?" Ben asked breathlessly. "Is it almost over?"

William's mouth pulled into a thin line. "Yes, it's almost over." He searched Ben's pockets, fishing for something.

"And Alice, is she okay?" Her father struggled to lift his head to search for her. "Why did you—"

"For her protection," William said.

Alice didn't feel like she was being protected.

"Alexander— I mean, William..." Ben whispered, struggling to catch his breath. "Thank you... for everything. For trying to save me. For being my friend."

Alice didn't know how the two of them could be friends. Perhaps William had only meant to give her father the elixir with the intent to cure his cancer. They had said before that this time around, the elixir's effects were worsened due to being completed incorrectly. Perhaps William originally had her father's best interests in mind and things unfortunately got more complicated. And perhaps all the lies were woven to protect Alice from it all as William tried to fix everything.

There was only silence as William kept his gaze locked on his feet. He had something in his hands, whatever he had found in her father's pockets. Silver flashed in the moonlight. "I'm sorry this didn't turn out the way we planned," William said as he finally looked up at Ben.

"It's okay…" It seemed like it was getting more difficult for Ben to speak, subdued and weakened by the second concoction William made him drink. "What else do I have to do?"

William exhaled a huff of air, twirling the silver object in his hands, a knife. He took the blade, hooked it under the collar of Ben's shirt and sliced, ripping the fabric right down the middle and exposing his sunken chest, his rib cage protruding underneath his skin.

"This next part you won't like," William said. "I'm sorry." He pointed the tip of the knife at Ben's sternum.

"What do you mean? D-do you need my blood?" Benjamin asked, his eyes darting between the knife and William's face.

"No," William paused. "I need your heart."

"M-m-my what?"

Alice tried to scream, but her throat burned in pain. Cutting out an immortal's heart would kill him. He'd promised not to kill her father. He promised. *He promised.*

She squirmed harder, thrashing on the ground. Tears and snot poured out of her face. The most noise she could make was a muffled screech inside her chest, but even then she ran out of air too quickly.

"Keep quiet," William said through gritted teeth. His hand stretched out to her without looking, and suddenly she felt the roots tightening around her even more. She whimpered from the pain and the fear of suffocation.

"Please," Ben croaked. "D-don't hurt her. Just... tell me what I need to do."

William turned back to him. "You don't need to do anything else, my friend." William placed his hands on Ben's shoulders, still clutching the silver knife in his fist.

"If I'm immortal, what will happen when you—" Ben gulped. "When you take my heart?"

"You'll be free of this curse."

"I will? How?"

Alice was somehow able to loosen the roots constricting her neck enough for her to speak. "He'll kill you," She coughed. "Daddy, if he cuts out your heart you'll die." The roots instantly tightened on her neck again, causing her to gag.

"What?" Ben struggled against his restraints as panic filled him once more. "You said you'd help me. You said you were looking for a cure." Tears fell from his eyes. "You promised to save me."

"There is no cure, Ben. I'm sorry."

Alice's heart shattered. There was no cure. This entire time, William was supposed to be searching for a way to reverse the elixir's effects, lying through his teeth about his intent, whispering promises into Alice's ear.

"You liar!" she choked out. "You've been drugging me, manipulating me—"

William grumbled under his breath. He checked his watch, rubbing his forehead as his annoyance increased. He knelt down next to Alice and pressed the point of the knife under her chin. "There are other ways people can be manipulated, Alice," he whispered, eyebrow arched. "No need to use herbs or drugs when someone like you is so easily convinced by other means." The roots tightened around her neck and another wrapped around her face, gagging her mouth. "Now shut up."

"W-why?" Ben pleaded as William returned to stand in front of him. "Why lie about... the c-cure?" Ben sobbed. "About everything?"

"You were going to die anyway." William pressed the knife against Ben's chest. "I'm sorry, but I needed you."

"And I needed you!" Ben cried with labored breaths, his consciousness fading. "You were my friend, and... you did this to me. You destroyed my life, my d-daughter's life."

"Alice only has herself to blame for getting in the way," he said with a clenched jaw. "I do care about you, Benjamin. Your story broke my heart when we first met last year."

"You mean you're not one of my old students?"

"No, I'm afraid not. I had been on campus looking for that book, but you found it first." William checked his watch again and looked up at the sky. "I truly am sorry, Ben." He moved the point of the knife, settling it in the hollow between two of his lower ribs.

Alice tried to scream, cry out, thrash around until she was free, anything to stop William from killing her father. "Please," she choked. "William..." She couldn't get any air. "You promised." Her sobs were stuck in her throat.

"It'll be alright," her father whispered, tears streaming down his face. "Look away, Little Bug," his voice trembled. "Look away..."

William plunged the knife into her father's chest. Alice squeezed her eyes shut, face pressed into the ground, but she couldn't escape the sound of her dying father's gasp, the cracking of his ribs, the choking sound of blood filling his lungs.

She couldn't breathe, her struggle asphyxiating her even more. Blood pounded in her ears and her lips tingled. Her vision tunneled into nothing but blackness as she fainted.

Moments later she came to, sweat dappling her forehead. She craned her bound neck to check the scene. William stood with her father's quivering heart in his hand, dripping with hot blood, and dropped it into the hole. When William stepped away, he revealed her father's body still tethered to the tree, slumped over with his rib cage cracked open and a huge cavity where his heart had been.

Bile burned up her throat as dizziness washed over her again. She clenched her eyes closed, but all she could see was the horrific image of her father's mutilated body in her mind's eye, burned into the back of her eyelids forever.

The clinking of bottles and shuffling of feet through the brush made her look up again to try and figure out what William was doing. With a long tree branch in his hand, he drew a circle in the dirt around himself. He sprinkled some dry herbs around the circumference. Then he sat, cross-legged with elbows on his knees, his hands steepled and resting on his chin, his eyes fixated on the hole in the ground.

A hollow screech sounded from inside, then clicking and gnawing, like heavily grinding teeth, followed by haggard drawn breaths. Withered hands reached out of the hole and clawed at the earth. Torn dress sleeves and ribbons of dead skin hung from wrists of bone which bent unnaturally as they worked to hoist the body upwards. The crown of a pale skull covered in strings of dried hair broke the surface next.

A long-nailed, atrophic hand seized at the collar of

William's shirt. He yelped, utterly shaken as he scrambled backwards. The circle on the ground must've been for protection. And apparently, it did not work.

"Wait!" William cried as he floundered away from the creature, unable to get to his feet. He backed into a tree, heels digging into the ground, and held out his hand to defend himself.

The corpse dragged itself towards William. Dirty tattered clothing and the remains of putrid flesh hung from its bones. The chattering and grinding of teeth continued. Fear seemed to paralyze William as it crawled nearer. He dug wildly into his pocket and then displayed a small wooden trinket, a carving of a bird. "Look!" his voice was pleading, breathless. "Look, I've kept it all this time."

The corpse cocked its skull sideways in curiosity, examining the trinket. It snatched the wooden bird delicately between its boned fingertips, turning it slowly. "Will-iam..." it said with a rattling breath.

The drawl of the creature's raspy voice caused ripples of goosebumps to erupt over Alice's skin. She no longer struggled to get free, and instead she didn't dare to move or make a sound, afraid to draw attention. The creature looked like those dead, but not quite dead, possessed women they had encountered before. This one though, it looked like it had actually been dead for a long time, somehow awakened by a ritual which required her father's immortal heart.

"Y-yes..." William whispered. "It's me. Victoria, it's me. William." He touched his hand to his chest. "Do you remember?"

Victoria. His dead fiancée. Now undead. She inhaled another ragged breath and released a groan, teeth grinding as she studied him. She nodded. "Will-iam," she croaked again, the tiny wooden figurine clutched in her boney hand.

"I'm sorry, I..." he stuttered, looking her up and down. "This didn't turn out exactly how I had hoped." William was on his knees now, both of his hands reaching towards her but not quite touching her, like he was disgusted by her corpse-like appearance. "You were supposed to be fully formed."

Victoria reached a gangly finger up to his face and stroked his cheek. Alice saw him gulp as he tried not to recoil. He was revulsed by the thing touching him, his supposed fiancée, but there was also something like grief and longing in his eyes.

"Don't worry, I'll help you," he said, breathless. His eyes darted back and forth as he thought. "You have the heart of an immortal, so in order to become fully formed, all you would need is..." William paused, his eyes finally settling back on Alice. "Blood." Only for a second did regret flash in his eyes before he pointed in her direction. "There."

Alice gasped, getting a face full of dirt as she tried to scream, still gagged and bound. The undead Victoria turned. Alice was stricken with bubbling fear as her gaze locked with the gaping black holes where eyes should have been, holes which bore into Alice's soul. Victoria lifted her fragile frame to a standing position, hunched forward with crooked shoulders. She shambled towards Alice, who struggled against the tree roots ensnaring her.

"William," Alice wheezed through the gag. "Stop... please..."

"I'm sorry, Alice," he said. "You chose this." William sat on his knees, watching with a blank expression on his face, his throat bobbing with suppressed emotion, implying maybe he actually did care for her in some way. Just not enough. Because he chose Victoria over her. He chose to lie and kill her father to bring back his dead fiancée. He never cared for Alice. How could he if he was about to let her die?

The foul smell of rotting flesh got stronger as Victoria closed the gap between them, her stained and tattered funeral dress dragging behind her. She hunched over Alice's body, their faces inches apart. Alice gazed into the black nothingness beyond the empty eye sockets. Rancid breath swirled around them as the creature examined her prey. Her skeletal hand gripped Alice's shoulder and yellowed fingernails punctured her skin. A helpless scream was caught in Alice's throat as hot pain throbbed from the fresh wounds on her shoulder.

Victoria pulled back her blood-coated fingers, lifted them to her mouth, and dipped them between her teeth. Her graying skin wriggled and crawled over her bones, like it was stretching out to cover more of her, reforming her. A swath of thin skin covered the sunken eye holes for a moment until it peeled back to reveal two glassy white eyeballs which had formed where there was nothing but blackness before.

Alice screeched as Victoria's claws were on her again, this time gripping her neck, tighter and tighter until they punctured her skin once more. Victoria squeezed, constricting her airway completely, threatening to slice through Alice's jugular.

She was going to die.

Alice closed her eyes. This time, she was ready, because she had nothing left to live for.

CHAPTER 23

A sweltering burst of flame catapulted Victoria off of Alice and into a crumpled heap of bones beside her. The roots binding Alice slackened. She clutched her neck, blood pouring through her fingers. Spots clouded her vision as she tried to sit up. The world spun around her. Where was Victoria? William? Who else was there? Was someone screaming?

Alice dragged herself out of the tangle of roots, unable to staunch the wound. Her eyesight darkened. She was losing too much blood, so much it was turning the dirt to mud beneath her. Victoria must've hit a main artery.

Two rough hands grabbed her shoulders, and Alice screamed. The person shook her. "Stay with me, girl." It was Arthur. "Keep your eyes open."

He hauled her behind a tree and laid her on the ground as shouting and cursing continued behind them. Alice's blurry vision swirled, and she broke into a cold sweat. Arthur pressed something cool and sticky on her neck, some sort of poultice to control the bleeding. He forced a gulp of liquid down her throat. It tasted different from the healing tea, thick and bitter and metallic.

Alice retched, but kept it down. Whatever was in the flask began to take effect, immediately improving her vision and dulling the pain. Alice rolled on her side, propping herself up on a shaking elbow. In the middle of the clearing was Natalie, covered in blood from scratches and bite marks, grappling with Victoria's regenerating corpse. New patches of skin stretched over her reformed muscles, and her pale cracked lips were smeared with blood.

Victoria swiped her nails down Natalie's face, slashing her from brow to lip. Natalie retaliated with a burst of flame which Victoria easily evaded. She was faster now, like Marie had been, scrambling across the ground on all fours like a wild animal, dodging the tree roots Natalie was summoning in attempt to restrain her.

"Arthur!" Natalie hollered as she stumbled backwards away from Victoria, wiping the fresh blood from her wounded face. "I need you!"

"Stay," Arthur ordered at Alice through gritted teeth. "Drink all of this if you want to survive." He shoved the flask into her weak hand. "Don't give up," he said as he gripped her shoulder before running off to assist Natalie.

Alice's lip quivered as she forced herself to drink the remainder of the disgusting thick liquid. She tucked her face in the crook of her elbow to prevent herself from throwing up. A strange buzzing feeling tingled its way up her body, starting from her toes and fingertips. When the sensation reached her head, her vision spun around her so violently she had to squeeze her eyes shut to maintain composure. And then, it all stopped. The dizziness, the buzzing, the throbbing pain in her neck. Her eyes shot open, and she drew in a gasping breath. She felt like she had woken up refreshed after a long night's sleep.

Her fingers clawed at the poultice and ripped it off. When she felt the skin of her neck, it was healed. Completely. Every open wound on her body was healed. Every ache and pain. Gone. Any ounce of tiredness was wiped away. She felt energized, as if she could run for miles. A fire had come to life inside her, roaring with vigor.

Alice scrambled to her feet, her brain swirling as she tried to think of how to help. Arthur and Natalie wrestled with Victoria on the ground. William barreled out of the brush, arm extended and erupting flames in their direction. Leander rushed out after him, launching himself at his brother, causing both of them to tumble over. Leander, with teeth bared in fury, fisted William's hair and pushed his brother's face in the dirt.

Victoria managed to wriggle free from Arthur and Natalie, leaving them on their knees clutching at their wounds, and she thundered across the clearing at Leander, galloping like some skeletal beast. She barreled into him with a snarl, knocking him off of William.

Alice stood frozen in place, suddenly reminded of her frail humanity as she watched them all continue to fight despite their mortal wounds. She felt helpless. Whatever she drank healed her and gave her strength, but she didn't know if it would protect her from further harm. Her eyes fell on her father's limp corpse still bound to the tree, and white hot rage bloomed inside her. Her gaze snapped to William with the taste of revenge on her lips.

As William tried to get to his feet, Alice threw her entire body weight against him, and they slammed into the earth. She had no idea how to gauge her newfound strength. But she didn't care. She wanted to hurt him.

"Alice, don't!" Leander yelled with a strangled voice as he struggled with Victoria.

She ignored him. Her hands gripped William's throat, and his eyes flared in shock as he registered how strong she was. Before he could even fight back, Victoria grabbed Alice by the ankle and yanked her off William. Her face smacked into the ground.

"Get away from him," Victoria said with a snarl as she dragged Alice across the clearing. Alice's fingers tore at the dirt, trying to gain purchase but with no luck. Victoria was so much stronger.

Leander ran towards them, but was cut off by William, who pinned him to the ground and started punching him in the face. Leander eventually gained the upper hand and pushed William over onto his back, straddled him, and returned the punches. Flames engulfed them as the brothers tried to burn and singe one another with each fiery punch, scorching their clothes and leaving fresh burns on their skin.

Alice kicked herself free and rolled over. Victoria hovered above her, looking more corporeal from the taste of immortal blood. Her hair thickened and began to regain its deep shade of red. Her skin turned from ashen to ivory, dusted with freckles and flushed with life. Her dirty, ragged dress hung from her newly formed, very alive body. Her clouded white eyes had turned to their original shade of blue, flashing with hatred.

As she scrambled backwards, Alice saw both brothers paused mid-fight, shocked at Victoria's new appearance. William's mouth was agape with adoration and disbelief as he beheld his lover's reformed body. Leander used the distraction to overpower William and tied his wrists behind his back with an inscribed leather strap.

Seeing William in danger once more, Victoria hurled herself at Leander, his own eyes flashing wide like saucers as he took in her fully regenerated form, like he had seen a ghost from his past. Except she was real. Alive. Over a hundred years later, like not a day had gone by to age her. No indication she spent the past century dead in the ground besides her threadbare clothing.

Victoria had her hands on Leander's neck, nails sharp enough to slice open his skin. He stiffened from the shock, unable to fight back. Arthur had regained some of his strength and ran to him, trying to wrench Victoria away.

William freed himself from his leather bindings and was on his way to defend his fiancée when Natalie interfered. She held up a quivering arm, gushing blood from a gnarly bite wound, and used whatever ounce of energy left to blast fire into William's face, knocking him back. William pulled himself to his feet and sent his own flames clashing with Natalie's, causing a pillar of fire to go shooting upwards into the sky, illuminating the forest clearing like daylight.

William charged at Natalie and slammed her to the ground. "Leave her alone," he threatened, squeezing Natalie's neck as she thrashed under him. "You know I'm stronger."

She spit in his face. "You bastard!"

He slapped her.

Natalie screeched and clawed at him.

Alice grabbed William by the shoulders and yanked him off Natalie with what little extra strength she had left. Whatever type of concoction she drank, the magical effects weren't lasting very long. William called on his magic, roots and vines bursting from the ground, ensnaring Alice once again.

A glint of silver flashed through the air as Natalie dove

at William's back and stabbed him in the left shoulder with his knife. He howled, back arching from the pain, before gripping the hilt of the knife and yanking it out. His fist flew through the air, catching the side of Natalie's face. She reeled backwards, and the back of her head slammed into one of the huge boulders. She sucked in a breath from the impact, rolled over on her hands and knees, and vomited from the concussion. It was an injury that would've killed any mortal.

William struggled to regain his footing as he headed for Victoria, who had left Arthur and Leander groaning and bleeding on the ground. William fell to his knees before his fiancée, and she knelt with him as they embraced.

"Victoria," he whispered into her hair.

"You brought me back," Victoria cried, clinging to him.

"I couldn't live without you." William cupped her face and pulled her lips to his.

"William," she whispered between kisses. "Oh William, I—" Victoria's voice was cut off with a choking gag as a leather strap was thrown over her head and tightened around her neck.

Arthur had snuck up on them, strangling Victoria as he pulled her off William. She sputtered in panic, kicking up chunks of dirt and grass. William froze, mouth agape. But when he regained his senses and tried to hoist himself up, Arthur pulled a centuries-old pistol from his belt holster and shot William in the shoulder, causing him to collapse backwards.

The gunshot echoed through the clearing, leaving a deadening silence besides Victoria's whimpering as Arthur continued to drag her by her red hair, the strap securely tied around her neck, weakening her from the sigils burned in the leather. He forced her to get on her knees and held her steady by her hair as she sobbed.

"P-please..." Victoria begged in her strangled voice, fingers clawing at her neck attempting to loosen the strap. "I don't want to be dead."

Leander stumbled over to William, who was clutching the gunshot wound on his shoulder, and forced him onto his stomach to retie his wrists behind his back with the leather bindings. With William's magic and strength diminished, Alice's restraints were loosened, and she scrambled free.

"Let her go," William grumbled into the ground. "Victoria..."

Arthur fumbled with something in his other hand, something white and glinting in the moonlight. William thrashed harder, trying to free himself to get to his fiancée. "Please... don't..." he cried.

"William!" Victoria screamed. "Will—"

"No!" The choking sob that escaped William's mouth was silenced when Arthur's arm whipped around, the white blade aimed for the undead woman's chest. For her heart.

Victoria twisted at the very last moment, her hand catching Arthur's arm under his elbow, causing the white blade to clatter to the earth. She yanked his arm to her mouth and bit down. Hard.

Arthur howled and released his grip on Victoria as blood poured from the deep bite wound. Victoria rounded on him, going in for the kill. He was on the ground, and her claws were on his chest. She was going to rip his heart out with her bare hands.

Without thinking, Alice catapulted herself at Victoria, and the two of them tumbled in the dirt. Victoria pinned Alice to the ground, a sinister smile playing on her perfect lips as one hand gripped Alice's neck while the other aimed for her ribcage.

Alice flailed beneath her, one hand clawing at Victoria's wrist, trying to pull her hand off her neck, while Alice's other hand grasped at anything she could use as a weapon. Her fingertips touched cool metal. Alice squeezed the brass eagle pommel as tightly as she could as she swung it around and thrust it up into Victoria's chest.

Victoria's mouth gaped open as she spit up blood. It dribbled down Alice's arms and soaked her shirt. Alice pushed the blade further into Victoria's chest, just to be certain she hit the right mark. Victoria croaked out a gasp. Her once flushed pink skin turned pale and ashen. Her hair became dull and brittle. Her muscles withered. Her blue eyes faded to the cloudy white of death.

With an exhausted shove, Alice pushed Victoria's limp body off of her. She sat up, her entire body trembling, as she looked down at her blood-soaked hands and arms and clothes. She could even taste the tang of blood on her lips. There was wailing in the background, but Alice could barely hear anything through the ringing in her ears. She felt dizzy. Sick. She'd killed someone. On purpose. Even though Victoria had already been dead. Alice was a murderer, like everyone else.

Natalie rushed to Alice's side, kneeling next to her and touching her shoulder. "It's okay," Natalie said with a quaking voice. Leander was soon at her other side, his hand cupping the back of her head.

"Alice, look at me," Leander said breathlessly. "You're okay. Everything is going to be fine."

Her mind reeled, and her gaze was blank. She couldn't feel anything. She felt detached from her body. Numb. Alice stared at Leander, her eyes wide and empty, and then she focused her attention on William. He remained in a fetal position on the ground, his wrists bound behind his back. His ankles were bound as well.

"Victoria..." William whimpered and sniffled, his entire body shivering with sobs. Alice had never seen such a pathetic expression of emotion from him.

Arthur hovered over William and glared down at his crumpled form. He used the toe of his boot to push William onto his back. William let him. He didn't care.

"I had her back," William cried. "Why did you take her from me?"

No words of consolation were spoken. Arthur grabbed William by the collar of his shirt and forced him to his knees. "I have no sympathy for the dead."

"B-but," William stuttered, his head hung forward, hair falling and covering his eyes. "I brought her back. She was alive."

"She was dead and should've stayed dead, boy. A product of necromancy will attract all sorts of dark things that don't belong here." Arthur yanked the white blade from Victoria's chest and spun it around to offer the hilt to Leander. "It's your decision."

Leander considered the gesture before taking the dagger. The two men shared a knowing look. Leander stood up rigidly, the dagger limp in his hand. He took a deep breath and swallowed before facing his brother.

Arthur crouched down with the girls to check their injuries. Natalie pulled her own flask from her pocket and chugged whatever was inside. She made a disgusted face as she wiped her mouth on her sleeve and offered the flask to Arthur who took a couple swigs. Alice didn't need it though. There must've been some lingering magic from the previous concoction she drank earlier since it had healed her newer wounds already.

Leander headed towards William. A knot formed in Alice's throat. She watched him fiddle with the white blade as he grappled with the terrible choice he was about to make. He was going to kill his brother.

"Don't look," Arthur said to Alice, adjusting himself to block her view. Natalie kept staring, wide eyed and unable to look away.

Alice tried to look around Arthur's shoulder. William, his face contorted in disgust and sorrow, looked up at Leander.

"Do it," William said through his teeth. "You'll finally be rid of me."

"Look at me," Arthur said as he grabbed Alice's chin. She struggled against him, trying to watch. "Look at me! Leander's going to do what he needs to do." His face softened. "You've seen enough death."

The idea made Alice's stomach lurch, but she still couldn't stop herself from trying to watch the scene unfold. William spent over a year poisoning her father's mind and soul, turning him into some evil murderous being, only to use him as a pawn to raise his dead fiancée from the grave. He lied to her, to everyone. He made her care for him, whispering half-truths in her ear before taking her in his bed, promising everything would be okay when it was all over. Then he cut out her father's heart.

And yet. *And yet.* Part of her wanted to scream for him, to make Leander stop. To make it all stop. William was so pitiful. His heart so warped and distorted through his pain. The way he clutched Victoria's face, the way he looked into her eyes. He had so desperately needed her. Maybe there was some sort of understanding in his madness, just as there was understanding in her father's madness. She remembered what William had told her, the night she first met him: *Sometimes bad things happen to people who don't deserve it, and they make regrettable choices driven by their grief.*

If Alice had been dying of cancer, or if the love of her life was murdered, what would she do if she knew magic was real? How far would she go? Would she kill? Is it worth taking one life in order to save another? And who was she to judge another's worthiness, to deem whether someone deserved to live or die?

Her father was a killer, and she was ready to forgive him. William was a killer, though she'd never forgive him. But in the end, how were they any different? William had been acting irrationally, driven by grief and obsession. Her father, intoxicated by dark magic. And now Alice, she was a killer too. She killed to defend herself, but a killer all the same.

"Alice," Arthur urged. She continued to resist his grip.

Natalie's eyes were glued to the brothers, who were motionless except for their heaving chests. She chewed her bottom lip and clutched her blood-covered body, like she wanted to interfere but knew she shouldn't. Couldn't. Natalie sat there helpless, watching the man she had once loved, and might still love, grapple with the task of killing his own brother.

"Look away, Alice," Natalie whispered, her voice cracking.

Look away, Little Bug... Her father's last words. Alice choked, unable to hold back her tears. But she couldn't look away, no matter how hard Arthur gripped her chin. She was able to see over his shoulder just enough.

With a grunt, Leander kicked William in the chest, and he fell back. Leander stood over him, one leg on either side of his brother's body and crouched down. The knife slashed down the center of William's ragged shirt, revealing the fresh injuries, including the gunshot wound on his shoulder. William clenched his eyes closed as Leander pointed the tip of the blade on his ribs.

Leander seized William's neck with one hand, and pressed the knife into his skin. William hissed, biting back his scream, his entire body tensing from the pain. But the knife barely dipped lower than the surface of his skin. Leander wasn't stabbing his brother through the heart.

No.

He was carving something into his chest.

CHAPTER 24

Leander dropped the white blade at Arthur's side, his eyes blank. William was left curled in a fetal position, wrists and ankles bound, shivering with quiet sobs. He made no move to escape, like nothing mattered anymore.

"Let's get out of here," Leander said, then went over to where Benjamin's lifeless, disfigured body was still tethered to the tree by roots and vines. He used his magic to release him, caught the man's frail body in his arms, and stood over the open grave Victoria had emerged from. Arthur nodded, and Leander dropped the body into the earth. He collected Victoria's corpse and dropped her in as well.

It was so detached, so inhumane. Emotionless. As if the two bodies that were tossed into the ground were never actually people. Her father. William's fiancée. They had been alive once. No matter what darkness had overtaken them. They laughed once. Smiled once.

"Let's get you home," Arthur said, hooking his arm under Alice's armpit and hoisting her to her wobbling feet. Home. Alice had no home.

Leander stood at the edge of the hole, hand

outstretched over the top. "Would you like to say anything?" He held a pained expression.

She shook her head, clutching her upper arms as she shrank away. No, she couldn't bear it. Not now. She couldn't walk over there and see his broken body unceremoniously dumped in some unmarked grave in a random forest. Because she knew if she got close enough she'd jump right in and ask Leander to put that blade through her heart as well. It was what she deserved.

With a nod, Leander sent a roaring flame into the pit, burning the bodies until they were unidentifiable ash. Alice squinted and cowered away from the blinding intensity of the fire.

"I'll get her to the car," Natalie said as she took over supporting Alice's weight. The after effect of the substance she drank had rendered her even more exhausted than before.

They shambled through the dark forest path in silence, only speaking when Alice stumbled over a rock or needed to stop to readjust her hold on Natalie. The beat up truck was parked askew at the closed gate at the front of the park. Natalie opened the rear door and helped Alice climb in.

"How did you find us?" Alice asked, leaning back in the seat with a groan.

"Leander," Natalie said as she handed Alice a bottle of water. "He heard you arguing outside the cabin, saw you drive off with William. So in a panic, he searched his brother's room to look for clues, which was empty of course, except for a scrap paper forgotten under the desk with a few details about the fortieth parallel. Leander knew immediately where it was."

Alice shuddered as she sipped the water. "He knew Victoria was buried there?"

"No," Natalie said as she opened the hatch of her truck. She tossed a towel to Alice so she could clean the blood off herself. "We had no idea what to expect when we got here. Leander just knew it was a location with strong magic."

The carved whorls on the boulders, the flowers blooming a bit too early for the season, the ring of mature trees, hidden in the back corner of the woodland park. A sacred place along the fortieth parallel. It made sense. Alice wondered if William chose the location on purpose to bury his fiancée. If he had been planning this since the day of her death. It was never about saving her father. It was always about Victoria.

Her hand lightly grazed her neck, the ghost of the pain from her injury still lingering. Another situation where she almost died. "What did Arthur make me drink?"

Natalie came back around to the rear door, standing in front of Alice with her hands on her hips, shifting uncomfortably. "A stronger healing elixir which has more immediate effects. It's only supposed to be used in desperation because of the ingredients and their potential side effects."

Alice hated this. She hated this messed up world of dark magic she had been sucked into. "Great," she sighed, her head falling back against the seat. "Let me guess, the main ingredient is something gross, like blood."

"Unfortunately. And it's gotta be fresh." Natalie shuffled her feet, the guilt radiating off of her. "It was Arthur's blood, since immortal blood has better healing abilities, mixed with some other herbs. Quite difficult to make actually."

Alice wanted to barf, remembering the thick, warm taste of it. Blood magic. Which had terrible consequences. "And the side effects?"

"It's different for everyone, and we rarely ever use it, so we don't really know for sure. Sometimes people get nightmares, visions. They don't last long, maybe a few weeks. And since it's blood magic, it can attract some unwanted attention."

"Wonderful," Alice huffed, closing her eyes. She tried to make sense of Natalie's reasoning, of why they rarely used it. Surely the negative side effects would be worth it if it saved someone's life. Unless the side effects were even worse than she was letting on. It still didn't make sense though, because there were times when they could've used it, and they didn't. Like the possessed woman in the garage. They let her die.

Maybe Alice was being too harsh, too judgmental with not enough facts. Clearly, their decisions weren't as simple as black and white, and they often had to function in the gray area. Maybe Natalie and the others didn't purposely pick and choose who they meant to save. She said the healing elixir was difficult to make, and the blood had to be fresh. How fresh, she didn't know. She didn't want to know. Alice's head throbbed. She was tired of trying to make sense of everything.

"Are you okay?" Natalie asked, offering a soft hand on Alice's upper arm.

Alice swatted her away. "What do you think?"

"I'm sorry you had to go through all of that."

"Yeah. So am I," Alice said dismissively. She didn't want to talk anymore.

Natalie bit her lip. "And I'm sorry I wasn't there for you. For the past few weeks, I noticed you were pulling away, spending all of your time with William. He's such a bastard. I should've known. I should've said something."

"He had everyone fooled," Alice whispered, more to herself. She was the biggest fool of them all. "He convinced me not to trust you. Any of you."

"I'm truly sorry. For everything."

Alice clenched her jaw, holding back her anger. The apology meant nothing to her right now. She had lost too much to care. Everything could've been so different.

The sound of muffled voices grew louder. William was being escorted by Arthur and Leander up the path towards the car. His ankles were unbound, allowing him to walk. His wrists remained tied behind his back. The two other men kept fierce grips on his upper arms to prevent him from escaping.

Natalie growled under her breath as the men drew nearer. She shut all of the doors to the truck, leaving Alice alone in silence. But when Natalie started to raise her voice, Alice could hear bits and pieces of what was said as she argued with Leander.

"...you're not putting him in there with her..."

"...how else are we going to..."

"...he killed her father..."

"...maybe you should've..."

"...don't want to talk about it right now..."

Arthur's booming voice silenced Natalie and Leander. "Put him in the back, and we'll talk about it later."

The back hatch creaked open once again, and Alice heard grunting and grumbling as William was awkwardly pushed into the space between the back seat and the hatch door. There was another groan as William tried to adjust himself into a more comfortable position, his wounds still untreated, bleeding, and not healing as quickly as they should've been for an immortal.

Natalie returned to the driver's seat, Arthur took the front passenger seat, and Leander slid in the back seat with Alice. He had the white blade dagger squeezed in his hand, his knuckles taught as he rested it on his thigh, ready to turn around and use it if William tried anything.

Alice hugged herself as Natalie drove off, her chin tucked down towards her chest. She willed her eyes to stay open, watching as the streetlights passed by the window, because if she closed her eyes, all she saw was death and blood—her body and her hands painted crimson, her father's chest carved open, a corpse come alive with blood dripping from her cracked teeth, blue eyes fading to white.

She drew in a shallow breath, afraid if she breathed too deeply her breaths would turn to sobs. Alice couldn't cry. Not here. Not in front of everyone. Not with William in the back, the reason for all of this mess in the first place. William Alexander Montgomery. He had been so good at pretending this whole time. Not only was she traumatized by violence and loss, but underneath that was heartbreak and broken trust.

Alice leaned back, and her eyes drifted behind the seat. She had an almost perfect view of William's face. His head rested against the hard plastic, rocking back and forth with the sway of the truck, his gaze focused out the back window up at the night sky. The streetlights illuminated his face every so often, the light beaming across his deadened eyes. His skin was coated in crusted blood and dirt, his shirt ripped open and dangling from his shoulders revealing the odd geometric symbol Leander had carved into his chest. But there was nothing on William's face that showed he cared, just the blank emptiness of someone who had given up.

William's eyes slid to hers. Nothing remained in his expression except a short-lived flicker of something she couldn't distinguish. Alice would never know for sure, but she thought it could've been regret. Or hatred. The pain squeezing her heart made her look away.

How her life dissolved into such terror, she didn't know. She never considered herself religious, similar to her father, but she always found herself cursing someone above during her worst times. Because how could so many terrible things keep happening to the same person?

She had even more questions about her beliefs now that she knew about magic and immortality, life and death. There was some sort of unknown power coursing through the veins of the Earth to make these things possible. And from where that power came from, she had no idea. She reckoned the others probably didn't either. If they did, they probably wouldn't tell her.

Anger coiled in her stomach the longer they were all packed in that truck together. Alice hadn't been paying attention to how long they had been driving. She didn't even know what time it was. She knew if she didn't get out of that truck soon, she was going to have a meltdown, either sobbing or screaming.

She balled her fists at her sides to contain her impulse to lunge into the back and strangle William. Leander noticed, his eyes flitting between her clenched fist and her face. He arched an eyebrow at her, as if to inquire if she was alright. She wanted to strangle him too. Of course she wasn't alright. She hadn't been alright for a long time. She grit her teeth so the harsh words wouldn't spill out.

Not only did Alice blame William, but she also blamed Leander. He was supposed to destroy the book. He said so in the vision Alice saw in the Grey. If he had been true to his word, there would have never been a book for her father to find. Her father would've gone on with the remainder of his short life. He would've died from his cancer within the year, but anything was better than this.

It would've been a simple and quiet death for her father. Alice would've grieved in the comfort of her childhood home. Aunt Jane would've come to stay with her again, or her friends could've moved in with her, or she could've moved out west with her extended family instead. It would've been hard, but she would've gotten through it, a chance to start over.

This though, this was a nightmare. Her house burned to the ground, nothing but ash and dust. She was almost mauled to death by the undead multiple times. She was stalked by *vagari* and daemons. She saw death in front of her eyes, caused death with her own hands, horror and gore that no human should ever see.

Leander and William, it was their fault. And she hated them.

CHAPTER 25

Alice didn't leave her room for days, except to use the bathroom, which was mostly in the middle of the night or whenever the house sounded empty in order to avoid everyone. She hadn't even showered since she first arrived back. She had spent an hour sitting in the tub scrubbing off the blood and grime until her skin was raw. Most of her time was spent curled up on the tufted window bench, looking out into the forest or up at the steely sky. It hadn't stopped raining all week.

Trays of food were left at her door three times a day since she refused to let anyone in. She wasn't eating any of it. She didn't care. The only time she ingested anything was when Violet forced herself in the bedroom and pressured Alice to at least drink some water and nibble on some crackers. The others continued to knock and attempted to talk through the door. Alice ignored them. They were all liars.

She hated Leander, and if he tried to show his face she knew she'd lash out at him for holding on to that cursed book instead of destroying it. She was mad at Natalie for always siding with him. She was mad at both of them for not doing something about William sooner, especially since they knew what he was like. They stood by and let him manipulate her. There were so many things they could've done to prevent it from ending up like this.

Alice was mad at Arthur for feeding her his blood. It kept her alive, but now any time she slept, she was jolted awake by vivid nightmares of her trauma. They had a darker undertone than usual. There would be shadows creeping after her in the background of the dreamscapes. Haunting her. And sometimes, she thought she saw them while she was awake. She felt like she'd be haunted forever. Sure Arthur saved her life, but maybe death would've been easier.

Michelle and James, they should've been there to help. They didn't come that night because they blindly trusted William. They should've seen through his act. They should've done more. All of them. If William was known to be a sneaky manipulative bastard, he should've been tracked down and killed fifty years ago. A hundred years ago.

She blamed them all for letting each and every event unfold, every little instance that led them to this horrible outcome, where she and her father were the ill-fated victims.

Most of all she blamed herself. She shouldn't have been so oblivious to the signs, about her father not acting like himself and about William being a liar. And she hated herself for thinking she was onto something when making that damn tincture. If she had never made it, then maybe William's plan wouldn't have worked. Maybe her father would've been able to escape. Maybe this all could have turned out so different.

Alice's lips were cracked from the dehydration. Her head pounded, and every time she moved she felt dizzy from lack of sustenance. This was better than feeling the empty depression though, the numb nothingness of her trauma. The physical pain was a distraction, but the pain fueled the anger, and it was becoming harder to manage.

As much as she wanted to be left alone, she was mad at the others because obviously they didn't care enough that she was wasting away up in her room. Maybe they never really cared about what happened to her after all. She wanted them to leave her alone, but she also wanted them to care at the same time. It didn't make sense.

They stopped knocking after a few days, everyone except Violet. Alice watched through the window as they came and went from the cabin. Leander and Natalie dressed in their suits, probably going off to meddle with the legal mess left behind, tying up loose ends regarding her father's disappearance and death.

She was another burden to them, another piece they had to put back together before shipping her off back to normal life. Five, ten, twenty years would go by and they'd forget about her, and she would be another name in their ledger, right next to her father's name where it would say *Deceased*.

Perhaps that was why Alice tolerated Violet and allowed her to come in. Because Violet was the only one still human in the house, living out the rest of her human years. She understood what it meant to have limited time. To be fragile. The two of them could bond on that level, even if they barely spoke. Alice and Violet were the collateral damage that faded away in the background.

Someone knocked on her door, someone that wasn't Violet. Alice knew because Violet had a particularly gentle knock, and this one was sharp and harsh. She ignored them. They knocked again. And again.

When Alice didn't respond, they let themselves into the room and cleared their throat. Curled up in a ball on her bed and back towards the door, Alice had to roll over to see who it was. Fury instantly ignited within her as she saw Leander standing at the threshold, arms folded.

"You haven't been eating or drinking," he said, his voice plain.

"Get out." Alice rolled back over and ignored him. It was either that or lash out, and she didn't have the energy right now. Her head was killing her.

"You really should—"

"No." She huffed. "I said get out."

"I have no idea why you're mad at me," Leander said with a sigh.

"I'm mad at everyone." It was true. And she didn't feel like explaining her reasons because nothing anyone said would make it better. "Just leave." Alice pulled the blanket over her head.

He sighed again, and it sounded like he was going to say something else, but he was cut off by a few sets of footsteps coming up the stairs. Great. Her open bedroom door was inviting everyone to come and check on her, some sort of intervention. Because for some reason, they only seemed to pretend to care about her wellbeing after she lost everything. They hadn't realized she already lost herself.

"Hey." It was Natalie. Alice didn't answer. "You have visitors."

"I don't care." Alice grumbled through the blanket. She knew it was a ruse to get her to engage with them so they could convince her to eat. She didn't care about eating, or drinking, or getting better. It didn't matter.

"Alice?" The girl's voice was gentle and kind, just like she remembered.

Whipping the blanket off, Alice propped herself up on her elbows. Pushing their way past Natalie and Leander and into the bedroom were her two best friends, Jenny and Caleb.

Alice gasped, swinging her legs over the side of the bed. She stumbled over to them, collapsing into Caleb's arms as a sob choked out of her mouth. She clung to him, and Jenny came up to hug her from behind, pinning Alice between them as she cried. She would've fallen to her knees if they hadn't been holding her up.

"It's okay," Caleb said in a tearful whisper as he smoothed the tangled hair on the top of her head. Alice didn't care if she looked a mess, if she smelled from not showering for days. Her best friends were here. It had been months since she had seen them or anyone from her personal life.

"How are you here?" Alice pulled away. "How'd you know where I was?"

Jenny nodded to Natalie and Leander hovering in the hallway. "They contacted us and told us what happened."

Alice's eyebrows jumped in surprise. "They told you?"

"Not everything," Caleb said. "We know you were involved in some sort of investigation, and you're still in witness protection."

"What else do you know?" Alice asked.

Leander gave a covert shake of his head. Of course there were more lies, and now she was part of it. She would never be able to explain the horrific things she witnessed. The darkness, the daemons, the death. They would never believe her.

"Not much," Jenny said as she exchanged a glance with

Natalie. "Only that your dad didn't make it. I'm so sorry, Alice." She pulled Alice in for another hug and Caleb did the same.

They held each other in silence for a few moments, and thankfully Leander and Natalie disappeared. Jenny informed Alice they were allowed to stay the night to keep her company, and they knew they weren't allowed to ask questions or talk about what happened.

Her friends seemed suspiciously calm about the entire thing, and Alice presumed they were given the henbane blend to make them more agreeable. Natalie and Leander most likely manipulated them to make sure they didn't freak out or ask too many questions. Even though she knew it was important to protect their secrets, Alice didn't like it, especially with the risks with taking henbane.

The three of them sat on Alice's bed, and Violet brought them a tray of sandwiches and snacks. Her friends finally convinced her to eat something, even though it wasn't much. They even convinced her to shower. Later in the evening, Violet returned again with more food and some hot tea for all of them. Alice's tea was a normal blend, because she continued to refuse the sedative. She assumed the tea brought for her friends was more of the henbane blend since Violet spoke to them in a mechanical way almost as if she had rehearsed the lines.

"Alice has been through so much," Violet said. "And I know it's even harder since she's not allowed to talk about any of it."

Alice clenched her jaw, steeling her face into neutrality. Keeping track of the lies made her want to pull her hair out. She knew the actions of her father sent a ripple effect into so many directions, and they were all trying to cover it up. Any bit of truth that got out would send the whole thing tumbling down. Every lie they constructed about their world and their magic had a purpose, to keep the normal citizens away. But there were people like Alice, like Violet, like Miss Dee... they all got roped into the world but weren't actually part of it, and yet they were still burdened with the monumental task of keeping it a secret. It was a lonely responsibility. And judging by Violet's detachment as she spoke, she felt the same way.

"It's okay," Jenny said, nodding along. "We understand. We won't ask you anything until you're ready to talk."

Violet stared at Alice expectedly, hoping she would go along with it. "I might not ever be ready to talk about it," Alice lied. She wanted so badly to talk about it. She needed her friends. She needed support. She needed to feel less alone. At one point she had felt less alone. With William. Before he killed her father.

"Whatever you need, Alice," Caleb said as he rubbed his hand on her back.

"It might be best if," Alice paused, thinking of how to phrase it, to get the lie to stick, to get them to eventually forget about it all. "Don't worry about me. I'll bring it up if I'm ever ready to talk about it."

Her friends nodded, eyes sleepy. Their faces looked completely neutral, no hints of questions. It was relieving and devastating at the same time. Alice was glad there was no risk of this story getting discovered, and yet she was utterly hopeless now that she knew she'd always have to weather this burden alone. That she witnessed such gruesome death. That she actually killed someone.

As her friends passed out from the henbane, they curled up under the covers in the queen sized bed. Back at college, they would do this when one of them had a particularly stressful or emotional day. They'd pile all their blankets and pillows on the floor, since the twin-sized dorm beds wouldn't fit them all, and watch old movies on her laptop until they fell asleep. It was a comforting reminder they were still there for her, even if they weren't able to know the details.

That night, Alice's sleep was again riddled with nightmares, and every time she woke up she expected William to be there. Reality would come crashing down when she'd remember he was the reason for her nightmares. The only thing that would sooth her would be her friends keeping her company, comforting her any time she needed.

Alice woke up some time in the afternoon with a pounding headache. The bedroom door was open. Caleb was missing, and Jenny was sitting on the window bench reading one of her anthropology textbooks. Alice groaned as she sat up. Her stomach rumbled loud enough for Jenny to hear.

"You hungry?" Jenny asked, closing her book and moving to sit next to Alice on the pile of blankets. Alice nodded. "Good," her friend continued. "Caleb went to get you something to eat. Do you want to go downstairs?"

"Not really," Alice sighed as she plopped back down, face first in the pillow. She didn't want to see any of them. She knew they would either pester her with questions or awkwardly stare at her from across the room.

"It might be a good idea to get some fresh air," Jenny coaxed as she placed a hand on Alice's upper arm. "It finally stopped raining."

"She's right," came Natalie's voice from the doorway.

"Please, Alice. For me?" Jenny said.

Another grumble escaped Alice's lips as she sat up. Natalie gave a soft smile and nodded at Jenny, urging her to give Alice some privacy. "We'll let you freshen up," Natalie said. Jenny walked over to Natalie, stopping to share another glance, and followed her out of the room. They must've planned this before Alice woke up.

She pulled her tired body out of bed and forced herself to shower and get dressed into something other than pajamas, although she still picked sweatpants and an oversized hoodie because it was the easiest. She realized she was much thinner than she had been a few months ago. The stress of worrying about her father, even before he died, took a toll on her body and eating habits.

Down in the kitchen she found Caleb and Jenny sitting on the stools at the island, and Natalie was making some peanut butter and jelly sandwiches at the counter. Alice sat on another one of the stools next to Caleb and glanced out into the living room. Everyone was there.

Most of them sat on the couches circling the fireplace. Michelle and James were on one couch, and Arthur was next to Leander on another. Violet was in a chair off to the side, staring out the window. Even Miss Dee was there. And they all abruptly stopped their conversation to look over at her. Alice held her head in her hands as Natalie shooed at them, trying to get them to stop staring.

They were probably going through more plans of how to clean up and manage the situation, and it probably involved more henbane and lies. Alice couldn't imagine how many people were involved in this, and how many of them would need to be compelled to believe a new story— multiple police departments, state and federal investigators, witnesses, families of the victims, local news stations. Alice wondered if half of the unsolved murder cases in the country went cold because of this very reason. Miss Dee had mentioned needing to clean up their messes time and time again, and this was just southern New Jersey.

When Alice lifted her head again, everyone had resumed their conversations in hushed tones. She wanted to forget everything. Maybe they could use the henbane on her.

Natalie placed a sandwich in front of her, but Alice pushed it away.

"Please, eat some of it," Jenny said with a frown.

"You said you would try," Caleb said.

Alice rolled her eyes, took a bite of the sandwich, and dropped it back down on the plate.

"More than that." Caleb folded his arms and arched his eyebrow.

They stared each other down for a few minutes before Alice eventually ate half of it. That was enough. She felt a little nauseated because her body wasn't used to eating that much. Jenny suggested a walk, and Alice promised to try to eat the rest when they came back in.

As Alice and her two friends headed for the back door, Natalie scurried up behind them and followed them out. Alice gave her a deadpan stare, knowing she was about to say something annoying.

"We have to head out in about an hour," Natalie said, her eyes drifting to Jenny and Caleb. The two of them nodded.

"Why can't they stay?" Alice snapped.

"We still have a lot of things to work out with the case," Natalie said.

"It's okay, Alice," Jenny said. "We don't want to get in the way."

"Why can't I leave with them?" Alice snipped. She didn't actually know what she wanted. She just wanted some sort of control back in her life.

"It's best to keep you here for now, for your safety."

Natalie's voice was light, but Alice could detect the command underneath.

"What if I don't care about that?" Alice stomped her foot. "I just want to go home." A home which she no longer had. Her lip trembled as she held back her tears. She turned away to hide her face.

"Come on, Alice," Caleb said softly, placing a hand on her back and guiding her down the garden path, away from Natalie.

"When this is all over, we'll figure everything out. You can stay with my parents," Caleb said. "Or Jenny's. You could come back to school whenever you're ready."

Alice shook her head, dismissing every one of his suggestions. She wanted none of that. All she wanted was her dad and her mom and her home and her old bedroom. She wanted her life back.

They reached the bank of the creek and she fell to her knees in the dirt, the dampness seeping through her pants. Alice was crumbling. Her body shook from her silent cries. Her friends knelt on either side of her, comforting her, not saying a word and letting her let it out.

If this is what her life would be, she didn't want it. She couldn't bear it. There was nothing left for her here. Alice loved her friends, but her trauma would just burden them. It would be easier for everyone if she disappeared.

"I can't do it," Alice mumbled through her cries. "I can't."

"Do what?" Jenny asked, her arm draped over Alice's shoulders.

"This." She buried her face in her hands, her shoulders hunched over. "Live, not like this. Not anymore. I can't do it."

"You'll only have to stay here a little longer," Caleb

reminded her. "We'll help you figure everything out when you—"

"No," Alice cut him off. "No, that's not what I meant. I..." she trailed off, the heaviness of the truth she was about to speak weighing on her soul. "I don't want to be here. I don't want to be anywhere." She could tell by the looks on their faces that their hearts dropped with the admission.

"Oh, Alice," Jenny said. She was crying now too. And Caleb. They hugged her, the three of them on their knees and wrapped in each other's arms on the ground.

Something had broken within Alice. She didn't know when, but it had been broken for a while. Even before her father died. Even before he was diagnosed with cancer. Perhaps it broke the same day that windshield shattered and sent shards of glass flying through their car in slow motion. The same day her mother died. The same day Alice died and was brought back to life.

And every day after that she had tried her best to hold it together. If not for herself, then for her father. And now that he was gone, now that everything was gone, Alice had no one to keep it together for.

Minutes passed as she continued to cry, falling apart in her friends' arms, her only lifeline to sanity as they squeezed their love into her. They knew everything she had been through in the past, and they knew she struggled even when she put on a happy face. And they understood her now, empty of all hope, no will to continue living, and yet they didn't leave her side.

Caleb had his cheek pressed against the top of Alice's head. "Please stay," he whispered into her hair. "Please."

"We'll help you get through it, Alice," Jenny added. "Please keep trying. For us. For your dad. Your mom. They would want you to keep going."

"I know," Alice cried into Jenny's shoulder. She was right. Her mom and dad would want her to keep living her life, to keep trying, no matter how hard things got. That was one thing her father taught her through all these years, to never give up hope, to see goodness when it seemed like there was none left.

They finally separated from the hug. Still kneeling, they faced the creek. Alice's head hung heavily from her shoulders. "I'll try."

Jenny walked over to some overgrown brush next to the creek where there were some pale yellow daffodils peeking through the dead, soggy leaves. Jenny picked a handful and returned to kneeling with the others.

"Here," she said as she passed a few flowers to each of them. "Maybe it would help to say something."

Alice held the flower stems limply, not convinced of Jenny's idea. It felt stupid, meaningless. "I don't know what to say." Because nothing she said would mend the hole in her heart.

"Dr. Foster had the best macaroni," Caleb finally said with a small laugh followed by a sniffle. "He could lighten the mood, finding any trace of good in a bad situation." Alice didn't smile, but she appreciated his sentiment. "He was a good professor, a good dad, and a good person," Caleb continued.

"He was kind," Jenny added. "He cared so much about his work and his students. And his family." She and Caleb looked at Alice, waiting to see if she had anything to add.

She didn't. Not really. Alice would never be able to put into words the pain she felt for losing someone she loved so much. For the second time in her life. All she could think of was the sound of his gasp as he died, the vision of his body strung up on the tree, the way Leander dropped his body into the grave like he was nothing.

"I'm sorry, Dad," Alice choked. It was all she could manage. She tossed the daffodils into the creek. Jenny and Caleb followed suit. The flowers floated lazily in the water, bumping into rocks and branches along the way before they disappeared around the bend.

CHAPTER 26

After Jenny and Caleb left, Alice slipped right back into her isolation. She would eat, drink, and bathe, but she refused to speak to anyone except Violet. Although, no one really tried to engage her in conversation anyway. They were all still too busy cleaning up loose ends, so she rarely crossed paths with anyone.

Leander and Natalie were off with Miss Dee settling things with the courts, such as paper trails and files regarding her father's case. Arthur was meeting with local police departments to quell the search, and he planned to connect with local news stations in order to stop the spread of the story. Michelle and James were traveling through southern New Jersey and Pennsylvania to meet with the families of victims. And each one of them were loaded up with supplies of the henbane blend to manipulate the minds of dozens, if not hundreds, of people. It was an extensive process. Until everything was cleaned up and a cover story in place, Alice was stuck there.

This left Alice with a ridiculous amount of free time to replay every terrible detail of the past few months over and over again in her mind. It also gave her time to decide what she wanted to say to *him*.

They told her to leave him alone, to avoid the basement, to pretend he wasn't even there. But how could she forget her father's killer was resting comfortably beneath their feet and had a fresh tray of food brought down to him every day.

This morning, the only person left at the cabin with Alice was Violet. And William. In the basement. So once Violet had her breakfast and departed for her usual routine of caring for the plants in the conservatory, Alice made her way downstairs.

Her footsteps were soft and silent as she descended into the basement, turning down the long hallway towards the iron door. No one had told her exactly where he had been locked up, so she assumed he'd be in the cell she had seen before. All the other rooms didn't seem secure enough for a monster like him. However, he should've been significantly underpowered due to the brand Leander carved into his chest with the white blade. She found out it removed his ability to use elemental magic, and it slowed his accelerated healing. It made him almost human again. She wondered how easily he could die.

Alice passed by the alcove with the large trunk and collection of jars that she now knew were full of exorcised demon sludge. Something so malevolent should've been locked away in a more secure place, but she didn't care enough to voice her opinion anymore.

Inching closer to the door, she wrung her sweaty hands. Her breathing was quiet and shallow, ears listening for any sign of movement from inside the cell as she approached. Alice placed her palms on the cool metal of the iron door and peered through the barred window. On the cot with the dingy mattress in the corner lay William, one arm rested behind his head as he stared up at the ceiling. In his other hand he fidgeted with something small, the carved wooden bird. He looked awfully relaxed for a prisoner.

"I was wondering when you'd come," William said. He didn't bother to look over at her.

Alice sucked in a breath. Everything she planned to say dissolved from her brain. Not that she had much planned to say to begin with. So she stared, hands gripping the bars of the small window. A lump formed in her throat as she was overwhelmed with sorrow and burning hatred.

Her extended silence was enough to pique William's interest, making him sit up. He pocketed the wooden bird before resting his forearm on his knee. They made eye contact. Her stomach twisted with revulsion. She had to look away. So many horrific memories came flooding back all at once, the emotions too much to bear. Alice turned to leave but paused when she heard the creaking of the metal springs of the cot and the shuffling footsteps of William as he moved closer.

He stood about a foot away from the door, arms folded and hand resting on his chin. He was dressed in neat clothes, and he looked relatively clean. His wounds had been healed. She scowled. He was getting treated much better than he deserved.

"Did you come down here just to stare at me?" William asked, his voice too cocky for her liking, so different from the way he used to speak to her. "Or to apologize for killing the love of my life?"

"No," she snapped.

"Then what is it?"

Alice was too flustered to find the right words. He knew the exact buttons to push to set her off like the conniving manipulator he was. She dropped her trembling hands to her sides to hide the evidence of her anxiety. He couldn't see her upset. He couldn't see her cry. She couldn't let him think she was weak. When truly, all she felt like was weak these days.

He responded with a grunt and shook his head. She didn't know what he was expecting from her. She didn't know what she was expecting from him. Alice questioned why she had even come down to the basement in the first place. Seeing him was making things so much worse, not better.

William headed back to the cot, ignoring her.

"Why?" she blurted out, stopping him in his tracks.

He looked over his shoulder at her. "That's vague."

Alice lurched forward and gripped the metal bars in the window again. The door clanged against its thick hinges from the force. "Did you even care about me? About him? About any of it?"

He faced her, an infuriating smirk curling at the corner of his mouth. William absolutely disgusted her. "I did."

"You're sick," Alice hissed. "You're a twisted, lying—"

"Wow, Alice," he said as he placed a hand over his chest like he was wounded. "So quick to judge me without hearing my side."

"There are no sides! You killed my dad!" Her face pressed against the bars of the window in the door, her teeth bared. She couldn't contain the rage any longer, the rage she had kept on a leash for days, weeks, months... maybe even years. Tears burned the corners of her eyes. "You killed him. He trusted you. I trusted you."

William stalked forward, reaching out a hand as if he was going to caress her cheek through the barred window. She recoiled.

"Don't touch me," Alice spat. Suddenly she felt dirty all over. Her entire body had been tarnished by his touch.

"I did care for you, Alice. I still do."

"Shut up."

"It's true, Alice. My feelings for you were real."

"You were going to feed me to Victoria."

William pounded his fists against the iron door, eyes flashing dangerously as grief shattered him from the inside out. Alice jumped back. This time it was his face pressed against the metal bars. "Don't say her name," he growled. A moment of silence passed as he reigned in his anguish, hiding it again behind his mask of indifference. "It was an unfortunate decision I was willing to live with. I cared for you, Alice. I just cared for her more."

Alice didn't understand why that hurt so much. She trusted him once, with everything. He provided her with such comfort and safety. He claimed his feelings to be real, and yet he was willing to let Victoria bleed her dry. Because he loved her more. Over a hundred years later, he still loved her more. And for some reason, it broke her heart. No one had ever loved her like that, desperate enough to do anything for her. Well, except her father.

"You turned my dad into a monster."

"He was ill, and I offered to help him," William argued. He stepped back from the door again, standing more composed.

"He became a killer. He murdered people. He tried to murder me!"

William cocked his head and narrowed his eyes. "Did he? When?"

"After he killed Dillion, when he locked me in the basement. The house fire—"

"Ah." His eyebrows flashed with realization. "That was me."

"You?" Alice stumbled back a few paces, clutching her chest with shock.

William rolled his eyes. "He killed the kid. I found your dad and got him out of there. I was trying to clean up when you arrived. I needed to dispose of the evidence."

"D-did you know I was down there?" she stuttered. "In the basement."

He studied her before responding. "Yes. You were part of the evidence that needed to be disposed of."

A choking sound escaped her throat. "I hate you," she whispered, stepping backwards.

"I know."

Alice couldn't tolerate being in his presence any longer. She spun on her heel, stumbling a bit before running back upstairs. She collided with Violet as she rounded the corner. The old woman clutched Alice's upper arms to steady her.

"We told you not to go down there," she said.

"I had to... I.... he..." Alice stammered, unable to find a reason. Instead she fell into Violet's arms and cried. That simmering rage had stirred within her for days, and finally confronting William relieved the burning ache inside her heart. At least for now. She knew her rage would return when the others eventually decided what to do with William, because it was unlikely they'd keep him down in the basement for eternity.

Violet led her to the living room, and they sat on the couch together. "William has that effect on people," Violet said, looking down at her lap. "He's good with his words. He makes you trust him. He's done it to all of us at one point."

"But why?" Alice asked through her tears.

"He's been alone and in pain for so long."

Alice frowned. It sounded like Violet was making excuses for him. She was about to argue, but then Violet continued.

"I think he used to have a good heart," Violet paused. "Back then, before everything. He wouldn't have been Chosen if he didn't. Once everything happened, his goodness faded. Now he's driven by his pain. It turned him mad."

"I guess I can see that," Alice said with a sigh. She still hated him. People could be in pain and not turn into devious, manipulative murderers. Alice had been through so much, and she never once considered doing evil deeds in order to relieve her misery. Even if she knew about this type of dark magic before, she would never resort to killing others for her own gain. William was sick and twisted, and he deserved to rot for it. "What are they going to do with him?"

Violet shrugged. "I don't know. I don't have much of a say in that." The old woman's eyes unfocused, stuck in some memory. "You should get some rest."

Alice slumped on the couch. All she did was rest. She wanted to fade away, full of trauma she couldn't escape. It exhausted her and drove her crazy at the same time.

"Would you like some of the tea?" Violet asked as she stood. "To help you sleep."

Alice considered it. It would help calm her nerves. It would reduce the horrific nightmares. "Sure," she said. "I just don't want to rely on something like that forever." Or maybe she did.

Violet returned a few minutes later with the tea. "You can drink it for as long as you need to, Alice. You've been through so much."

She sipped it and leaned against Violet's shoulder as the

tiredness came over her. Violet unfolded a blanket and covered Alice with it. She ran her hand through Alice's hair, such a loving gesture that it made her tear up again.

"What happens when you die?" Alice asked, starting to feel sleepy. If there was magic, and it was possible to be immortal or come back from the dead, what did it actually mean to die? And more importantly, what did it mean for her dad?

"No one knows for sure. And I'm probably not the best one to ask about it. But I do know the Grey is a transition realm on the other side. Spirits pass through it. Then they either go somewhere else or get stuck, like the *vagari* and *exsugo*."

"How could they get stuck?"

Violet rubbed her chin. "Have you ever been in one of those carnival fun houses, with the mirror maze? You know when two mirrors face each other and their reflections go on forever. They say it's like that. Spirits and creatures in that realm sometimes get trapped if they can't find their way. It's why Miss Dee needed you to be the anchor. You can get lost in there."

Alice's stomach flipped, imagining how perilous Grey-walking had actually been, especially when she went alone as a novice. Her spirit could've been trapped there forever. What would that have meant for her body? "No wonder people don't like to do it," she said.

"It's why the Grey is also referred to as the Mirror, because the essence of the physical realm is reflected there. And sometimes, the essence of the Grey can be reflected in the physical realm."

"Like seeing *vagari* or the daemons in mirrors and windows?" Alice asked with a gulp, remembering those hollow eyes staring back at her in the glass.

"Exactly. Sometimes we can see reflections of them. Greywalkers can see them more clearly because of their connection to the Grey. Although all souls and beings are connected to the Grey somehow."

"And what about my dad? Do you think he—"

"I'm not sure what would've become of him, Alice. I'm sorry."

Alice knew people who believed in eternal torment, in some sort of fiery underworld. She hoped something like that didn't exist. For her father's sake. It was the elixir that made him a killer.

Violet put her arm around Alice and squeezed. "It'll be okay."

It didn't feel okay. She didn't think it would ever feel okay. Not after the things she had seen. The things she had done.

People had been telling her for her entire life that things would be okay, that she should keep going, keep holding on. That it'll all get better one day. That it'll make sense one day. It was the biggest lie, since every year of her life things seemed to get progressively worse. She couldn't imagine how things could be better.

"How do you do it?" Alice asked with a yawn, the sedative tea taking hold. "How do you deal with everything?"

"Honestly, dear, sometimes I ask myself the same question." Violet sighed. "Because some days it feels too hopeless."

"What stops you from giving up?" Alice would never admit how close she was to giving up. It felt like endless loneliness, going down the path of her life that led to nowhere.

Violet pursed her lips, as if she'd never stopped to consider the answer before. "I guess I want to help as much as possible, because helping people is what I've always done. It's why I joined the Army Nurse Corps, and it's why I'm still here involved in all this. Because maybe I can make a little bit of difference, bring back a little bit of hope, any way I can."

Alice let out a quiet sob. She could almost feel the pain and sadness radiating off of Violet, and yet the old woman found a way to make each day mean something. Violet was a simple human with no special powers. She still tried. She still cared.

Violet was the only person Alice had truly trusted in the cabin. The only person she felt like she could really connect with. The only person she thought truly understood her. Violet had been through horrific things on her own, signifi-cant loss and trauma throughout her long life, and she was still here. Maybe Alice could keep trying too.

* * *

When Alice woke up, she was still laying on the couch in the living room. But she wasn't alone. Ming the cat was curled up next to her, purring. The embers of the fire still crackled in the fireplace. A soft light glowed from the kitchen. She could hear quiet conversation from the other room. The clock on the mantle read just after midnight. There was no shadowy figure in the hallway.

She got up and stretched. Her feet padded towards the kitchen, but she took a moment to hover in the dark hallway to listen.

"How much longer should we keep him down there?" Michelle asked.

Alice stiffened.

Leander cleared his throat. "As long as it takes."

"As long as it takes for what?" Alice asked as she stepped out of the shadow.

Everyone seated at the table tensed, holding their breath.

Arthur squared his shoulders and kept his face neutral. "For Leander to decide what he would like to do about his brother."

So it was Leander's decision. Alice clenched her teeth. Leander had the chance to kill his brother when they were in the forest, and he didn't. The only remaining choices were to keep William in the basement indefinitely, or eventually let him go. They didn't care what Alice thought. They didn't care that she would rather see him dead.

Leander avoided eye contact, peeling the label off his beer bottle, as if he could sense her fury and distrust.

Natalie coughed to dispel the tension. "We're almost finished wrapping everything up, which means soon you can go uh—" she faltered.

"Home?" Alice's voice cracked. Her anger evaporated into worry. She had no home to return to.

"We figured you could reach out to your friends and stay with them," James said. "They could help you get ready to go back to school."

Stay with her friends. Go back to school. None of it seemed real. It felt like a different life. The idea of returning to the world felt so strange, and Alice would have to exist around people who would have no idea what she'd been through, no idea that she watched her father get his heart carved out of his chest.

"Isn't that what you wanted, dear?" Violet asked.

"I don't know," she whispered. Her vision tunneled. Alice thought she wanted to leave, wanted to escape this hell. She loved the idea of freedom, but forgot the fear that came along with it. Sometimes a cage felt safer.

"It might be helpful for you to be around familiar people, get into a routine," Natalie suggested.

Alice nodded, her face blank. People who endured trauma were always encouraged to return to some kind of normalcy, even if the normalcy made them feel empty on the inside. Alice figured she could do that. She did it for almost her entire life after her mother died. But stepping foot out of this cabin and stepping back to her old life seemed impossible, because her old life didn't exist anymore.

Her eyes drifted to the kettle on the stove and then to the jar of herbs and extra mug on the counter next to it. "Are you going to wipe my memories?"

No one spoke for a moment.

"No," Michelle said. "Not without your consent."

They didn't seem to care much about consent before. Although things were different now. She was part of their world, a Greywalker. There were things she *needed* to know.

"We can if you want us to," Leander added.

Alice considered the peace of forgetting, but then imagined living with the dread in the pit of her stomach, knowing the misery would always reside deep in her soul even if she no longer had the words to describe it. She wrung her trembling hands.

Violet stood and walked over to her. "You don't have to decide anything right now, dear." She put her arm around Alice's shoulder and guided her to an empty chair at the table.

The others looked at her like she was a wounded animal. She shrunk down in her seat.

"It's okay Alice," said Michelle. "We're here for you. You're not alone."

Alone. Alice remembered when she told William that perhaps it wasn't always easier being alone. But alone felt safe. Familiar. Perhaps not so much anymore. She didn't realize there were tears falling down her cheeks until Violet started rubbing her back. Maybe this entire time she hadn't been alone, she was just too blind to see it, too lost in William's lies, too stuck in her self imposed isolation.

James poured some brown liquor into a glass tumbler and slid it across the table to Alice. "No decisions tonight, no more tea, just booze," he said with a cheeky smile.

Picking up the glass, she gave it a sniff. Her nose crinkled. Alice wasn't much of an alcohol drinker, and whenever she did drink, it was always some sort of fun fruity drink that completely masked the taste. She swallowed a sip, appreciating the burn as it made its way down, but she couldn't hide her grimace. "Thanks," she said with a cough. "What is it?"

"One hundred year old plum brandy from eastern Europe," James said as he took another sip. "A farmer had given me a few bottles of his homemade stock as I was passing through."

"Oh, wow, uh," Alice stumbled. "Thank you for sharing it with me."

"Of course." James raised his glass and winked at her. "Speaking of Europe, let me tell you a story—"

"Here we go," Natalie said with a laugh, pouring another glass of the brandy for herself.

"Don't worry, Alice will love this one," James continued. "It was when I snuck into a garden party at Buckingham Palace, and one of Queen Victoria's yappy little dogs sniffed me out and bit me on the arse."

Alice couldn't help but smile as James prattled on, his accent sneaking out more and more. It was a comforting distraction to hear some lighthearted nonsense. Michelle had to interject a few times, because apparently James was known for exaggerating certain details. After being engrossed by the tale for quite some time, she caught Leander staring at her from across the table. The side of his mouth quirked up as they shared a glance.

The buzz of the brandy seemed to loosen everyone up quite a bit, and Alice was surprised to feel a glimmer of fondness blooming within her. Despite the anger and confusion and trauma she endured while in their care, they did their best to ensure that she survived. They made sure she had warm meals in her belly and a safe place to sleep.

As the lighthearted conversation continued, Alice realized that everyone carried immense pain with them every day, and they all had likely been Chosen in response to some sort of terrible tragedy, even if she didn't know all of their stories. They had all been where she is now in one form or another. Yet they hid it well.

Grief felt lonely, that much she knew, ever since a young age. Alice knew they felt grief too, likely much deeper than her own. But grief had brought all of them together, joined by some unspoken understanding and a mission to help others and prevent them from experiencing the same.

By this point, James was absolutely trashed and ended up knocking over the almost empty bottle of brandy. Natalie, equally drunk, howled with laughter while Leander took the responsibility of grabbing a dish towel and cleaning up the mess. Even Arthur was laughing as Michelle tried her best to prop up her protesting husband as he stumbled to bed. The energy then simmered down as everyone took a moment to help clean up the rest of the drinks and snacks before wandering off to bed themselves, each one of them with an easy smile on their faces.

If they could be okay, if they could live through horrors and death and grief and hopelessness through decades and centuries, maybe there was something Alice could learn from them. Somehow, they kept going. They didn't give up. They weathered countless bad times, and yet made sure to remember the good times. They found purpose in helping others, in helping Alice. So Alice decided that the first step in moving forward would be learning to let people in, learning to accept help from others, and learning that she really doesn't have to do it alone.

ACKNOWLEDGMENTS

Like most writers, I've been a daydreamer ever since childhood, and I'd create stories in my head about anything that made me curious. In order to get here, I have to give many thanks to all those who stood by me and encouraged me to share my weird and haunted stories.

To my husband Dan, thank you for loving my weirdness, reading my manuscript multiple times, listening to my endless brainstorming sessions, and helping me make the hard decisions on my publishing journey.

To my parents, grandparents, and very large extended family, thank you for always telling me to be myself and to never give up. I especially want to thank my Dad, Nanny, and Poppy for bringing me down to the Delaware River as a kid to take me fishing and to teach me how to skip rocks.

To my friends Janna, Rachel B., Rachel W., Emma, Alice, Kat, Shannon, Kate, Doretta, and Chris, thank you for being my ultimate cheerleaders, giving me pep talks when I needed them, and making me laugh when I felt discouraged.

To my developmental editor Fiona, thank you for going on this journey with me and helping me flesh out this story with your creativity and skill. Not only are you amazing at what you do, but you also seemed to love my story and characters just as much as I do, and I appreciate that so much.

To my beta readers Kennedy, Ari, Sherry, Brylee,

Breanna, Thiffa, Tessy, Kimberly, Ruchi, Alicia, Cassandra, Vivian and many others who read snippets here and there, thank you for giving me amazing feedback and compelling suggestions, because this story wouldn't be what it is today without you.

To my creative writing professor Carla, thank you for helping me grow as a writer, calling me the "master of creep" in your class, and encouraging me believe in myself.

To my cover designer David, thank you for fitting my request into your very busy schedule and creating something beautiful.

To the many Reddit communities, Facebook groups, and book discord groups I am part of, thank you all for answering my endless questions and providing me guidance where I needed it.

Thank you all so much.

ABOUT THE AUTHOR

J.P. Flynn, also known as Jess by her friends and family, lives in New Jersey with her husband and two cats. She works part time as a licensed professional counselor and owns her own private practice. She has a bachelor's degree in psychology and a master's degree in clinical mental health counseling. In her free time when she's not writing, she enjoys riding her bike, gardening, playing video games, reading, and doing anything crafty.

Coming soon
- Books 2 & 3
- Prequel set in the 1800s

Follow J.P. Flynn on social media for more updates:

Instagram @jpflynnauthor

TikTok @jp.flynn

www.ingramcontent.com/pod-product-compliance
Lightning Source LLC
Chambersburg PA
CBHW021806130726
47987CB00010B/3030